THE LAST MAY-DAY

A novel of tight-rope tension, and of five people, all dedicated in their own and completely divergent ways.

STEPHENS: Commander of the U.S. Sub *Skate*. All he had to do was cut through Soviet naval defences in the Black Sea, wait until Kirov was brought to him, and then get out – all without anyone knowing

KIROV: power-maniac, now deprived of power. Ex-premier of the Soviet Union, once butcher, now eager to escape butchery

UZZUMEKIS: taciturn, strong-arm agent, employed to smuggle Kirov through the network of Soviet security police and thence to freedom

MELINA: companion and lever to Uzzumekis. Loyal, astute, cool under pressure, who gave her beautiful body . . .

HALE: underwater diving expert. By the time he reached the scene, the nuclear button was about to be pressed. And he only had an experimental machine and a lot of courage to save them all from death

For P, Z, S, R, B, etc.
With thanks and apologies
to the U.S. Submarine Service
and with admiration

The Last May-day

Keith Wheeler

CORONET BOOKS
Hodder and Stoughton

First published in Great Britain by
Hodder and Stoughton Limited 1969

Coronet edition 1970
Second impression 1970
Third impression 1975

Printed and bound in Great Britain for
Coronet Books, Hodder and Stoughton,
St. Paul's House, Warwick Lane,
London, EC4P 4AH
by Hazell Watson & Viney Ltd
Aylesbury, Bucks

ISBN 0 340 12961 1

I

FOR three days the nuclear submarines U.S.S. *Skate* and U.S.S. *Triton* had stalked each other in the NATO submarine exercise area stretching in a vast and deep intra-Aegean lake from Akagria on the Greek island of Andros, 110 nautical miles into the Turkish Gulf of Kuşadasi. This playground of the nukes provided plenty of water under the keel, better than 4000 feet in the deepest of the sinks between Ikaría and Sámos, averaging around 300 fathoms, with the 100-fathom line running so close ashore that any time you came to periscope depth the pale parched baby mountains of the islands and headlands were in plain sight. The point was, however, that you came to periscope depth only in the most rigorous circumstances, knowing, as you did, that the radar of hunter-killer destroyers and U.S.S. *Hornet's* planes were patiently waiting for you topside. This was a listening game of blind man's buff, with the probing electronic tentacles of the enemy's sonar groping for you as, in turn, your sonar groped for him with a lover's searching jealousy.

Between any two American attack submarines this game would be played in deadly earnest. Between *Skate* and *Triton* it was almost more than a game, for these were jealous ships and in a service where pride ran high and hot they nursed a brand of it that came close to arrogance—surpassed arrogance. Though the deeds were somewhat in the past, these two nukes felt serenely that they had sound reason to hold themselves queens among their sleeker and newer sisters. After all, who but *Skate* had shouldered through four feet of pack ice to heave herself to the surface at the North Pole, and who but *Triton* carried in her log the record of eighty-four . days around the world on Magellan's track, submerged every mile except that quick regretful surfacing off the mouth of Rio de la Plata to offload a sailor writhing in the agonies of a

9

ruptured appendix? And so, now, *Skate* and *Triton*, though pregnant only with dummy torpedoes in their tubes, were grimly bent upon reciprocal slaughter.

Commander David Stephens, captain of *Skate*, with his ship rigged for silent running, with his crew sock-footed, moving often almost dead slow to suppress the bank of lights which, when they twinkled, betrayed cavitation noise from the screws, felt complacent about his location of a zone of shrimp beds where, when the enemy seemed likely to feint him into a vulnerable situation, he could hide forever, shielded by the cacophonic twittering uproar broadcast by millions of busy nibbling pincers. I like 'em as well as any man dipped in hot red sauce between the martinis (ten-to-one) and the steak (rare), but I like them a damned sight better down here when their orchestration keeps somebody from sinking a torpedo in my gut, he thought. On the other side of the court, Commander Walsh Kelly, captain of *Triton*, congratulated himself on discovery of a temperature inversion which, with *Skate* closing off his port bow on an attack approach, had saved him in time. He had gone down considerably further than 400 feet, which was all the Navy would officially admit he could go. Down there, he knew because his own sonar went inversely dead at the same time, *Skate* would have lost him when her sonar pings began bouncing futilely back from the abrupt cold-water layer he had penetrated. It was, as much as anything else, a guessing game in which evaluation of the other guy's psychological mix dictated your maneuver.

Once Stephens had first eluded Kelly and then nearly got him by running up to the reefs around Kalógerio Rock and going to ground to wait there, dead silent, in a mere sixty feet of water with only two feet of margin left under the keel at periscope depth. It was, he admitted to himself, probably a little foolhardy in fact since the charts were not sure, within a mile, just where the rock was from the latest fix of its position in 1947. Still, he knew, that in actual war this kind of reckless sneak thievery was sometimes just the ticket. Kelly came looking for him, as he had expected, but being perhaps more sensitive to the chart's dangerous vagaries, had shied off before getting into reasonable range for *Skate* to take a poke at him. So then it was Stephens' turn to come out of his lair and go on the prowl again.

All this was a source of considerable curiosity to Stephens' guests for, in this exercise, he was carrying courtesy observers from the navies of allies. They were Captain Warren Brown of the Royal Navy, Herr Kapitan Wilhelm Mueller of the West German Navy, Commander Stavros Cavanides of Greece, and Capitano di Fregata Garibaldi Nicolai of the Italian submarine service. Nicolai's title of rank slightly amused Stephens for it seemed to him a little fancy, not to say pretentious, way to describe a rank which was, in fact, the same as his own, which was to say, plain "commander."

Captain Brown was aboard to observe American submarine dogma while awaiting his own nuclear submarine, the *Royal Oak*, still on the Vickers-Armstrong ways at Hebburn-on-Tyne but with the English-Electric reactor already in her belly. The British had installed an American reactor in their first nuke, the *Dreadnaught*, but thereafter had turned to home products as Her Majesty's nuclear navy gradually saw its tribe increase.

The other three were staff officers. Nicolai and Cavanides, whose Greek Navy had recently received a couple of Guppy-class, obsolescent conversions of World War II fleet boats, as a free gift from the U.S., were without personal submarine experience. Normally they were no-seagoing political-type officers, but their governments had sent them along anyhow in answer to the U.S. invitation to cruise with *Skate*.

Of the four, Kapitan Mueller was clearly the most sophisticated in the nuances of submarine tactics and, this being his first nuke, was experiencing some difficulty concealing his avid interest in *Skate* beneath the cloak of austere dignity which was his armor against the world. Now and then his shield sprang a rivet or two, and he would be unable to suppress an enthusiastic "Wunderbar!"

Although Kapitan Mueller was now a staff officer, it was

only because of age and infirmity. In World War II he had won both renown, as the sinker of 129,000 tons of Allied shipping, and personal survival as skipper of the *U89*, although toward the end he did lose his boat and all her crew except himself.

Coming out of the risky shelter of Kalógerio, to his everlasting shame, was what cost Commander Stephens the ball game. He hadn't really expected Kelly to lie doggo, silent, hovering, listening, broadside to his own course of 120°, but he came out with all the caution he would have exercised if he had expected him. They were still rigged for silent ship, with 120 men catfooting around in their sock feet and captain's mast awaiting the offender who so much as flushed the john. At that moment Steward's Mate Second Class Willard Billings and Cook First Class Josh Collingwood were setting up the wardroom for a buffet supper of shrimp curry and cold cuts. What occurred then was totally unaccountable, since Billings and Collingwood had long been as skillfully meshed as a prima ballerina and her partner at getting in and out of the narrow door between pantry and wardroom without friction. But this time they collided, Billings with a stack of ten plates balanced on his right hand and a fistful of flatware in his left, Collingwood with a sterling silver commissioning gift platter, insulated with aluminum foil against acid staining by the five pounds of curry it contained. Plates and platter hit the deck with a horrendous clatter, loud as a reverberating, ricocheting salvo of artillery, in an atmosphere otherwise so tensely quiet that even the air conditioning was shut down.

"What the hell was that!" came Captain Stephens' bellow of outrage, plainly audible from the control room a deck above and two bulkheads aft.

In stunned horror, Billings stared down at the shattered wreckage of crockery around his feet. He saw that blood was seeping through his white cotton sock from the neighbourhood of his great toe, port side. He looked up at Collingwood, his technical superior.

"Man," he said in an icy tone. "I am going to kill you!"

"Man," Collingwood replied. "You are going to be dead before you get the chance."

In *Triton*, Captain Kelly heard the uproar coming in on sonar, got the range and bearing and depth while the weapons officer, Lieutenant (jg) Dean Klass cranked this intelligence into computers which passed on what they knew to the Mark XXXVII acoustic torpedoes in the six forward tubes.

"Shoot!" said Captain Kelly, wearing a look of satanic glee.

"Fire one," Lieutenant Klass told the microphone connecting him with the torpedo room as he pushed down the red firing button. The ship shuddered only minutely as the torpedo went on its mission.

"Shoot," Captain Kelly said again.

"Fire two," said Klass and pressed the button again.

In all they sent a spread of four, practically boresighted at a mere 1500 yards. It was so dead certain that Kelly didn't bother to wait for official confirmation. He merely called Stephens on the underwater telephone—so close they were—and observed, "Five-seven-eight. Paisan, you are daid!"

Sunk in dejection, Stephens ordered secure from general quarters and left the officer of the deck, Lieutenant Grady Johnson, to secure from rig for depth charge and to surface the boat where, no doubt, he would take his bitter lumps by signal from Vice Admiral Dewey Hart, the task force commander with his flag in *Hornet*.

He went wearily forward and down the ladder and into the wardroom, taking off his cap with the scrambled eggs and tossing it on the sideboard as he slouched into a chair, not even bothering to take his own armchair, to which rank entitled him, at the head of the table. He was vaguely aware of Collingwood and Billings eying him in frozen apprehension from the pantry door.

"How about a pot of hot water?" he asked. In defiance of all navy tradition, Commander Stephens drank coffee only at breakfast and on other occasions of thirst drank plain hot water. This habit filled his shipmates with awe, being close to sacrilege.

"What happened?" Stephens asked, almost idly, as Billings set down cup, saucer, and steaming teapot full of the captain's virginal favorite brew. He looked up and caught Billings and Collingwood glaring at one another in baleful accusation.

"He . . ." they started simultaneously.

"Never mind . . . I don't suppose you did it intentionally . . . I'll have to get you some paper plates, that's all."

"Aye, aye, sir . . ." they said simultaneously, right arms jerking involuntarily, as if aiming subconscious salutes of gratitude.

Well, he mused in resignation, hell will freeze over before I hear the last of this in Naples . . . New London . . . Holy Loch or Norfolk or Pearl Harbor, for that matter. They'll know me forever as the guy who got sunk by an armload of crockery.

He looked at the depth repeater on the bulkhead, saw that they were at twenty-nine feet and thus would have all the sail and a small walrus back of deck out of the water. Surfaced, he could feel a slight sea motion in the contrast to the living-room steadiness of the ship in the depths. He got up, retrieved his cap and started for the bridge. He passed into the control room, glanced around at the quiet efficiency proceeding there, noticed that Lieutenant Johnson was gone and asked, "Bridge got the con?"

"Yes, sir," replied Chief Bos'n's Mate Joseph Cate, a spike-haired, lantern jawed old-timer, swinging in his swivel chair throne at the bank of toggle switches, where, as chief of the watch, he ruled over alternate air or seawater in the ship's main ballast and seven different varieties of trim tanks.

Stephens went up the vertical ladder through the two hatches inside the *Skate*'s thick pressure hull, emerged into the still-dripping sail, climbed two more ladders, and, with Lieutenant Johnson's feet in view, yelled, "Permission to come on the bridge!" Hearing Johnson's automatic "Aye, aye, Captain," he slid himself backward and up into *Skate's* little chamber pot of a bridge, now, on the surface, with its streamlined steel cover jacked open. The sea was shimmering, a kaleidoscope of gold and steel gray in the low sun of late afternoon. Off to the east he could see *Triton's* black rectangle of sail. Damn him!

Westward, silhouetted against the sparkling light two miles away, reared the great, ungainly bulk of *Hornet*, seeming mountain-tall from his low perch only a dozen feet above the surface. A signal light, brilliant even against the sun glare, was snapping its lascivious winks from the bridge. Stephens could read the Morse himself, but he knew he was not as adept as the signalman perched on top the sail, leaning against the risen fairing of the radar antena, swaying comfortably with the slight roll of the boat.

"What's he say?" he asked.

"Yes, sir, Captain," the signalman said. He was already writing, though, Stephens knew, he was perfectly capable of remembering a hundred-group signal verbatim. In a minute, the signalman handed the paper toward him and Stephens was reaching for it when he saw, with a kind of curious apprehension, that the sailor was blushing a furious dark red.

He took the message and thought, No wonder he wrote it out. He read, "FIVE-SEVEN-EIGHT. FM BLUEGRASS. TRUST YOU ARE ABLE TO EAT FROM HANDS. OTHERWISE CAN SPARE YOU EXTRA DINNERWARE. ACKNOWLEDGE."

Stephens flinched, knowing perfectly well that *Triton* had read the signal too, over his shoulder, so to speak.

"Acknowledge it," he grunted at the signalman, then added, send this, "BLUEGRASS. FM FIVE-SEVEN-EIGHT. THANKS. WE NOW ON DIET."

Hornet's light was blinking again, and while the signalman watched and wrote, Stephens, mouthing the words as they came, spelled out, "FIVE-SEVEN-EIGHT. FM BLUEGRASS. I AM IN RECEIPT SPECIAL ORDERS FM COMSUBLANT DETACH-

ING FIVE-SEVEN-EIGHT SPECIAL TD IMMEDIATELY ON RE-
CEIPT. ACKNOWLEDGE."

"Acknowledge," he told the signalman, conscious as he did
so of rising surprise and curiosity in himself. He knew this
hunter-killer exercise was scheduled for two more weeks
before returning to Naples. Only himself and *Triton* were involved. They couldn't very well play hide and seek with only
one submarine. It sounded funny, but *Hornet*'s light was
busy again, winking more slowly and deliberately, as though
making sure he got it all and got it right.

"FM COMSUBLANT FOR FIVE-SEVEN-EIGHT. UPON RECEIPT
FIVE-SEVEN-EIGHT TO DETACH FROM BLUEGRASS. PROCEED
TO TEKE POINT OF GALLIPOLI PENINSULA THERE BOARD
TURKISH PILOT NAVY CAPTAIN BURHAN EMEK. PROCEED SUB-
JECT HIS DIRECTIONS TO ISTANBUL. REPORT TO AMBASSA-
DOR RUSHMORE AMERICAN CONSULATE FOR FURTHER
ORDERS. FM BLUEGRASS. FIVE-SEVEN-EIGHT ACKNOWLEDGE."

"Acknowledge it," he told the signalman automatically.
He was baffled. This didn't make sense. There hadn't been an
American flag submarine through the Dardanelles Strait
since he could remember. For that matter, ever . . . so far as
he knew. He didn't dig this and despite his confidence in the
signalman, wondered if there must not be some screw up
somewhere. He hated to ask for a repeat, fearing to appear a
greater boob than the crockery matter already had estab-
lished him as being. But still . . . this was a baffler.

"Get him to repeat that," he told the signalman.

Hornet did so, this time even slower, as though in controlled impatience spelling things out for a dull child.

Stephens acknowledged again and received a curt, "FIVE-
SEVEN-EIGHT. FM BLUEGRASS. EXECUTE."

Puzzled but at least convinced he had heard aright,
Stephens had a sudden worrying thought.

"Send this," he told the signalman. "REQUEST ADVICE
WHAT DISPOSITION SHIP'S PASSENGERS."

The answer was even more explicit. "FIVE-SEVEN-EIGHT.
FM BLUEGRASS. TAKE 'EM ALONG. EXECUTE IMMEDIATELY."

He turned to the OOD. "I don't yet know what this is all about, Mr. Johnson. We'll find out, no doubt. Turn her around and head generally north until I give you a course. We'll submerge then. I'm leaving the bridge now."

"Aye, aye, sir," replied Johnson, a husky, crew-cut blond, whose more or less constant smile rendered his round face attractive despite the scars smallpox had left on him (a rarity in his time, but he had by some mischance escaped vaccination). As Stephens jackknifed himself forward and down into the narrow depths of the sail, Johnson spoke into his mike. "Left full rudder, come to ooo degrees. All ahead standard."

Like an echo his words came back from his speaker followed by "Aye, aye, sir." *Skate* began to swing to port, leaving a slick of smooth water inside the turn and aft.

Reaching the bottom of the ladder, Stephens heard the talker telling Johnson, fifty feet above them and with the signalman—the only man aboard in open daylight, "Passing zero-one-zero degrees, coming to zero-zero-zero, sir." It's a smart, well-handled boat, he thought as he often did in affectionate pride . . . only damn the crockery . . . damn the crockery to hell. He moved to starboard, around the raised pulpit of the con, past the radar scanner to the chart table where Chief Quartermaster Ray Guernic lounged, endangering his thick black beard with the stub of a cigarette smoldering to the last economical five-eights of an inch.

Nearly everything in a nuclear submarine has a reason, and Chief Guernic's beard was not an exception. It was, of course, a source of aesthetic satisfaction to him but, more important, it was a declaration of moral protest. The chief's skin under that rug was tender and easily abraded. In his stays ashore, which were rare, he had discovered that the only shaving lubricant his hide would tolerate was a particular brand of menthol-cooled lather dispensed from an aerosol bomb. The nuke, conversely, would not tolerate any such thing; in fact, the whole new undersea navy abominated *anything* stored in an aerosol can.

"Chief," the officer in charge of the sub's internal atmosphere said apologetically when Guernic came aboard with a can of the lather among his gear, "I know you've got a touchy chin and I sympathize. But if I let you bring the stuff on, I'd have to let anybody else as well. You know that would mean roughly six hundred pounds of freon gas roaming all over the ship. The air scrubbers got plenty to handle the way it is, what with such freon as we can't avoid in the refrigerators and air conditioning, getting rid of the goddam carbon dioxide and monoxide—manufacturing oxygen and soaking up the crummy BO our best friends wouldn't tell some of us guys about. Nope, Chief, I am sorry!"

"We need a course for the Dardanelles, Chief," Stephens now said.

"Aye, Captain. This chart'll do it," Guernic said, tapping the Aegean Sea projection already pinned to the table. "Let's see, now." Chief Guernic, who had taught navigation to numberless classes of ensigns and neophyte quartermasters in sub school at New London, had the uncontested officer's job of putting the *Skate* where she was supposed to be for the perfectly legitimate reason that his knowledge of the electronic complexities within SINS (Ships Inertial Navigation System) and its feeder satellite NAVDAC (Navigation Data Computer) was more intimate and loving than any other man's knowledge of his mistress' erogenous zones. He reached for his parallel rulers and bent over the table. After a minute, he looked up at the captain, simultaneously discarding the butt which had gone out without committing arson on him.

"It's a clean run, sir," he said. "Steer three-three-three to about thirty-nine degrees ten minutes, then zero-five-zero degrees straight into the mouth of the strait."

"Water enough to stay submerged?" Stephens asked. He could do any of this himself, but he believed in letting specialists specialize; it was one of the things, he knew, which gave him a happy ship.

"All the way, Captain . . . that is, almost. It shoals to

18

twenty-four fathoms off Bozcaada Island . . . about twenty miles out."

"Very well, Chief," Stephens stepped up to the con pulpit and, out of habit, took a quick swing around the horizon through Number One periscope. He called the bridge, "Mr Johnson, set course three-three-three and prepare to submerge." He heard the orders, parrotlike, being repeated back and forth among the helm, con, chief of the watch and bridge and, as he stepped down and returned to Chief Guernic's table the diving klaxon sounded its repetitious warning squawk. The world's loudest razzberry, he thought.

"Chief," he said to Guernic, "we got a big-scale chart of the Dardanelles?"

"Afraid not, Captain. We've never had any need of it. And I didn't suppose we ever would." There was nagging curiosity in the chief's eyes, although Stephens knew full well that he would never commit the breach of etiquette of asking his skipper where they were bound, far less why. This time Stephens, who would have remained silent had he himself known, decided to let the chief share his own bafflement.

"I haven't the faintest idea," he said. He turned and left the orderly, fantastically complex business of the con and climbed the ladder—really a stairway in the relatively commodious entrails of his 2360-ton command. He was about to inform his guests of this radical change in the program. Captain Brown and the Italian, Nicolai, were already in the wardroom in desultory conversation over coffee. I guess I should have requisitioned an expresso machine for the Wop, Stephens thought; mere hospitality. He sent Billings off to roust out the others, meanwhile asking Collingwood for a pot of hot water.

Within a few minutes the Greek, Cavanides, appeared, sleepily rubbing his eyes.

"'Allo, all," he said. "Captain, when I was invited to cruise with you I was, to be frank, scared. I am attached to the submarine force, yes, but to tell the truth, I am at heart a staff man. And then, of course, I knew this was an atomic vessel and that scarced me even more. But now . . . a week of it . . . and this little spy you so graciously pinned on me"—he flicked the radiation counter looped to his belt—"doesn't even have the grace to flicker a little and give me, at least, the excitement of a little apprehension that I am being radio-activated. I regret to say it, my Captain, but I am afraid I must: Your atomic submarines while no doubt wonderful as weapons to destroy the world, are somewhat less than a thrill to live in. In fact, Captain, a bore."

Stephens grinned. "I admit it's no roller coaster."

Kapitan Mueller, correct in uniform even to tunic, a tall, somewhat stiff figure with a straight mouth and alert, level gray eyes, entered.

"You asked for me, Captain?" he said. With professional interest, his eyes went automatically to the course and depth indicators on the bulkhead. "Ah," he said, "I see we are submerged again. Do we now continue the exercise?"

"No, Herr Kapitan," Stephens replied. "That's why I called you gentlemen together. When we surfaced after . . . after the misfortune"—he grimaced—"after the misfortune which caused our opponent to locate us on sonar, the flagship transmitted orders summarily detaching us from the exercise. The orders were urgent, and there has not been time to inform you earlier. I regret it."

Mueller's gaze went back to the course repeater.

"I see we are proceeding north, northwest. Is it permitted to ask, Captain, where we are bound?"

"Certainly. You are our guests. It would be discourteous to shanghai you without, at least, telling you where we are going. We have been ordered through the Dardanelles to Istanbul."

The Greek's eyes were no longer sleepy, but bright with curious sudden interest. "Constantinople? How could that be? We are a warship, no?"

"Yes, I can't answer why or how it has been authorized because I don't know, gentlemen. I assume we moved with

20

Turkish assent. We are to pick up a Turkish pilot at the mouth of the Strait."

"So?" the German broke in, as his eyes went back to the repeaters again. "We cruise submerged. Is there a reason, Captain?"

Stephens smiled his sudden sunny grin. He was for the most part a soundly organized man with a ready sense of humor. "Only the usual one, Kapitan Mueller. We brag that our modern nuclear submariners are a superior breed of men, and they are. Highly trained, specialists, as you know. However, living submerged most of the time as we do, we have regrettably lost one of the seaman's cardinal virtues. Nuclear submariners are not comfortable on the surface. They get seasick."

The Italian looked up with a beatific smile. "So, Istanbul, eh, Captain, you could not have pleased me better. I was there for a month last year. Ah, lovely city, lovely. Do you know the Klub Kit Kat? Ah! It stands in a cellar on the Cumhuriyet Cad. The food is passable, the music atrocious, the liquor violent. But the girls, ah, yes, the girls! Did you know they dance there without the foolish impediment of clothing? Such grace, such lovely sinuous grace. Such breasts and other things. I was fortunate to make a friendship with a person called Marida. Hers is a speciality, a belly dance they call it. For me the ordinary belly dance is an abomination . . . but in the case of Marida! Ah, gentlemen, I will tell you . . ."

Grinning, Stephens left the wardroom and went back to the con and stepped up on the pulpit.

"Take her down to 250 feet and all ahead full, Mr Johnson," he said. "We have aboard a gentleman in a hurry to get to Istanbul. We may as well give him at least as fast a ride here as he seems convinced he will get there."

Skate surfaced the next dawn with Bozcaada Island off her starboard beam and ran in at fourteen knots toward the rocky, soaring headlands guarding the entrance to the Dardanelles. Off Cape Teke, on the European side, in response to a blinkered signal from the beach, Stephens told Lieutenant

Peter Zink, his weapons officer, who had the deck watch, to slow to one-third speed and come to 048 degrees to rendezvous with the pilot. At seven A.M., Zulu (or Greenwich) time, *Skate* hove to as the pilot boat, a fast launch, became visible against the mountainous shielding backdrop of the cliffs, mainly because of the high white bone in her teeth.

"He's moving like a bat out of hell, Captain," Lieutenant Zink observed as the launch came on. As it neared, Stephens went below, then back up to the deck hatch on the starboard side of the sail. Considering that everything so far about whatever he was doing was unusual, to say the least, Stephens thought he might as well go down and welcome his Turkish guest—or temporary boss, he didn't really know which—personally. After all, he isn't an ordinary pilot. Besides, I guess a Turkish captain outranks me. Since, according to law, we're going to be trespassing we may as well be polite about it.

The launch eased in alongside, and a sailor in *Skate*'s deck working party heaved it a line. Stephens saw a stocky figure in the cockpit working his way out of a suit of spray-shiny oilskins, and then, with a hand from the submarine's men, he clambered up the steep camber of *Skate*'s round side and, at length, stood erect on the minuscule expanse of the submarine's flat deck. Stephens stepped forward with a hand outstretched.

"Albay Emek? Welcome aboard. That is the correct Turkish title for Captain, is it not?"

The Turk, short, heavy in the shoulders, round and somber of face, with a black mustache and sharp, intelligent eyes, met Stephens' hand with a powerful grip.

"And you are welcome to Turkey, Captain Stephens," he said. "And the title is correct, yes. I presume we can get under way at once?"

"Ready when you are, Captain. I assume you'll want to con the ship from the bridge."

"Yes, if you will be so kind to lead the way, Captain," the Turk said, a curious formality in his manner.

"Of course. I'm afraid you will find it a little unconventional in this ship, a little awkward. We must go below and then back up . . . through the sail . . ." He slapped the plating of the tall, black finlike tower, uncluttered anywhere on its surface.

"No matter," the Turkish officer said, and followed him down through the deck hatch and then up again through the levels of the sail.

On the bridge, he introduced Lieutenant Zink, an introduction acknowledged with a short but polite nod.

"Captain Emek will con the ship, Pete," Stephens said. "Take your orders from him. We'll stay on the surface, of course?" he added, turning toward Emek.

"Yes, Captain. There is enough water to run submerged most of the way, but it shoals at two points. In any case there is much traffic in the strait. It is better to see—and be seen."

"We are fortunate to have you help us," Stephens said, agreeably. "You may wonder at it, Captain, but we don't have proper charts of the Dardanelles aboard."

"That is no cause for surprise. I understand that under ordinary circumstances you wouldn't need them."

Well, Stephens thought, that's a polite way of putting it.

Stephens heard Captain Brown's unmistakably British voice from the level below. "I say, permission to come on the bridge?"

"Come ahead, sir," Zink answered.

The Britisher's lined and weathered face appeared at their feet and then, after some contortion, the long gaunt body followed. Once up and on his feet, Captain Brown towered above the short Turkish officer and even over his host's rangy five eleven and a half.

"Had to see this, you know," he remarked after introductions. "Gallipoli, you know. Huge piece of our shared history, eh, Captain Emek?"

"A bitter time," the Turk acknowledged.

"It was up there, wasn't it, Captain?" Brown gestured toward the steep and rugged rise of cliff looming to port.

"Dug in for eleven months up there, God knows how many regiments half destroyed, we even had submarines in this gut—not that they did us much good. Your Turks fought like demons, you know. Magnificent."

"Yes, I know," Emek acknowledged.

"You know, we nearly lost a great man out of history here. Pity."

"How so, Captain?" Stephens asked.

"Churchill, you know. Old Winnie—First Lord of the Admiralty then—was absolutely convinced the Straits could be taken. Disgraced himself, what? Would have been a thundering tragedy if he hadn't managed to live that down. Bloody miracle he did."

"That's an understatement, Captain," Stephens said. "It is strange how circumstances, luck or something, produce great men when they are needed. But Churchill's time of greatness was a time of real giants. Churchill himself, Roosevelt, Stalin. It wasn't necessary to like them. The ability to attract adoration was never an essential element of greatness. I suppose, under these terms, even Hitler was a great man, paranoid or not."

"We, too, have our great ones, Mehmed II, Kemal Attaturk," the Turk said. He turned to Zink. "Lieutenant, you will please come right to zero-eight-five degrees off the Gelibolu beacon. Then left again to zero-four-five as we debouch into Marmara . . . in approximately three miles."

"Aye, aye, sir," Zink acknowledged, then passed the pilot's sailing direction down to the con.

The walls of the gut had been spreading almost imperceptibly, but now they flared wide until they fell away entirely and they were riding the island dotted Sea of Marmara, one of the world's most beautiful bodies of water.

"If that girl Hero was as breathtaking as where she lived it was no wonder that Leander used to swim across back there to get his hands on her. She must have been something magnificent in bed . . . but I wonder what kind of shape Leander was in after that long swim," the British captain said.

"Swimming drains the arms and legs and lungs," the Turk replied. "Fortunately it does not exhaust or even measurably deplete other essential organs."

Skate, under Emek's direction swung left to 032° and entered the Istanbul channel at 1630 hours. Creeping along at three knots, she threaded her way through the waterway's bustling traffic, commuter ferries shuttling back and forth be-between Istanbul and Uskadar on the Asiatic side, between Istanbul and the lovely green humps of the Prinkipo islands, freighters standing out of the Bosporus or standing in, the white grace of millionaires' yachts, the battered utilitarian handsome-ugliness of fishermen's boats with painted eyes staring downward at their appointed function of locating the still-uncaught catch.

Skate crept into the Golden Horn under the loom of the bosom-round hill on the European side where soared the domes and spiked minarets of the Blue Mosque and Aie Sofia. They tied up on the Galata side near the Turkish navy yard in the berth, Stephens remembered from a long ago midship-men cruise, once occupied by the rusted hulk of *Yavuz*, Turkey's only and spectacularly unlucky battle cruiser of World War I. The old wagon, five times rent by British mines, had lain there for more than a quarter century, kept afloat possibly as a reminder of naval shame or, perhaps she wasn't worth the trouble to tow her out and sink her.

Now *Skate* took her place. Zink, too young ever to have heard of *Yavuz*, watched, as down on deck the line handlers of the special sea detail went expertly about their chores of laying out the two-inch nylon hawsers and raising cleats and winches from the recesses where they had been pocketed to maintain the hull's sleek streamlining when at sea. By 1715 *Skate* was moored, bow and stern and spring lines.

In his cabin, Stephens was informed that an officer messen-ger from the consulate had awaited them with the ship's mail, flown in from Naples by MATS, and with a verbal mes-sage for him, to be delivered personally. Soon a Marine lieutenant, spotless and tall in knife-creased khaki, knocked at his cramped stateroom and was told to come ahead.

"My name is Grady Matthews, sir," he said. "Ambassador Rushmore is flying in from Ankara this afternoon to see you. He is expected to land in around an hour. He has instructed me to invite you for cocktails at the consulate at nineteen-thirty. He also told me that your guests are invited, too, if they care to come. We will have two cars at your disposal on the pier at nineteen-fifteen."

"I'm sure they'll be pleased," Stephens said. "That is, all but Capitano di Fregata Nicolai, the Italian. I think he has a somewhat different diplomatic mission here, which he regards as urgent . . . Tell me, Lieutenant, did you ever hear of a place called the Kit Kat Klub?"

Matthews abruptly went unmilitary and whistled.

"Sir," he said, regaining his composure, "the Kit Kat is so hot we expect it to go up in flames any night—spontaneous combustion. If your Italian guest is bound in that direction, it is eight to five you'll never get him back—at least not in the original condition."

Stephens grinned. "He says he survived it once before with no lasting ill effect . . . Incidentally, have you ever heard of an entertainer there, Marida is the name . . . belly dancer or something like that?"

Matthews whistled again, even more emphatically.

"Blow torch, sir, pure blow torch."

"Well, you may be right about our Italian friend going in harm's way. I suppose we'll just have to be philosophical about it. He doesn't look as though he could be dissuaded. Too bad, a staunch ally and a good shipmate. He was a great cribbage player until he learned we were coming here. Now he seems a man with something on his mind . . . or in his pants."

"I could get the shore patrol to watch over him, if you wish, sir," Matthews offered.

"No, I think not! he's of age. Every man to his own poison."

26

Matthews turned to go, then abruptly turned back, fetching a pale blue envelope from his shirt pocket.

"Oh, I nearly overlooked this, sir. A letter for you. Came in the pouch mail. I must be getting absent-minded. Or maybe it was the Kit Kat that bemused me."

"Thanks, Lieutenant," Stephens said, taking the envelope, recognizing the source even before he touched it. This was from Peg, back in New London with the kids. He wondered how Peg, had managed to piggy-back her letter with the diplomatic mail. Resourceful girl, he thought.

He opened the letter. It was a long one, four pages of Peg's crowded, miniature handwriting. Peg ought to be engraving the Lord's Pray on pin heads; he felt a sudden wave of affection and loneliness. The subs make a lousy life for a Navy wife, he mused, as he often did. Stay home and mind the kids and get your jollies writing letters. He guessed she must have picked up that tiny handwriting crowding a maximum cargo of information on the old-style V-mail folders.

He read the letter through twice, learning he was beloved at home—which he knew anyhow—that Peg was lonesome —which he also knew. That it would be lovely to be in bed together again, sleeping raw. And how ! he agreed. That the braces would be off Peg junior's teeth in another three weeks —"thank the Lord, you know she hasn't dared to smile in the two years since Dr. Reasoner clamped them on." Then the bad news, washing machine going to pot just after the guarantee had run out and it had cost a whopping $76 to resurrect it—and that only one week after the color TV blew its picture tube.

"I swear I think the things just lurk and wait and conspire with each other to go blooie en masse just when you're brokest," she had written.

Gal, you're so right, he thought. That's another dandy thing about the Navy. It wasn't starvation level, exactly, but didn't it seem a little ironic to put a thirty-nine-year-old guy in charge of a $69 million enterprise—which is what *Skate* was at the minimum—and pay him $13,000 a year before taxes? Still, he admitted to himself, he wouldn't change jobs with any $75,000-a-year executive if he had the chance. And, he knew with gratitude, Peg wouldn't want him to. She'd prefer to skimp and keep him the way he was. It sounded trite, they would both admit, but pride was sometimes intrinsically more dear than money.

Still, reminded by his absence from his family, Stephens sometimes turned to wondering what he really was, or rather what his job was.

He was, he knew, a superbly trained human being, entrusted with a superbly contrived instrument and the lives of some 120 men. He had in him, he recognized, a strong pride in the instrument and the men, pride in the submarine service, pride and confidence in his own finely tuned professionalism. There was a powerful satisfaction in knowing his intricate job and knowing that he did it well. That came first, doing it, understanding his orders and seeing that they were carried out.

Stephens was not ignorant of the political world and the frightful dangers for mankind inherent in it. And he recognized that *Skate*, he and his crew, altogether, comprised a political instrument. However active they might be, however rightfully confident in their abilities, their assignment in the human cosmos was essentially negative. If they ever were called upon to do in serious anger what they so well knew how to do, they could account themselves a failure. They were what the world had learned to call a deterrent which meant in effect that success for them was exactly measured by the degree to which they helped to persuade the other side to do nothing.

That goes for *Skate*, he reflected. It goes even more for her bigger, more lethal cousins, the Polaris boats with their sixteen missiles per boat, taken as a fleet, enough to wipe out the world twice over.

The Greek was right, though halfway joking, *Skate* and her relatives were lovely instruments to destroy the world.

But if they ever did have to destroy it, they would become less than nothing, a damnation rather than a reason for pride. We don't produce; we don't contribute to the good of man, he thought. All we do is stand here with the whip in hand and a well trained eye, and tell man he'd better not get out of line. The job was necessary, given mankind's paranoid temperament, but nobody could say it was a positive contributor to mankind's betterment. They were there merely to keep mankind from getting worse. What that makes me, truly, is a con man in reverse.

II

THE summons came on teletype from the Pentagon and reached Vice Admiral Jacob March, USN, Annapolis '41, ComSubLant, about noon in his office at the Norfolk Navy Base. He sensed an air of formality as well as urgency in the message, and so Admiral March changed from his khaki working uniform into blues. He ordered out a single engine Cessna service plane, which he distrusted on the principle that it operated in a fluid medium not to his liking. He considered air insubstantial; it didn't have enough salt in it. His prejudiced dislike was confirmed . . . somewhat lefthandedly . . . because the hangar door trolley jammed in its tracks and the ground crew delayed him twenty minutes getting the plane out into the open. A little put out, he reached the office of Admiral Michael Engel, USN, Annapolis '36, Chief of Naval Operations, at 1430 hours local time.

He was greeted cordially by his superior who, in adherence to Navy custom, called for coffee before getting around to relieving his Atlantic submarine boss of his curiosity. Even with coffee and some service chitchat out of the way, Admiral Engel seemed strangely hesitant to get to the point; meanwhile Admiral March fidgeted inwardly and wished the chief would get with it. At length he did, talking without interruption for fifteen minutes, while Admiral March's jaw, ornery in the most felicitous circumstances, grew grimmer.

When Admiral Engel paused at last, the submariner was having trouble absorbing what he had heard. Being solid Navy he made a conscious effort to suppress, at least so far as his surface was involved, both his dismay and a rising surge of icy anger. He succeeded pretty well with the first but Admiral Engel, having had practice with this man before, recognized that his subordinate had hoisted a hurricane warning. The fury aboil in that leathery frame, he saw, was about to be decanted. It was no wonder, he thought. Nevertheless...

"This can work, Jake," he said soothingly, not really expecting March to be in any degree soothed. Actually, except that he was a political animal, which March was not, the professional seafarer part of him was as appalled and indignant as March. But he had to say something, if only to make a space in time until, as professionals, they both cooled enough to accept the proposition that they were dealing with orders and orders were not to be gainsaid, however unpalatable, however, indeed, murderous.

"Yes? It can work, can it?" It had been longer than he could remember since Admiral March had been intimidated by a superior. "Play hob with a treaty that's been standing, more or less unaltered, for better than a hundred and twenty years? Screw up the rules of the road as more or less laid down in international law? Run up on a hostile beach in peacetime . . . which I guess is what we call it? Navigate some of the trickiest water in the world and do it blind? Surface where the radar will have you cold . . . if sonar doesn't have you cold already? Do all this for a bum who has been flung out by his own people and here will serve no purpose except, perhaps, give people something beside race riots to think about for a few minutes. It can work, can it? Mike, who dreamed up this monstrosity?"

It may as well be said at once that some admirals get to that exalted rank by polishing up the handle on the big front door, and others largely by outliving their classmates. Neither circumstance indicates that they are necessarily bad admirals. In fact, the U.S. Navy, by and large, ends up with a disproportionately high average—compared to other industries—of senior officers endowed with superior competence. On the other hand, inevitably, it does make its goofs and sew tons of gold braid on knuckleheads.

None of the categories could be said to fit Admiral March. Bad-tempered, single-minded, utterly without fear, totally dedicated to the submarine service, he had got to be an

31

admiral simply because he was too good at his work to be passed over. All bureaucratic organizations, of which the Navy is one, naturally resent genius; their problem, of course, is that when genius is thrust upon them they are often forced to put up with it. But genius takes its toll; in the case of Admiral March its toll was measured in almost total and completely outspoken disrespect for officials, particularly those chosen by the voters of America.

Admiral Engel stiffened; he did not often need to listen to that tone from the mouth of a junior. He could flatten them when the need arose. But he was not yet ready to pull rank on this particular junior. In the first place they were old friends; in the second place he had to get something done whether he liked it or not, which he didn't. He borrowed a little space, waiting to calm the irritation of being talked back to, by gazing around his office in the Pentagon's E-ring, reseeing the proud painting of a Navy, all the generations from U.S.S. *Constitution* engaged with *Guerrière* to U.S.S. *Nautilus* surfaced through the ice at the North Pole.

"The lot. He had us all over there. State . . ."

"State! That man may not be an idiot but the proposition is unproven. He may have a brain, but, if so, he has not yet had the guts to use it. He's a freshly diapered, clean, and winsome, obedient child."

"All right. I'm not fighting you . . . Defense . . ."

"Him? I should have known it!"

"The Joint Chiefs . . . a guy from the snoopers, the head snooper as a matter of fact; he was the one who had the word. They talked about other ways: through Germany and over or under the wall; out through Finland; an airplane into the Caucasus. All too risky. The cargo is valuable . . . and too old and fat. Also, as you could guess, they want to impress him."

"Who wants to impress him?"

"HE does."

"I should have known that, too."

"Anyhow, along in all this, our own Secretary came up with this . . .."

"Our own Secretary, as you know, Mike, was a catboat sailor on Lake Geneva outside of Chicago. Which may be his qualification . . . aside from the fifty thousand clams he put into the last campaign. He and State, as you know, were the big spenders. I have heard it reported, although out of loyalty I put it down to malicious gossip, that he got seasick in any breeze over Force Two."

"You aren't carried away by enthusiasm for the leaders, are you, Jake?"

"Nope. Are you?"

"It had to come to a decision. He made it."

"That one I suppose." It wasn't a question, really, but the thumb hooked out and across the Potomac did whatever honors Admiral March thought were indicated.

"That one. We were in the Oval Room, which apparently gives him some sense of purpose . . . or destiny. He's a great one for destiny, you know. You ever been there?"

"No."

"In his bedroom, along with his masseur, he keeps a painting of the cabin he was born in. Only he can't quite get his primitives straight. He wants to be Abe Lincoln, all right, but he can't quite abide the idea that, when he was a pup, nobody in his neighborhood had the price of paint . . . he's willing to have come from the poor . . . but he has trouble getting honest into the equation. That painting is some artist's rendition of the new cabin he has built which is his own version of the Oklahoma shack he was actually born in."

"If you're selling him to me, don't bother, Mike. I know he's Commander-in-Chief. That's what it says in the book."

"He had the alternatives to pick from. He picked your people."

"I submit he's pretty free with my people." Admiral March knew his place but did not intend to keep it. "What does he know about water? Beyond flinging empty beer cans off a private yacht into a private lake that the taxpayers dammed up for him? Does that qualify him in submarines?"

"Come on, Jake. You know he doesn't have to qualify in anything. All he has to do is listen and make a pick. And, to tell you the truth, I'm not any too sure he listens first. He likes to go it big, Western style."

"You sound a little disloyal, Mike."

"Compared to me you're subversive. He's still C-in-C."

"Yes . . . And it's my kids he's likely to kill."

"No, he's not out to kill them. He's out to make heroes out of them . . . heroes next to him, of course."

"All right." The more Admiral March pondered this, the harder it became to keep a grip on the quality the Academy had striven to breed into his bones . . . decorum. Duty, yes, but politeness? The hell with it. "You know as well as I do . . . sir." The submariner got back a corner of the proper decorum. "You know as well as I do we stick a seventy-million-dollar submarine in there, and if the Turks don't shoot us out of the water, the Russians sure as hell will."

Admiral March had been wholly and single-mindedly in love with submarines ever since he had got out of the Academy and had been ramrodded through sub school under a looming wrath that became a reality with the first torpedo launched at Battleship Row in Pearl Harbor. In the beginning it had been an unrequited affair with a cranky mistress; his first boat as a downy ensign had been a battered, cramped, sweating, un-air-conditioned, unreliable old S-Boat operating out of Dutch Harbor in the Aleutians. It was wretched duty in the resurrected relic and the crew, patrolling in the murk and chill around Kiska, had to get used to the chronic misery of one venomous cold after another, always teetering on the brink of double pneumonia. But the affair had blossomed into enduring passion one black night as Ensign March kept the OOD watch on the bridge while charging batteries. He had only just made out a looming profile, high forward, probably military, Japanese as sure as sin, in time to scream down the voice tube, "Captain, to the bridge!" and send the boat to General Quarters. Even in the dark and with minimum sea know-how in his locker, young March was able to conclude that these two strangers in the night were on a collision course. The captain, wearing a sheepskin but no pants over his long handles, barefoot, and nose dripping like a leaky garden hose, had got there just in time to figure a range and bearing and sink two torpedoes out of a spread of six into the other ship. The explosion was a glory to the heart and gave a quick blast of light bright enough to confirm that this thing, now with a broken back and headed for the bottom, was a Japanese destroyer indeed. March's future was sealed. Now he loved his wife, was devoted to his country, tolerated —just barely—the leaders of his government—and considered submarines the most exquisite handiwork of man and fully admired the men who took them to sea and under it.

Now he could foresee one of his boats—he still thought of them fondly as boats even though the tonnage of submarines had gone up so nearly to that of a light cruiser that the Bureau of Ships had ordained, in its wisdom, that modern subs must be accorded the dignity of being called "ship"— dispatched into grave jeopardy for no prize more substantial than a political whim.

"You believe he'll stick to this harebrained idea? Think he'll insist?" He still hoped unassailable logic must somehow be brought to bear to mitigate the stupefying illogic of a powerful and bullheaded landlubber.

"He'll insist. The polls show him far down since a year ago. He's poll-sensitive, and criticism gives him a bellyache. He needs a propaganda spectacular and the way his skull works he sees this as just the ticket. He'll insist until he's proved wrong." The chief looked glum and worried. "You know, and I do, that proving him wrong could cost a ship."

"And the men in it," March added grimly. "This isn't getting us forward any. Have you looked at the charts?"

"Only a quick once-over. I ordered them up as soon as I got back from the White House. They came just before you did. Let's look."

35

The chief paused, thoughtfully scratching the seat of his pants.

"You know, Jake, the British put their subs into the Dardanelles in nineteen-fifteen while Churchill was trying to force Gallipoli—and they had to push through the Turks' nets to do it . . ."

"Yes, I know it. But those were E-boats, about a third as long as a nuke and a fifth the tonnage. It won't help this crackpot business to dredge up ancient history. I'd like to have a top navigator in here to study these things."

"We can't; this is top secret, absolutely on need-to-know status—and for my money too damn many people need to know already."

"I wish I didn't," March said as the two admiral's, both graying but otherwise unalike physically, moved to the chief's huge chart table, far roomier than anything afloat.

"May as well begin here," Engel said. "It's also where we could finish." He stopped before a Mercator projection of the Aegean Sea, bottom contoured, scale 1-to-768, 450 at latitude 38° north. March, slender, still reasonably lithe from his years of moving fast up and down the vertical ladders of American submarines, hard of eye, pugnacious of jaw, bent over the chart. Admiral Engel, heavier, going to gut, usually genial of mien (at least on the surface; Washington contained a lot of politicians and other kinds of people he had to get along with), put both hands on the table ledge and let them take up a share of his considerable weight.

"There's water . . . enough," Engel said, lifting one hand to run a lightly boned, well-cared-for finger along the narrow, crooked, precipitously walled forty miles of the Dardanelles Strait.

"Most of it, yes. But not all. Down to fifty-four feet here in the bend below Cannakale, shoals nearly clear across the channel. And higher up below Gelibolu it shoals again, smack in the middle of the channel, down to three fathoms with deeper water on both sides of the shoal. Tricky. It's enough, of course, depending on how you go about it. Nine

36

fathoms isn't anywhere near enough to go through submerged, not for a boat drawing thirty feet surfaced and nearly twice that submerged to periscope depth. And that brings up the next questions; just where does the brain trust think we're going to stand with the Turks on this?"

"State says they can be persuaded. Guarantees it, in fact. He's flying out to Ankara tomorrow to make his pitch personally."

"State again," March's remark was a noncommittal grunt. "I'm not current on the Montreux Convention; never had need of it and didn't expect to. But I seem to remember it rules out ships of war in peacetime unless damaged and making for drydock. We sure don't fit that qualification . . . not going in, anyhow, but we may need a shipyard on the double coming out—if we come out."

"State's idea of cover is that, on the surface, our sub will be making a courtesy call at Istanbul, showing the flag to a stout ally. That's State's version; and he says he's sure the Turks will buy it, will anyhow when they know what the guts of the mission—after Istanbul—is all about."

"So the Turks are on the need-to-know list, too, are they? Mike, you know I think this whole idea's potty at the minimum, and it looks leakier by the minute."

The chief's voice was a little testy.

"From Istanbul and until the ship gets back there with the cargo, it'll have to run, maneuver, and navigate submerged—except for that one quick surfacing. When the sub leaves the Golden Horn, ostensibly going home, it'll have to submerge outward bound in the Sea of Marmara—to make it look good—before making its turn for the Bosporus. We can rationalize that on grounds we're showing off for our Turkish friends. The rest of the operation isn't even marginally feasible without Turkish agreement and a lot of help. You can call it complicity if you want, because that's what it amounts to."

"I know that. And I confess I don't see how they can afford it, much as they may agree with our brass on the attractions

37

of giving the Kremlin a zing by getting that man out right under their noses. The Montreux Convention protects the Turks from potentially hostile shipping sliding through their front yard. But at the same time, the way it stands now, it also protects the Russians from unfriendlies making free with the Black Sea. If we get caught, we'll be handing the Kremlin one of the loudest and most legitimate beefs in history."

"I know, I know. State has convinced the guy the Turks will co-operate. Certain, he says."

"Certain? If I were the Turks I wouldn't let a canoe through there. Not if it mounted so much as a bee-bee gun."

"That's up to the politicals. If the Turks won't buy it . . . please God . . . you won't have to send your ship." The chief paused for thought, rump now propped against the chart table. "Unless they go really loopy and try to sneak you through the Bosporus without the Turks knowing . . . they're weird enough to think of it. But I suspect we could legitimately refuse that one. We can't prove this won't work but we could make out a hell of a prima facie case against that one. Anyhow, let's look at it some more." Letting the Aegean chart lie, he slid over it a larger-scale projection of Marmara and the Bosporus twisting a score of miles northward to the Black Sea.

"You ever been in Istanbul?" he asked. "Did you know that the local sports' idea of a big time in Marmara is to go out and shoot swordfish with a bow and arrow? The big ones come up and sleep on the surface."

"Now look at this corkscrew," March said, bending to the chart in that section where the Bosporus opened into the Black Sea. "Physically we could get through without help . . . on the surface. But I suppose that's out of the question. It would be tougher submerged; the channel is less than half a mile wide, and the currents must be fierce. If we tried it on the surface, that man over there," Admiral March jerked a thumb over his shoulder, aimed more or less across the Potomac again, "might as well ring up the Kremlin on the red phone ahead of time and give them date, hour, and port

38

of arrival. We'll need a guide, on the surface, for several reasons: the soundings allow enough water for our boat to submerge but not deep enough to clear all surface traffic. Great spot for a collision. The guide would have two jobs at the minimum, keeping other traffic clear of us for one, furnishing camouflage for the periscope for another. I can't see one of our captains going through there entirely blind; he'll need a ten-second squint now and then. And, of course, the guide ship can't be one of ours."

"A Turk, of course . . . another reason why they're on need-to-know status. I thought of using some American vessel under Panamanian or Liberian flag, but that wouldn't deceive anybody much."

"The ship, commercial for sure, should be an old rust bucket . . . attract less attention. It had damn well better be under total radio silence until the mission's completed—if it ever is completed. I don't like anything about this, Mike. What's to keep the Turks from blabbing after it's over? The proper thing would be for the Russians never to know how we got the cargo out of there."

"You're asking too much," the Chief of Operations said. "If we keep them ignorant *until* we've gone in and out, that's about the limit we can realistically hope for. They'll know eventually. They knew about the U-2, but they never said anything until they actually shot one down. Their situation is the same as a man who's morally certain his wife's cheating, but unless he can catch her in the act it's just as well to keep his mouth shut, in public anyhow. Too humiliating . . . especially if he can't prove it and she doesn't have to admit it."

"That's one of the few situations where I feel some scant sympathy for heads of state; when they get caught with their pants at half mast and have to confess adultery—Ike and his U-2, Kennedy and his Bay of Pigs."

"The worse contingency we have to think about is the chance of our submarine actually getting hurt. I wonder if

39

there ought to be an ASR outfit aboard the Turk, an American ASR unit. What do you think?"

March frowned. "If they get hurt at all, they're probably dead. If they're not dead, they're sure in Russian territory. That means they can't holler for help. No distress signals, no SOS, no MAYDAY. They let out a peep and they're in worse trouble. What remote chance might there be, do you think, that the Russians would put up with us staging a rescue operation in their waters, trying to help a boat of ours that had no business there in the first place? What would you plead? That it got off course by accident? If they swallowed that—which would be incredible—you'd still have to convince them that it had any legitimate business in the Black Sea. Especially considering that, by that time, they'd know beyond question who we had aboard. I am willing to agree that we should put an ASR outfit aboard—with the DSRV along, which would be its only chance—but I wouldn't give it hell's bare bones of a chance to do much good, especially considering they'd be hunting a target struck both deaf and dumb. Our people are going to have to go it cold . . . unless that one over at the end of Pennsylvania Avenue gets his marbles back in time."

"You're getting subversive again," the chief said. March grunted. The chief went back to the chart and frowned.

"We have to get around to it eventually," March said. "Where and when and how does the brain trust expect to deliver what we're sending somebody to fetch—and what guarantee are they prepared to give that they can deliver?"

"Their notions are fuzzier than we can accept as tolerable. We'll have to cooper our own. They wanted to—believed they could—or were told that he could be delivered at the mouth of the Dnepr. My understanding from the snooper was that his getaway has been arranged—or, in any case, has been put in the hands of a savvy American expatriate—fellow who's been there since the war. The position was that the river would be the safest, cleanest route. You know, of course, that these people are not sailors. They've been looking at maps—not charts."

"That's obvious." Admiral March's angular, angry face mirrored his disgust. "Sailors they are not—I say again, sir—this nightmare is purely landlubber. The Dnepr—Odessa!" He snorted. "The bay at the river mouth is a sandbar with too little water to float a champer pot. The closest you could conceivably get a nuke to the river mouth would be offshore from Il'ichevsk south of Odessa—and that would have to be on the surface. And then, after you'd done your dirty work, you would have to run over a hundred miles south on the surface before you'd have a virgin's prayer of getting under. I trust even they don't really expect us to run up to Odessa on the surface—in the dredged channel—board a distinguished guest at our leisure, spin around on the keel with one engine ahead and the other astern because there isn't sea room to make any other kind of turn, then cruise blithely away with a thank-ye kindly, ma'am. Good glittering God!"

"They're not stupid, Jake—merely ignorant. They began to understand after I explained the facts of ships and shallows." The chief smiled a thin smile, shorn of humor. "I must say they were reluctant to give up something they never would have put in motion if the snoopers had asked first. They hoped we could do it their way. They don't want to communicate—with whoever they do communicate with—very much or often. Don't want to complicate things. Every word and every change is a risk, they say."

"Then why didn't they ask before going off half cocked? Talk about risk! They'll risk my boat and my people—well, what's next? I take it they'll compromise—compromise, that is, on something that's at least remotely possible."

"The snooper fella said he thought it possible—though dangerous—they could sneak him overland into the Crimea. It'll be hard intercepting him; been on the river—in a coal barge, for Pete's sake—a week already. They'll get it into the pipeline to intercept somewhere downriver and plant him

41

where you want him when you want him. They suggest the pickup offshore from Sevastopol."

"Still working with the Esso road map, I presume," Admiral March said sourly. "I don't suppose it occurred to them—our country's in the very best of hands—that the bay offshore from Sevastopol, twenty-five miles out from the beach and fifty miles deep, is a gunnery range, clearly marked 'prohibited' on any chart? When I get back to Norfolk, Mike, I'm going to reread *Alice in Wonderland*—and, I swear, believe every word of it."

The chief permitted himself the thin suggestion of a smile. "I told you, they're not sailors."

"They ain't. So then?"

"I made a tentative suggestion. Not one I like particularly —and entirely subject to your agreement. South of Sevastopol, around the cape and roughly eight miles overland, is Balaklava. Roads and the railroad run into Sevastopol and that is risky. The place is a military base, full of navy. Getting into Balaklava is a job of putting one foot ahead of another, I imagine. But Balaklava is only a small fishing port and resort these days—about the equivalent of Martha's Vineyard —but just now the off season for tourists. It's a possibility— but a skinny one."

Frowning, concentrated, Admiral March bent to the chart again. "It's another prohibited area," he muttered once and continued to study.

"But the water's deep," the chief said.

"Ye-es," doubtfully. At length Admiral March stood erect. "It seems barely possible—that is, if State, that celebrated necromancer, can promise that every Russian for a hundred miles around will be either sound asleep or mesmerized by sex. There's better than three hundred feet of water within eight miles of the beach—outside of the 'prohibited' zone— and better than six hundred feet ten miles further out. It's decent submarine water." He scrubbed his eyes and went back to the chart. "Barely possible. Just barely."

"Any idea what ship you could use?" Admiral Engel asked.

"Yes. We need something that can maneuver; the new ones won't do; they're clumsy in the pinches. It'll have to be one of the two-screw boats. So we begin with *Nautilus*."

"Isn't she in New London?"

"Yes. Some new gear and a fresh charge of the hot. She's out. Anyhow I'd prefer a smaller, more nimble boat. That leaves *Skate*, *Swordfish*, *Sargo*, and *Seadragon*."

"Which one?"

"*Seadragon's* in the Philippines—out of reach. *Swordfish* is in Mare Island—refit. I know you haven't forgotten that *Sargo* is off Murmansk—what we call 'intelligence,' snooping, in fact. So that leaves us . . ."

"*Skate*."

"Yes, *Skate*. Just now she and *Triton* are in the Med with Admiral Hart. Fleet exercise and a bunch of NATO dagos aboard to look on and admire us."

"Who's in *Skate*?"

"Young guy, name of Stephens."

"Is he good?"

Admiral March bristled. "They're all good," he said coldly.

"All right, it's *Skate*," Admiral Engel said.

"It's *Skate* if we have to go through with this. But I lay my commission on the line. I will not order any submarine or any captain in my command to make that landfall unless he believes—and convinces me—that he does believe the mission is feasible. And, even if he does, I'll still feel like Cardigan after he ordered the charge of the Light Brigade in the same neighborhood."

III

It's cold—for this far south—even if it is only April, Uzzu-mekis thought, and wondered if it would be worth the trouble to get up and move nearer the tiled porcelain stove that filled one corner of the small room to the ceiling. Down here the edge ought to be coming off the winter's long cold. Possibly it was a hangover from their days on the river, the wetness, the fog, the long monotony that fabricated a chill aimed straight at the bones. It sometimes seemed to him that he had never got properly warmed up after that winter in the German prison camp which had followed being captured in a cellar on the outskirts of Bastogne in the Battle of the Bulge; twenty-two years of the shakes; stop it, you're being ridiculous. More likely what now worked to numb his marrow, muscle and brain alike, was natural child to the buildup of tension; he would have preferred some risk more quick and decisive rather than this impatient game of patience. Not that the journey had not gone well. Perhaps it had gone too well, and that was it. The uneventful way of their passage so far had left him with an untidy moraine of unease. Superstition, he sneered at himself; you don't have room for it. When you needed to travel light and agile, a load of fear could weigh as heavy and bulk as awkward as a trunk full of lead bricks. You can't afford it, he told himself. Alert, yes; afraid, not if you can help it.

Actually, I ought to congratulate us, he thought. They hadn't been so smart as they had been simple—or at least they had been ultimately simple ever since fetching the Dnepr at Yartsevo. He had, with reason, worried about getting that far, the first two hundred miles by train from the outskirts of Moscow. That had been touchy and he did not believe, at first, that it could be done at all. He had considered disguise; but as baby-sitter (he thought of himself in those

44

terms) to a face as unmistakable in Moscow, Idaho, as it was in Moscow, U.S.S.R., he had decided that camouflage would be fatuous. It had occurred to him that perhaps it could be done wide open—on sheer gall. They both had recognized that no hairpiece, or whiskers, or dark glasses, or putty nose would successfully alter that figure and set of features. He did not think of the way, he had the old man try it as an inspiration; it was a test; if it worked, well and good; if it didn't, little harm would be done since, clearly, there had been no attempt at deceit. The old man merely boarded first class as himself and from then on played himself superbly. He had been effusive, making jokes, initiating conversation, retreating occasionally into brooding isolation suddenly broken by a return of high humor. He was himself so openly that if his captivated audience wondered at his presence here they probably thought, perhaps with some pity, that the old man was going a trifle potty, considering how far he had fallen—been pushed, rather—toward oblivion. He had so disarmed the small world of the first-class carriage—that even the authorities neglected to ask for the internal passport, required of domestic travelers, which he did not possess. These, after all, were not his jailers and perhaps, for common men, something remained of the thunderous charisma of which he had been formally stripped.

And so they had fetched Yartsevo without event, and the old man, he remembered, had been egregiously puffed up over his success as an actor. Once a ham, always a ham, Užžumekis had thought in sour humor.

While they were on the train he had stayed well clear of the old man's compartment. Since this was, primarily, a test, it would have been pointless, an unnecessary complication, to be identified with his charge, a circumstance that would need explaining lest it rouse speculation and there was no rational explanation why he, an émigré Lithuanian-American, should be in the company of a fallen Russian god. So let him play at being a god alone; let him have his last pathetic view from a pretended Olympus. His own work would begin in earnest when they reached the river, that would signal the beginning of punishable deceit. The punishment, if success failed him, would be terminal, he knew. But he allowed himself an occasional bleak inward smile to consider the bitch of a MAY-DAY occasion they would be handing the Kremlin if it did work—if it did.

It was foggy midnight when the train clattered across the bridge over the Dnepr and huffed into Yartsevo. Uzzumekis stepped down into shadows sparsely relieved by murky yellow lights above the platform. Like that guy in the White House, he mused with wry satisfaction, the Russians don't believe in wasting electricity. He waited for the old man to break away from the small cluster of his traveling companions and walk alone along the platform behind him. It was a moment which could arouse dangerous curiosity, he knew, but there was no help for that. Play it simple, play it simple, he kept reminding himself. So long as they could successfully pretend that the old man was as unremarkably nobody as any ordinary traveler, perhaps others—for long enough anyhow—would permit the old relic something like the precious anonymity they craved for themselves.

Uzzumekis turned into a narrow, nearly lightless street, unpaved, muddy between wooden walls overhanging at the second floor. Given daylight, he knew these walls would be paintless, weathered gray. He waited for the old man to draw abreast.

"And now?" the old man asked. It was the first word between them since the empty coeducational washroom where they had boarded the train outside Moscow.

"We walk," Uzzumekis answered. "Six kilometers. Can you make it?" The question was genuine but not sympathetic; from the beginning this had been a serious concern for him, the degree of the old man's stamina. The worry was practical; he couldn't guarantee the bastard a ride on the cushions all the way.

The old man chuckled. "This isn't all fat. You need not fear. I do not need to be carried, not yet."

"I'm sorry," Uzzumekis said, relenting a little. "It is best not to make needless exposure. Now, in the night, we will not be noticed."

"It is nothing. We do as you say."

They went on in silence until they reached the river. Uzzumekis knew where he was, but it took some casting about, like a puzzled hound, to locate himself exactly in the lightless murk. He was relieved when, using a pencil flash sparingly, among the night-clustered sameness of the river barges, he found the number he sought. Moving along the pier, picking his way among the unseen hawsers of the mooring lines, he came abreast the squat cabin aft and hailed softly. When he hailed the second time, a dark figure detached itself from the black shadow and moved across the deck toward them.

"Yes?" The voice was guarded, suspicious.

"Uzzumekis," he said. "With the package."

"A moment. The plank is forward. Here, now, follow me."

Uzzumekis led the way, catfooted along the narrow gangplank, and stepped down carefully. The old man followed but, leaving the plank, he came down hard and the steel deck resounded under his weight.

"Careful!" their guide hissed.

"My pardon," the old man muttered. "I could not see."

The cabin was dark when they entered.

"Wait," the guide said. Uzzumekis and the old man stood in the warm blackness, inhaling the heavy, though not stale, odors of cooking. A match flared and the wick of an oil lamp slowly gathered up the flame and they could see the rude, cramped dimness of the wooden walls around them. They heard a stirring behind the blanket curtain and a woman's voice came, querulous.

"Dmitri?"

"Go back to sleep, Anya. They have come."

"Oh." It was more than only a sigh. The sound carried the mourning tone of resignation to millennia of danger, visited upon generation in and generation out until it became an essential element of the bloodstream. Uzzumekis glanced at the Menorah on a shelf above the iron stove and thought again how little love these, their hosts, must hold for the fat old man. A lot of this sort of thing would never be possible without Jews, he thought. Perhaps the old one was less a devil to them than the dark, mustached Georgian who had preceded him, but he had been monster enough in his own time. But now they would help, out of no love for the guest, but out of loathing for the system from which he fled. They had not asked why he fled—and Uzzumekis could not have answered for him if they had. And he didn't know whether even the old man could answer fully for himself. It was enough that he had known they would be here at the rendezvous and that they would not talk. Or, for that matter his cynical mind told him, from this moment of welcome onward they would not dare talk—for now they were in it, too, up to their necks. They would earn their fee.

The man, dark, unsmiling, heavy-shouldered, with calloused, unclean hands regarded them somberly.

"It is better if you change your clothing at once," he said. "I think nobody will be about before dawn, but it would not be wise to wait." Crossing the cabin, he bent and rummaged under a board counter and brought forth two tied bundles, faded cotton, not clean. "You may change here," he said.

"Change?" the old man asked, eying his bundle not with distaste but curiously.

"Sorry. These won't be as comfortable—or as warm," Uzzumekis said. "But now the charade begins. Your being recognized on the train was a risk we took because we had to. It went all right—or seemed to—but the time for that is past. From now on, we are rivermen."

Without speaking, the old man dropped his fur-collared coat, his astrakhan hat, shrugged out of the wide-lapeled, double-breasted jacket, cravat, collar, and white shirt, the floppily cuffed, pin-striped gray trousers and the shined black high topped shoes. Stoically, he arrayed himself in a riverman's smock and baggy, stained pants and heavy boots, pulled on and roped around his middle a quilted cotton jacket, and topped off the ensemble with a shapeless cloth cap.

"How do I look, hey?" he said with a sudden grin, a kind of wry delight real in a face often unreadable even at its most animated because the steady, pale blue eyes seldom said anything whatever. "No mirror, yes?"

"No mirror, sir," Dmitri mumbled, gathering up the rich discarded clothing. He tied the bundle firmly, slipped through the door and came back quickly with a jute sack which, when he lowered it, met the deck with a solid thump.

"What's that?" the old man asked.

"A stone. It is a pity—this fur, this fine material—but we must sink it now."

"Ho," the old man chuckled. "There goes my other self." Turned suddenly somber, he watched as Dmitri stuffed the clothing into the weighted sack. "Good riddance," he said at last.

Now, you old goat, Uzzumekis thought, you won't like it but you're going to get something to chew on, a mouthful of the kind of muscle work you probably never heard of. I hope he can stand up to it, he thought again. For now the disguise began, the only really effective way to place this fallen deity beyond mortal man's recognition : hard, sweating labor— and dirt, specifically coal dust.

"I have arranged your quarters forward," Dmitri said. "Not in comfort, I fear, but"—he nodded toward Uzzumekis —"he wanted no flaw. If you must now appear a roustabout it is regrettable but necessary that you appear one in all things. Follow me, please."

Dmitri blew out the lamp and blindly they followed him on deck and heard splashes as he dropped the two bundles of clothing, rich for the old man, undistinguished but adequate street wear for Uzzumekis, over the low freeboard.

"Come, hold my hand," he hissed. Uzzumekis grasped it and in turn reached back to guide the old man. They stumbled forward, groped down a ladder into even blacker darkness, and stood unseeing at the foot until Dmitri guided

49

them by turns and pressed them down until they could feel a pile of blankets, rough, chilled, damp with the river's dampness.

"It will be better if you sleep together—for the warmth," Dmitri whispered. "We will cast off at dawn. This morning I will handle the lines and the woman will handle the helm. It would not be wise for you to show awkwardness on the dock. During the day I will attempt to show you what you must do when we moor or cast off. You need not be expert, I think. Only adequate will be enough."

Thus had begun the time of punishable deceit, and it had gone entirely too well for Uzzumekis' peace of mind about the future. This old man, fat and accustomed to rich idleness of the body while the brain manipulated half a world with ruthless skill, in the misty dawn confronted what his body must perform in the next weeks whether or not his brain chose to idle: coal. It lay in the hold, bagged in the same coarse jute which had carried his sable-collared coat to the bottom.

"We'll have to unload this stuff when Dmitri tells us. Where and how much he will explain. I think, sir, it will be necessary that you appear busy. Or maybe it would be better if we passed you off for drunk; in that case it would be necessary for Dmitri to curse you. I too. But you will understand it is a necessary part of the charade."

"I have no settled prejudice against getting drunk," the old man said. "But perhaps it is not necessary. You see, young man, here my life comes full circle. Or at least nearly so. It is a little at variance with state planning, I suppose. But I am not at total loss here. You may not be aware of it, but I grew to manhood with coal as my every day's companion. The difference, here and now, is that in youth I was in production. I mined the coal, with a carbide lamp on my cap. And now"—he chuckled deeply—"I find I am in transportation, distribution if you wish. A step toward capitalism, you might say. But still"—he stood in the hold regarding the mounded sacks which, even untouched, carried a fine, sifting, acrid

50

gray mist which quickly clogged in the pores and made fine black traces in the lines around eyes, in the forehead and from nostril to corner of mouth—"but still—coal."

"That was a long time ago," Uzzumekis protested. "You're not as young—I'll try to spell you. I am strong, you see."

"Yes, you are strong indeed. In fact you are a mountain of man, and I envy your youth," the old man said, surveying Uzzumekis' six feet four. "But do not deny me entirely the remnants of my pride of youth. I was never so big as you, but believe me, I was strong also. And once again, my young escort, I ask you to remember this is not all fat." He thumped the prodigious barrel above the pouted gut. "Moreover, if I survive it, this may be good for me. Who knows what I must do to live when I reach your country? If I do," he grinned. "I promise you, if I am in a union, I will be militant—against the capitalist exploiters." He grinned, mocking, laughing . . . without any mirth whatever.

They were fourteen days to Zaporozhe, and by the time they moored there Uzzumekis had nearly ceased to marvel. And he had entirely given up the apprehension that, at any moment he would be relieved of his responsibility by the old man succumbing to heart seizure although, in the beginning, brooding on that morbid prospect, he had wondered moodily what they could do with the corpse . . . this corpse of all corpses . . . if worst did in fact come to worst. Weight him and sink him—like the clothes; a seaman's burial.

It was true, the second night, when they finished unloading at Smolensk the old man was haggard even under the grotesque mask of black dust, glued into the furrows of his face by sweat. And the stubby, soft hands were raw. But he would not quit, nor even coast, though both Uzzumekis and Dmitri, bitten by the sardonic knowledge that it would be even worse to be caught with this one dead than to be caught with him alive, kept at him to ease up.

"You forget, my capitalist snob," he grunted at Uzzumekis, "this is the land of the worker."

By Gomel, he was handling mooring lines with passable dexterity and, leaving Kiev, Uzzumekis went aft to find that Dmitri had let the old man take the helm.

"Ho, you see . . . I am thinking of giving up the remainder of the journey. Here I have employment. That is the one thing my prospective hosts—your people—have not offered me. So perhaps one should hold to the sure thing, yes?"

"You turn into a Volga boatman and a hell of a lot of people are going to be unhappy as hell," Uzzumekis grunted. "Especially that poor bastard waiting out there in a submarine."

"I was joking—or partly joking," the old man said. "But it is a fact, obvious, no, that I am a little antique for an immigrant. And, the truth is, I have enjoyed this—this, freedom. This is the first vacation I have had in fifteen years."

"Some vacation," Uzzumekis muttered.

As day followed uneventful day of hard labor upon the commerce-laden river, Uzzumekis was not lulled exactly, for indeed the very lack of event sharpened his already alert senses in readiness for trouble. But he could not help beginning to hope that, if matters kept up this even tenor, they stood a reasonable chance of making it all the way to Odessa. There he would have to leave the last tough lap to the gods. The plans were laid. The boat, hopefully, would be ready. Exposure would be cut to the minimum by boarding directly from the barge under way in the ship channel—and then, if the damned sub played its part, the job would be done. If. If. If. The Ifs had no end.

The If was waiting for them on the pier in Zaporozhe as Uzzumekis and the old man snubbed the fore and aft and breast lines to bollards and then paused to gaze curiously at the drear provincial skyline. A figure, a woman Uzzumekis noted idly, was standing against a warehouse wall. She was watching them, he realized, and grew instantly alert with the quick instincts of those who expect to be hunted . . . and do not intend to be caught.

At length she moved toward the barge, seemingly reluctant. Uzzumekis, pretending concern with the lines, moved to the old man and nudged him.

"Get out of sight."

"Yes? What is it?"

"Just get the hell out of sight! I don't know what it is. Maybe nothing. Move!"

The woman waited, diffident, at the gangplank. Then, apparently making up her mind, she stepped aboard and moved aft where Dmitri still stood near the tiller. Uzzumekis' hand went nervously to the pistol under his smock. Then he withdrew it. What the hell, here in daylight, on a working waterfront?

He could see, while affecting no curiosity, that the woman was in earnest conversation with Dmitri. He moved aft, shambling along the deck. I never really thought this out, but just exactly what do I do when and if the real pressure comes on? Abandon the old bastard and take care of myself? Well, of course. But that's a little silly, isn't it? If they're on to him, it's ten to one or worse they're also on to me. He felt the muscle tension creep like a chill across his shoulders.

Who is she? How the hell can you tell, he asked himself in nervous irritation. Young . . . or seemed to be . . . sort of young. Fair . . . he glimpsed a tousle of dark blond hair loose from the scarf that covered her head. Not well dressed, but that didn't mean anything. He saw Dmitri nod and lead her toward the cabin. The bastard, is he going to turn us in? And immediately the truth came back hard: he can't! Turn us in, he turns himself in.

Dmitri came for him then.

"Please," he said, nodding toward the cabin.

"What is this?" Uzzumekis grated.

"Please," Dmitri repeated. "She will tell you."

"She'd better." Uzzumekis' fingers were back on the pistol as he followed Dmitri. And he felt a fool. He could kill them; that would be easy, but then what?

The woman was standing against the rough wooden table in the cabin. He got an impression of gray eyes, a large mouth, an air of strain. Dmitri muttered something he did not catch. Uzzumekis turned to the woman, holding his voice level with an effort.

"Yes, madam?"

"You are . . . ?"

"Yes, madam?"

"This is nonsense . . . I know who you are . . . I have been sent."

"By whom?"

"That does not matter. I have the word you will recognize."

"All right, nonsense, if you say so, madam. I don't understand this. What word?"

Whispering, so low he could scarcely hear, she uttered a word, and Uzzumekis felt a surge of relief mixed with quick anger. God damn it, why couldn't the snoopers leave well enough alone? Did they think he needed a welcome wagon at every port they touched? What had they sent her with? Doughnuts? Clean socks? Razor blades?

"I have been sent to tell you a change has been made in the plan. I have been sent to assist you."

"Change? What change?" Uzzumekis felt anger tightening in his throat. God damn it, why did they always have to monkey with things? Couldn't they get it through their fat heads that the only nearly reliable thing was simplicity? Every change, every complication spelled a new way for something to go wrong, for some cog not to mesh. "It was all understood. Everybody necessary knew what he was to do and when to do it. Now! What change?"

"I do not know why. I know only what I am told. It is necessary to leave the barge here. You . . . we, for I am told to guide . . . now go overland. Into the Crimea."

"For the love of God," Uzzumekis exploded. "The Crimea. That means exposure. We can't take that chance. This far from where he belongs. Every soul in Russia knows that face. And what of the rendezvous? How, now, will anybody know where and when? This is an insanity!"

54

"I only know that I am told the other plan is impossible now. And I am to assure you that the others will be able to keep the rendezvous. We have time. It will be at one o'clock in the morning, one week from tonight. I am to see that you reach Balaklava and to arrange for your boat and boatman. That I can do, that last. Reaching Balaklava in acceptable privacy may be more difficult."

"Difficult? Offhand, I would say it sounds impossible."

"Perhaps not, we will see."

"And transport?"

"There is the train."

"The train is a danger."

"Here, yes. The express stops here, but the station is large and well guarded. Your . . . your man might be recognized."

"I'd bet my last ruble on that," Uzzumekis said.

"And an auto is dangerous . . . there are not many . . . and the police would be curious."

"That doesn't leave much . . ."

"Possibly just enough. There is a town, a village almost, Mikhaylovka, seventy-five kilometers from here. Twice a week —usually—a train arrives in Mikhaylovka and leaves again. It stops in all villages and towns, and its final destination is Sevastopol."

"What kind of a train?"

"It is slow . . . and uncertain. But not so . . . so conspicuous."

"Tell me, is the train only for passengers? Are there goods wagons also?"

"Mostly goods wagons. A few carriages, always the third class, or almost always."

Back to my youth in Chicago, Uzzumekis thought. Riding the rods, by God. He felt a tinge of rather spiteful pleasure at the idea of the rude discomforts to which this journey was putting the Russian god. He studied the girl thoughtfully; she seemed bright enough about some of the elementary things, like not being too visible in the wrong places or to the wrong people.

55

"You know that we cannot take a train to Sevastopol. Big town. A navy base. Full of military and busybody officials. It would be a form of suicide."

"Yes, I know. I don't know what to do."

"Does the train stop at any village near the city?"

"Oh, yes. Many."

"I don't mean just any village. We would still have to get around Sevastopol and overland, somehow, to Balaklava. It would probably mean walking. The man is not young."

The woman looked worried. "There is Bakhchisaray. It is on the outskirts of the city, just to the north."

"What kind of country?"

"Small farms. Some hills. Some woods."

It could work, Uzzumekis thought. If I knew where there was a church I'd make a novena. Maybe two. If I had anybody but this bastard in tow I'd brazen it right through the big towns, the bigger the better. Can you imagine a worse liability than that face for a guy on the run? The whole damn plan had a million holes in it and now he remembered another one.

"This Mikhaylovka? How do we get there? Tiptoe through the daisies?"

"Pardon? Oh, I see. I forgot. My brother-in-law lives in this city. He drives a truck for the state, taking supplies to the farms, the collectives, and bringing back produce to the markets. I have spoken to him in this affair . . ."

Damn it, another leak! Uzzumekis thought.

"What have you told him?" he demanded sharply.

"Only that I wish to take a friend to the village . . . I did not tell him more . . . because knowing might frighten him . . . and knowing might be dangerous."

Smart girl, Uzzumekis thought.

"And he agrees without knowing?"

"He loves my sister very much."

Stupid sod, Uzzumekis thought.

Now in the gloom of the heavily curtained small room,

with its one feeble bulb hung from the center of the ceiling and contained within a bead-fringed shade of hideous-hued stained glass, they were, for the moment, simply waiting. Waiting for the woman, Melina Pelavin, who had gone out to fetch food and to discover, as discreetly as possible, the plans of her brother-in-law. Uzzumekis, under a surface he had thought to seem impassive, was in a rage of restlessness. Hurry up and wait may be all right for the dogface, but waiting is plain hell when you can only guess what they know or suspect or are, in fact, doing in and beyond the Kremlin. By this time, of course, they had to know that the old man was no longer where he was supposed to be—in what, to all intents and purposes, amounted to a semi-polite imprisonment in his home. Next question, what were they doing about it? His first-class ride to Yartsevo must, by now, have been explored in detail. Uzzumekis was reasonably confident that the scent had been cut off there—quite literally in water and coal dust. But he knew they wouldn't let it rest there, merely give up and go home like baffled hounds. They didn't handle matters that way—not and keep their jobs, or, for that matter, their heads.

He found himself staring at the old man squatting on the hard chair across the room: squatting is really the word for it, arms folded across the belly, thick legs apart, and feet flat on the floor. He seemed as immovable and as impassive as a carved Buddha. He had always thought of that fat, button-nosed face as piglike, as it was. It could be a wonderfully articulate face—in bombast, in rough humor, in calculated fury—but to Uzzumekis none of these things ever seemed to go any deeper beneath the surface than their owner and operator intended them to go. The small eyes were the give-away—or rather precisely the opposite. The eyes were unwavering and they gave away exactly nothing about the man behind them.

Uzzumekis admitted to himself that he now possessed a lot more physical respect for the man behind the eyes than he had felt when this strange fugitive journey began. The old man had guts and he was no quitter and, so far as you could tell, he didn't scare worth a hoot. But like him? How could you conceivably like him? One way or another, given the way he had run things while he had it, the old hooligan could probably put a half million corpses to his own account—that is, if anybody kept that kind of vital statistics under his peculiar system. And the corpses, likely as not, had included as many avowed buddies as acknowledged enemies. Not that Uzzumekis objected to ruthlessness in necessity, nor murder. He had killed when it was necessary—and would again. But there was something basically appalling, no, even more, revolting about wholesale slaughter in pursuit of a question-able political goal. And now the old one was a has-been and on the lam to boot, and I, though I have trouble believing it, am his shepherd and responsible for his well being—though if I had a choice he would probably be one of the last sons of bitches alive for whose continued good health I would care. But I don't have a choice, not in this matter.

It's a strange, half-assed way to close out a half-assed career, he mused, baby-sitter for a failure, for you couldn't describe him as anything more than that. A powerhouse run out of power. He supposed his people back home could get or thought they could get some tangible use out of having the old bastard for a house guest, a former First Secretary of the Communist Party of the Union of Soviet Socialist Republics —but never forget the word "former." The old man was as former as they could get. You didn't make a comeback under that system. So here they were, at the mercy of a woman, almost a girl, at the mercy of luck, at the mercy of everything they couldn't count on—running for their lives. He won-dered whether they would take the trouble to liquidate the old man if they were caught; he could bloody well imagine how the old man would handle matters if the positions were reversed. As for himself, he suffered no illusion; he knew how they would deal with him if they caught him convoying the old sport to political asylum in, of all places, the U.S.A.

It had been a long road leading to this unlikely destination, he reflected. The German prison camp. The Red Army getting there ahead of Patton. The long trip east to Moscow, a free man, sort of. Not quite free because the Russians quickly discovered that he spoke and wrote their tongue; he had been brought up on it in that immigrant home Back of the Yards. The Russians had wondered whether they might get some use out of that unusual facility in an American dogface. And so they had subjected him to a kind of persuasion which was just short of force. And he, for his part, hadn't resisted too vigorously. He had had all the war he wanted, and the thought of hastening back to be shipped out to the Pacific was singularly lacking in appeal. They had put him to work as a translator and interpreter in The All-Union Institute for Scientific and Technical Information, which cumbersomely designated organization performed the grub work of extracting documentary intelligence for the KGB and other Soviet users. He hardly noticed at first that he had become, in fact, a neophyte spy against his own country. He woke up to the fact with something of a start when they assigned him to work full time as translator for a seedy-looking German physicist, three times a defector, from his own country, from England, from the United States.

By that time he was in love with a dark-haired, dark-eyed temptress, and she seemed hugely more important than anything the German traitor had to say or not say. Anyhow he regarded the brooding, suspicious Kraut as a certifiable nut and could not believe that anything he had to communicate could bear any useful significance. In this, he came later to understand, he was in grievous error. But by that time he had Nina, as he called her, although her real name was something else and close to unpronounceable even in his fluent Russian.

He hadn't, up to that point, thought much about personal comfort, but he found that he hated to have his love cooped up in the barren two-room flat they shared with a family of three. He wanted her all to himself and, vigorously in rut as well as in love, he hated to look up from his love-making to discover himself being gravely observed by the other couple's runny-nosed six-year-old. It was too rottenly undignified; besides the snotty kid had a talent, probably realized with glee, for stultifying his passion in full freshet. He began to think about going home.

It turned out to be impossible if he intended to take Nina along, which he assuredly did. The months dragged unbearably as he went back time and again to the Foreign Ministry and confronted the endless run-around of begging for her exit visa. And he knew, even if he did get it, he would then face another challenge in trying to persuade OVIR, the military control, to permit them to approach any border in the Soviet Union.

The futile, infuriating search at length took him to the American embassy in search of help. He had not been near the place in years. His fellow countrymen proved curious about him. Why had he never gone home? Did he realize that technically he was a deserter from the Army of the United States and would face appropriate discipline if and when he got back? How had he been occupied all these years?

At length the consul turned him over to a nondescript functionary of indeterminate years, who appeared to have no special duties but seemed vaguely attached to the commercial attaché. The questions now became more penetrating, more personal, more exhaustive. Where had he traveled within Russia? Who did he know? Why had he stayed? Did he consider himself loyal to his homeland? What sort of work did he do for the Russians? Translating? Translating what? Documents? What sort of documents? Technical journals? What sort of technical journals?

In the fifteenth year of their marriage, still childless, still in the two-room flat, with the leaky-nosed youth now grown to a callow majority and no longer much interested in his neighbors' sexual activities which, in any case were now noticeably both less frequent and less ardent, still without an exit visa, Nina divorced Uzzumekis.

It was probably the divorce as much as anything that con-

verted Uzzumekis from a not particularly essential spy for the Russians into an active agent for his own country. Nina's defection from the difficult circumstances of their marriage had left him quietly bitter and had compounded all the anger at the Russian system which had been accumulating, like acid in his vitals, during the long frustrations of trying to obtain her visa. Besides language, his seventeen years in Soviet service had won him a certain confidence from his superiors and considerable privilege not enjoyed by other Americans. He had traveled freely, both on jobs for the Russians, and as a tourist. He knew his way around the country by train and bus and riverboat. He had made friends, though not particularly introspective about himself, he had an extra sense about others. Through instinct, coupled with a wary native caution, he could sense men who were disgruntled or, what was even more useful, greedy. Over the years he had become a specialist in furtive and effective movement and, under the particular direction of Steed—his inquisitor, whom he had finally come to recognize as the CIA personified—he performed numerous useful errands for his own country.

But this sort of thing could not go on forever. There had been small signs for the last year or two that his cover had worn perilously thin. It was time to pack it up and go.

And now, for his swan song, Steed had handed him the heaviest commission of his career. He had feared the assignment and, even worse, thought it idiotic and nowhere near worth its potential cost, his neck. But here he was, outward bound, homeward bound, charged with delivering this fat old has-been, Kirov, alive and healthy to an American submarine poaching against a Russian coast in the Black Sea. Crazy, he thought. Insane. The only reason I'm doing it, or reasons rather, is that, one, I probably have the know-how to do it better than anybody else available and, two, that, if I pull this off, it wipes out everything outstanding against me back in the States. That was Steed's promise.

And now they waited for this woman, Melina, whom he

61

did not know but must blindly trust because she had been sent to him with a word he knew and that she could not very well know unless she had got it from the authentic source. But what if the authentic source had been penetrated? He did not fully trust the snoopers, Steed and his works. He did not fully trust anybody. But take this woman he must. This was unfamiliar territory, terra incognita to him despite his cautiously amassed fund of knowledge. He wondered about the train at Mikhaylovka. If it was possible to stow away in a boxcar, at least in daylight, they just might manage. At night, he thought, it might be possible in third class where the light was next to nothing and the peasant mobs so crushing that the individual human being virtually vanished in the press of flesh. Well, they would see.

The old man, long silent, now stirred slightly and spoke.

"I know I am in your hands, yours and such friends of yours as we encounter," he said. "I consented to it, for there was little other I could have done."

"Not much else. It was me or nothing," Uzzumekis grunted.

"This woman? You know she is to trust?"

"No, I know that nobody is to trust. But we have her—and nothing else. The plan was changed by others after we left Moscow. I do not know why ..."

"I have been thinking . . . This business of the submarine . . . It would have been difficult—for political reasons —to bring it through the Bosporus into the Black Sea."

"I don't know about that. Why would it be difficult? All I know is that I was informed it would be there and would rendezvous with us. Getting it there is the Navy's business. Once we are aboard my work is finished."

"You perhaps would not know about it, but I do. The Bosporus is prohibited to warships by hard law. No warship has a right there without Turkish help—no submarines whatever." The old man chuckled. "I know. I worked long enough, threatened enough, planned and intrigued enough to open it to my—to our—major military vessels. And failed."

"Maybe you should have failed. The way you people have been waving your muscle around for years. It is not my affair, I say again. We get there; the sub is supposed to be waiting. If it isn't, I have no further suggestion. Swim perhaps?"

"Does it ever strike you that you Americans are too much devoted to elaboration? It occurs to me, this might have been more direct and possibly more reliable to do it in a simpler fashion. A submarine, I admit, sounds romantic but perhaps cumbersome. Tell me, do you know that your submarines can be so exact as to find us precisely in the dark?"

"How would I know . . . sir? I have been in your country twenty-two years. And even if I had been at home I doubt if I would have known anything about submarines."

"But you will confess this scheme is elaborate, and being elaborate it is complex, and being complex, some essential part can fail?"

"Sure. But they consider you what we call a 'big shot' or a VIP, which is to say a very important person. They probably want to impress you."

"I am impressed, young man. But also I am aware that my —forgive me, our—coastal defenses are effective as well as alert. They ought to be; they cost enough. Would it not have been more reliable to proceed much as we have done so until now? A simple fishing boat along the coast or directly across to Kerempe Burnu on the Turkish side?"

"You wouldn't last a day in an open boat," Uzzumekis said flatly.

"You are difficult to convince, young man. I submit I have lasted well thus far."

Yes, you have, you old bastard, Uzzumekis thought. I never would have believed it, and I'm not sure I do yet.

Then Uzzumekis went tense at a sound outside, and his fingers went instinctively to the pistol. But the door shoved open from the dusk of early, fogged night outside and the woman Melina Pelavin entered.

IV

In a long career, rising to one glory with election as chairman of the board of the enormous inherited farm machinery plant started in Milwaukee seventy years before by his great-grandfather, and to a still greater one with appointment as Secretary of State—for which he told himself that he had not paid, although the party had quite properly appreciated that $100,000 donation—the Secretary had never suffered a more frustrating interview.

Moreover, he was tired and his head ached and he felt a little nauseous. He hated being rushed and even more he hated flying. He could never sleep on airplanes; instead he remained alert to every bump, flutter, or minor change of tone in the screaming engines. Every flight left him nervously exhausted, which he hoped the President did not know or even suspect. Consequently he preferred to dispose of the business of his office at home in Washington and employed, when possible, various stratagems to lure other foreign ministers and heads of state to come to him, rather than the other way around. The delicacies of diplomacy, he felt strongly, were best conducted on familiar ground. Moreover, he occasionally told himself, why shouldn't they come to him? After all, he represented the place where the money was.

Now, sitting in the ornate gold and plush chamber, under a glittering crystal chandelier in the Dolmabagché Palace— once a harem for the sultans, he had been told—he eyed the man across from him and tried to conceal his resentment.

"You can scarcely ask me to pretend that what you propose can be described as a right of innocent passage," said the Prime Minister of Turkey, a heavy man with hard eyes and a reputation for being elusive with ambassadors as well as newspapermen.

64

"We do propose it as one of Turkey's firmest—and most generous—friends. As for whether it constitutes innocent passage, we propose also that it should never be known."

The Prime Minister made no effort to conceal his scoffing disbelief. "Have no fear, it will become known. Anything known by any two persons, especially in my part of the world, eventually becomes known to all. How much faster would be the dissemination of public knowledge of a fact known to hundreds? Every man in your submarine crew, for example?"

State had, for two exhausting hours, tried everything he knew: appeal as an ally, the incalculable propaganda benefit to be reaped by all the free world, reminders that Russia was Turkey's ancient enemy, reminders of the Marshall Plan, appeals to national pride. He had even tried a little delicate muscle in mentioning that hundred million dollar loan which, for the last two years, Turkey had failed to get in spite of hiring a prominent former state governor as its lobbyist. Nothing worked. Every maneuver—which State felt he usually handled rather cleverly—banged itself to frustrated nothing against those obsidian eyes.

"We have already, perhaps, compromised our position by authorizing a *friendly* visit by your submarine to this port. Some newspapers have attacked us for exposing our people to the peril of radiation. The opposition in Parliament is shouting criminal outrage. You, yourself, understand that Turkish governments are never entirely secure. Remember Menderes."

"Mr. Prime Minister, my government assures you that a nuclear submarine imposes absolutely no danger to its surroundings." State wondered if that was wholly true; he knew damned well he would never ride in one himself.

"For myself, I accept your assurance. On the other hand, what counts in these affairs is what is believed by the public —not what is true."

"Mr. Prime Minister, I cannot conceive of any possible way

65

that what we propose can jeopardize Turkey's position. After all, your part of the operation would be—"

The Prime Minister interrupted. "You cannot conceive? Let us look at what you propose. You intend to take a nuclear submarine clandestinely, submerged, through the Bosporus, run up to invade Russian territorial waters and there commit what, at the least damaging, would be intepreted as an international kidnaping—"

Now State interrupted, "Kidnaping? Impossible—the man has asked asylum, to be rescued—"

"Once again. It is not what is true, but what is believed. Now for this adventure—this is something close to an act of war—you ask me to provide a Turkish vessel as escort and conveyance for a rescue crew and its apparatus. No, Mr. Secretary, we have done enough. If you persist, you go on from here without any help from Turkey—except this one dangerous concession—we will look the other way."

"But the submarine cannot possibly penetrate the strait without escort. And some means of rescue—in the unlikely events of emergency—must be at hand."

"I am sorry. That is your problem. As you know, the Montreux Convention imposes strictures on the passage of war vessels through the Straits. These strictures are particularly rigid in the case of submarines. The Convention can be interpreted as forbidding such passage altogether. Even if they should be permitted to pass, authorized by my government, they must do so on the surface. Above all, the purpose of a warship's passage must be *innocent*. You are asking us to participate in an act of international piracy. We cannot afford it."

"But . . ."

"A moment. We have to live next door to the Russians. You do not. It was dangerous enough when we let you install your Thor missiles here, and nobody could have been happier when you took them out."

"The missiles were here for your protection," State protested.

66

"Yes? Not yours?" The hard eyes were skeptical.

"Our mutual protection, of course," State interposed. "I want to make it clear, Mr. Prime Minister, that the free world, of which your country is a most vital part, has its resources arrayed in a position of defense. Neither your nor my country seeks aggrandizement; but we do seek to save our own. We must save it. Thus, as you know, sir, we must depend upon one another. It is the essential condition of survival, of all those things vital to their left.

"If you had time to get out of the cities—or, for that matter, even to take a good look at the cities—you would find, Mr. Secretary, that your way of life in the United States is considerably dissimilar to the way of life in Turkey today. Do not try to tell me that we of the 'free world,' as you describe it, particularly resemble one another. It does not, I fear, illustrate anything much that I know a *hadji*, green turban and all, who is drunk twenty-three hours of every day—and keeps his congregation together quite successfully. His interpretation of the Koran is that it forbids wine—as we all know —but says nothing whatever about hard liquor."

"Isn't that somewhat irrelevant?" State asked.

"Certainly. I stipulated that before I began," the Prime Minister said. "But, since I have visited your admirable and —as you say—generous country and have toured it quite extensively, even including the back yard of Chicago, I know that you run somewhat more to washers, dryers, television sets and outdoor steak fries than we do. We do not abominate these niceties, but we can't afford them, despite all your generosity."

"On the other hand"—State was getting a little indignant on top of his other more physical infirmities—"I have never held that color television is the absolute epitome of civilization. And I do not believe that washing clothes by hand in the nearest stream—even using rocks for bleach—is degradation. If I must be frank, Mr. Prime Minister, you have been taking it from us for something over twenty years. I do not suggest television—which is an abomination anyhow—but

67

why do you not let a little of our despised largesse leak down to where a woman in modest circumstances can have at least a hand wringer for her old man's overalls—or whatever you call work pants hereabouts?"

"This way of life has been working for centuries," the Prime Minister said. "I fear that you do not understand physical poverty; if you are bred to it, the condition is less odious than your Sears & Roebuck catalog suggests."

"I buy quite a number of things from Sears," State said. "Here again we get close to the point of dispute. If you fiddle around with tools, which I do, you would recognize that Sears has contrived to combine quality with modest price. Just don't buy any shirts there; they won't fit."

"They won't?" the Prime Minister asked.

"No, they won't." State, who was by no means a dummy, although his chosen boss frequently accused him of being one, thought it was time to get back to cases, whether the Prime Minister's collar strangled him or not.

"The United States of America, as you know, is firmly bound to your vital interests. We would tolerate no action taken against Turkey—unlikely as that is—which might derive from this operation."

"Yes? The same way you guaranteed the territorial and political integrity of the Arab states in the Middle East? I am sorry, sir, if I seem to take your guarantees a little lightly. And I must leave now; I have a cabinet meeting this afternoon in Ankara, and my plane is waiting." The Prime Minister heaved himself to his feet. "Good day, Mr. Secretary."

State's mood was depressed as he went about his next business in a limousine driven by a Marine orderly from the consulate. They rode past the great cannon cast by a gifted Hungarian bronzemonger to help Mohammed II bring down the corrupted Byzantine Empire in 1453.

Big damn things, State reflected. There they are, monsters, created long before my time, to saturate this soil with more blood than it is usefully able to absorb. Eastern Church,

68

Roman Church, Crusaders, Tartars, God only knew how many kinds of Baptists, Rosicrucians, Puritans, Methodists, Congregationalists, Orthodox Jews and Reformed Jews and some who cheated on both ends, Calvinists, Maronites (who were Catholics but were not quite sure of it), Muslims (the only way in the world to find out what was wrong with Islam was to send an Islamite to investigate), Buddhists, and to get right down to the core of it : people . . . dying old, dying in infancy, dying crazy, dying by a neighbor's displeasure, dying by their own idiocy. But first they had to be born, and State guessed that was his business. And it was. Moreover, since his heart held more worry than it really had room for, he was a reasonably good Secretary of State in a world where nobody could have been good enough for the job. They drove on down along the Bosporus, along the cobbled street, jarring enough by itself, made worse by street car tracks and unmended potholes. Not with much curiosity, State noticed an ancient, though magnificent, ruin on the bluff to their left.

"What's that?" he asked the driver.

"They call it Roumili Hissar," said the Marine, who, in a three-year hitch at the Istanbul consulate, had grown sufficiently discouraged about the availability of quality Muslim girls and sufficiently depressed by the quality of those others who were available, to turn to history—somewhat. "They built it in the fifteenth century, the Ottoman Turks did, sir. They emplaced those big cannons we saw back in the park. They used them to cork up the Bosporus, and it worked all right, I guess. They were the first cannon big enough to do it—without blowing up and killing the gun crews."

They have something else to cork it up with now, State reflected, a convention written in 1936 to cozzen the Turks out of joining up with a rampaging Germany again and, of course, even more to keep Communist Russia from making too free with the Straits. The trouble with diplomatic coups, he often considered, was that sooner or later they were likely to lash back at you in a pinch. Now he had done his manful best to unsnarl a backlash for the sake of brief convenience and had, he acknowledged half bitterly, failed.

"We're here, sir," the Marine said, pulling up on a dusty verge.

"We're where?"

"Where you're expected, sir. Up there." The Marine got out and opened the door for him and pointed. Above them rose a vertical cliff, and far above, State made out some sort of structure, impossibly hanging out over space. There were steps in the face of the cliff, hairpinning back and forth as they rose.

"Good Lord," State said. "What is it?"

"That's where Mr. Dessin lives, sir. The head of USIA here. That's his house, sir. I was told to bring you here."

"Good Lord," State said. "How do I get up there?"

"Climb, sir, I'm afraid. That's the only way to get there."

"Good Lord!" State said.

"It's only a hundred and twenty-four steps, sir," the Marine said cheerfully.

These idiots with their psychotic notions about security, State thought. He went doggedly about it. Even though he stopped to rest at every landing, his lungs were burning and his thighs quivering when finally the steps turned into the cliff and up onto a platform.

"Sorry, Mister Secretary, I know its inconvenient." A smiling young man with a rugged face and tousled hair met him on the platform. "The ambassador told the admiral about my place, and the admiral thought we'd best come here. You'll need a drink after that climb. What can I get you?"

"Anything," State gasped.

"A screwdriver?"

"What could that be?"

"Vodka and orange juice, sir."

State winced. "I can try it. Is the admiral here?"

"Yes, sir. He and Commander Stephens. They're waiting on what we call the porch. This way, sir."

The young man led him outward onto a wide, glassed-in

veranda, a pleasant room, State saw, light, furnished but not overfurnished with rattan chairs, carved teak chests bound in brass, vast beaten copper trays set on low legs. Two men were standing at the windows, looking out. They turned and State recognized Admiral Jacob March. The other, slender, youngish, relaxed, smiling, crew cut, State did not know.

"Mr. Secretary," the admiral said. "This is Commander Stephens. He runs our sub."

Good Lord, he's just a baby, State thought as he shook hands. Do we put those things in the hands of children? Give them the red buttons to blow up the world? And I, there in Washington, with no way to keep them out of temptation. Good Lord.

"Come over here, Mr. Secretary," March said, taking his elbow and leading him toward the expanse of window. "This is the damnedest view you ever saw."

And it was, State had to admit through his headache, his tiredness, and his worry. They were, he realized, in the part of the structure he had seen from the bottom, cantilevered crazily out over space. And below them, startlingly blue, shimmering in the sunlight, lay the narrow neck of the Bosporus, perhaps, State thought, less than half a mile wide. Upon it went a motley commerce, up and down, forever active. Ferryboats, the commuter trains of Istanbul, chuffing busily from station to station. The slatternly but businesslike little craft of the fishermen. Two freighters meeting and passing. A sailing yacht the tips of whose tall masts, State thought, must be nearly on their level, sails white and glistening. A destroyer passing upstream.

"Who does that belong to?" he asked.

"It's Russian," his host said.

"Russian?"

"Yes, sir. They pass between here and the Med. They have to give notice, of course, and there's a limit on tonnage. No capital ships, no aircraft carriers, no submarines—or at least not any submarines that they admit."

"It seems to me the Montreux Convention has been tin-

71

kered with so often and in so many ways that it is nearly impossible to interpret with any accuracy," State said, sighing inwardly and with some resentment at his too-recent defeat. "I know, of course, that the Russians would want access to the Mediterranean for combat ships. I suppose it constitutes something of a toehold on their old yearning for warm water. But what do they do with them once they get them there?"

"They pester our people now and then," Admiral March reminded him dryly. "Like to get in the way of our fleet maneuvers. They're snoopy. Also, I guess, putting a few ships in here helps support that favorite fairy tale of theirs that they're standing up for the Arabs."

"Oh yes. Of course. What's across there, on the other shore?" He gestured toward the buildings, misty in the distance, perched on steep slopes, among dark trees.

"Scutari. That's where Florence Nightingale worked up a lasting reputation," his host said. "I'll get you a drink, sir."

He returned in a few moments with a glass of yellow liquid, clinking with ice.

"Thank you," State said and sipped it cautiously. It nearly separated his head from his neck.

"I'll leave you gentlemen now," the host said. "There's ice, orange juice, and dynamite on the tray. Help yourselves and if you need anything, just yell."

"Remarkable," State murmured. "Why here?"

"The consulate has been bugged twice—that they know of," Admiral March said. "They're sure this isn't. It's been double-checked. How did you make out with the P.M.?"

"Not well, I'm afraid," State replied, feeling the heat of his resentment rise anew. "They categorically refuse to furnish an escort vessel of any kind."

Admiral March's normally hard jaw took on a few more degrees of reinforced concrete.

"They do, huh? Can't you put the pressure on them, Mr. Secretary?"

"None that they seem ready to yield to—at the moment.

They insist they can't afford to step on Russia's toes. They have a case there, although naturally we can't afford to acknowledge that, not at least in the present circumstances. The most they will agree to is not to interfere with our submarine —rather deliberately fail to detect it if it goes through the Bosporus out of sight, that is, submerged."

"That's impossible!" Admiral March stated curtly. "Mr. Secretary, look out that window. See how jammed that roadway is? And the water under all those ships is shallow. A submarine of *Skate's* tonnage draws nearly sixty feet just barely submerged. Some of those surface ships out there draw all of thirty. There are places where the Bosporus is only about a hundred and thirty feet deep in the center of the roadway—and the rules of the road would require traffic bound for the Black Sea to hold to port—to the left side of the channel—where there are some tricky shallows. Even if there were no strictures on us, you cannot navigate a ship like *Skate* scraping the bottom, dead blind, to keep out of collision with other ships."

"I can understand that, Admiral. But there must be some way."

Admiral March permitted himself to scowl. "There is only one way. That is an escort ship which can go through on the surface without challenge and without offending anybody's tender sensibilities. Mr. Secretary, I have made that clear from beginning.

"Moreover, this mission demands a dangerous penetration of an unfriendly coast. *Skate* could very possibly get into serious trouble. I'll tell you frankly, sir, I will not order her into the Black Sea without some feasible rescue backup."

State had come away from the Prime Minister in a state of suppressed resentment, which he now felt turning in a new direction. This smelled of insubordination.

"Admiral March, do I need to remind you that the President, who is the Commander-in-Chief, has ordered this mission carried out?" His tone was icy.

March's reply this time smelled of barely controlled fury.

73

"Mr. Secretary, the C-in-C can . . . no, let that ride. But I can tell you, sir, the Navy has accepted those orders with the greatest reluctance. My personal opinion is that this so-called mission is damn foolishness in the first place. I know as much about orders as anybody, and a damn sight more than most about what is possible at sea and what is not possible. With adequate escort and rescue capability, the mission is barely possible; without that protection, it's impossible."

State tried a new tack. "I thought these nuclear submarines were virtually independent and practically invulnerable. The Navy has bragged about them enough."

"They're pretty good. They ought to be for what they cost. But they are not miracles."

State made an honest effort to hold down his push toward anger. This grim sailor seemed as impermeable as battleship armor, but he knew he was not in a position to challenge his competence. Two stubborn men in one tough day was putting it on a bit thick, he thought ruefully. But he recognized that at least 50 per cent of his own job was patience and nosing, first one way and then another, until a way could be found to get around, through or under seemingly insuperable obstacles. The trouble was, he recognized, that here he was dealing with a set of esoterica entirely unfamiliar to him.

March was talking again. "I have two C-141s leaving Westover Air Force Base today. They carry an SR crew and a DSRV and its crew and trailer and support equipment."

"A what? Admiral March, I'm afraid you have me at a disadvantage. After all, I'm a landlubber, you know. It will help me if you will explain your terms."

"SR means Submarine Rescue," March said patiently, thinking, At least he's trying to get his mind around it. "This outfit will be coming from the New London sub base. They're good. Under a Lieutenant Hale. He's a mustang, but he is also the best in the business."

"Mustang?"

"Not an Academy man," March explained. "Up through

74

the ranks. Unlike some Academy men, the mustangs generally know where the shovels are kept."

"I see. A professional. And this other you spoke of—D.S. something, I believe you said."

"DSRV. Stands for Deep Submergence Rescue Vehicle. It's a thing the Navy and Lockheed have been monkeying with the last five years or so . . . the last I heard the bill was around twenty-five million dollars—so far. What it is, actually, is a small submarine designed and equipped to find a disabled sub, seal onto the escape hatch and take off whatever crew is still alive."

State thought he might be seeing some light, but he was still on totally unfamiliar ground and knew it. The only way through for him was to keep on asking questions even if, to a professional, they made him seem a little slow.

"A submarine, you say? Self-propelled?"

"Of course, Mr. Secretary."

"You recognize I have to proceed in ignorance, Admiral. But why can't the rescue submarine merely follow the other submarine—and be on hand—in the event of the difficulty you anticipate?"

"Perhaps I failed to tell you," March said. "The DSRV is designed to carry only twenty-four men at a time, whereas *Skate*, with her passengers, would be carrying more than a hundred and twenty. What is more, it is not an inexhaustible nuke like *Skate*; it is driven by batteries and batteries get exhausted. Its range is short and its speed slow. Something has to piggyback it to the scene of the wreck. That is why, even aside from essential escort through the Bosporus, we need a ship."

State mulled it over, knowing that he had to clutch at straws in another man's private maelstrom and embarrassed at the predicament.

"We have ships in the Mediterranean. Isn't it possible to call in one of our own surface vessels?"

"You have already had your troubles with the Turks," the admiral reminded him. "I doubt if it would work to ask for more of the same. Of course, it is certainly legitimate for a U. S. Navy surface vessel to ask authority for passage through the Straits. But, remember, the Turks already know what we propose to do with *Skate*. They have agreed to ignore it. But would they also agree to the passage of an American naval vessel which they would instantly deduce was going along just to hold *Skate*'s hand? Moreover, even if they did permit it—which they wouldn't do in a hundred years—the Russians certainly would not stand for an American destroyer, say, mysteriously hanging around their twelve-mile limit off Balaklava. No, it won't work."

"Will anything?" State asked. The further he explored this unfamiliar alley, the more it looked like a dead end.

"Just possibly," March said, scowling again. "I had hoped for a Turkish ship. Since that appears to be impossible, let's explore what may be possible. We need a ship, nondescript, neutral, Liberian registry . . . or one of the other half-breeds. And we need it quick."

"And where"—the Secretary's tone had got back some of its ice—"do you propose we get it?

"Buy it? Where? With what?"

"Mr. Secretary, I don't give a damn what we do for money. The United States must have some around somewhere; it blows enough. But we can't buy a ship here; the Turks would catch on in a minute. I'd say Greece—or Lebanon. They're both close and they'll both sell anything—if the price is right."

"Don't you think it equally likely that somebody would suspect something odd about the United States government shopping for a foreign ship in a foreign port—on the spur of the moment?" State asked.

"They would, of course, if the government was doing the buying. We can get an agent to do the buying. He can buy under the name of some bastard shipping line."

"That, of course, is subterfuge," State said.

"The whole operation is subterfuge," Admiral March said

crisply, thinking privately that State ought to know something about subterfuge—the racket he was in.

"I have no objection to being slightly misleading," State smiled thinly. "So long as a good enough cause is served and the act is sufficiently discreet. Admiral, you have raised problems which, frankly, I did not anticipate, since I thought there was sufficient reason to believe the Turks would cooperate. Before we go further, I believe I should advise the President."

"Why don't you call him then?" March asked testily. "We must have a ship. Either we get a ship or we'll have to forget it."

"I wonder if I can call from here."

"I don't know. Dessin may have a telephone that can be hooked through the consulate scrambler and go straight to the boss. If he hasn't it may be necessary to do it from the consulate. The ambassador certainly has whatever you need." He turned to Stephens. "Commander, would you be good enough to find Mr. Dessin?"

"Sure, sir." Stephens, who had listened in fascinated silence while his betters debated, got up and left the room. This whole business sounds weirder and weirder, he thought. Right through the looking glass. And how do I feel about it? I don't know yet? It sounds wild—and it could be a terrible risk to my boat. But then, I have to recognize my boat was built for terrible risks, not pleasure cruising. As far as *Skate* was concerned, he knew he had total confidence in the ship and in her men.

Going down all those steps, which he found was nearly as wretchedly exhausting to the thighs—and even worse on the backs of the calves—as going up, within half an hour State found himself in the home of Ambassador Rushmore who, being a career man and mindful of his career's prosperity or the lack of it, quickly mustered the necessary facilities and got through on his own hot line to the State Department which, in turn, set up a private relay to the Situation Room in the cellars of the White House in Washington.

In Washington the President, grumbling a little because it was time for his daily swim in the White House pool, permitted himself to be escorted to the Situation Room and seated himself in the soundproof booth at the red telephone and picked it up and spoke without preliminaries.

"All right, Alec, what is it?"

"Good morning, Mr. President. I'm sorry to call; I know your time is pressing."

"Then get with it, Alec."

"This is a rather strange situation, Mr. President."

"Nobody ever pretended it was normal. What's your problem?"

"The Turks will—well, look the other way is the way they put it—if our submarine goes through the Bosporus. But they absolutely refuse to provide escort. Categorically."

"Losing your touch, Alec?" The President's voice, State was uneasily aware, was something short of cordial.

"No, sir. They simply insist that they cannot risk offending the Russians by becoming an overt party to this—mission."

"Didn't you assure them we'd back them up?"

"Of course. He said it wasn't enough."

"Wouldn't listen to the old crap, eh? Can't say I blame him. Well, what's next?"

"Admiral March wants—demands, in fact—that we buy a ship."

"What kind? And why?"

"One adequate to escort our submarine on the surface. And to provide a rescue capacity."

"Why? What makes him think he needs rescue?"

"In case the submarine got into trouble. He considers it possible."

"You think he's a little white-livered?"

State had to think about that; it might offer a way to get off his own hook with this demanding employer, but he decided it wouldn't stand up under investigation. He knew the man in the White House had a way of looking for *all* the

78

reasons why anything displeased him—and generally finding them all.

"No, not that. He says the peculiarities of the mission demand it. The admiral, of course, knows his business, while we—I do not."

"Well then, let him go shopping."

"Mr. President, this is a strange situation, really unprecedented. The admiral intends, once he gets a ship, to put an American Navy crew aboard it. I'm not an expert in maritime law, but I fear we can anticipate some difficulty there. Then there is a question of funds."

"I say again, nobody pretends this is normal, and it doesn't sound so strange to me. If it's money, use the counterpart funds. That makes more sense than some horny congressman blowing it on dames while he investigates the status of emancipated womanhood around the world. Get with it, Alec. Good-by, I've got business."

"Good-by, Mr. Pr—" State began to say, but realized he was talking to a dead line.

Negotiating those steps the third time was nearly enough to make State wish he was back in Milwaukee forevermore. He found Admiral March and Stephens still in Dessin's overhung veranda, down on their knees studying charts.

"How'd it go?" Admiral March asked, without formality.

"He said to go ahead and do it whatever way you think the situation demands. Admiral, buying ships is not my field. I'll need guidance."

"You furnish the money, Mr. Secretary, and I'll take care of the finding and buying."

"I am curious what you intend to do with the crew, which, of course, may be with the ship you find."

"Pay them off and kiss them good-by," March said. "I can have a full crew of Navy out of Naples in a matter of hours, I will not send any ship anywhere on a job like this crewed by people I don't know and won't trust. If we ever need that ship, we're likely to need it bad."

79

"What about uniform, Admiral?" Stephens asked. "If that ship is laying off and on for any length of time, and just outside their territorial limit, the Russians are going to look it over."

"The crew will be in civvies," March said.

"Isn't there something in maritime law about that?" State asked. "A U. S. Navy vessel under a foreign flag—with the crew in disguise? Are we looking for trouble?"

"There's probably something in maritime law about everything—except perhaps cuckoldry. I know there's nothing particularly legal about any of this. But if we have to do it, we'll have to do it in a way that has a chance to work. Not screw it up.

"If you want, Mr. Secretary, we can show you roughly what's involved. Please get down here, sir. Stephens will trace it out for you." Although, of course, you're not likely to understand one word of it, the admiral thought privately. "Go ahead, Commander."

State's legs, already abused without mercy by 372 steps up and down from Dessin's cliff dwelling, bent unwillingly under him. And another hundred and twenty-four to go, he remembered, and suppressed a groan.

"You see, Mr. Secretary," Stephens began, "*Skate* is berthed here—in the Golden Horn." He pointed out the spot on a big scale chart of Istanbul's harbor. "We'll back out into the stream—here. Then we turn and head out into the Marmara, ostensibly going back to the Med. We get out to the twenty-fathom line here—still in plain sight of the shore and of all the shipping going in and out. That's a little shallow for diving, but we can manage that. No sweat.

"Once under, we turn. That's fairly simple because *Skate* has twin screws and is very maneuverable. Meanwhile the escort ship has picked us up. We go out through the Bosporus with escort right alongside to camouflage the periscope if we have to stick it up. The Bosporus is only twenty miles long, but it's narrow and crooked and full of traffic.

"The next part is a cinch. Straight across on a course of

zero-seven-four degrees to Cape Kerempe on the Turkish side. That's a hundred and eighty-eight miles. Turn there and run right up to Balaklava, right across the belly of the Black Sea. Course zero-zero-five degrees, another hundred and forty miles. Speed? No problem, except what the escort ship can make. Whatever she can do, we can do more. We stay submerged all the way, of course . . . There's one thing, of course, sir." Stephens turned to Admiral March.

"What's that, son?" March asked.

"Sonar and radar in the escort vessel."

"Tricky," March said. "Anything we buy will likely have search radar. The DSRV has sonar, of course, but that's no help until she's in the water."

"Could they put her over the side and tow her, say the last fifty miles?"

"I don't see why not. Maybe I didn't tell you, but I'm going with the escort ship; I'll work it out with Hale."

"You're going?" State interrupted. "Why . . ."

March may have smiled but, to State, it looked more like a snarl. "I'm going. You think I'm going to let this kid have all the fun? Well, get on with it."

"We drop the escort here," Stephens said, placing a pencil point on the chart. "That's about thirteen miles offshore. They can pretend machinery trouble. Anything plausible. I surface here." The point of the pencil was even more precise. "But before I surface I turn so that I am outward bound when we hit the top. Course a hundred and eighty degrees exactly. We run in with silent ship . . ."

"What do you mean, silent ship?" State asked. This jargon confused him. As why should it not? This wasn't his field.

"Dead slow to keep down propeller noise. No air conditioning; that's noisy. No banging around or clattering inside the ship." Stephens remembered the shattered crockery and winced inside himself.

"What possible difference does noise make under the sea?" State asked.

"A hell of a lot," Admiral March said curtly.

81

"This is the rendezvous spot," Stephens said. "At one A.M., May second, a week from today, three miles out of Balaklava harbor, a hundred and eighty degrees from the white flashing beacon on that windmill. You can see it here, sir, on the chart." Stephens pointed to a cabalistic symbol, while State peered.

"That seems very exact," State said.

"It is," Stephens acknowledged with confident pride. "A few years ago it would have been ridiculous to shoot for something that precise. But with the navigation gear we carry in *Skate*, we'll make it. No sweat."

"Remarkable."

"The only real problem is the craft we are to meet. We are assured they'll make the rendezvous and any competent fisherman who knows the local waters ought to be able to do it. Ought to. But we can't be sure. For that reason, we're going to give them a little leeway. We'll stay on the surface not more than twenty minutes. If they're close, good. If they're in the area, we should be able to latch onto them with radar. If we don't have them in twenty minutes, we submerge and skedaddle, and somebody will have to think of some other way to get the man out."

"You mean abandon the mission? We can't. The President . . ."

"Stephens can't hang around," March said flatly. "That twenty minutes is stretching things just about nineteen minutes too long. That's a military area, declared prohibited by the Russians."

"What does that mean?"

"Off limits. Under radar surveillance. You don't think the Russians sleep on their radar, do you?"

"Well," State said, creaking back to his feet. "It seems a great adventure, young man. I almost wish I could go along."

"You could come with me on the escort ship," Admiral March said, grinning evilly.

State ignored that. And he thought a little graceful lying

82

might bolster Stephens' morale, if it needed bolstering. He had detected no sign of need, but it couldn't hurt.

"The President asked me to convey his personal admiration for you and your ship. You are making history, young man."

"Oh, I wouldn't quite call it making history. A little unusual perhaps, but not history," Admiral March said with that smile which State uneasily confused with a sneer. "The Bosporus has had submarines in it since the middle of the fifteenth century."

"How was that?" Stephens asked with a grin, suspecting something.

"It was a result of a habit the sultans fell into: screwing themselves out of a job. Some of them had as many as a hundred wives and mistresses, which is twenty-eight better than the seventy-two houris the Koran promises to the bravest and most pious warriors in Paradise. With all those dames available, there were bound to be a lot of brats growing up for the next generation. They had no firm law or custom governing succession. So when a new sultan got the job, he was in trouble from the start, because it was considered reasonably legitimate for some brother or cousin to knock him off and take over the job.

"So many sultans got murdered that Sultan Mohammed II passed what he called the Law of Fratricide, which meant that as soon as a new man took the throne he was supposed to have all his brothers and cousins and other potential competitors strangled.

"And then, just to forestall the proliferation of other potential rivals, they tied the opposition women up in sacks, with their heads sticking out and rocks in the bottom, and heaved them into the Bosporus. They submerged to periscope depth almost at once. The current carried them down to Seraglio Point, where they went aground by the hundreds. My boy, I wish you better luck than that."

V

A YEAR after he was deposed, Kirov's wife died of cancer and despair. This left him with no living relatives he knew of—barring perhaps some distant cousins in the Ukraine—except a forty-year-old son, Nikita, whom the old man considered such a no-good that he, himself, had long ago sent him off to semi-respectable exile as a clerk in the Soviet embassy at Ulan Bator in Outer Mongolia. This would, he had hoped, keep his offspring from always getting into the woman-and-vodka embarrassments that had been his specialty around home. At least Ulan Bator was far enough away so that if the kid kept it up, it wouldn't fret his mother because she wasn't likely to hear of it.

After her death, when he was alone with one superannuated manservant, whose cooking he detested, Kirov seldom stepped outside the villa on Moscow's southwestern outskirts to which he had been dispatched by the triumvirate which had succeeded him. Instead he stayed indoors, received hardly anybody, read *Pravda* and *Izvestia*, and grew increasingly bored and even more increasingly disgusted with his successors. They had thrown him out and more or less locked him up; that he could understand, since he had, on occasion, done the same to others. In fact, he often thought, they had been foolishly softhearted about him; in their place, and considering the stature of the victim, he would have done something a good deal more terminal. But the way they had failed to handle China infuriated him and the insults they swallowed from Albania even more. And they had got themselves entangled with that loony, Castro; not to mention a number of places, like Syria and Egypt, which could absorb any number of pieces of military hardware but did not seem to know what to do with them except let the Israelis either smash them or swipe them. And this business of building automobiles, nylon stockings, canned dogfood, cosmetics, and television sets instead of concentrating on the sinews of the country struck him as the primrose path to ruin. Indeed, almost the only thing in the new order of which he approved was what, in the West, was called a miniskirt; it saved material.

At length he decided to get out. He did not think of it in terms of defection. What he did believe, with all his soul, was that his successors had things so bollixed up that somebody had to step in and get rid of them. He knew he couldn't successfully carry out this intent from his present point of disadvantage in a suburban villa. But an exile, particularly one of his own still-remembered stature and in a place of respect and honor, conceivably could do a lot. Given an Olympus, he could still cast down thunder and bolts of lightning; he did not particularly want his former job back; what he wanted was to tell the man or men who held it how to manage affairs and policy. And, though I may be old by many standards, he considered, I am young enough for that. He knew the nation, huge as it was, was pockmarked with disaffection. Given a voice and a place from which it could be heard, he might well coalesce that mighty force and turn the rascals out. After all, Lenin had done it; why not Kirov?

At length he decided. Certain arrangements were made. Steed, the CIA man with an outwardly innocent job at the United States embassy, had the directing hand in these arrangements. For his part, Kirov was no fonder than he ever had been of the U.S.A., but it was unquestionably the highest Olympus he could think of.

Because Kirov so seldom appeared outdoors, the guards, stationed there in relays as much to keep the curious away as to keep the old man under surveillance, grew careless about their work. They were a slovenly lot anyhow, as Kirov knew, having plenty of leisure to observe their deportment. He knew they vanished often, presumably, it occurred to him, to relieve the tedium with tea at the *stolovay*, a sort of standup cafeteria a few squares away. And he suspected that even when they kept physically to the job they were often deep in vodka and spiritually far away.

In consequence, it was four days after he slipped out the back gate and into a nondescript Moskvitch automobile, before the guard got around to knocking on the front door which, eventually when it was not answered, he broke open and found the old manservant locked in the kitchen pantry and Kirov gone. Uzzumekis, who had come to pick Kirov up, held no ill will for the manservant and, though he threatened to come back and tear his head off if he made a racket, had decided on the pantry as a prison because it held both food and drink. Moreover, it was deep inside at the back of the villa and windowless, and he doubted, in any case, whether the old bag of bones could make enough noise to attract attention.

Thus the fugitives had a fair head start. They might even have had more, for the guard, abashed at discovery of the consequences of his negligence, seriously thought of going over the hill himself rather than do his duty—report Kirov's absence and face the music. He was prevented from this prudent course only because the guard corporal, making his own rounds, came by at the time and finding his man away from the sentry box and the villa door open, entered for a look around and caught the unhappy sentry in *flagrante delicto*.

The word came up through channels and reached Sobelov, the head of KGB and thus Chief of State Security, at five o'clock the following morning, thus increasing Kirov's and Uzzumekis' lead to 117 hours, every minute of which they were going to need. Even so, the news made pretty fast time considering the amount of apprehension, recrimination, and thus nervous procrastination it stimulated at each step of the way. In fact, it was a wonder the word got to the top at all.

Sobelov listened in silence to the colonel who brought him the report. The colonel was visibly upset.

"Gone, eh?" Sobelov said at last. "Where?"

"We don't know yet."

"Do you have any idea why?"

"No, sir."

"It may have been innocent. I have suspected he was going a little off his head since his wife's death—and the other thing."

"I could not say, sir."

"Well, find him."

"Yes, sir!"

Now, Sobelov thought, I'm going to have to tell *them*, and I wish I knew how to put it. He remembered all the times he had traveled with the old man in the past, Belgrade, Delhi, Jakarta, the UN, Los Angeles, Camp David, a silo somewhere God knew where in Iowa, shielded him, propped him up when he was on the bottle, practically wet-nursed him around the world. Suddenly he was angry. Why would the old bastard do this to me? he asked himself.

Five-thirty now, he thought. He knew the First Secretary disliked being rousted out at any such hour. On the other hand, he would resent not getting news of this magnitude as soon as it was known. Sobelov remembered the First Secretary's anger on another occasion when, out of consideration for the boss' rest, he had delayed in telling him of the fiery death of a pregnant woman cosmonaut. He sighed and rang for his aide.

The First Secretary, ordinarily urbane, was now grim as well as in his bathrobe and unshaven.

"When did it occur?" he asked.

"The servant, who was in the dark and had no clock does not know exactly. He was sure it was in the evening and that it must have been some days ago."

"Doesn't he know what day this is?" The First Secretary's frown was deepening. "Or that one was?"

"The idiots who first questioned him did not think to add one thing to another. I will know in a few minutes."

"Kirov wasn't alone in this?"

"No, some man was with him. The servant got only one glimpse before he was knocked on the head. All he knows was that the man was huge. That may be his addled memory—out of fright."

"Was Kirov co-operating with the man? Or was he kidnaped?"

"That is another thing the nincompoops forgot to ask. They should be asking him just now."

"You have no trace of him from the time the servant was struck?"

"None whatever. But my people are working."

"They had better be working," the First Secretary said grimly. "This could be nothing, of course. Kirov may, for the devil knows what peculiar reason, have just decided to go off on a holiday—although he knew perfectly well he was not supposed to without proper arrangements being made. Security—of course. But I—we—cannot tolerate not knowing precisely what took place and why. You understand that, Comrade Sobelov?"

"Of course. That's why I thought it necessary to awaken you."

"You were right. Which way do you think he may have gone?"

"Until now—no idea."

"But you will find out?"

"Naturally, sir."

"How?" The First Secretary's face was growing grimmer, a condition in no way improved by the dark bristle around his jaw.

"We begin with means of transporation : roads, autos, railroads, by air, even afoot. Do not forget, sir, Kirov is practically impossible to disguise."

"That is correct. Body of a bull, face of a Poland China hog."

"Poland China? What is that?"

"Excuse me, I forget. You are not an agriculturist and even if you were in our—in some ways—benighted land, you probably wouldn't know about pedigreed livestock. The Poland

China is a pig, a particularly porcine-looking pig. I learned of it while touring American farms."

"I see. I may have seen some example of this beast myself when I accompanied Kirov to Iowa. Not that I noticed, for I was preoccupied with keeping him sober or, at least, concealing the fact that he wasn't.

"But now, back to business. I may have a lead within a few hours. Perhaps even already. They—my men—would not interrupt me here . . . with you."

"You have what resources you need?"

"They are already at work, those who could be reached at once. Others within hours. I have good men, sir."

"I know that. East, west, south, north? Which way could he have gone? And why?"

"I don't know that—yet. I will know it, be sure of that. With your permission, I leave you, sir, and get to it."

"Do so."

Sobelov left, and the First Secretary, yawning, headed for his bath and a shave, but first he rang for his servant and instructed him that he desired a pot of tea.

"Strong," he said.

"Of course, sir," the servant said. He knew that the boss liked tea. He also always knew precisely when moments of crisis came upon the Soviet Union, for, to confront emergencies, the boss liked his tea with the wallop of an irritated crocodile's tail.

Sobelov returned to his austere office inside the Kremlin walls and summoned his aide.

"How many men on the job now?" he asked.

"Fifty. All that were immediately available."

"What progress?"

"This is Tuesday. The escape—or kidnaping—whichever it was, took place about eight o'clock Thursday evening."

"Hmm, he could be anywhere by now."

"Or still in Moscow."

"Moscow is part of anywhere," Sobelov said irritably.

"Yes, sir," the aide agreed. He knew, to his sorrow, that

despite Sobelov's mild appearance, with his round face, shiny pince-nez, and shiny bald head, his wrath could be awesome.

"We may need a hundred and fifty men before this is finished. Or five hundred. Or a thousand. To begin with I want men in every port, at every airport, at every border crossing point—railroad or road—in Berlin, particularly Berlin, and particularly at the place they call Checkpoint Charlie. I don't know that he is running away, but if he is, Berlin is the route that comes first to mind."

"Yes, sir. May I ask, sir ... ?"

"Ask what?" The eyes behind the pince-nez glinted dangerously.

"What general instructions to give the men if . . . in case ... that is when they do find him?"

"Bring him back."

"If force is required ... ?"

"Use what force is necessary. Only that. Don't hurt him. He is an old man."

Alone in his office, Sobelov settled himself to the task of trying to read the mind of his former boss, the ex-First Secretary of the Communist Party of Soviet Russia. It wasn't a very fruitful effort, for, to begin with, the man now so furtively vanished was by no means the same man—although he had the same body—he had once watched bully half the world.

Defected? It was hard to swallow for, if he was sure of anything, he was sure that Kirov was a patriot, heart and soul committed to Mother Russia. And he was a proud man, who would not stoop to flee from any enemy. But you had to consider defection, for when any prominent citizen mysteriously vanished out of the system, you had to consider the twin possibilities that he had either run away or had been discreetly knocked on the head. However, he knew, *if* Kirov had been knocked on the head he, Sobelov, should have known about it since he probably would have been commissioned to do the knocking. But then, also, he admitted he couldn't know what Kirov's humiliating fall from power and his subsequent confinement had done to the old man's spirit.

Pride entered into that, too. Or might this be some mysterious maneuver aimed at the recapture of power? It was hard to think how that could be possible although he knew—and who knew better?—that across the vast sweep of the Soviet Union there were pockets of disaffection which could be summoned up to action by a strong leader. He'd better get his agents into those pockets, too, as quickly and discreetly as possible.

He got his first break at dusk that same afternoon—or what, at first seemed to be a break. It was sooner than he could have expected.

Excitement illuminated the aide's face as he knocked and entered without his usual ceremonious waiting for permission to be called to him.

"What now?" Sobelov grunted in annoyance.

"We have something," the aide said, forgetting to sir him, "Gagarin is here to report... He says..."

"He is here?" Sobelov demanded. "Send him in then. I don't want it secondhand."

The agent, a soldier in the ranks of Sobelov's unseen underground army, followed the aide into the office and stood waiting.

"Well, talk. What do you know?" Sobelov demanded.

"Five nights ago, within an hour of this hour, Comrade Kirov boarded a westbound train at Sychevka," the agent began.

"West, eh?" So, Sobelov thought, Berlin after all. "Who saw him?"

"The guard of the train. Four other persons in his compartment. He was recognized. He made no attempt at disguise."

"Was anyone with him?"

"Not that we know, yet. He was in good spirits and talked freely with the others."

"Who told you that?"

"The train guard."

"Why did the guard not report this at once?"

"He did not think it necessary. There was no concealment."

"What kind of papers did Kirov carry?"

"The guard did not know. He was astonished to see Kirov on the train, but, since he was there openly . . . and because Kirov is a personage of great importance he was embarrassed to ask."

"A personage of even greater importance than he thinks . . . I trust you have taken care of the train guard?"

"Yes. He is in a cell. For your disposition."

"Find out everything else he knows. All of it. Also find out *what* he is, the guard. Then we will see."

"Naturally, sir."

"When was the last the guard saw him?"

"At Yartsevo. He left the train there."

"Yartsevo, eh? Who was with him?"

"Apparently nobody, so far as the guard says. Two others left the compartment there, but they did not appear to be with Comrade Kirov."

"Who were they?"

"Merchants, the guard says."

"Trace them."

"We have begun."

Sobelov turned to the aide.

"I want a hundred men in Yartsevo by midnight, no later. More if you need them, but it is not too big a town. I want everything checked out of there, rail, airplane, roads, rivers. It is on the Dnepr. I want the town itself searched, house by house. Talk to everybody, particularly of the railroad. It is impossible for a man like Kirov simply to vanish."

"Yes, sir! Now at least we know which way he went, sir."

"You mean we know which way he started. Out of Yartsevo there are the same directions as there are out of Moscow. North, south, east, west, and all the compass points between. In any case, double the force in Berlin. I want him found— and quickly."

"Yes, sir."

Sobelov turned back to Gagarin.

"About the train guard, wring him dry. I don't like that excuse for not asking for documentation—even less for not reporting."

"Yes, sir. At once."

"If he has anything of substance—or is anything of a substance I would not like—report direct to me. Otherwise tell *him*." Sobelov jerked a thumb at his aide.

Sobelov settled down to think. Did he have anything or didn't he? A short train ride, no attempt at concealment, a train guard who was either fatheaded or in cahoots with the old man, a couple of unidentified merchants, no more. What did it amount to, except that Kirov had actually been seen after leaving the villa? There was still all four points of the compass and half a world to look in, maybe an entire world.

J. Edgar Hoover should have my job, he thought bitterly.

VI

"GLORY be to God," the pilot, an Air-Force major, said to Navy Lieutenant J. N. Hale. "What've you got in the package?"

"Oh, a trailer and some other junk. And twenty-four men," Hale said.

"I don't mean the trailer. I can see what that is with my very own eyes, although a little peculiar-looking for a trailer. I mean the Christmas parcel, that doodad over there."

They were on the apron at Westover Air Force Base in Massachusetts, vastly foreign to Lieutenant Hale's normal surroundings at the New London, Connecticut, Submarine Base. They were standing in the shade, sheltered by the vast aluminum overcast of the wing of an Air Force C-141 cargo airplane. A hundred feet or so behind them the transport's cargo doors swung open on the gloomy maw of its eviscerated abdomen. The major's interest, however, was not at the moment on his airplane but on a monstrous object, swathed in tarpaulin, mounted on skids and held aloft by six big fork lifts, three to a side. The thing looked about fifty feet long and a dozen thick and vaguely cylindrical, though hunchbacked.

"Oh, just something we're not supposed to blather about very much," Hale's tone was noncommittal. "We're just supposed to take it along."

"Yeah? What's it weigh?" the major asked.

"Oh, around thirty-one tons—a little over. Think you can carry it?"

"If it'll behave we can carry it. It ain't alive, is it?"

"No."

"Then we can carry it. We can carry anything, except maybe a submarine."

"How long will it take you to make Turkey?" Hale asked.

"Oh, we plug along," the pilot said. "If that thing's as heavy as you say we'll probably have to refuel at Wiesbaden.

Say twelve, thirteen hours, depending on the winds. You ain't in a hurry, are you? We're a little on the plodding side on account of being somewhat pot gutted."

"From what I hear, that should do it," Hale said. "Are we ready to load the planes now?"

The pilot raised his cap, scratched a nap of short-cut, curly red hair and squinted again at the cargo. "Sure. Otherwise we're fueled and read to go. I swear, I sure wish I knew what that doodad is, bub, if you'll pardon an old man's curiosity."

"Consider it pardoned," Hale told the major, easily fifteen years his junior, though a rank higher. "Also consider it unsatisfied."

Hale, who ran the sub base escape and rescue school at New London, had received orders, through the flotilla admiral, to load up the experimental DSRV and get it to Istanbul with as little commotion as possible. Nobody really expected the thing to go unnoticed, but as much privacy as feasible seemed advisable; thus the shroud. Hale was not told what he was expected to do with the DSRV once he got it to its destination, and, although he was curious, he was too old a hand at carrying out Navy orders to let it unsettle him.

"What means of transport, sir?" he asked the admiral.

"There'll be two air-force transports . . . the big ones, tank carriers . . . ready to go tomorrow at Westover AFB," the admiral said. "It would be a lot simpler to piggyback it on a ship, but I gather they're in something of a hurry."

Somebody is always in something of a hurry, Hale reminded himself.

"The designers say an airplane can carry it, sir," he said. "But we've never tried that."

"I understand we don't try it this time; but do it."

"Aye, aye, sir."

It had been a long night run from New London to Westover AFB. Proceeding by the simplest and most direct route, the business of getting the DSRV to Westover would have been simple, a mere matter of some seventy miles. But two

95

things that were clearly incompatible were that the DSRV weighed thirty tons bare-naked, and its trailer and tractor weighed Lord knows how much more, while some of the bridges on the more direct path would probably collapse at anything over ten tons. And so, instead, it had been necessary to take the heavy highways, the Connecticut Turnpike to New Haven, then skirting the city onto U.S. 91, again roaring over Springfield on the thruway, finally turning off for the air base entrance on Highway 202 at Hadley Falls. Altogether the trip had used up 125 miles, crossing the Thames (home of the subs) and Connecticut rivers, bypassing Old Saybrook—home away from the sea for many a submariner, penetrating the heart of Revolutionary War country without stimulating a single patriot to fire a musket from behind a tree or stone wall.

It's probably a good thing they bulldozed out the trees and stone walls a long time ago, Hale thought. Still, I guess it was best to take it at night. It does look pretty weird. Except for that hump in its back, people might take it for a missile, but I'm not even sure they're used to those in this part of the country. But with that hump it looks like a camel with cramps.

"How do you go about loading your planes?" he asked the pilot. "Do you back up to the . . . the doodad?"

"Nope," the pilot said cheerfully. "These birds, if you can call them that, handle pretty good in the air but they're bloody beasts on the ground. We haul, but what we haul has to come to us instead of the other way around. We'll manage."

Loading the trailer and a prepackaged and palletized McCann rescue bell, its winches, anchors, buoys, compressors, nylon cables and lines aboard one of the two C-141s, borrowed from the Air Force by the interservice cajolery of Admiral Engel at the Pentagon, proved a fairly simple operation, involving few matters more complicated than sweat. The hooded DSRV was another matter, but not impossible.

The fork lifts trundled their burden behind the airplane's

gaping anus and then lifted it. Their synchronization was a little clumsy, and Hale caught his breath while the DSRV wobbled on its skids.

"Belay that!" he yelled at the lift operators before he realized that these Air-Force types were unlikely to savvy Navy nomenclature. But the lifts steadied down and, at last, the bulk of the DSRV, still safely in its disguise, was level with the C-141's interior deck. Winches anchored at the head of the cargo hold were hooked on and, inch by painful inch, the burden slid into the plane, supported by rollers sunk in the floor. Lashed down all around, it was ready to go.

Go where, I know; go for what, I haven't the faintest damn idea, Hale thought as they lifted out over the Atlantic. Hale had been in the regular Navy for twenty-five years, twenty-three of them in submarines. Now, at forty-two, he had been a commissioned officer for twelve, earmarked forever as a mustang by the tattooed hula dancer on his right arm and the word MOTHER engraved in Gothic script on the left. For the last nine years he had specialized in the esoteric business of submarine rescue. He knew whatever there was to know about finding a downed submarine and wished he knew far more. In practice, he had, in command of an ASR (Auxiliary Submarine Rescue), carried out successful rescue operations with the old diving bell which winched itself down to a sunken submarine's escape hatch and took off its trapped crew seven or eight at a time. Until development of the DSRV, the bell was the latest thing the Navy had since its first moderately successful use on *Squalus* off the New Hampshire coast in 1939.

Thirty-three men were got out alive from *Squalus* after she essayed a test dive and went right on down to the bottom in 243 feet of water and refused to come up. It was the most successful submarine rescue in history but, even so, it accounted for only slightly more than half her crew. Twenty-six had died when *Squalus* flooded in her dive.

Hale thought probably that very few people realized how generally bankrupt his profession was, if you could call it a

97

profession. Throughout the history of submarines, which went back at least as far as Alexander the Great, those that went down for good very seldom yielded up any live men. Generally the only point in salvage operations was to get the boat back and find out what went wrong and, if it seemed profitable, repair it and put it back in service with a new crew after, of course, first burying the old one. The Confederate Civil War submarine *Hunley*, for example, hand-cranked by eight men, sank three times and drowned the crew on each occasion. Her final sinking was accompanied by success since she took the Union blockade vessel *Housatonic* with her. The nuke *Thresher* illustrated a new generation in the problems of saving men who went down in submarines not wisely but too well. It had taken nearly three months even to find the crushed wreckage after she went down in 8400 feet of water.

It may have been a streak of perversity in him, he thought, that had moved Hale to take up an occupation with such bleak prospects of success. He wanted to demonstrate that it could be done and spent untold hours brooding over ways to do it better or improve the methods the service already knew. One of the things he had worked out in theory was a method to latch onto an automatic gear rigged to a sunken submarine's stem — "bull nose" — and tow it back to the shallows and safety. Perhaps his most powerful motive for becoming a rescue and salvage specialist, though he never thought of it in those terms, was that he was a submariner, and submariners as a genus were as clannish and mutually protective as a family of Kentucky mountaineers.

Now he had the DSRV and held fond hopes for it. In its simplest terms, the DSRV consisted of three pressure spheres mounted in line, interconnected by pressure hatches, the whole caboodle sheathed in a streamlined outer housing. The center sphere, with a skirt like the old rescue bell, operated by sealing onto the disabled sub's escape hatch. Once sealing was done, water was blown out of the lower skirt of the sphere. Then its inner hatch was opened, as were the upper and lower hatches of the submarine's escape chamber. Thereafter, if all went well, the DSRV could take off two dozen at a clip. Aside from its greater passenger capacity, the huge and most significant difference between the DSRV and primitive bell was that the new craft was both sentient and mobile. It carried a crew and instrumentation and it could go under its own power. Moreover it was designed for deep work, down 3000 feet or better.

Hale had operated the DSRV in practice, and all had gone well. But then he knew practice was one thing and doing the same job under pressure was another. For a major consideration, he wondered how the DSRV would perform on a disabled sub which lay at such an angle of list that the sealing surface of the escape hatch was considerably off level. Could the DSRV be trimmed down accurately enough to accommodate the tilt? He knew he could do it reasonably well with the bell when the escape hatch was as much as ten degrees off the horizontal. But, in this, the bell was another breed of cat. He didn't know how well the DSRV would work and he hoped to God he never had to find out.

They landed in Wiesbaden a little after five A.M., local time, which considering their take off at four P.M. from Westover and the five-hour time differential, was not bad at all, at all, as the jaunty major explained. An eight-hour passage, considering the pot-bellied state of their airplane and the bulk of the doodad and a twenty-knot headwind halfway across the Atlantic was pretty close to commendable. The two big planes were half through the fueling operation, and the sun was winking over the horizon, when a jeep brought a message for Hale from the flotilla admiral at home.

"HOLD UP UNTIL FURTHER ORDERS," it said. Hale showed it to the major.

"Hey!" the major said. "Does that mean we offload?"

"I doubt it," Hale said. "If they wanted us to offload, they'd say so. We just park and wait."

"Well, the Air Force is unlikely to be pleased," the major said. "They keep needing guns, tanks, and the like in Vietnam. Fetching the blessings of democracy to those people is a slow business, and it seems to me we poor slobs in the transport business have to fetch an awful lot of it . . . without, I must say, ever witnessing much result of the fetching. Would you suppose that anybody ever thought to wonder whether the Viets really want our brand of that democracy stuff? It sometimes seems to me that what setting a people free mostly requires is killing them off . . .

"However, though the Air Force may be disgruntled, my motto always has been to take the bad with the good and vice versa. I was stationed here for a while; I know a fraulein in town . . . charming girl . . . not greedy . . . old family and all that. She has friends. I could, I think, arrange a date for you tonight. Guaranteed co-operative"

"Thanks, no," Hale said, for a moment feeling a wistful twinge of youth. "I'd like to, but I think I'd better stay with the doodad."

"I thought you told me it wasn't alive," the major said.

The message holding up the DSRV's approach had originated with Admiral March in Istanbul and had been routed through the Pentagon, his own chief of staff in Norfolk, the flotilla admiral in New London, and, at length, to Lieutenant Hale in the dawn at Wiesbaden.

"We are going to attract enough gawking as it is," he told State. "Right now I'd rather have Germans wondering what's inside those two airplanes than have Turks . . . and their friends and neighbors . . . speculating. When they pull in here we're going to have to offload and snake that trailer and its load twenty miles into town over rotten roads and then pull it through this town's impossible streets down to the docks and hoist it aboard ship.

"By the way, has anybody been out to lay a tape measure on that gate through the old city wall? We'd be in a hell of a social fix if we had to ask the Turks to blow a hole in a monument."

The Admiral's major problem, of the moment, was that he

still didn't have an escort ship for *Skate* and mother hen for the DSRV, and he was icily determined not to permit *Skate* to go without.

At the moment of sending the message he was some 168 hours short of the rendezvous off Balaklava. He had the scouting resources of Navy and the diplomatic services and the Defense Intelligence Agency organized on emergency status but their operations were, he knew, limited by the necessity of concealing, for at least a week, that the prospective purchaser was the United States government.

They got an offer from Salonika, but, upon investigation, the vessel proved to be an ancient, straight-stemmed Hog Islander laid down sixty years ago for the west-coast lumber trade. If they wanted something down at the heel in appearance, this ship certainly met the admiral's qualifications in that cosmetic respect. Her iron was so rust-bitten that, nearly anywhere, it was possible to lay a finger so flat in one of the pits in her scabrous plating that a ladybug could have crawled across without exertion. Her engines were close to the point of beyond redemption, and even her present owners, an inter-island shipping syndicate in the Aegean, wouldn't claim more than seven knots for her.

"Five would be closer," Admiral March said when the vessel's condition was relayed to him. "If that bucket can do seven knots it will have to be downhill."

It might have been possible to put up with her speed, in a terrible pinch, but it went without saying that the ship did not carry even the most primitive radar.

"That lets her out," March said. "It also lets me out of being hated forever by the crew I would have put aboard. Besides we need something faster," he told State. "I don't need to remind you that time is chewing on our rears. We need at least a day to get the DSRV aboard and secured and show a new crew where the levers are. Hell, that tub would take nearly all the time we've got just to get here—not even considering the other three hundred and fifty-some from here to Balaklava. Keep looking."

They were down to 140 hours, and the admiral was growing desperate, when, all at once, the problem was solved. A Lebanese broker in Beirut, the acuteness of whose commercial instinct and profit motive had come down through his genes three thousand years from Phoenician forebears, called on the commercial attaché at the embassy. The attaché, when wearing his other hat, was also the local CIA man and thus had something more than an inkling of what was afoot.

"You need a ship, sir. I believe I have what you require."

"Where is it?"

"At the moment, in Rhodes."

"Hmm," the attaché said. "Interesting. What kind of ship is it?" Privately, he was interested. Rhodes was about as close as you could get to the ship's first destination without actually being on Turkish territory.

"Excellent. Sound vessel, sir."

"I asked what kind, not what shape?"

"A trawler. Two thousand tons."

"What registry?"

"Panamanian."

That's good, the attaché thought. It's a good thing all ship-owners are crooks and never register anything at home. Taxes. Insurance. All the little annoyances of patriotism avoided simply by hoisting the flag of some pipsqueak nationality insignificant enough not to give a damn—so long as you paid their fees.

"How old is she?"

"Sound vessel, sir. Beautiful condition."

"How old?"

"Clyde built in, I believe, nineteen-thirty," the Lebanese admitted reluctantly, seeing a sale in danger of going glimmering.

"We'll have a look at her," the attaché said. "Can't buy a pig in a poke, you know."

"What's that, sir?"

"*Caveat emptor*, that's what. Oh, never mind. Can you wait here a little while? I must consult."

"Of course, of course. At your service."

The attaché left the Lebanese in his office, thoughtfully sipping a tiny cup of thick Turkish coffee, and went to the embassy radio room where he put through an emergency call for State at the consulate in Istanbul. As it happened, Admiral March was with State when the call went through. State promptly gave the telephone to the admiral, thinking, with relief, that buying ships was an activity so far afield from his office as almost to constitute an open affront.

March listened intently, then spoke.

"Who are the present owners?"

"A Lebanese holding company. Some of these firms do everything, banking, shipping, agents for European and American manufacturers, opium peddlers . . . literally anything. I know this outfit. They're a medium-size one, doing business in the Med and as far east as Iran."

"Are they reliable?"

"Reliable, yes, honest no."

"I don't care whether they're honest or not. Are they discreet?"

"You can keep them discreet as long as you need to by holding out part of the price until you don't care any more."

"By the way, what do they want for it?"

"Two million clams. That's their asking price."

"Gawdalmighty, what do they think they're selling us, the *Queen Mary*?"

"I know. Ali Baba and the forty thieves. That's why I think, if the ship will do the job, we may go for the whole price, or something near it. If they think they're in for that much sugar, they won't squall so much about having to wait for part of it."

"You're probably right. You and that agent meet me in Rhodes, as quick as you can."

"How quick?"

"This afternoon. I'll take this embassy plane. You take your ambassador's. If he wants an okay, have him call the Secretary here. Right away."

Whew, the attaché thought, it's no wonder this guy's an admiral. It's a wonder he isn't President.

"Oh, this last," Admiral March said. "Do they know we're going to dump the crew?"

"Sir, they wouldn't give a damn about that, not around here. These sailors got no union."

Under any ordinary circumstances, an admiral would have delegated such chores as finding and buying a ship in a hurry to his staff and to the Defense Intelligence Agency, who were equipped to do it and whose sensibilities might be wounded if they were bypassed. An admiral, he knew, ought to reserve himself for more rarefied levels. However, March was by no means an ordinary admiral.

He would normally have admitted it, except to a most trusted friend, but the fact was that desk duty itched him. He preferred sea duty. Thus, whenever it was feasible to elude the snares of red tape, protocol, and high strategy that enmeshed his high office, he much preferred to be a do-it-yourself admiral.

And this time, he told himself with satisfaction, he had an excuse that ought to hold up. The fewest possible people were supposed to have any idea whatever concerning the errand upon which *Skate* was bound. Therefore he felt perfectly justified in playing hooky long enough to buy a ship himself, without having to defer to the inevitable aggravations of going through channels.

At five P.M., wearing civvies, as he had ever since leaving Norfolk, Admiral March, the CIA man with his pseudo-attaché label, and the Lebanese broker reached the docks in Rhodes and went aboard the *Queen Zenobia*. The ship was dirty, they saw at once. That's all right if it's only sloppy housekeeping . . . even better, Admiral March thought. But it's something else again if slop topsides also means slop in the engineering spaces. The admiral's primary interest lay in four matters: the condition of the engines, deck space for the DSRV, sufficiently powerful hoisting gear sufficiently well maintained to handle the DSRV, and the condition of the radar. Sonar, of course, would be beyond hoping for.

He went below and inspected the engines, two big diesels. The engineroom, like topsides, was unkempt, but that did not necessarily mean anything. He had the agent tell the engineer to start them up which the engineer, looking puzzled, did. They came to life with deep-throated roars and then, throttled back, steadied into a quiet drumming. Watching them, March listened intently for foreign noise but could detect no sign of impending demise.

"They sound all right, in here. Under way may be something else," he told the agent. "I'll want to take her out of the harbor."

"Anything you wish, sir. Anything," the agent assured him. "You are welcome, sir."

The radar room, markedly out of mesh with the rest of the ship, was spotless. March told the agent to have the operator warm up, so he could see how it worked. He did so, and March intently watched the slow, sweeping line of light, set to close-up scale, sweep around and around the darkened screen, bringing up the bright pips of nearby buildings, the hills behind, caïques setting into and out of the harbor. It's old-fashioned, but it'll do, he thought with satisfaction.

Topsides, he let his mind calculate berthing room for the DSRV. There was enough he reckoned. There were two derricks forward, rigged amidships with, evidently, enough reach over the side to handle the DSRV's dead weight and length enough in the well deck to set her down on her cradle. The bulwarks, he noted with pleasure, were breast-high. They would be that much help in concealing the nature of *Queen Zenobia*'s burden. Still, he knew, we'll have to do some more camouflaging on her. Damn, I wish there was time enough to do this job up right. We'll have to jury rig a dozen things and most of them while we're under way.

He got the agent to get the captain to rig out the hoisting gear and try it out on a pair of heavy freight-moving tractors on the docks. It worked, although with some hitching and complaint. Finally, under March's critical eye, the captain took his ship out and put her ungainly, sway-backed bulk up to all ahead full. March estimated she was good for between fourteen and sixteen knots. Better than I could have hoped. He was already beginning to feel fond of the frumpy little ship. Damnedest thing the Navy ever owned, he thought. Wonder what we'll do with her when we're finished. Give her a Simoniz job and then give her to the Kremlin for a souvenir?

Back at the docks, he took the commercial attaché aside.

"Go ahead and buy her," he said. "Quibble about the price only enough so they'll keep their traps shut after the deal's made. Hold out whatever you're convinced is necessary to make sure they do keep their traps shut.

"I ordered a crew in from Naples before I left Istanbul. They should be here by midnight, maybe before. Captain's a lieutenant commander named Dave Gottfried. Good man. They'll all be in civvies. Tell Gottfried I want that ship in Istanbul as fast as he can make it. Tell him flank speed. Meanwhile get hold of that Willie Sutton of an agent and make sure she's bunkered full—I mean fueled to capacity. See about fresh water. I want her ready to sail as soon as Gottfried is aboard.

"Now, another thing. Paying off the crew, as I understand it, isn't our responsibility. However—you speak Arabic?" The question was abrupt.

"Yes—enough."

"All right, I want you to do this personally. That agent I wouldn't trust any farther than I could throw him. Tell the crew you're paying them an extra month's pay—over and above whatever they may get out of the owners—to stay aboard, provision the ship, and stay long enough to brief Gottfried and his crew on where things are and how they work. Got all that?"

"Yes, sir. You satisfied with her, sir?"

"She'll do," March said as he went over the side.

VII

LIEUTENANT COMMANDER Richard Oulahan, *Skate*'s executive officer, had a number of things on his mind, all of which disturbed him. To begin with, *Skate* had now been four days in Istanbul. Unlike the normal good-will visit, few guests were coming to tour the ship; that, in itself, was not particularly abnormal since he knew that a lot of people in lots of parts of the world still nourished a mortal dread of atomic fission. On the other hand, he could detect no evidence that any American officials were trying to propagandize the Turks out of their apprehension and into a desire to be neighborly.

And then he couldn't, for the life of him, savvy why they had been pulled out of a long-planned fleet exercise in order to go ripping off on a good-will mission in a port where *Skate* was not particularly welcome.

Moreover the old man, Commander Stephens, was spending a good two thirds of his time ashore dashing around on Lord knew what errands about which he was keeping his lip buttoned. Oulahan was perfectly well aware that a ship's captain could get secret orders which he was not permitted to divulge to anyone, friend, foe, or executive officer. However, he and Stephens were solid friends as well as exec and captain and he wished the boss would loosen up a little. After all, he could keep a secret too.

Of one thing he was certain; something was under way and wasn't merely a matter of cossetting the Turks.

Another thing. Oulahan had now served with Stephens for nearly two years in *Skate* and had known him for a long time before, all the way back to the Academy. He knew the small signs of the captain's moods, and he knew that Stephens was intensely preoccupied with whatever was afoot. Possibly even worried.

And so, when they were alone together in the wardroom

after lunch had been served and cleared away, he took this rare opportunity to pry a little.

Oulahan, an extraordinarily lean man with a face deeply and prematurely lined, always made Stephens think of a cheerful cadaver. He was cheerful. He was also an extraordinarily good officer, a quality which he plainly needed as second in command of *Skate*, responsible for more matters, large and small, than he ever had been able to count.

"What's up, Dave?" he said. "You've maybe got something you can't talk about, but, hell, I'm the exec. A little light won't do me any harm."

"What makes you think something's up, Dick?" Stephens answered with a question.

"For one thing we've been four days in this blasted port, and nobody is doing a damn thing except you, running around like a demented monkey. For another, you've got that muley look."

"What muley look?"

"The one you get when you get stubborn."

"Lousy actor, huh?"

"Oh, possibly not too lousy. I just happen to know you better than most."

"Is the boat ready to sail?"

"Never readier."

"I'll tell you this. I think we pull out tomorrow."

"Going where?"

"I'll tell you when we get to sea."

"Go to hell, old buddy. What're we going to do with that bunch of trained seals we got aboard?"

Stephens looked at him gravely. "Frankly I don't know yet. They're under consideration and the decision isn't mine."

"When will we know?"

"When we sail."

Oulahan sighed. "You know, Dave, secrets are absolute hell to keep. I'll tell you something you possibly don't know. You know Chief Cate, he keeps his eyes open."

"I know. What about him?"

"He was out to that airport with the funny name yesterday. He saw that mustang, Lieutenant Hale I believe his name is, and recognized him from New London. You know the guy I mean, runs the rescue and salvage school back home.

"It's funny enough for Hale to be here. It's even funnier that he came in with a crew aboard a couple of oversize airforce transports."

"Hell!" Stephens grunted.

"Hale and big airplanes got anything to do with us, Dave?" Oulahan's question came slow and somber.

Stephens considered it for a long moment and returned Oulahan's straight browed gaze.

"Maybe. You'll get the word as soon as anybody does. Sooner."

Oulahan sighed again. "Okay, Dave. You win. You know there's always some sonofabitch who doesn't get the word. This time I seem to be him."

"Sorry. I really am sorry."

The first night in Istanbul, Stavros Cavanides was a proper and gracious guest of the United States government and attended Ambassador Rushmore's cocktail reception in the soft spring dusk on the roof of the consulate. This location offered a splendid view of the waters rounding away from the Golden Horn and to the Bosporus. Afterward Cavanides remembered it had been about as dull as most diplomatic affairs, except for the drinks, which were fine.

On the second night he succumbed to the blandishments of Garibaldi Nicolai and accompanied him to the Kit Kat Klub. The drinks were relatively awful, but nobody could say that the smiling blond German girl who danced without any clothing whatever was as dull as the ambassador's reception. She had a sinuous and beautiful body, but the pink-tipped breasts dipping down nearly to the floor as she knelt in some semi-tribal rite at the close of her dance were what nearly got him. Later, however, when she had her clothes on again, he asked her to dance and found that she still smelled from the exertions of her solo turn. He was introduced to Nicolai's belly dancer, Marida, and thought he would be charmed to beat his Italian colleague's time with her, but Nicolai had the look of a potentially enraged water buffalo, so he merely wondered, a little wistfully, why the ballet-skirted Greeks had been able to chase Mussolini's black shirts almost at will up and down the Albanian mountains in 1940, while here today, he, a Greek, felt himself to be intimidated by this particular Italian. Marida, he considered, was close to being worth another intra-Mediterranean war.

However, after leaving the Kit Kat alone at five A.M. and abandoning his companion to his fate, he met the Italian coming aboard *Skate* at eleven A.M. Nicolai's eyes were puffed and red, his legs wobbled, and he wore a fatuous grin somewhere between remembered delight and imminent collapse.

"I trust your trip ashore was enjoyable," Cavanides said politely.

Nicolai made a noise that sounded like the gurgle of a defective flush tank and staggered off toward his cabin without other reply.

On the fourth night Cavanides decided to pay a discreet visit to an old friend and colleague. The visit had to be discreet because Cavanides' friend was an extraordinarily indiscreet choice for a man in his position to make.

In the frequently messed-up political structure of the Mediterranean world, particularly the Balkans, Cavanides was a mutation, a dangerous freak. After the Germans were chased out of Greece and the struggle for power began at home, Cavanides, scion of a family long prominent in the military and political affairs of Greece, became so enraged at the brutal excesses condoned by the Papandreou government —particularly the massacre in Constitution Square—that he sneaked away and committed similar but opposite excesses of his own. North of Larisa on the slopes of Mount Olympus he found Markos, the Communist leader, and threw in his lot with him.

He was with Markos or members of his furtive and deadly followers through four years until the Greeks, with American weapons and active American military aid, finally cornered the wily Communist and slew him. During those four years Cavanides got personally involved in only one frantic atrocity, the literal wiping out, by bayonet, machine gun, and flame, of an entire village northwest of Salonika. The village, almost entirely dependent for its economic life on a leaping mountain stream and the mill wheels it turned, was cut off on all four sides by the Communists. No one was spared, not old men, nor pregnant women, nor the unborn in their bellies, for no witnesses were to be left to testify. The carnage made Cavanides physically ill, for his turn of temperament was more toward intrigue than physically carrying out the fruit of his intrigue. He plotted some things, like the murder of a too-nosy American correspondent in Salonika Harbor. And he performed other useful chores for his mentors, particularly liaison across the hospitable borders of Albania and Yugoslavia, where the Greek guerrillas, when too hard-pressed, could retire for rest, refreshment, and re-arming under the aegis of Enver Hoxha or Marshal Tito. In these refuges, the Greeks found that their chief suppliers, training officers, and instructors in the dogma of their faith were Russian.

Cavanides was much taken by the Russians, particularly their ruthlessness, their cold efficiency, and their seemingly absolute commitment. These qualities were finalities and admirable the more because he never did know quite what he himself was. He wished he had it in him to be so unbreakably certain of himself.

With Markos dead, his bands disbanded and fugitive, and the cause, whatever it really had been for the Greeks involved in it, irretrievably lost, Cavanides got back to the paramount business of seeing to the safety of his own skin. Even in the universal confusions of those times, it was not easy for a Greek to reappear on the other side. But Cavanides managed; managing that sort of sleight of hand was his peculiar talent. Both inside and out he had the attributes of a chameleon.

The family name and honorable record helped, of course. By the time *Skate*'s invitation was tendered he was, so far as modern Greece was concerned, not only rehabilitated but moderately trusted. The invitation called for a naval officer, and that Cavanides was, although not a seagoing one. The general staff sent him out to be Dave Stephens' guest and watch how the nukes played their skilled and deadly game in the waters of Ulysses.

But he was still, under a polished and proper exterior, a man of wretched confusions, beset by old angers that he had never fully understood, still wistful for victory in a war that long had been lost. Now, for old times' sake and perhaps some thing else, he wanted to see again Serge Ivanov.

Of the Russians at the Yugoslav sanctuary, Ivanov had been the one Cavanides most liked, personable, spoke a Greek as pure as Cavanides' own, a man whose steel internal fiber wore a garment of perfect disguise.

Now, from the diplomatic list, Cavanides knew that his one-time friend had become cultural attaché at the Russian consulate in Istanbul which, for practical purposes, was almost more Turkey's capital than Ankara was. It was certainly the place where more things, frequently devious and often traitorous, took place. Cavanides telephoned from a public booth at the Istanbul Hilton, the most private kind of communication he could think of. Ivanov was delighted and wanted to meet immediately.

"Let me buy you dinner, old friend," the Russian said.

"But where?" Cavanides hesitated. "You know . . ."

"Of course I know. I knew long ago you had, so to speak, jumped back across the fence."

"And so . . ." Cavanides was embarrassed and hoped his voice didn't betray it, although, of course, it did as Ivanov recognized.

The Russian chuckled warmly. "Don't fear, my friend. I know a place. Quiet, out of the way, discreet. Now take these directions and meet me there in an hour. It is near the Blue Mosque. The proprietor is a Bulgar. Ask for him by name and he will bring you to me. He is Petrof." Ivanov chuckled again. "Have no fear. I use the place often and Petrof values my—my patronage."

The place was small and aromatic of Balkan cooking which, despite his nervousness, quickened Cavanides' palate. The portly owner led him to a small booth, so curtained with hanging glass beads that their many-colored twinkling effectively hid whoever might be inside, while, from the inside against the lighted interior of the place, the delicate curtain permitted a fair view of whoever might be outside.

Ivanov rose to greet him with a smile and warmly outstretched hand.

"We'll speak Greek," he said. "I don't believe Petrof knows it—but even if he did it wouldn't matter. Not with the way I pay him. And nobody else who comes in here is likely to know it." He eyed Cavanides up and down, smiling. "You are looking fit, my friend, after all these years. That uniform becomes you—more, I suppose, than our guerrilla rags from the old days."

"No fitter than you. Don't you ever age?"

"Ho, of course I age. I am now ancient."

Ivanov didn't look ancient, Cavanides thought. A little gray around the temples, perhaps, a trifle heavier. But then, back in the Yugoslav mountains, none of them had been eating as well as the Russian probably was now. Ivanov had a taste for good things: two-hundred-dollar Brooks Brothers suits, which he had the Russian UN mission order for him in New York; Havana cigars, which came from Cuba in partial payment for machine guns; Haig & Haig pinch bottle, which was a little more difficult but by no means impossible for a man of his standing to acquire. Ivanov's rank on the diplomatic list was deceptively modest, but his other job in KGB, Sobelov's vital eye and ear on the Turkish Straits, was something else again and allowed him, among other perquisites, to indulge his costly vanities.

Ivanov eyed his guest with outward twinkling good humor. "For a backslider, old friend, you've come a long way.

113

Guest of honor on an American submarine, nuclear no less. Staff officer in the puppet Greek Navy. Improbable but admirable. In the old days I expected you to get shot any week."

"Things change," Cavanides said. "Sometimes it is necessary to change. One must accept inevitability and adapt to it." Cavanides was feeling slightly on the defensive.

"Of course, of course—or at least appear to adapt. By the way, how are you enjoying your pleasure cruise? I am envious. I doubt if even my best American friend—and I do have several—would be likely to invite me to make a similar trip."

"To be frank, the trip is boring. I could not have believed how boring."

"Boring? How is that possible? In the midst of secrets that half the world would give a fortune to possess—and still bored? Incredible."

"They don't tell us the secrets. And probably"—Cavanides smiled ruefully—"I would not recognize one if I saw it face to face—which I suppose I do do every day."

"A pity. Think how I could pump you. Merely in the name of old friendship, of course."

"A dry well, I fear." Cavanides' smile was deprecating.

The food, when it came was delicious and redolent of home, and they ate with gusto.

"I even believe Petrof has retsina," Ivanov said. "Shall I ask?"

"Of course. It would be a strange Greek who didn't like it."

Ivanov called Petrof and sent him for a bottle of the dry, powerful wine, its taste unmistakable witness to the resin which lined the casks. Ivanov was thinking privately that this was a strange Greek indeed, half one thing he remembered, now half something else. Which was he most of? They finished with thick, sweet Turkish coffee and almost equally thick and sweet Metaxa brandy. Ivanov offered one of his rich-smelling Havana cigars, but Cavanides refused.

I'd better not try to lead him very far into anything, Ivanov

114

was thinking. Nothing overt at least. He may belong to that fancy uniform more than I suspect. But sometimes a man can learn a little something useful even from the innocent. One thing is certain; he isn't enchanted by that accursed submarine, which possibly means he's not enchanted by the crew either.

"You've been here four days now, which seems a long time just for a friendly visit, and, I must say from what I hear, the Turks don't seem overly friendly about the visit."

"I'm long accustomed to Turks not admiring Greeks," Cavanides said. "And the reverse also."

"I doubt if this aloofness is directed at you personally. You know, of course, there are many who object to the entire idea of atomic submarines. They fear them."

"I did, too, when I received orders to travel with this ship. I recovered from that. Now I am merely bored and wish it was finished."

"When will that be, my friend?"

"I don't know. These people even keep secrets from one another. I overheard the captain and his first officer talking today. The first officer wanted to know where the ship was going but the captain refused to tell him."

"Close-mouthed, eh? Did he say when?"

"Not that I heard." Cavanides wondered a little uneasily whether he was possibly being indiscreet. But then he shrugged the notion off. It was literally true that, although he knew his friend was prying, he couldn't give away any secrets if he wanted to for the simple reason that he didn't know any.

"Voyage to nowhere beginning no time, eh?" Ivanov chuckled. "How long is your personal sentence to this floating palace of nothing-to-do?"

"Again, my friend, I don't know. My orders from the general staff were to join the ship as an observer. The orders have not been rescinded or altered. You must know that—with some delicacy in my own past career—I am not likely to

115

be cavalier about making a personal interpretation of what my orders mean."

"No, of course not. You have my sympathy. Swallowed up in secrets and nothing to be known. No wonder you are bored."

"Swallowed up in secrets is correct. You eat, you sleep, you read, you watch motion pictures until your eyes bleed. I didn't even know we were coming to Istanbul until we were on our way."

Ivanov raised an alert guard over his quickening interest and said casually, "That sounds somewhat discourteous to me. What are you, my friend, guest or hostage?"

"Hostage to ennui, surely. We were told the submarine was on fleet maneuvers in the Aegean. I suppose, in fact, we were. But then suddenly we find ourselves coming through the Dardanelles and to here."

Ah, even from innocence, Ivanov thought. And thereafter he led the conversation away from the submarine and back to their shared memories of the dangerous but exciting months in the mountains of Yugoslavia and on and over the borders of Greece. He had what he wanted, or at least something. And it wouldn't do to dig enough to alarm this Greek. He doubted there was more to be mined out of the man's discontent in any case. It occurred to him that this, his old friend, was just barely worth his contempt. He certainly wasn't worth hating. How could you afford more than mildly despising a man who didn't know what he was beyond the immediate discomfort of his circumstances?

Well, Ivanov thought, it was an excellent dinner and, he suspected, well worth the price. He sat in the booth, musing and slowly sipping brandy after Cavanides had discreetly departed before him.

"It will be better if you leave alone," Ivanov had said. "This meal was innocent and blameless, but there are those here in Istanbul who tend to look upon me with suspicion. Petrof has been told to get a taxi for you. If by some remote chance you should be recognized leaving here alone, it will not matter. Every kind of tourist in the world comes here to the old city to shop and ogle." He laughed. "That peculiar quality makes it the safest place in Turkey to meet an old friend. And I have been delighted to see you again—even if you have changed sides since we last met."

So now the Greek was gone, and Ivanov was thinking. An American submarine up the Dardanelles, unbelievable enough on the face of it. And, the Montreux Convention being what it was, impossible without Turkish consent and probably connivance. Moreover, a submarine which suddenly broke off serious fleet business to pay a courtesy call which could only be described as frivolous. He already had advised Moscow of the sub's arrival and, subsequently, the arrival at Yesilkoy of two monstrous American military transports which, for two days now, had remained unexplainably parked on a remote corner of the field. Most U.S. military aircraft in Turkey, he knew, did their comings and goings from the military air base at Adana, in the south.

Now, to these fragments, what did he have to add that was useful, or seemed to offer some potential of usefulness? And there it was : a captain who refused to tell his chief lieutenant —what did they call it in the American Navy?—executive officer—where his ship would be bound when it did sail. All this was interesting. Very. But did it add up to any pattern? Did it portend anything of importance to himself or to Sobelov?

Or was it even wildly feasible that it had anything to do with Kirov? That was insane on the face of it. All the same, Kirov was missing, had been for more than two weeks. Sobelov had let him know as soon as the hunt had begun. The message was precautionary to all heads of KGB missions everywhere, but he knew it was far from routine. Sobelov owned and operated a big net, and he certainly would not leave any gaps in it which it was feasible to patch.

Ivanov returned to the consulate and thoughtfully encoded

a top-priority advisory to Sobelov in Moscow. Even as he did so, he was thinking, I may be adding two and two and getting twenty-two—if so, I'm merely being stupid, which Sobelov pays me not to be. But he knows more than I do where he is and I really think he ought to know about this.

VIII

SOBELOV did not expect the hunt for Kirov to be impossible —he was a good cop and confident of his abilities and the breadth of his resources—but he did not expect it to be easy either. But as the days went by his frustrations grew apace. This was, in part, because he got a daily summons to the presence of the First Secretary, now often accompanied by the Chairman of the Council of Ministers and the President, and all three were clearly nervous. He knew his army was out methodically and efficiently eliminating every conceivable possibility. In the end, he knew, they would find the one which could not be eliminated. All the same it was humiliating to be called to the Kremlin carpet time and again and be forced to report that he had nothing to report.

The train guard had been so thoroughly shaken out that, in the end, it had been necessary to transfer him to a hospital. Sobelov was convinced there was nothing more to be wrung out of the man who could, at worst, be described as sloppy and a bumbler. The same went for the relays of guards who should have been constantly on duty at Kirov's villa. They, too, had been wrung out, not so much in the hope of getting any useful clue, but more in the nature of reprimand for inefficiency. He doubted if they would ever be inefficient again —in the unlikely event that they ever got the chance.

The two merchants had been found, but they were no help. On the train Kirov had been friendly, even occasionally effusive, being Kirov every inch. They had, of course, been astonished to find themselves in such formerly illustrious company; they had also, it was plain, been flattered by it. And, of course, they had been curious, but not sufficiently so as to attract any official attention to themselves by reporting their unusual encounter. They could not remember that Kirov carried any sizable luggage and they had merely supposed that he was either on his way to some party function where his presence was required or was bound upon some private business of his own.

Private business, indeed! Sobelov told himself.

The last they had seen of him, Kirov had said a pleasant good-by and left them at the station turnstile in Yartsevo. Again and again they were requested to search their memories for any indication that Kirov had been accompanied. Particularly was there any recollection of a man, with Kirov or not with him, of extraordinary proportions? No, no such recollection. So much, Sobelov thought bitterly, for the old servant's impression that he had been hit on the head by a huge man. Life would be much simpler in this work, he thought for perhaps the ten-thousandth time, if eyewitnesses were ever worth the powder to blow them up.

The trail had simply evaporated in that Yartsevo railway station. If any one thing was clear in this wretched conundrum, it was that Yartsevo was the place where the thread had to be picked up again—unless Kirov had suddenly sprouted wings and flown off into the Russian night. Sobelov had known the wily old fox to pull off some remarkable stunts in his time, but he doubted whether he was that close to angelic powers. Broomstick perhaps, he thought, wings never.

He had sent Gagarin, whom he knew to be both shrewd and persevering, back to Yartsevo to cast about for the trail at the head of a sizable task force. But a week passed. Then most of another. Nothing.

"Find him," the First Secretary demanded daily.

"We are looking," Sobelov would reply with what patience he could still muster.

"That is not enough," the First Secretary would say.

Meanwhile, in Yartsevo, as the days became weeks, Gagarin was beginning to get the glimmer of a theory. This was based upon a process of throwing away things that he was beginning to consider impossible or, at least, transparently unlikely. A key element in his line of reasoning was the growing stretch of futile elapsed time. Unless Kirov had got clean away by some sleight of hand he could not understand, Gagarin thought he must either be in hiding or must be using some extraordinarily slow means of locomotion.

As for the quicker methods of getting about, he had eliminated Aeroflot early on the supposition that Kirov could not have boarded any airliner anywhere without being recognized and reported long ago. The same theory applied as well to the trains. True, he had traveled this far by train, but that had been a bold gesture—and here he had vanished. That left automobiles, but it seemed to Gagarin impossible that a man of Kirov's high recognition quotient could have got through the hundreds of road check-points alerted to intercept him in the last two weeks. He thought it equally unlikely that a pirate plane, sent by who knew what agency, could have spirited him away; somebody would surely have seen such a plane and reported it.

Kidnaping? Who would want to kidnap him? For what purpose? Moreover, Kirov obviously had left Moscow under his own steam.

What did that leave? In hiding? It no longer seemed likely. With hundreds of men at his disposal, he had combed not only Yartsevo's 50,000 souls but every town and village for a hundred miles around, house by house and room by room.

You could probably also eliminate hiking overland. For one thing Kirov was an old man, no longer too well endowed for skulking from ditch, to forest, to hayrick, living off the land. It would take him forever to get anywhere that would serve his purposes, whatever those were.

That left him with one clear possibility, the river. The Dnepr, navigable from its headwaters all its fourteen hundred miles to Odessa, was one of the world's heaviest laden traffic arteries. He had, of course, considered the river a strong possibility from the first, but now the passage of so much time seemed to have eliminated or rendered unlikely most other avenues for Kirov's flight. The river now seemed the place to concentrate. But here again that constant bugaboo of the search, Kirov's unique recognizability, got in the way of theory. How *could* the old man possibly have hoped to travel hundreds of miles on the water without being recognized and betrayed? Impossible. He would have to be desperate to the point of lunacy even to consider it. And Gagarin did not think Kirov a lunatic.

He decided to return to Moscow and consult with Sobelov. His boss, having for years been personally responsible for Kirov's safety around the world, probably understood the working of the old man's head better than anyone else alive.

"You are correct. He is not a lunatic," Sobelov sat stiffly in his office chair and regarded his lieutenant through the shiny pince-nez. "If he is crazy, it is crazy like a computer. All the same, he is a courageous man; he is not afraid to take chances when the game is worth it."

Gagarin, a gray man, one of whose more valuable professional attributes was his total unnoticeability, was still bothered by Kirov's reverse of his own protective coloration.

"But, Comrade Sobelov, it is impossible for him not to be seen. Why else would he have been so open about traveling to Yartsevo?"

"True. But the fact remains that you have not been able to find anyone who has seen him since."

"We have combed the river all the way to Odessa. Every kind of vessel."

"Including the barges?"

"Of course. But there are literally thousands of them. It takes them weeks to make the voyage downriver—and weeks more to return. Any one may be in one river port today or in another tomorrow or tied up in the same port for days or downriver bound or upward bound. Checking them all, making sure none are missed, is a task for giants."

"Nevertheless, you are now convinced he got away on the river?"

"I see no other real possibility."

"Then he had confederates."

"I have considered that. And I have not forgotten that some person or persons helped him escape from the villa."

"Here is something which should interest us," Sobelov said. "It came to my desk, almost by chance, this morning." He lifted a sheaf of papers from his center drawer. "I do not know that there is any connection, but there are two certain similarities. You will see them instantly."

Gagarin sat forward, alert.

"In nineteen forty-five, we took an American private soldier out of a German prison camp, and he was brought to Moscow. He spoke Russian, having learned it as a child. He showed no interest in returning to his own country and, because of his language ability, certain authorities considered that he might be of some use to the Soviet Union. It developed over the years that he was of very considerable use.

"Now, because he was technically a defector from his own country, a military deserter, and because he was gradually doing more sensitive work for us, his loyalty to his new employer—that is, the Soviet Union—became a matter of continuing interest to this bureau. Such people, as you know, are not always reliable, and it sometimes pays to keep an eye on them. Of course, no such bureau as this can afford to expend its entire energies on surveillance of marginal cases. Primary responsibilities for the activities of such people rests with those in constant contact with them—in this case the All-Union Institute, which employed this man and used his certain talents. Anything unusual in his behavior should have been reported by them to us."

Sobelov sat back and regarded Gagarin thoughtfully.

"That man," he now said slowly, "has been missing from his place of employment for the last fortnight. That is one similarity. You will recognize the other at once when I tell you that he stands something over two meters tall and weighs more than a hundred kilos—in short, a giant."

"Ah," Gagarin breathed. "Of course."

"The failure to report this earlier is, of course, unforgivable negligence. Steps have been taken to correct it."

"As you say, it may be only coincidence. But still, remarkable coincidence—if it is. What is the man called, Comrade Sobelov?"

"Uzzumekis. An outlandish name. Of course, Uzzumekis, if it was he who struck the old man, would hardly be in a position to escort Kirov—wherever he wished to go—without additional aid. Therefore your search is aided by only this one confirming clue. You still have to find them. I agree with your theory that the best place to look is on the river. Do not abandon other avenues, but look most closely there—as though with a microscope."

"The barge people are difficult," Gagarin mused. "A clannish lot, secretive and surly, living in no settled place, but existing only on and within the river. They don't like to get involved with authority."

"I know," Sobelov agreed with a thin smile. "Stalin did little to increase their affection for authority. However, I am confident you will find the means to win their cooperation—one way or another."

On the sixteenth day of Kirov's absence from his villa, Gagarin struck oil. A barge captain tied up in Smolensk, one of a thousand interviewed that day, recalled with some persuasion a coal boat that had been moored across a pier from him many days ago had been crewed by an odd pair of men, one short and pudgy and the other a tower of a man. The thing odd about them, he remembered, was their awkwardness; any riverman could tell at a glance that they were new to the water, not bred upon it. With a little more persuasion, he remembered the boat's number. Afterward he felt an uneasy sense of betrayal but still he felt relieved to have come off no worse in this encounter with these strange, hard men with their inexhaustible questions.

Dmitri, when they got him that night tied up downriver at Rechitsa, was tough enough so that Gagarin almost admired him and actually might have if he could have spared the time.

Dmitri's face went gray under its permanent cosmetic overlay of coal dust when they took him off, leaving his wailing wife behind with a guard. At first he would yield only an occasional involuntary grunt of agony to the blows. But repetition wore him down, and by midnight he was moaning constantly and twice he fainted. But he did not scream until they brought his wife to watch the treatment and his screams echoed her own. But he did not break until, around two in the morning, they stripped off her clothes and began to administer the same treatment to her. At the first sight of her blood, he talked.

He did not talk enough to suit Gagarin, but he talked enough to help. He had advanced a long way along the trail when a special plane came to fetch him to Moscow to report to Sobelov.

"Yes, he had them aboard. I'm sure it was they although he insists he was never told their names. But the description fits," he told Sobelov. "I think I believe that about not knowing the names. Not because I am convinced he is an entirely truthful man but because if I was conducting the same type of operation I would not bandy the names about either."

"How close are you to them?"

"Much closer. Exactly how close I hope soon to discover."

"You must hurry, you know."

"I know. They left him at Zaporozhe, although earlier he had been told to take them to Odessa and put them aboard a small boat which would rendezvous with the barge in the ship channel."

"Why did they leave?"

"A woman came to get them. She had some password which apparently satisfied the big younger one. Uzzumekis, I suppose."

"Who was the woman?"

"He says he doesn't know. Again I believe him, because that is the way I, too, would do it. But if I am wrong, we still have the barge man. In the end, we will know everything he knows."

"Why did he do it?"

"I can only guess. You know, Comrade, there are those among us who will do such things. In addition he was paid."

"Who paid him?"

"Again he swears he does not know. An American. He thinks probably a diplomat. I have not yet got out of him precisely why he thinks that. He said the man was sturdy, of medium age, graying hair, wearing dark, horn-rimmed spectacles."

"If we knew who it was, we could find the identity of the woman and their destination with Kirov," Sobelov was thoughtful. "And I could make a guess, if it really was a diplomat. We have, for a considerable time, taken an interest in the American commercial attaché—a man named Steed."

"I could get him for you," Gagarin offered. "We could find out."

"I am afraid not," Sobelov replied. "Steed left for Washington yesterday."

IX

MELINA PELAVIN supposed that her husband was dead, and for all the good he could do her, he might as well have been. He had been manager of a state collective fishery. His actual job was running a processing plant in Balaklava, where the sturgeon catch was brought in, weighed, gutted, the caviar salted, and the less valuable flesh smoked for markets as far away as Murmansk. The caviar, except that spooned off en route for the delectation of important persons and their important guests, went into the export trade and was a valued earner of hard currency, including Yankee dollars, which were not despised nearly as much as their source.

Uri Pelavin had not much to do with the actual fishermen —after all they knew their work better than any bureaucrat, which Uri was intelligent enough to acknowledge—and he had still less to do with the mushroom growth of heavy industry around every river mouth and port on the Russian littoral of the Black Sea. In particular he had no responsibility whatever for the shipyards, steel mills, and chemical plants which, after the savage devastation of World War II, had risen out of the rubble of Sevastopol just around Mys Kheronesskiy to the north. Thus it would have been hard to say that Uri was to blame for the acid putrefaction the plants dumped into the waters from which the raw material for his own factory was drawn. And nobody, absolutely nobody, could reasonably hold him to account because the sturgeon took offense at this industrial cesspool of chemical pollutants and moved over to the Turkish coast, where all they had to contend with was a steel mill which Prime Minister Adnan Menderes, since hanged for other errors, built with U.S. money where there was neither coal, coke, nor iron ore. Since the steel mill made no steel and was thus no contributor to man's inalienable right to poison the waters around him, the sturgeon were happy there. And production in Uri Pelavin's plant fell off year after year until the State in alarm decided to try him for criminal mismanagement of the enterprise. To his surprise, but that of scarcely anyone else, Pelavin was convicted. The three-judge people's court, presided over by a young woman party member whom Uri had once courted but had abandoned in favor of Melina because his mother warned him against having any but the most casual relations with a *shiksa*, determined to deal sternly with him. It was a year in which affairs had gone badly nearly everywhere; agricultural production was down; steel and oil had failed to close the gap with the West's output, as the last party congress had promised it would; young men in Moscow had taken to wearing pointed shoes and peg-top pants and were contemptuously dubbed *stilyagi* by *Pravda*'s editorial writers; and the Kremlin was red-faced over a bad guess in backing Egypt against a combination of the French, British, and Israelis. An example was needed, and Uri Pelavin provided it. They sent him off to explore the possibilities of establishing a productive fisheries industry in Lake Baikal, approximately 6500 kilometers to the northeast, and told him not to come back until he did.

Thus Uri did not expect to see Melina soon again. And she, after eight years of periodic appeals to the chief judge, from whom she did not expect much mercy for her husband, did not expect to see him again, at all.

"You should understand," the judge told her. "A man who squanders his energies on women—a woman—is a creature the state cannot afford to coddle. Perhaps, where he has been justly sent, your husband will learn to keep his pants buttoned up."

Yes, Melina thought, if he had kept his pants buttoned up around you, you spiteful bitch, he would not be where you sent him. She longed to say it aloud but did not out of reluctant prudence; after all the bitch *was* powerful.

At first she had missed him in aching agony, even forgetting that he often came home smelling unpleasantly of fish. She was a steadfast woman and did not forget him, although the abrasion of time and weariness gradually dimmed the sharp lines of his face until she had trouble remembering exactly what he looked like. And she felt guilty when, at last, she came to realize that what she missed most was the maleness of him. But, though her body often cried with need, she did not take another man. She believed it would be unfair. But in part, she acknowledged to herself, her abstention grew up from an instinctive revulsion; the only men available to her, whether they wished it or not, had to stand as symbols of the system which had ruined her life, and Uri's, with such casual brutality. And, because she was a woman and recognized bitchery when she met it, she hated the judge with unforgiving venom.

With all, she loved her country, but could not abide what had been done to and with it. Learning of her, studying her with shrewd patience, Steed at length recruited her. It was, he explained, the one small blow she could strike for her husband—perhaps not so small as she might imagine. Until now she had been given only minor courier chores to perform and Steed might not now have entrusted her with this extremely touchy commission if he had had available an agent of greater maturity and experience. But one thing that helped his choice and gave him some cautious optimism was that she knew and had been befriended by—after her husband's misfortune—the fishermen of Balaklava; if anybody could lay hands on a boat to deliver Steed's cargo to *Skate*, she stood as good a chance as anybody, perhaps better than most. Anyhow, with the fatalism of a trade in which sheer chance often made a monkey out of skill, he picked Melina because she was all he had to pick.

If Steed was dubious, Melina Pelavin was appalled at this strange mission now in her hands. It was not merely the danger; she was aware of that potential but willing to endure it. It was the nature of the man whose life was now, in part at least, committed to her keeping. She would not shirk the assignment, though her first impulse had been to refuse it.

This—this Kirov—had he not for years been the very touchstone of the callous machine she abominated? Was he not the personification of that system which condoned—no, more than condoned—deliberately created and fostered the kind of offhand cruelty by which a man, Uri, could be ruined, not for real crimes of either omission or commission, but really for climbing into a bed of his *own* choice? She ought, she told herself, to hate and betray this fat old man. Fat? More like granite, she thought—and shuddered, thinking of that inscrutable, cold-eyed creature sitting beside the stove in her sister's house.

That concerned her, her *sister's* house. By what right, in the name of heaven, had she dared to expose the innocent? There was not one chance in a million, she thought, that *they* would ever discover that her sister's roof had been used to shelter *this* fugitive. But what if they did? She knew it would do her sister little good to plead her genuine ignorance that Kirov, in flight, had been allowed to take refuge there. She had used it, she acknowledged, since it was there to use and there was no other. It had been there to use only because her sister was away in Kiev with an aunt. But could that excuse this unforgivable abuse of a trusting hospitality? And giving, of all improbable things, shelter to this monster, unmoving, a cold malice in the corner by the stove.

She knew she was confused, hectored by terrible doubts. There sat the living testimony of her husband's degradation; it could not have come about but for the calculating savagery of which this man had been high priest. But, on the other hand, this chill presence was now itself fugitive, running away from the thing she herself feared and despised. No matter now that Kirov had perpetuated if not indeed helped create the thing. But she would not betray him. She had no reason to suppose the man himself had changed, learned any vestige of humility or honor or pity, probably not. But his defeat and flight had worked some sort of alchemy with him —probably more in herself than in the essence of him, she admitted. He had become her fellow creature, a victim.

And that strange man who had convoyed him, that man even more outlandish than his name. Huge, powerful as a bear, suspicious, trusting nothing, in his very quietness an air of controlled threat. An American, she had been told that much. What guests the times had sent her! Nine years ago, she reminded herself with a wry inward glance, who could have believed this of me, Melina Pelavin? The last would certainly be Melina herself.

Melina's brother-in-law was a carefree and careless fellow who drank too much and, when her sister was not around to police him, preferred to spend his off-duty hours getting tanked with his friends. He was also, Melina often thought, not very bright, and she wondered why her sister had married him. Now she had found him where she had expected, in the tavern, and well over half lit up. It worried her but quite evidently did not cause him any apprehension.

"Not to worry, my duckling," he gave her jovial assurance. "I can drive drunk or sober. Indeed, I sometimes think I drive better drunk. My skill improves."

"Nobody else thinks so, Andrei."

"Ho. Who is this friend of yours whose skin is so precious?"

"I told you, Andrei. It is better not to ask."

"A lover, hey? And you want nobody to know because of Uri? Is that it?"

"You can think what you like. Just don't ask."

"You don't need to worry about me." He winked lasciviously. "I know what it is to get along without it. You have waited long enough, my duckling."

"Stop it, Andrei. And you had better stop drinking, too."

"Don't try to ruin a man's life, sister. I go at eight to load the truck. You and your friend can expect me to come by about ten."

"There are two, Andrei."

"Ho. Two now? One lover is not enough? You kick over the traces at last, my sister, and now it takes two to satisfy you. Ah well, it has been a long time. I sometimes get a little temptation and wish, for a little, I was not married to your sister."

"Andrei, you're a fool. You'll be there, you're sure?"

"Never worry."

Going back to the house, she bought a loaf of coarse bread and a fat chunk of aromatic sausage. It was not much but then they wouldn't have much leisure for the amenities of eating; this they could consume on the run. For the moment, there was the stew she had left simmering in the house.

It was now dusk, and misty, and in another hour or so she thought it might be safe to move—if anything was safe. If anything was . . .

She looked back as she reached the entrance to her sister's narrow, unpaved street. She had been uneasy and all the time she was out, she had found herself looking back and to either side. I don't know whether I'm nervous or only learning good spy habits, she thought wryly. She did not think she had been followed.

Uzzumékis did not visibly start as she entered with her bundle, but even across the width of the room she could sense the wary tension of him. He is like some wild beast, ready to spring, she thought.

"Well?" he said.

"It is well," she said. "My brother comes at about ten when he starts his ordinary round. The distance is not great but it will take some hours since he must make deliveries at the villages. It will be dark and we will not arouse curiosity since he often gives rides to farmers and villagers."

"What have you told him?"

"Nothing . . . except to stop for us. He is drinking."

"That's not good. It's bad enough with a stranger . . . but a drunk stranger. I do not like it."

"Do not be overly concerned about it. Andrei is usually drinking."

"What does he think? Or does he? Doesn't he even wonder about this?"

Melina wondered if she blushed. "He thinks we are lovers."

132

"A splendid time for love," Uzzumekis said.

"Now, we will eat," Melina said. "There may not be time for it later."

Kirov stirred. "I wish I could wash," he said. "A bath would be even better."

"Not a chance," Uzzumekis said sharply. "That coal becomes you. Moreover it's the best disguise you could hope for."

"I suppose so," Kirov sighed. "I am getting accustomed to taking your orders. It is a change from giving them."

It was not to be doubted when the truck arrived. It came into the street with huge roarings and clankings and lurched to a stop under groaning brakes. Good God, that thing will open the cemeteries, Uzzumekis thought. As though the truck itself was not enough, it was followed by pounding on the door and a happy bawl of voice.

"My duckling, come along now! Fetch your lovers." Then came a bellow of delighted laughter.

And a clown, too, Uzzumekis was disgusted.

"Can't you make the fool shut up?" he demanded of the girl.

"We will go; and then he'll be quiet."

She turned off the one bulb, went out ahead, and Uzzumekis heard her urgent whisper. What's she whispering for? he wondered, instantly suspicious. Then she called him softly and he went out, first pressing Kirov's wrist and whispering, "Wait."

He knew the man was peering at him curiously but knew, in this light, he couldn't see much.

"We go, now, my friend," Andrei said. "And also my congratulations. How is she? A good one, hey?"

Uzzumekis could smell him. Probably could smell him as far as I can hear this rattletrap. I wonder if the cluck can drive.

Andrei went toward the cab, first asking the woman, "You could ride with me, but probably you prefer your friends rather than comfort?"

133

"Just go ahead, Andrei," the girl said sharply. Uzzemekis hissed at the doorway, and Kirov came out, softly shutting the door behind him. "Do you want it locked?" Uzzumekis asked the girl.

"Yes," she said. "Here is the key."

The truck motor clattered alive, and Andrei, leaning from his cab, bellowed at them to get aboard. Uzzumekis looked at the truck; from what he could see in the wet darkness it seemed to be the equivalent of, perhaps, a Chevy one-tonner, vintage 1927 or thereabouts, with a high, boxlike back like a grain wagon. I wonder if the damn thing has seventy-five kilometers left in it; I doubt it.

"Come on," he said, boosted first the girl into the high back, then gave the fat old man a leg up and vaulted aboard himself. He banged an ankle against something and swore briefly.

"Here. Forward," the girl called him. "Andrei has made us a place."

He fumbled ahead, feeling his way around obstructions. As nearly as he could make out, the truck body was half loaded with bales, crates, and empty milk cans. He found the girl and Kirov crouched in a cul-de-sac behind the cab.

"It will be cold," the girl said. "But at least we will be out of the wind."

The truck was now lurching through the streets, heading, Uzzumekis considered, generally east and south, though he could not be sure.

"How many stops does he make?" he asked the woman.

"Seven or eight—first the police post."

"Police?" Uzzumekis was instantly alert. Damn her, is she trapping us after all?

"Police?" he demanded. "What police? What is this?"

The girl grasped his arm, hard and urgent. "Do not worry. It will be all right. They know him. They see him every night and they know he often carries people to the villages and farms. They will not search, you will see. It will be all right."

It had better be, Uzzumekis grimly told himself. He felt

for the pistol and shifted it to the outer pocket of his smock. If it isn't all right, I'm going to have a cop killing on my record.

But it was all right. The truck rattled and clanked its way through the city and turned full south in the outskirts. There they were hailed and, with his complaining brakes, Andrei lurched to a stop.

"Ho," they heard him bellow. "It's me."

"Come ahead then with your ancient barrel of bolts," they heard a voice call.

"Do not speak rudely of my chariot. I adore her and, besides, she is older than you are and deserves respect," Andrei shouted. Uzzumekis had the pistol out, held down between his knees out of sight but ready for use.

"What have you got this time?" the voice called above the rattle of the engine. He's closer, probably alongside the cab, Uzzumekis thought. I'll wait—maybe we'll get through.

"The usual—oh, and my sister and her boy friends," Andrei laughed lewdly. "Better not disturb them. No telling what they're doing to keep warm."

"You've got a dirty mind. And you're half drunk, also as usual."

"Ho, why not be drunk?" Andrei retorted.

"Go on then. And try to stay on the road," the voice ordered. Then Uzzumekis saw the figure at the back of the truck, faintly outlined against a dim light cast, he supposed, from the sentry post. He stiffened and began to inch the gun up, thinking, Even blind I can probably get him with the first one. But the figure—Uzzumekis could now plainly see the peaked official cap—merely glanced into the truck bed and turned away. Uzzumekis did not relax until the truck had once more meshed its antique bones and shuddered into motion.

Their stops were usually brief and, once he had learned the routine, failed to set Uzzumekis quite so much on edge. They would take aboard full cans of milk and offload empties. Occasionally there were sacks of potatoes or beets or cabbages to be picked up for the market. Now and then one of the bales or crates would be offloaded, jute sacking for vegetables and repair parts for tractors, Andrei explained. Andrei would get up in the truck and handle that end of getting and giving while some dim figure worked from the ground or a loading platform. All this would be accompanied by a running commentary from Andrei, cheerful, usually bawdy, and grunted, often surly replies from the ground. Nobody paid much attention to the fugitives.

It went that way until, Uzzumekis estimated, they must be more than half way to Mikhaylovka. Then, in a huddled little farm village, there was an interruption, and Uzzumekis didn't like it. The milk cans were exchanged, and Andrei jumped down, but instead of the engine convulsing into asthmatic life, they could hear some urgent conversation on the ground. At length Andrei climbed into the truck bed again and stumbled forward to talk to Melina in, for once, a low voice. Uzzumekis tightened up again, heard it.

"These people—they want to ride," he told her.

"Impossible, Andrei," she hissed. "Who are they?"

Andrei shrugged. "Just an old man, his sick wife, his daughter who must have been too much with some man about eight and a half months ago. Such a belly." He swept his hands outward over his own. Better just listen, Uzzumekis told himself. Let her handle it, it'll make the bastard suspicious if I stick my oar in. I'd rather have him stewed with his mind on sex instead of having it on thinking.

The woman turned to look at Uzzumekis questioningly.

"It is impossible, isn't it?" she asked.

"I don't know. Where are they going?"

"The same as you. They are going there for the girl to have her brat and to get a doctor for the old woman," Andrei said.

"It might be worse for him to turn them down," Uzzumekis muttered to the woman. "I don't care for it much, but it's still dark."

"All right, Andrei," Melina said reluctantly.

"Do they need help?" Uzzumekis asked. Andrei said it

looked as though they could use it and went to get out of the truck. Uzzumekis whispered to Kirov, "Keep quiet. Pretend you are asleep," and got up and followed Andrei.

On the ground, in the dim lights of the truck station, he saw the family huddled together. The old man, thin and bent, was standing, leaning on a cane. The two women were squatting, huddling against the wall. Beside them was a huge bundle which appeared to be wrapped in blankets and tied with rope. When the old man moved, Uzzumekis saw that he was crippled and moved, with the cane, in a sort of shuffling stagger.

"Can I help you?" Uzzumekis asked.

"We would be grateful," the old man said. "She is sick, my wife, and cannot walk. The girl—you see. And I am, as you see, useless."

"Let's heave this up," Uzzumekis said to Andrei, who must have had a cache of his favorite elixir somewhere about, for he stank afresh and had a noticeable tendency to lurch to starboard. He reached for one end of the great blanket bundle, and Andrei, with a little fumbling, managed to secure the other.

"One, two, three. Let it go," Uzzumekis said, and grunted with the weight as the bundle swung aboard. Then, gently, he picked up the sick woman in his arms and deposited her on the truck bed. Hell, she can't weigh a hundred pounds. The girl was next, and she was a different proposition; gawdalmighty, Uzzumekis grunted, as he hefted her, she's going to have a litter.

"It looks as though you could use a lift, too," he said to the old man.

"I am ashamed to say it, but I could indeed," the old man said.

"I'll go easy," Uzzumekis promised, and got the old man under the knees and shoulders and hoisted him aboard.

"You are kind," the old man said. Uzzumekis could hear the pain in his voice.

"All right, Andrei," Uzzumekis said. "Let's roll."

137

They did—until the last village before Mikhaylovka, and there, an hour before dawn, Andrei's beloved chariot, long past her time, died a natural and honorable death, nor could be, although Andrei gave it a manful try, cursed, prayed, wrenched or kicked back to life.

"Pour in some of the stuff you've been pouring into your gut. That will revive her if anything will," Uzzumekis suggested. He had been trying to help and now had generous gouts of grease to beef up his coal-dust make-up.

"It is too late, I am afraid," Andrei sighed in mourning tones. "I have seen this coming for perhaps five years. She was expiring."

"Twenty years would be more accurate probably. She was of the walking dead."

"Now she needs the embalmer. I am sorry, my friend. I had hoped to do better for your honeymoon."

"What honeymoon? Oh yes, I see. It was a splendid effort, however, and I am grateful. How far from here to Mikhaylovka? Can we walk?"

"Easily," Andrei brightened. He was, on the Beaufort Scale, now only about Force 3 plastered. "It is only five kilometers, a mere stroll. For me, I must see about saving the milk—if there is any ice in this blasted mistake of a village. And I must get word back to Zaporozhe. How to do that, I confess, I do not know. Well, perhaps if they don't have ice they at least have vodka. It is a necessity of life."

"I'll talk to the others," Uzzumekis said. "How about them?" He cocked a thumb at the old man and his burdensome family.

Andrei shrugged. "I don't know. They are not easily moved."

"I don't know either," Uzzumekis grunted. And damn it, he didn't and they weren't his responsibility.

He went to the back, climbed aboard, and went forward to where Kirov and Melina were huddled in their cubbyhole. Kirov was asleep and snoring, but the girl was awake, crouching with her arms around her legs and her head on her knees.

Uzzumekis nudged Kirov; a snore ended in grunting protest, and he was instantly awake.

"The truck is a disaster. Finished," Uzzumekis said.

"So now, then?" Kirov asked.

"We walk. It's not far, five kilometers or so. I know you've got that much in you, old man," he added with a little spite.

"More—if I don't have to carry you, young man."

"There is another problem—this family of misfits," Uzzumekis said. "I've been wondering about them. What do you think, Melina?"

"Poor people, peasants. With so many problems they can't spare time to wonder about somebody else. How do they concern us?"

"They don't—only—"

"I'm sorry for them, but I don't see how we—"

"They're a nuisance, but I think we can use them," Uzzumekis said.

"Use them! Are you mad?"

"Not more than usual. It'll be daylight in less than an hour. It's already graying up. There'll be people on the road and they could be curious about us, two men and a young woman. But if we had the cripples along, were doing their work for them, we might attract attention, but not much busybody butting in."

"And why not?"

Uzzumekis grunted a sour ersatz laugh. "People don't go looking for work they can avoid. If they see a bunch of derelicts with two able-bodied men to do the shoving and hauling, they'll stay clear for fear of being asked to lend a hand."

"I see. You don't believe much in people?"

"No." Uzzumekis got up and went to wake the old cripple, who was wheezing in his cold sleep more than snoring.

"We must go another way," he said. "The truck is dead."

"Where are we?"

"Five kilometers from Mikhaylovka. Do you think you can walk that far?"

139

"After a fashion I can. Slow but with movement. The girl also can walk. But my wife, no. It is her heart."

"What is in the bundle?"

"What we own, not counting the clothes on our backs."

"You need it, eh?"

"If to live, yes. Leave us. Perhaps there will be another way."

"And perhaps not. Let me see what I can do."

He got down and found Andrei who, having repaired to his cache, had a pint bottle of vodka in his right hand and, bracing his left elbow against the radiator, was holding a mournful wake for his expired chariot.

"Sober up a minute," Uzzumekis snapped.

Andrei turned an owl's questioning gaze upon him. "Why?"

"Because I tell you to. I need some kind of transportation. You know this village, don't you?"

"Like my wife's navel," Andrei said. "Why?"

"I want a cart or something. Something with wheels that two men can push or pull. You know of anything like that?"

Andrei regarded him solemnly. "There are such things, naturally. All farmers have them. But how would you get it now? — Everybody is asleep. You do not intend to st—"

"Hell, no. I want to buy. Now, here's money. Go wake up some friend of yours and buy me a cart."

Andrei took the money and shambled off into the dusk, muttering. Uzzumekis sent a tight-lipped grin after him. I've seen worse, drunk or sober.

Twenty minutes later, Uzzumekis heard a creaking of unoiled wheels, and Andrei came out of an alley, pushing a rickety farm cart whose high wheels, with several fractured spokes, rotated in a number of erratic planes, none perpendicular to the road.

"Bah, what a shambles. I hope you do not hope to go far with this monster."

"I don't intend to need it long," Uzzumekis said.

"Here is the rest of your money," Andrei said. "I did not need it all, and even what he did take was a banditry."

"You'd better keep it. Who knows how long you will be marooned here? You'll need it for vodka."

"Ah yes, the bread of life. I thank you," Andrei said pocketing the money. "Now, how can I help you?"

"To get that abomination loaded. First the bundle, then the women and the old man."

They started off, the old man hobbling on his cane, the girl walking pitched backward against the great swaying weight of her belly, Melina toting an extra small bundle tied in cloth and the brown paper parcel of bread and sausage, the great blanket bundle overlapping the sides of the cart with the sick woman precariously perched atop it and Uzzumekis and Kirov pushing. The cart was exceedingly cranky about any sort of locomotion, and small stones and ruts in the road constantly threatened it with imminent extinction.

This is the original one hoss shay, Uzzumekis thought sourly. When the damn thing goes, any minute now, it'll go down to the last bloody atom. And then what?

Andrei watched them up the village road, bottle in hand. Did you ever see so much insanity in one pile? Andrei asked himself. He bade them bon voyage.

"What a honeymoon!" he bellowed in farewell. "My duckling, I warn you, the backs of those two will be useless after this. You face another period of dreary continence."

"Continence yourself, you goddam sot!" Uzzumekis yelled back at him.

It was slow going. Uzzumekis and Kirov might have shoved the cart along more expeditiously but for the fear of its total collapse. But, in any case, it was evident that the plodding progress of the sway-backed girl and the old man's painful shuffle were going to set the pace. For the pain that was obviously in him—and probably had been for many years—he's a pretty cheerful cuss, Uzzumekis mused.

"I got these in the Great War," the cripple offered. "A devil of a machine gun stitched me like a mad tailor. Ever since I get about on these broken sticks."

"What great war?" Uzzumekis grunted. It couldn't have been the last one; that's incredible.

"Nineteen-twenty. After we decided not to fight the Germans any more, we had a lot of fight left in us, so we began to fight each other. I was in Wrangel's army at Sevastopol. I was standing in the food line—we hadn't much to eat late in the siege—when the machine gun, the devil, made stew of my legs."

"You! A White Russian?" Uzzumekis exclaimed. "What the devil are you doing here?"

"Oh, they couldn't kill us all," the cripple chuckled. "Although sometimes it seemed that was what the Bolsheviks would have liked to do."

Kirov grunted. Uzzumekis jabbed him with an elbow, and he said nothing. Probably smart enough not to, anyhow, Uzzumekis supposed.

It was full daylight now, and the sun had broken through the mist. Occasionally they met other pedestrians on the road or were passed by farm wagons drawn by oxen or spavined horses. As Uzzumekis predicted, the little group attracted stares, but nobody spoke and nobody offered help. Kirov kept his head down and up against the blanket bundle at these encounters. You're learning, old duck, Uzzumekis silently assured his companion.

They were going up a hill, and the cart fought them every step. Uzzumekis was sweating when they breasted the top and stopped for a blow. He noticed that Kirov was not even puffing.

Just like the perverse old bastard, probably showing off out of spite.

At noon they stopped beside a brook to eat the bread and sausage. Melina, whose hands were relatively clean, tore the bread into chunks but was baffled by the tough-skinned sausage until the old man, grinning, handed her a clasp knife.

"I go to get water," he said. From somewhere in the

mysterious depths of the great bundle he fetched a small tin bucket and limped down the gravelly banks of the stream. Uzzumekis found he was famished, and when he had wolfed his share and washed it down with hungry gulps from the bucket, he felt he could easily have put away three times as much. He looked up to see the old cripple with his hand out.

"Here, my friend, take this," he said, offering what must have been half his own portion. "You're doing the work; you need fuel for the engine."

"Thank you, but no," Uzzumekis said, admitting the sore temptation to himself. "All engines need fuel, yours included."

The old man tried to insist, but Uzzumekis, perverse probably because of the intensity of his hunger, refused gruffly.

"Don't be an idiot. Take it," Kirov muttered. "You lean ones don't have my reserves. Like a camel, I could probably go a week, though I wouldn't enjoy it." Fondly he rubbed his vast expanse of gut.

"What will you do in Mikhaylovka?" Uzzumekis asked the cripple, curious about what possible salvation these helpless ones could anticipate. They certainly weren't his problem, but he thought it had to be a lousy system that allowed the defenseless to go shuffling along the roads, roofless, probably moneyless, unfed, forgotten.

"There is no real problem," the cripple said. "An old comrade, from the wars of many years ago, has a farm on the outskirts. I sent word to him, and he has let me know that his hay barn, which is unused until the harvest, is empty and we can shelter there. Doubtless, although he is not rich, he will spare us a little food—until—"

"Until what?"

"Until I make the arrangements for them," the old man nodded at his two unspeaking women. "There is a hospital of the state near Mikhaylovka. It is possible to get them admitted there. You can see they are in need of it, my wife especially."

That girl and about four pups are going to be in need of

it, too, Uzzumekis told himself. God, what if she should decide to spring it here? Somebody ought to be following her around with a washtub.

"Well," he said, getting wearily to his feet. "Let's get on with it."

At one-thirty they breasted a final hill and looked down a gentle slope to the village, lying quiet in the sun. From this distance, set among farms and gentle, wooded hills, the place was pretty, but, close up, Uzzumekis knew it was more likely to be drab.

"This is the last. And all downhill," the old man chuckled. "I do not know how it is possible to express our gratitude."

"Never mind," Uzzumekis said.

Half an hour later they left the road and shoved the creaking cart along a lane between rows of dusty cypresses. They found the barn, a gray and weathered shack, innocent of paint, at the end of the lane. Uzzumekis looked around curiously for other buildings.

"Where does your friend live?" he asked.

"Why, in the village, of course," the cripple said.

While Kirov steadied the cart, Uzzumekis reached up and lifted the woman down and carried her into the barn. He put her down on a bale of hay and said, "There you are, Mother. Now, you'd better rest." As he was turning away he felt her bony fingers close on his wrist and looked down and saw she was staring up at him and tears were spilling down her cheeks. He turned away.

Now what, he was thinking. Where do we go from here and how do we go about it? I've never been here and I don't know what the score is. Maybe the girl knows enough; she'd better. The trouble with this damn job is that every turn in the road could be the end of the road altogether. He found the cripple beside him.

"Will you come with me for a few minutes?" the cripple said. "I have a few words for you—alone."

Wondering but impatient to get at whatever they were

going to do next, Uzzumekis followed him out the barn's back door and into a copse of ancient cypresses, standing tall and almost black in their foliage. Only four days and half a night to the rendezvous, he remembered. They had to get on with it, and no fiddling around.

"I do not wish to seem impertinent," the cripple said. "But will you allow me to ask what you will do now?"

Uzzumekis stood silent, staring coldly into the old man's eyes. What the hell's he getting at? he wondered.

"I ask because I have been thinking. I think you will want to go on, perhaps by the train?"

"What business is it of yours?" Uzzumekis' tone was harsh.

"None, perhaps. On the other hand, you may not know the train here is unreliable. You could stay here, with us, until it comes. Here, at least, there is shelter. You might not want to go into the town."

"Look here, old man, I don't know what you're getting at. Just exactly what have you got on your mind?"

The old cripple nodded toward the barn and spoke again, almost a whisper. "You see, I know who he is."

The pistol seemed to jump into Uzzumekis' hand and, from two feet away, held rock steady on the cripple's chest.

"Put it away," the cripple said patiently. "No threat could frighten me less. For most purposes, I am dead already."

"I can kill you now," Uzzumekis said. "And I assure you I am ready to." That in his eyes told the old man it was so, but he did not flinch.

He shrugged. "What good would it do you?"

"It would shut your babble, old man."

"Listen to me, then, before you shut it. I told you the train is unreliable. Nobody knows exactly when it will come until it gets very near. It has many towns to visit and some work in each. You cannot, with him, go into the town. The people are not blind."

"So we stay here and wait for you to turn us in? Is that it?"

"After last night and today, you should know better. Put the pistol away. You do not need it."

Knowing this was true, that he could if necessary break the old cripple's neck like a matchstick, a little ashamed, Uzzumekis slid the weapon out of sight.

"It is possible you saved my wife's life. She is very frail. One does not repay a priceless gift with treachery. If you do not stay here to wait for the train, where would you stay? You cannot send the young woman into the town, not safely, for she would arouse curiosity. But nobody would be curious, at least not care, about one like me. Moreover, I am known here. No, my friend, what else can you do?"

"The woods, I thought, perhaps that. Something surely."

"I can think of nothing."

And, damn it all, he's right, Uzzumekis knew. They had come this way blindly because no other path was open. Surely this town, as every other living thing everywhere, offered peril. He had been bulling ahead because he had to, trusting blind luck when every assessment of the odds ran incredibly against him. Now, here was this offer. Was there any yardstick in the world you could lay upon sincerity and get the right answer? No, there was not.

"Why do you offer this?" he asked. "You know this could cause you trouble, very serious trouble."

"I have lived with trouble a long time," the old cripple said.

"And you would let him get away? Help him?"

"Remember who else pushed the cart?"

"All right, we'll try it," Uzzumekis said. "And thanks."

"Welcome," the cripple said.

X

THE bite-sized chartroom of the trawler *Queen Zenobia*, in which two could have been reckoned a crowd, held all the people and paper it could handle. They were Admiral March, Lieutenant Commander Gottfried, Lieutenant Hale, and Commander Stephens. The papers were a map of Istanbul and environs including Yesilkoy Airport to the west; a chart of a portion of the Black Sea (U.S. Oceanographic Office 4177, Odessa to Sevastopol, Scale 1-to-400,000 at latitude 44° north) which included the approaches to Balaklava; a chart of the entire Black (or Euxine) Sea (British Admiralty 2214, Scale 1-to-1,366,000); a chart of the Bosporus and Istanbul harbor (U.S. Oceanographic Office 4167, Scale 1-to-36,170) showing practically everything there was to know about the crooked 20-mile waterway whose average breadth was a mere half mile, the damnedest bottleneck in all of the history of seafaring. Stephens was the only one in uniform, but even his were unostentatious working khakis. The admiral was in a civilian suit. Gottfried and Hale wore rather shabby versions of merchant seamen's garb, hastily acquired three days earlier in Naples.

Beyond the chartroom, out the forward windows of the trawler's wheelhouse, down in her well deck under the now-secured derricks, rested a bulky, humpbacked shape whose identity was rapidly being still further obliterated by a working party of U.S. Navy sailors who, using half-inch plywood, were trying to make whatever it was look like a gaggle of lashed-down crates.

Thus the *Queen Zenobia*, lacking only a Jolly Roger, was a pirate ship by the measure of law. She lay a few hundred yards off the Galata Quay, a little around the bend from but almost in the entrance to the Golden Horn. She had loaded the DSRV at the quay, using her own derricks, finishing the job at three o'clock that morning. Loading might have been —surely would have been—a lot simpler if she could have gone into the Horn, past where *Skate* lay and to the Turkish navy graving docks but, as Admiral March knew rather resentfully, *Skate* and her mission already had strained the rivets of official Turkish hospitality. They had been lucky to get permission for a few hours alongside the busy quay, and that only on grave assurance that the work would be accomplished in the darkest and most deserted hours of the night. Even so, getting the DSRV aboard and lashed down had been a breeze compared to Lieutenant Hale's nightmare of getting it and its trailer and appurtenances off the two C-141s at Yesilkoy, getting them mated, hitched to the biggest prime mover that could be hired in all Turkey, and snaked over a tortured route, then through the pinch of the Yedikule gate in the ancient wall, then through the narrow streets of an ancient city and at last to the Galata Bridge, which he feared would collapse under the DSRV's weight and drown everything—including both *Skate*'s mission and U.S.—Turkish amity—in the Golden Horn. The journey had taken, he reckoned roughly, eighteen miles, and every mile had cost him a year of life expectancy.

The jaunty Air-Force major had bidden him good-by and god-speed as the C-141 was delivered of her pregnancy.

"You sure you still can't tell me what the doodad is?" he asked.

"I'll write and tell you," Hale said.

"Well, good luck with it," the major said. "Just don't ask me to tote it around any more. I'm busy enough toting freedom and democracy to the Vietnamese." He cocked a suddenly suspicious eye at Hale. "You sure that doodad ain't some new-fangled kind of democracy we're going to use to alienate the Turks?"

"I hope not," Hale said. "And thanks. I'd have told you if I could. Anyhow, I still don't know what I'm supposed to do with it. All I know is we got it here, for which I thank you. Most sincerely."

148

And now, in *Queen Zenobia*'s baby crib of a chartroom, Lieutenant Hale was learning for the first time what he was supposed to do with it. It was appalling knowledge.

Stephens had the Bosporus chart on top the sheaf of its mates, and now he laid the point of a pencil on it and turned to the admiral.

"I can back out of the berth with a little finagling. But I was wondering about tugs. It's a little tight in there. Any social implications? Or political?"

"I can't see why we can't have tugs," March said. "After all, this is the finish of a good-will visit. You have certain courtesies coming to you."

"That'll help," Stephens said and turned to Gottfried. "Look, Dave, it seems to me that only the first part of this is going to be tricky, but that'll be tricky enough to last all week.

"The tugs can swing me out and turn me around. That'll save time. I'll pass you when I come out of the Horn and round Seraglio Point. You'll still be here, over toward the left side of the channel. I'll submerge here." He put the pencil point down. "Roughly on a course of two-ten between Cape Zeytin and the Princess Islands. There's twenty-five fathoms in there, and that's enough. For play-acting purposes—if anybody still thinks this is theatre—that ought to be convincing enough. Anyhow, when I go out of sight, I'll be headed in the socially proper direction—home."

"The problem is going to be picking you up," Gottfried said.

"Exactly. That's the first and almost the biggest tricky part. Time and place. It would be better if you could follow me out, make the turn together after I submerge. But of course we can't. You start out one way, then turn around and come back, people would either think you're nuts or figure out what's really going on."

"We're shaping up a big enough credibility gap as it is," Gottfried agreed.

"And, since you haven't got sonar, I'll have to find you,

rather than the other way around. I'd say give me two hours from the time I round Seraglio Point heading in that innocent direction. When I come back, natch, innocence will have fled. You can't even come downstream far enough to sheep-dog me through that rat's nest of cable crossings. But I guess I can make it. There's an average of twenty fathoms in the middle of the stream. We ought to make it through unless we tangle arseholes with the keel of a Russian destroyer or some other encumbrance."

"Let's see. You're going to have to get through some ferry crossings below me," Gottfried pointed out. "There's all that stuff moving from Haydarpasa on the Asiatic side to the European side and the Princess Islands. All I can say about that is, God go with you because I can't. But I want you latched onto me before we have to deal with the waterbugs crossing back and forth from Uskadar."

"You see this thing they call Leander's Tower, over on the Asiatic side just below Uskadar? The water between there and your anchorage here runs twenty-one fathoms. That's enough for me to stay under, although I admit not comfortably under."

"Yeah?"

"What if you picked up your hook and got under way slow a little out from this anchorage? If I came up on your port side and stuck up the scope for a quick squint about in there I could pick you out from all the other traffic. And, if you kept a tight watch to port you'd know I had you because you'd see the scope."

"I hope to hell nobody else does," Admiral March said.

"That's a chance we'll have to take, I guess," Stephens said. "We've got to get married somehow—even with a shotgun."

"This is a damned peculiar waterway," Gottfried said. "This business of driving on the wrong side of the road strikes me as a little nutty."

"The whole operation is nutty," the admiral said. "Nevertheless the waterway belongs to the Turks; if they say northbound shipping has to keep to the left, we're not in a position to argue."

"Okay, we go left-handed. The only other things we have to contend with are foul water, shoals, prohibited anchorages, and traffic. That place has more traffic than the New Jersey Turnpike on the afternoon of Labor Day."

"What speed do we want to make through the gut?" Gottfried asked.

"I'd say six knots," the admiral suggested. "For the hot rods, the legal limit is ten. I'd rather keep *Skate* safe than decapitated. Are we agreed?"

"Okay, that takes us roughly five hours from the time I round Seraglio until we're in the Black Sea at Rumeli Fener. From there on it's a piece of cake," Stephens said.

"What speed do you want to make from there to Cape Kerempe?" Gottfried asked.

"Whatever you can with this here speedboat," Stephens said, grinning. "Anything you can do, *Skate* can do better."

"Oh, I don't know," Gottfried grinned back. "We were doing sixteen knots all the way in here from Rhodes. No sweat. She may be old and dirty, but she behaves nice."

Admiral March looked at his watch, thinking that if anybody could pull this off, these people could. He had the first team working for him.

"I don't think it's necessary to argue about speed," he said. "It's now oh-nine hundred, April twenty-ninth, which makes it just about sixty-four hours until you take aboard our fat friend. There's roughly three hundred and fifty miles to go, which gives you leeway enough. How soon can you get under way, Captain?" he asked Stephens.

"As soon as I get back aboard and you can put tugs alongside, sir," Stephens said. "Make it somewhere between noon and thirteen hundred." He turned again to Gottfried.

"I think I'd better surface off Kerempe, just for a last check with you—that is if the coast's clear. Why don't you stop your engines if there's nothing showing? That'll be enough of a signal, and I'll come up alongside—within hailing distance."

"Pretty pleased with that pig boat's navigation, ain't you, bub?" Gottfried said sarcastically.

"Yup. So would you be if you had Ray Guernic to tell you where you are."

Admiral March turned to Hale.

"You're the problem that everybody hopes we never have to solve," he said.

"Amen, sir," Hale said fervently.

"What could you do—if you had to?"

"All I can say for certain is what we've done in tests. We have emptied a sub's full complement in sixteen hours—a little more. But those were ideal conditions."

"And these, of course, are not."

"They certainly are not, sir. Say *Skate* got into trouble, God forbid. But if she did, we'd probably be eight or nine miles from her. That's stretching it for the DSRV, possible but difficult. We're slow for one thing. For another that long a trip would pull the batteries so far down we'd have to get a fresh charge between trips. That means at least two hours hooked up to the chargers on the trawler between each round trip. I'll be optimistic and guess it would take between forty and fifty hours to empty the ship. That is, after we found her."

"Finding me wouldn't be easy," Stephens said. "If *Skate* ran into any kind of trouble, I'd shut down everything until we were out of it. You can't expect me to make a peep. No SOS, no hammering on the hull, no voice MAYDAY, quiet as a clam—or quieter. Any finding us castaways would be entirely up to you—except for one itty bitty thing."

"You wouldn't have to yell very loud for us to home in you—but, then, yes, I guess you couldn't. What's the *except*?"

"You ought to know approximately, say within half a mile, of where we would be. I'll turn around and be heading out before I surface to make the pickup. You know where the rendezvous point is. I'll be coming away, diving hard, on a course of exactly one hundred and eighty degrees. From that point on, it would be up to you and your sonar."

"You know that it isn't easy to find a silent target—even with sonar."

"You bet I know it. And you also know that—if we did have trouble—there'd probably be others besides you looking for us. I'd just have to bet that you are better at it."

"We're not bad," Hale acknowledged. "Not perfect either."

"Well," Admiral March said, "let's get it on the road, gentlemen."

Two tugs, fuss-budgeting around in the way of all tug-boats, had lines aboard *Skate* by 1145 hours. The line handlers, skillfully surefooted on the submarine's tiny top-sides' working surface, had the lines singled up and, as the tugs began to take up the slack, cast off their last tether to Turkish soil. Out in midstream, one tug cast off and chuffed around to the starboard bow, while the other moved in and gently leaned her muscle on the port quarter. Slowly, almost imperceptibly at first, *Skate* pivoted on her axis until she was headed downstream for the two bridges which, courteously interrupting the discourteously resentful flood of midday traffic between Stambul and Galata, opened their drawbridge sections to let her through.

Lieutenant Grady Johnson, pock-marked, smiling, knowing his business and quietly proud of it, had the con in the sail. Stephens stood beside him and a signalman sat behind them on top of the sail with his back against the periscope fairing. Below, at their feet and around the back-straining bend that led off the bridge and down into the sail, a tall young talker kept calling up the depth of water under the keel in a sten-torian voice.

"Niner feet, sir," he bellowed.

"Very well," Johnson said.

"Ten feet, sir," the talker yelled.

"Very well." And then, quietly into his microphone as the bridge rose and the tugs backed off. "All ahead one third."

Skate slowly gathered way and passed under the bridges

with their impatiently horn-tooting and bell-ringing and cursing stalled traffic.

"Those people up there aren't much pleased with us," Stephens observed.

"No, sir. They're not," Johnson said. Then to the microphone, "All ahead slow. Come to zero-nine-zero degrees."

"Fifteen feet, sir," the talker declared.

Through the bridges, which came ponderously down to the relief of their impatient patrons, *Skate* came abreast of Seraglio Point and Johnson called down a change of course to 170°.

The signalman, lolling comfortably at his post, suddenly sat up straight and gave tongue. "Sir . . ."

"What is it?" Stephens asked.

"There's a ship speaking us, sir," the signalman said. "Off to port." His voice sounded puzzled.

"What ship?"

"That little tramp over there, sir," the signalman said, pointing. Stephens turned his head and saw the *Queen Zenobia* lying at anchor, prow pointed upstream, and the blink of an Aldis lamp twinkling at them from her bridge. Damned fools, he thought, can't they keep their big traps shut?

"What's he say?"

"He says Good Luck," the signalman said. "He signs it Jake."

"Don't acknowledge," Stephens said.

"Aye, aye, sir," the signalman said, still sounding puzzled.

Skate came due south, then again to south southwest as the hazy humps of the Princess Islands began to separate themselves from the hazier humps of the mountainous hills of Asia off to port.

"We'll be submerging about there," Stephens said to Johnson, pointing.

"Yes, sir," Johnson acknowledged.

"I want to be about halfway between Antigoni—that one there"—pointing again—"to port—and Cape Zeytin"—

pointing once more—"over there to starboard. We'll go down on two-one-zero."

"Aye, aye, sir."

Stephens relaxed in the thin spring sunshine, letting himself roll easily as the first swells of the Marmara began to take hold of *Skate*, giving her the slight sea motion she felt on the surface. He let his mind roam over what lay ahead for his ship and himself. He was accustomed to what were called intelligence missions; the nukes were not built for peacetime playthings—too expensive, too much brain went into them. They were work boats. But this, clearly, was a different brand of work. Intelligence? Observing a potentially hostile coast for detail? Exploration? Finding new navigable waterways under ice or storm? No. None of these. *Skate* was now, under his command, en route to pull an out-of-work politician off an unfriendly coast for the pleasure of other politicians who still had jobs. And what would their pleasure serve of use to man? Their jobs were temporary, their judgments open to question. But his franchise to question those judgments, he had to acknowledge, was limited to his single vote. He was a technician, expensively trained and penuriously paid by those same judgments, and his right to work was totally circumscribed by what he was told to do. He had made a choice and the choice contained as an essential ingredient his obedience to other judgments. But then, at sea, his own judgment was supreme, freed from the restraints of the land except for the essential of carrying out his orders. Within that framework he held autocratic power to dictate such matters as life or death to the people under his command. This was enough responsibility for one man, he considered, particularly a man whose wife also had to deal with such corollary judgments as a busted-down television and a mortgage which seemed to consist more of taxes than of principal. Still, put it all together as well as you could, the mission which now carried *Skate* was a challenge to both skill and luck. He knew he had the skill. He hoped for the luck. And he knew the orders were nutty.

"This is about it," he said to Johnson. "Come on to two-one-zero on the nose and take her down to sixty feet. I'll give you a new course when you get below. I'm leaving the bridge."

"Aye, aye, sir," Johnson said as Stephens jackknifed himself down to the next level and started down the ladders. You get to be a hell of a good ladder climber in this business, he thought as he went down rung by rung. I wonder what the legal minimum pay is for ladder climbing.

He went into the wardroom and asked Collingwood for a pot of hot water and got it. Oulahan followed him down from the control room as the diving klaxon let off its squalling uproar.

"Everything shipshape?" Stephens asked.

"What'd you expect, Captain? Chaos?" Oulahan said.

"Only a reasonable amount. Your brand," Stephens said. Jesus, what men we get aboard these glorified sewer pipes, he was thinking. Where else would you find men like this? Buying it all, doing it right, asking no questions.

"We're changing course as soon as we get under," he said.

"To what, Captain?"

"Back the way we came. You wanted to know where we're going. So now I'll tell you. We're going through the Bosporus and into the Black Sea. We'll steam up the Turkish side on zero-seven-four to Cape Kerempe and turn north on zero-zero-five to Balaklava on the Russian side and surface and pick up a Russian refugee and then submerge and get the hell out of there. That's all."

"That's all?" Oulahan said. "If it's that simple why didn't you tell me earlier?"

"All right, old cock, you know why I didn't," Stephens said, a sudden sunny smile on his face. "After we're through the Strait I'll brief you in detail. You know I could come down with the grippe and you'd have to do this little chore by yourself."

"Oh, sure. You look like a born grippe victim," Oulahan

said. Then sudden consternation came to him. "What about the freeloaders? We got them along, you know."

"I know too damn well," Stephens said. "I got the orders this morning. We take 'em along, silly as that may seem."

"And it does. Why?"

"A couple of reasons, neither one of which appears to make much sense. Maybe the first one does, a little. That was if we offloaded them, it'd stir up curiosity. I guess it would. The other, some people think if we keep them aboard and carry out this little gimmick, it'll involve a lot of what we like to call the free world in this operation. Give it a certain flavor, so to speak. You know. Not just one nasty little sub coming up to fetch the guy, but most of the Western world doing it. Cute, huh?"

"Whose idea?"

"You really want to know?" Stephens was suddenly and entirely solemn. "The President of the United States."

"I'm impressed," Oulahan said slowly. "When do we tell our guests the honor which has been bestowed upon them? Did they give you the medals to pin on?"

"I guess it doesn't matter—now that we're under—when we tell 'em. You do it, will you, Dick?"

"I feel the grippe coming on myself. Oh well. Aye, aye, sir."

Stephens finished his hot water and went back to the control room, skirted around the pulpit and found Chief Guernic at the chart table. From the pulpit and the other side of the room he heard the repetitious drone of orders given and orders repeated.

"Fifty-eight, coming to fifty-nine, sir."

"Very well," from the diving officer.

"Chief," Stephens said to Guernic, whose cigarette was down to its customary frugal length, "you are going to incinerate yourself one day."

"Yes, sir, Captain. Not me. You want to know why?"

"Sure."

"Well, sir, this is the age of chemical miracles as you know.

I got the idea when a neighbor's kid set her dress afire. I did a little research and had my whiskers fireproofed."

"Honest? All right, I'll believe you—for now. Now look, Chief, we got a little navigating to do. You'll note we're coming about. I want you to get us through the Bosporus submerged. Here, I brought you the chart."

He handed the folded paper to Guernic, who spread it out on his table and studied it.

"Twisty as a snake's gizzard," he observed at length.

"That isn't all," Stephens said. "Right here—just off that statue starboard of the freeway—we're going to stick up the scope and pick up a neighbor. Once we get him, you stick with him—a little to his port."

"Radar?" Guernic asked.

"Radar, my foot. We're working, Chief. You hang onto him with sonar, and he isn't going to hang onto you because he hasn't got any."

"What about traffic, Captain?"

"That's his responsibility."

"Well, it ought to be okay then. If he knows his business."

"He does."

Guernic went back to the chart and studied it.

"Twisty as a snake's gizzard," he mused again. "We got shallow water here—and here—over on the port side. He know about that, sir?"

"He'd better. Oh hell, he does. He was briefed until his eyeballs were dripping."

"All right." Guernic discarded his incendiary cigarette and shook another out of the pack propped against the back of the chart table. "I'll squeeze us through—that is, if we don't run into anything."

"If we run into anything, Chief," Stephens said solemnly, "I'll make you eat it."

"Aye, aye, sir."

"Bon appétit."

Stephens left the chart table and circled around to the port side and squatted beside Chief Cate at his console.

"We make this at periscope depth, Chief," he said. "But we keep the scope under—except for once. In about half an hour I'm going to take a look. The thing is we're going to be slow for about four hours and there's a lot of stuff overhead. The water's going to be churned up. Can you keep depth?"

"How slow, Captain?"

"Six knots."

"She wobbles a little that slow."

"There's also a lot of current running into us. And nobody knows what that does, nor exactly where it does it."

"Passing sixty, coming to fifty-eight," said the talker.

"Yeah, I see what you mean, Captain," Chief Cate said, reaching for his console to swallow 500 pounds of water into a forward trim tank to keep the 58 from suddenly blossoming into 55. "I can't keep her inside inches, Captain. How much room do I have?"

"Just don't let her broach."

"I'm not about to."

"I didn't think you were. The pep talk was for me, not you."

At 1340 Stephens stepped up to the pulpit and Johnson moved aside to give him room at Number One periscope. Stephens pushed the button and saw the oiled tube slide upward until the grips were at his hands. This was always a perilous depth for submarines—within collision distance of anything that might be on the surface—and so, instinctively, he first ran the periscope around the compass. A freighter there, outbound for the Med; a ferry crossing to Prinkipo with a load of tourists and week-enders; a tanker upbound for the Black Sea; a fat-assed mahogany-and-chrome sport cruiser using up half of his lens and not more than 200 yards away; a destroyer coming downstream circumspectly slow. The jack at the bow identified her, solid red, bearing a big white star, a smaller red star enclosed within that, and again enclosed the crossed white hammer and sickle. As she came abreast he saw the ensign at the stern, white field, hammer and sickle emblazoned red, a pale blue stripe on the bottom hem. Well, what did you expect? he asked himself.

The Russian destroyer was moving in a crowd, decorous and holding to the center of the freeway. He could imagine the yowl in the Turkish press if the Soviets, by mischance, ran down anything around them, from work boat to mahogany rich man's yacht. He swung the scope to starboard and over there—smeared, decrepit, and blessed by God—the *Queen Zenobia.*

Right on his starboard side, right on the nose, he thought. Just under way. From this precinct Gottfried gets a full count, and, if necessary, we'll stuff the ballot box or burn it, whichever seems preferable. He went to Guernic.

"You got that fixed, Chief?" he asked.

"Aye, Captain."

"Stick with it."

Guernic turned to the sonar man who had been called back from his off-limits shack to the chart table. He was, Stephens thought, impossibly young, impossibly innocent. What was his name?

"Quill," Guernic said. "You got that blip. Well, keep it; if you drop it I will personally kill you."

"Aye, aye, sir," the lad said, turning to go back to his instrument.

"Who is that kid, Chief? He looks new," Stephens said.

"He's so new he's still red-assed," Guernic said. "We got him as a replacement the last time in Naples. He's fresh out of submarine school."

"Can he handle the sonar? Looks like a baby; they get younger every year."

"He went to school for it. I've qualified him on it. He may not know much else, but he knows that. Anyhow, I'll keep on him."

Stephens looked thoughtfully at the closed door of the sonar room, hearing the steady, repetitious pinging, audible as the instrument's broadcast echoes bounced back from the hull of the *Queen Zenobia.* I guess he'll do, he thought;

Guernic sure wouldn't put him on it unless he knew he could do it.

Oulahan came up from the direction of the wardroom.

"I told 'em," he said with a grimace of distaste.

"How'd they take it?"

"The Englishman, all right. You know, old unflappable. About the Kraut, you never can tell. The Italian is still woozy from that babe of his and I doubt if he even got the message; if you ever saw a spent buck he's it. That other one, Cavanides, is sore as hell, demanding to be put ashore and all that."

"What'd you do with him?"

"Told him to go to hell. Politely, though. Said I was sorry and all that, but if he don't like it, it's tough tit.

"By the way, you never told me who we're running off to fetch away from the Roosians. Maybe I ought to know—in case you do come down with the grippe."

"A guy named Kirov. Ever hear of him?"

Oulahan's eyes popped and his mouth fell open.

"Brother! You do pick some lulus, don't you?"

"I didn't pick him. I was handed him."

"Anybody with him?"

"Yeah. American escort. Name of Uzzumekis. Something like that. You'll recognize him because they tell me he's about nine feet tall and wide to match. Kirov, of course, you'll know on sight."

"How do we make the pickup?"

"They're supposed to meet us with a small boat—exact place. I'm counting on Guernic to put us there on the nose. The question, of course, is whether whoever is running their boat can also hit it on the nose. But if they'll just get into the general neighborhood we can pick them up on radar. It's not too big a problem, but, naturally, we don't want to spend any more time on the surface than we absolutely have to."

"You can say that again. Again and again and again."

XI

THEY had arrived at the barn in midafternoon of April 27. They still had, Uzzumekis remembered, at least 350 kilometers to go, more like 400 the way the railroad probably snaked around. And, at the end, a shanks mare end run around Sevastopol and over the hill and through the woods to Balaklava. And, so far as he knew, no train in prospect for God knows how long. One hundred and six hours to rendezvous at one A.M., May second, three miles out of Balaklava Harbor on a course of two-one-zero degrees until directly south of the white flashing beacon on the big windmill at Karan and with a flashing green beacon east of it. At least the girl said it was a big windmill and the flashing beacon a bright one. So what if it's raining and you can't see the beacon? Or foggy? We will never make it, he told himself. It is absolutely impossible.

Then, on the other hand, the prospect of not making it wouldn't bear thinking about. It was impossible either way. Impossible to make it, impossible to find another way out when they didn't.

Then the boat? The girl was sure of a fisherman, once one of her husband's men, who would take them to the rendezvous. The man wouldn't ask why, only where, she said. And, after he did know, it wouldn't make any difference. But there was a hole in that a mile wide. What if the guy saw Kirov's face and balked—or got scared? What if the weather was lousy? What if the guy couldn't be found at the crucial time? Or was drunk? What if, what if, forever.

Uzzumekis wondered if they could steal a boat in crisis. But if they could, what would they do with it? He doubted if his own two brief youthful seasons as a deck hand on an ore boat between the Duluth docks and Republic Steel in South Chicago qualified him to navigate in the dark, out of a Russian harbor he had never seen, to a precise spot. For God's sake, what was he thinking? A few dozen watches at the helm of a fat ore boat waddling down the length of Lake Michigan? Insane!

The old cripple hobbled off toward the village a kilometer away as soon as he saw that his sick wife had fallen asleep on a blanket bedded in hay.

"She is very sick," he told Melina before he left. "Very tired."

"I know. I will watch her," Melina said.

"Just let her sleep. It is the best thing." Then to Uzzumekis, "I will find out what is known about the train. Perhaps it comes soon."

I hope that's what you're really after and not, after all, the cops, Uzzumekis thought bitterly. Uzzumekis was by nature a loner; every instinct rebelled against being forced to depend on outsiders, the girl, Andrei, even Dmitri on the barge. And he didn't like burdens; on the other hand, once having taken one up, however reluctantly, he was just as reluctant to put it down.

"You'd better take this," he said, pushing a wad of paper money into the cripple's hand.

"No, no, I will not need it. Perhaps later for your tickets. It would not be wise to buy them until the train actually comes. Somebody might wonder."

"Don't be absurd. You'll need it for food. I, for one, am close to starving."

He watched the cripple shuffle painfully away. Probably the most humiliating thing of all, he thought, is having to pile the load on an antique cripple who can scarcely navigate his own body, much less tote groceries. He's a brave one, and I guess generous—that is, if he's on the level. Well, we'll see. If he isn't squaring with me there's one little consolation; we won't be much worse off than we are already. Some consolation!

There was, of course, the possibility—a thin one—that if it was a double cross he could shoot their way out. The cops in this little burg weren't likely to be the world's toughest or smartest. But then what? They'd still need transportation. About one thing the cripple was surely right; he wouldn't dare expose Kirov in the town in the light of day. These people might be rubes, but, as the cripple had said, they weren't blind.

He kept watch. He might be caught, but he didn't propose to be caught asleep. And near dusk he saw a figure approaching in the distance. He tensed. But then he saw, as it drew slowly closer, that gimpy gait was unmistakable. It was the cripple, and, so far as he could tell, he was alone. Doesn't necessarily mean anything, he reminded himself. He could just be setting us up and the law will be along later. He wondered if there was a telephone in the town; probably not. Still, he remembered, if an alarm was to be raised the railroad would surely have the telegraph. All the same, watching that limping approach, he could not suppress a small sigh of relief, reservations or not.

He got up from his sentry post in the shadow of the barn doorway and walked out to meet the old cripple in the lane of cypresses.

"Here, let me take those," he said, as the man stopped and stood panting. Uzzumekis relieved him of a bundle tied in a rough cloth sack hitched with cords over the old man's shoulder and a milk can tied by its bail to his belt. "You've done your share—about six times over."

"Only a small problem," the cripple said. "I have been functioning many years. Slowly, as you know, but functioning."

For a moment Uzzumekis suppressed his anxiety for news to yield to curiosity. What will you do—after the hospital and the women are attended to?"

"I will manage. It is my specialty. Besides the girl is young and strong. When she is finished with this, she will work."

"Then who will take care of the baby?" Whoops, Uzzumekis thought, I came close to using the plural.

"I can do that. All except the breast. That is *not* my specialty."

"What did you learn in the town?" Uzzumekis asked.

"Some. Only a little, I am afraid. The train was expected yesterday. It did not come. It was expected today and did not. It is expected tomorrow—and may."

Uzzumekis felt the sickening weight of impossibility surge up in him. Another twenty-four hours to wait, at the least. What would that leave for all the impossible rest of it, eighty-two? And, even yet, there was no guarantee the train would ever come, although he supposed it had to—sometime. And if it was already two days late into this hick wide spot in the road, how long might it reasonably be expected to need to reach Sevastopol?

"There is no other possibility? A bus perhaps?"

"There are buses. Nearly as irregular as the train. Would you be willing to risk that?"

"Not unless there was absolutely no other possibility at all. Maybe not even then."

"What will you do, then?" the cripple asked.

"To be truthful, I do not yet know. Something, surely."

"I wish you luck."

They ate, goat cheese, black bread, a raw cabbage, raw rutabagas. They drank the milk. It was filling but somewhere short of gourmet.

"It would be good if we could have built a fire," the old cripple said. "But I think not very wise."

"You're right," Uzzumekis told him.

After the meal, Uzzumekis called Kirov and Melina out of the barn.

"It looks dismal," he said, and gave them the old man's lack of news. "From tomorrow afternoon we have only three and a half days to get all the way to the rendezvous. And we do not know that accursed train will arrive even tomorrow."

"It must," Melina said. However Kirov—or his past—might be repellent to her, she was committed now. After all this, the risk, the risks yet to come, they could not fail, they dare not fail.

"There is no law says it must," Kirov said. "An oversight. I should have attended to that while I had the opportunity. And, I see now, I should have spent more on railroads. Perhaps taken it out of the rocket program. I could get to the moon quicker than this."

"It's no joke," Uzzumekis said.

"I do not suggest that it is. Do we have an alternative?"

"No good one, at least that I can see now. There is a bus, but even dirty you're not safe with a busload of people."

"If we miss the rendezvous?"

"We miss it."

"I suggest, in that case, we return to what I suggested on the barge. We wait until a train does come, steal a fishing boat, and sail across to Kerempe Burnu on the Turkish coast."

"What do you know about boats?"

"Very little, except that I don't get seasick."

"Sounds like suicide."

"There are worse kinds of suicide than drowning," Kirov reminded him. "If we don't make it, we don't. As for her," he looked at Melina, "she can go back to her old life unharmed. I do not think she can have been compromised."

"No, no. We *must* reach the rendezvous," the girl insisted.

"How?"

"I don't know. Oh, I don't know," she said wretchedly.

The night passed—somehow. Lying on a pile of hay, trying to relax, knowing he was going to have to sleep or collapse, Uzzumekis could not. He had known of soldiers going to sleep in the midst of battle because there was no other possible reply to the hell going on around them. His problem was different; it was up to him to anticipate the hell and keep them out of it. He was astonished when, in the dawn, the old cripple woke him.

"I go again into the village," the old one said. "Perhaps today it will really come."

"If it does," Uzzumekis said, "observe everything you can

166

about the circumstances. They will do some switching probably. Moving cars to different tracks. Try to see if you can spot an empty goods wagon. Watch the guards. Watch the people of the train and see how they do their work, especially if they inspect the cars."

"I will do what I can," the cripple promised. I must have got two or three hours sleep, Uzzumekis supposed. I'm still pooped but better. He wolfed down some of the remaining cheese and bread and took up his vigil in the barn doorway.

The sun rose high and the day got hot. He was not conscious of moans from the sick woman on the blanket behind him, nor that Melina was trying, with only a little success, to get some food into her. The vastly pregnant girl sat impassive, brooding over what was going on inside her. Kirov came to the doorway now and then, but Uzzumekis, fiercely keeping up the standards of prudence now that their usefulness had become nearly futile, savagely warned him to stay out of sight. Kirov obeyed, wordless, inscrutable, not fighting when there was nothing to fight except frustration. He had been through that battle before and had learned to save his emotions for when they were useful.

The day dragged, and his helplessness turned Uzzumekis' temper savage. When the girl tried to urge him to eat something he turned on her. "Get back to your damned nursemaiding," he snarled and turned back to watch the valley. He kept pulling out his watch which, for prudence, he no longer wore on his wrist but kept out of sight in a pocket. Three o'clock; eighty-five hours left. To do what in? About a mile to the station. Around four hundred kilometers to the outskirts of Sevastopol—divide by eight and multiply by five—around two hundred and fifty miles, something like ten miles afoot dodging around the city, getting a boat and somebody who knew how to run it and finding a place three miles out in the bay in the dark. Around two hundred and sixty-four miles if his arithmetic was worth a damn and that made it a little over three miles an hour. A man ought to be able to walk on his hands that fast. Oh yes?

He heard it before he saw it at just after five o'clock. The whistle was an asthmatic, mournful squeal, far away. With a kind of savage satisfaction compounded with an impatience bordering on despair, he watched a toy train puff out of the curve of the valley and toward the village. He wanted to jump up and run for it and told himself, Quiet down, you idiot. The train heaved itself into the station, and he saw the puff of steam from the whistle long before he heard it or the distant clanging of the bell. It acts like the dog that just caught the rabbit. I wonder if they ought to wheel out a cannon and fire a salute for it being only three days late.

He strained his eyes, trying to see what was going on. He saw the engine uncouple and move off toward a water tank rising bulbous on spindly legs. They'll be here a while, judged on past performance, he thought. There's nothing to do but wait for the crip. Anyhow, we can't wiggle until it gets dark; two hours anyway, probably more.

Kirov came to the door.

"So it has come, eh? Good."

"We're not on it yet. And if we were, it runs like a turtle with two broken legs."

"I am usually lucky. It is on my record."

"If you were still lucky, we wouldn't be where we are."

"True."

The cripple came at seven, again carrying a parcel and the milk can, and again Uzzumekis met him in the lane and relieved him of his burdens.

"What do you know?" Uzzumekis demanded.

"As you can see, the train is here. You will go now. It is good."

"When? What is the situation? When does it leave?"

"About ten o'clock, perhaps later. I did not talk to the authorities but to those who did talk to them. I thought it better not to seem too curious."

"Right."

"Do you want tickets?"

"Not if we can stow away. Even in the dark I prefer to avoid people."

"There are goods wagons, more goods wagons than carriages for people. About a hundred people are waiting there for only the two carriages. It might be possible to disappear among so many."

"I would rather not take that chance if the other is possible."

"I think it may be. They are moving wagons from one track to another. It goes slowly. The carriages for people have been left at the station. They are leaving the goods wagons to remain here on the center track and placing those to be taken with the train on the far track."

"How about the guards?"

"There is one soldier in the station where the people are. He does not go near the rest of the wagons."

"And the men of the railroad?"

"They are engaged, on top and between the wagons. I did not see them open any."

"Could you tell whether the goods wagons were sealed— locked?"

"No. I was too far. I am sorry."

"Never mind. You have done well, and I thank you." It won't be the first time I've busted open a freight car, Uzzumekis reminded himself, but I hope it's the last.

"When we go, in about an hour when it is full dark, I will guide you to where the goods wagons are. We must cross the tracks but that will not be too difficult. We will go well below the station. It is fortunate that the third track comes near a little wood. We will not be seen."

"It is time," the old man said from the doorway. Uzzumekis joined him and looked down into the valley. It was dark now and the village showed only dim flickers of light. There was more light around the railroad station, but nothing brilliant. They could still hear the occasional distant clanging of the bell as the engine chugged about its chore of switching.

It ain't the Congressional Limited, Uzzmekis thought, but, Christ, I hope it runs. Kirov, silent, stood ready. Where's the girl? Uzzumekis wondered and went back into the barn and called her.

"Here," she answered. "In a moment."

He heard her murmuring and a cracked whisper in reply. What's she doing? he wondered. Then it struck him. She's saying good-by to the old woman, and, by God, she's got her talking.

In a moment the murmur stopped and she joined him and they started out, first down the lane of cypresses which they knew. But then the cripple, in a low voice, guided them across the main road and to another path.

"You will not see much. Follow my voice," the cripple called softly. Uzzumekis grasped the girl's hand and she in turn Kirov's, and they moved ahead. They crossed the tracks without incident at a point that Uzzumekis thought must be at least a quarter mile below the station, behind the shuffling locomotive. No person interfered.

"Hist!" the cripple whispered. "Now we follow the track. Not on it but in the verge. Until we come to the wood."

They followed him in silence. It was no longer necessary to grip one another, for the cripple, hobbling through the pain he had lived with for nearly half a century, was faintly silhouetted against the lights around the station and the engine.

"Hist," he presently said again. They had drawn within a couple of hundred yards of the station. "Now, we leave the tracks. To the left. Go in among the trees."

Five minutes later he stopped them. Now they were out of sight of the station, whose lights were blocked by the silhouettes of a line of wagons parked on the sidetrack a hundred or so feet away. The cripple tugged at Uzzumekis' sleeve.

"Those are the wagons that will go with the train. I am certain they are, but pray the Virgin I am right."

You're in the wrong country, dad, Uzzumekis thought. She's off limits here.

"I cannot do more," the cripple said. "It is too little, and I apologize."

"Wait here," Uzzumekis said. "I'll take a look." Long time since I hopped a freight; I hope I haven't forgotten the basics. All that's necessary is to avoid the dicks—and keep from under the wheels.

Walking upright, but stepping carefully, pausing every few steps to listen, he crossed the verge and came to the first of the line of cars. He felt for the door. Unfamiliar. He had never paid much attention to the difference between a Russian goods wagon and a Chicago and North Western freight car. Ah, there it was. No, the hinge side. He found the lock; it was sealed. He cursed under his breath and moved on to the next car. It, too, was sealed. I'll break one of the bastards if I have to, he told himself savagely. But the next was unlocked, merely clasped on the hasp. He swung it open, listening. Nothing. He eased himself over the sill and felt around in the blackness. Nothing. Something on the floor. Straw? No, but something that rustled. Papers, perhaps, left over from some lading. It didn't matter. He slid back over the sill, closed the door and felt his way back into the darkness toward the waiters.

"I have a place," he whispered. "Follow me. Where is the old man?" he asked.

"He is gone," the woman said. "He told me to say you should go with God."

"Hell!" Uzzumekis almost exploded. "Well, maybe it's just as well. I don't know what I could have said to him anyhow. But I wanted to give him something. I don't know how those people are going to live. He is a gutty guy."

"I did," Kirov spoke softly. "I knew he wouldn't take anything. I gave it to the girl to give him when he couldn't give it back." He chuckled. "Young man, you never seem to believe I am capable of carrying any of my weight."

"Maybe because you weigh so much, Grandpa," Uzzumekis grunted. "Let's go." They crossed the verge without incident, returned to Uzzumekis' found chariot, and with him boosting first the girl, then giving the fat man a hand up, they got aboard without difficulty. Uzzumekis softly closed the door.

"Now," said Uzzumekis, "we make a novena."

Kirov chuckled with as near to mirth as he ever got. "And also I suspect you think I don't know what that means. I've been making one ever since we left Moscow."

It may have been a time for thanksgiving but not, certainly, one of immediate spiritual salvation. They were in thick darkness, and seeing a watch was out of the question. The shuffling of the engine, the plaintive ringing of the bell, the crash of coupling against coupling seemed to go on forever. Around nine o'clock when we got aboard, Uzzumekis thought. That would leave them 79 hours and the same old 264 miles minus one. That raised their necessary speed to three and a half miles an hour.

Something hit their car from the end, and the girl's head banged back against the wall. Kirov stirred. Uzzumekis gave thanks. They had been coupled on; they were going to move. And they did. At first the jolting, metallic smashing back and forth of couplings as the locomotive gathered its meager muscles together and got the train rolling set their nerves ajar even more. But slowly the noises grew more rhythmic, a chuckling of couplings, a repetitious clank as wheels passed over the rail joints.

Here we go, Uzzumekis thought, lulled by the racket. I could get sleepy even listening to one of those idiot long-hair bands. They were moving and, moving, they were safe for so long as movement lasted. He let his back slide down the wall of the car and he was asleep.

He awoke each time the movement stopped and was replaced by the locomotive's laborious shuffling about, officiously depositing one wagon here, another there, hooking onto one, dropping another. But each time they began to move he returned to sleep, uneasy but an unimagined medicine of restoration, lullabied by the clink and clank and thunk of turning wheels, however flat.

Nobody bothered them. Uzzumekis had worried that their car might be set out on some siding some God-knew-where and held himself ready to find something which would continue. But it had not been necessary. Kirov snored. Whether the woman slept, Uzzumekis did not know.

They came, around four in the morning, to what seemed to be a bigger yard than most they had stopped in. They were there an interminable march of eons and Uzzumekis began again to count hours in his head. If his psychic alarm clock was any good they were down to about seventy-three hours. He wished he knew where they were and woke Kirov and cracked the door for a furtive look.

It was still nearly full dark and the former First Secretary of the Party shook his head.

"I make a guess that this is Melitopol, but you understand that I guarantee nothing," he said. "I was the boss—neither a railroad man, nor a cartographer."

"If it is Melitopol, where is it?" Uzzumekis asked.

"Roughly one third of the distance from Zaporozhe to Sevastopol."

"We're not going to make it."

"I was always aware that that was possible."

"So was I, of course. But one dislikes losing."

"One gambles."

"Not with loaded dice—unless he has the opportunity to do the loading."

"And you propose to load them?"

"If an opportunity offers—or can be manufactured."

"I propose to return to sleep while you go about patenting your device. For me, I confess I am shorn of ideas."

"Okay, granddad. Sweet dreams."

"What did you say?"

"Nothing of importance."

At last the train got into motion again. Kirov was asleep and snoring when the door to their car banged open. Kirov's snore broke off in a strangling grunt and he sat up and a voice, startled and peremptory, called out, "Who is that!" A flashlight, feeble with weakening batteries, aimed a yellow eye at them. Uzzumekis' hand was already on the pistol, but he forced himself to relax. There was a scrambling at the door, and a figure, scarcely visible behind the light's frail beam came into the car and moved toward them. Kirov and the woman rose to their feet. Uzzumekis stayed where he was, on his haunches, with his back against the end wall. His hand touched something. Cloth?. The woman's head scarf? He set his hand to gathering it up, crumpling it into his palm.

The voice behind the flashlight sounded both scared and angry.

"Who is this? What do you do here? Answer!"

"Nothing. We ride only," Kirov said.

"It is not permitted! Go to the carriages."

"Without money?" Kirov's voice was bland with innocence.

The figure came closer and, in the shifting of the light, Uzzumekis saw that it was not in uniform.

"And you!" the figure said. "Get on your feet!"

"And what would I do on my feet?" Uzzumekis made his voice sound thick, drunken, he hoped. It would have been a good time to be Andrei.

"Up!"

"Don't want to," Uzzumekis mumbled and let his head fall back against the car wall.

"Up!" The voice now sounded more confident and more threatening. It moved toward Uzzumekis, and he could see, behind the light's feeble blinding, an arm upraised. Something in it. A club?

Keep coming, buster, he said softly to himself. Just keep coming. Just another couple of steps. Keep coming, you bastard!

As the light centered on Uzzumekis, Kirov and the woman went into shadow, and the arm, suddenly, was coming down. Uzzumekis' right foot went out and up, and he felt it sink where he intended. The voice made an agonized scream, and Uzzumekis was on his feet.

"Close the door!" he hissed at Kirov. Then he was astride the writhing figure on the floor. He pinned whoever it was face down, with his knees digging into the kidneys. The scarf was now in both hands and he twirled it into a cord. There was no thought of mercy now, nor of asking questions. The corded scarf went under the voice's forehead and chin and Uzzumekis felt briefly and expertly for its placement. Then, with the ends crossed and wrapped around both fists, his right knee now between the shoulder blades for leverage, he brought his hands apart with a smooth powerful jerk. He heard the sound of the larynx crushing and after that the struggle was brief and not noisy. He stood up, dropping the twisted scarf.

"He is dead, is he not?" Kirov said.

"He's dead," Uzzumekis said.

The woman was gasping.

"Get that light!" Uzzumekis snapped at her.

"My countrymen have now begun to pay for my ticket," Kirov said.

"Listen, you still haven't got a ticket to anywhere. Here, help me drag this to the other end of the car. We don't have to sleep with him."

"Who sleeps after this?"

"Probably you. The way you've been going you would sleep through judgment day—in which, of course, you do not believe."

"I think, perhaps, I will now begin to believe in it a little." He turned the light, which he had taken from the girl, onto the broken figure on the floor. "I suppose he now does."

The woman had stopped gasping. "Who is he?" she asked.

"Brakeman, probably," Uzzumekis said. "Or maybe an inspector. If they begin looking for him, we're in trouble."

"Perhaps we ought to leave the wagon," Kirov said. "Take another."

"We can't now. It's daylight. Now we have only around

seventy or sixty-nine hours. Does this local train anywhere join the main line? Do you know?"

"I am not sure," the woman said. "But I think it must at Dzhankoy."

"Where is that?"

"It is after the causeway where the rails pass over the Sivash into the Crimea."

"Sivash?"

"The marshes. The part that is called the Putrid Sea."

"How far?"

"Perhaps another eighty kilometers."

"We're going to have to get off this junk heap there and find something else. This thing will never make Sevastopol in time."

"What else?" Kirov spread his hands palm upward.

"I do not know yet. How could I? Maybe the bus—if I could think of a way to make you look like nobody—or Gregory Peck—or Eisenhower—anybody. If you weren't so damned fat you probably would look like Eisenhower—a little."

"I am not entirely sure that is a compliment."

"It wasn't meant to be. Now, let's get some rest. We'll need it."

"With him—with that there?" the woman asked.

"Of course. He won't bother you. I wish there was some way to jam the door. So it wouldn't be so easy to get it open. I don't want to arrive with a carload of corpses."

"You are not a merciful man," Kirov said mildly.

"Were you? I would be if there was time for it. This man," he flipped the light toward the body, "simply ran out of luck. If he had been tougher—or smarter—where would you be now?"

"I do not quarrel. It was necessary. And it was quick. You are proficient."

"I doubt if that's a compliment either."

With the dead man's flashlight, Uzzumekis went to inspect the inside of the door. He was pleased to find that it was fitted with a simple hasp and peg. He dropped the peg in place with satisfaction.

"If I had known about that in time, the poor slob would still be alive. I'm going to get some rest. You two had better also."

He lay down at the end of the car, away from the body. He did not really believe he could sleep, but all at once the effort and the fact of murder left him exhausted. The killing had drained him emotionally if not physically. He regretted it but he did not quail from the knowledge. He was simply as tired as he had ever been. And then, trying to plan, knowing he must, he was asleep, asleep as though drugged.

Before long Kirov was snoring again. Melina, lying on the floor between the two men, thought she would never sleep again. She lay, cold, involuntarily shuddering, seeing as vividly as though in full light the broken body a few feet away. She wondered about the huge man beside her, that incomprehensible mixture of gentleness and swift bestial savagery. She didn't believe it was mere cruelty for cruelty's sake. He had been astonishingly compassionate with the sick woman and the cripple after he had first said he was only using them for a disguise. The old cripple had seemed to discern something in him, some quality beyond Uzzumekis' acknowledged cold self-interest. And perhaps something was there. She didn't know what it was; she did know he could be as expertly brutal as a wolf.

She woke up in his arms, and she knew at once he was still asleep or more than half asleep. She began to recoil and then did not. I must have moved against him in the cold, she thought. He is all relaxed now, soft, defenseless. She did not move away, but wondered . . . feeling the slow quickening of her own breath. She felt without will, without purpose. She had been this near to no man since Uri's exile. I ought to get away, she told herself fiercely, and still did nothing, or had she moved closer to that warmth? Perhaps, she did not know.

The arms around her tightened, and still she believed he

was sleeping. Kirov's snores rolled over them. No sound came from that other, at the far end of the car, nor ever would. Ah, what does it matter? she thought. She opened her blouse and drew Uzzumekis' head down toward her naked breast.

"Uh?" he said. Then he was awake and said, "I'm sorry."

"It is all right," she heard herself say. "It is all right."

"I'm dirty," he said.

"You'll be clean some day. Now it is all right." And it is, she thought as she felt him move against her. Somehow it is gloriously all right, and I know it should not be. Her body felt loose and accepting and at the same time straining toward him. They kissed . . . for a long time . . . and her thighs opened and took him into her. Kirov, his snores; the dead man, his silence; the train, its clattering progress, they all had ceased to exist. At the end they lay in one another's arms, content.

It was pitch black in the car, and when Uzzumekis went to look, first unclasping the hasp, it was dark again outside. The train was stopped. They were in a railroad yard. He called the woman and Kirov.

"Is this it?" he asked.

"As you know, I don't know," Kirov said.

"I am not certain. I think it is," the woman said. "I will go and ask."

"No, you don't," Uzzumekis said. "I'll go." He didn't know how he felt about her, except for this little tenderness lying beneath his iron determination to get Kirov on the submarine alive.

"No," she said. "Nobody will pay attention to me. If they are looking, as we know they may be, you will be too visible. You are too big. I will go."

"All right, but talk to nobody who looks like an official. And be back. Don't hang around."

Taking her hands he lowered her over the sill and she trudged away in the dark, moving toward the muddy lights of the station. Kirov touched his sleeve.

"You know, we are going to have to take her all the way now. With us on the submarine."

"You're out of your mind," Uzzumekis said shortly.

"I am not; we have to take her now."

"Why, for Christ's sake?"

"Because of that," Kirov jerked a thumb toward the huddled figure in the far end of the car. "It will be found. The connection will be made. They will, sooner or later, find them all: the barge and the man on it and his wife, the truck driver, the house in Zaporozhe, the cripple, his women."

"Why the hell do you think they will find them?"

"Because I know my—our people. They will have started working along the skein weeks ago. They may not catch up with us in time for them, but sooner or later they will find them all."

"Perhaps. But I doubt it," Uzzumekis said. "The submarine can be a dangerous thing. It is not a place to take a woman."

"It is better than leaving her here."

"It makes everything more awkward," Uzzumekis said. "This is going to be tough enough as it is, just getting your carcass onto that sub. That's my job; my job does not, emphatically, include picking up strays along the way."

"Have you forgotten so soon that you slept with her last night? Does not that imply some responsibility?"

"How the hell did you know?"

"I don't sleep all the time."

"Some responsibility, perhaps. Some debts have to go unpaid. I did not harm her, and I don't, whether you believe it or not, know how it began. Accident maybe. Then, maybe she began it."

"It doesn't matter. Either way, it was begun."

"Why should you care?"

"Perhaps I don't. I don't condemn. I don't envy you, although if I were younger, I probably would."

"Then drop it!"

"No. There is a matter of my pride, if you don't mind."

179

"What does your pride have to do with her?"

"You can put it any way that satisfies you. Perhaps it is that, when they are through looking, I would not want it known that I was shepherded as a fugitive by a woman. Almost a girl. They would deal with her, but also they would laugh at me."

"My aching ass! Pride now."

"All the same, we take her with us."

"I'll decide that."

"It is decided already. She goes, or I do not."

"That way, huh?" Uzzumekis said thoughtfully.

"That way. Yes."

They heard the woman coming along the track, although at first they did not know it was her feet crunching in the cinder road bed and Uzzumekis pulled Kirov back into the depths of the car until he heard her urgent whisper at the door and went to grasp her wrists and lift her over the sill. She was gasping and excited.

"The express is coming," she said. "It will be here in moments. It stops a little time and goes directly on to Sevastopol."

"Too bad we can't take it," Kirov said.

Uzzumekis, once more, was doing simple sums in his head. Sixty hours now, no more.

"We are going to take it. We have to," he said. "Otherwise we're finished."

"How?" Kirov demanded. "You forget. As you say, I have the misfortune to be unforgettable."

"Let me think," Uzzumekis said. "Maybe the answer is to make you even more unforgettable. Melina," he turned to the girl, "do you wear anything white? Cotton?"

She thought she might be blushing and then thought how absurd that would be. "Yes, my underskirt."

"Get yourself out of it and give it to me." Then to Kirov, "You got a knife or anything that will cut?"

"A penknife. A souvenir which I kept."

"Give it to me. Melina, get out of that skirt."

180

He took the knife, got the flashlight and went to the corpse. I don't suppose the bastard will bleed much now, he thought, but I won't need much. Just a little red and if it's stale it's just as well. More realistic maybe.

He bent over the body, then went back and got the cloth from the woman. Then he rubbed the cloth in the wound he had made and, tearing the skirt into strips, he went back to the other two.

"We're going to wrap you up like a mummy," he told Kirov. "A bloody mummy. Then we're going to pile into third class in that express and when anybody asks, as they sure as hell will, you have been in an accident. The woman will do the talking. All you have to do is keep your trap shut and grunt a little now and then. We are your daughter and her husband, and we are taking you home. Come on now, give me money for the tickets. Melina, see if you can bandage him up so his own mother wouldn't know him—or want to."

XII

"WHAT have you got to tell me?" Sobelov asked Gagarin, who was telephoning from Sevastopol. It was shortly after ten o'clock in the evening of May 1. Sobelov, pressed by the urgency of his problem and a growing sense of uneasiness, had stayed at his telephone throughout the day and ignored the glories of the May Day parade. Despite his worries, his voice remained calm, as Gagarin could discern even above the humming of the long-distance wire.

"A good deal. But I fear the time has grown very short."

"What is it?"

"You had my report earlier today that a trainman was found dead in a goods wagon on the route from Mikhaylovka this morning. I did not then know what it meant to us—if anything. Now I believe I do."

"Why?"

"He did not die of a natural cause. He had been garrotted."

"That doesn't necessarily help us. But I suppose it could."

"Yes, I believe it does. I have just now received a report from Dzhankoy. In the early hours of today, two men and a woman boarded the express there—among many others. The dead man was found in the railway yards there."

"How does this relate with the two men and the woman?"

"One was a huge man. The other was bandaged about the head."

"The woman?"

"No particular description. Young. Blond. She described to the train official that the bandaged man was her father and that she was taking him home. She said he had been hurt in an accident."

"What was his appearance?"

"Short. Stout, or so the train official thought. Peasant clothing. That is all, except for the bandage, which, the train official said, was the only reason he noticed him in the throng in third class."

"Our train officials are not very observant," Sobelov said. Gagarin was aware of the cold irony in Sobelov's tone.

"That is correct."

Sobelov tapped his desk blotter with a pencil. His eyes behind the glittering pince-nez were narrowed.

"Where were the passengers bound?"

"The train official believes the tickets were for Bakhchisaray. He is not too certain of that. He said the third class was very thronged."

"Did they leave the train there?"

"Again he is uncertain."

"You have his name? Have him discharged."

"Of course."

Sobelov tapped the blotter again.

"So now we deal with murder. And three fugitives. Do you have much doubt who they were?"

"Very little. Some, of course. There are such things as coincidence. But now, if I am correct, we must be fewer than twenty-four hours behind them. And we know, within a radius of fifty kilometers, where they must be."

"Twenty-four hours may be too much—more than we can afford. The same may be said of fifty kilometers. That must be narrowed. And drastically, you understand?" Now there was no mistaking the cold finality in Sobelov's voice.

"It is being narrowed. I have spread five hundred men through this region."

"I assume the train already has reached Bakhchisaray. Otherwise you would have intercepted it there."

"Yes. An hour ago. I ascertained that as soon as I received the report from Dzhankoy. The report was delayed."

"Fools. Idiots," Sobelov muttered. "Never is anything done as it should be."

"I am sorry. The telephone line from Dzhankoy was out of repair."

"Sorrow is of little use."

"We, of course, are searching from there. And from here in Sevastopol."

"We deal with conjecture, of course. And conjecture can lead to gross error," Sobelov mused. "But matters begin to fit, in a rather insane way. Did you know that an American nuclear submarine was in Istanbul until yesterday, which it left shortly after noon?"

"No."

"Naturally. You have been engaged, as I know. And I do not know what significance that may have to our errand. It may have none. Still the presence of an American submarine in Istanbul, having come through the Dardanelles, is unusual, to say the least. It had to come there with Turkish consent. There could be no other way."

"You said until yesterday."

"Yes. It sailed about noon—westward bound through Marmara, toward the Dardanelles." Sobelov kept tapping the desk top.

"Of course," he added, "the submarine sailing westward does not necessarily mean anything. It went under the water while still within sight of Istanbul. Where it went after that we have no way of knowing."

"You suspect it could have been sent for Kirov?"

"Anything is possible. But where?"

"Kirov—and his companions—were on the Dnepr.

"But they left the river. Or appear to have left it. In any case, no submarine could safely approach Odessa. The sea there is shallow."

"I do not imagine it could approach Sevastopol either, since that is heavily guarded. Kirov would not dare to appear there in any circumstance. He was extremely lucky—if it was indeed he—to escape recognition with that stupid disguise, the bandage."

"By the same measure, he could not move about much after he left the train—whether at Bakhchisaray or elsewhere. He cannot move far and wherever he does move it must be done with extraordinary caution. That helps us, narrows the circle."

"I know little of submarines."

"Nor did I—until after I got the message from Ivanov in Istanbul. Since then I have consulted the navy—on the conjecture, until now hazy—that the American submarine might have some connection with our problem. I have explored its possible approaches, again on the same conjecture. The conjecture then seemed outlandish. It now appears less so. Any foreign submarine, as the navy sees it, would encounter formidable problems making a furtive approach to a Russian coast on the Black Sea. Odessa, for example, would be out of the question, since the sea there is too shallow. This leaves only the Crimean coast, where, the navy insists, the ring of defenses outward from Sevastopol is so rigid that an unfriendly vessel, bent on a hostile errand, would need to be extraordinarily bold to come near at all."

"On the other hand, we know the limitations on Kirov. He does not have a free choice of where to make a rendezvous with anybody. But he is doubtless attempting to make one," Gagarin said.

"Nor does a submarine enjoy a free choice. It requires deep water, for one thing. It needs a definite point precisely because Kirov—or those with him—must be able to find that point. It needs to come close to shore for it is almost inconceivable that Kirov could travel far out to sea. The point must be somewhere where it is possible for Kirov to get some conveyance to take him to sea. Yalta, perhaps?"

"Possible, of course. But Yalta would place an almost intolerable burden on Kirov and his companions—again if, indeed, the bandaged man was Kirov which, personally, I do not much doubt. But if he left the train at Bakhchisaray, which is as close as the railroad approaches, he would still be more than sixty kilometers from Yalta, also through the mountains. He has had luck—so far. But one cannot place too much strain on luck. It is never guaranteed."

"You are right. Kirov has enjoyed the devil's own amount

of luck. But he is a bold man and would gamble. But we must now—and quickly—arrange that he runs out of it."

"Would you consider Balaklava possible?" Gagarin asked. Sobelov considered it for a moment.

"Scarcely. It is extremely close to the navy base. Also it is a prohibited area, a naval gunnery range. It has radar at Mys Feolent and sonar at Mys Ayya. Our own naval vessels are active there. The harbor is bracketed. A submarine would have to be commanded by a fool—or a genius—to come to the surface there."

"It is clear, however, that we are not here dealing with an ordinary situation. As I have said, I have men in the area. In the mountains, on the roads, moving toward every town and village on the sea. It is difficult to believe that a mouse could get through."

"This mouse must not."

"He will not, Comrade."

"Now, of course, since it becomes possible that we deal with the sea, even likely that we do, I return to the navy," Sobelov said. "After all, they have a responsibility too." Sobelov's tone allowed itself a faint edge of bitterness. "I will see that destroyers, other naval vessels, immediately establish a close surveillance of that coast. The American submarine may be a figment of conjecture. But Kirov is not. And he must be there somewhere." All at once Sobelov, who was both noted and feared for his composure under pressure, dropped his pencil, raised a well-manicured fist, and slammed down on his desk with a resounding thud.

Gagarin, far away, looked startled as he heard Sobelov's momentary betrayal of emotion.

"For myself," Gagarin said, "I suspect Balaklava. We know Kirov is bold. The submarine—if it exists—may be bold also. Also it is near where it is likely he left the train—and it is possible to get around Sevastopol, not easy but possible. If it should indeed be Balaklava, there may not be much time, only a few hours perhaps. The other possibilities are not being ignored, but I have certain knowledge there, certain connections. With your permission, I myself will go there at once."

"See that the other possibilities are not ignored—none of them. I distrust the idea of Balaklava, as I have said. But if you consider it feasible, go there. Get a fast car. This mouse must not get through. Kirov is somewhere near you. Bring him back."

"Alive?"

"If possible."

XIII

STEPHENS stuck up Number One periscope long enough to get a good look at all the traffic emerging from the Golden Horn and moving up and down the Bosporus and, against his will as captain of a United States Navy vessel, shuddered. He took a particularly good look at the unkempt and sway-backed little *Queen Zenobia* which, for the moment, he looked upon as a relative, a close relative, perhaps even his mother. He pushed the button and sent the scope down into its well.

"You take the con," he said to Lieutenant Commander Oulahan. "You're three years younger than I am and consequently that much braver. I am going someplace and cower like a coward—which I am. That little bucket out there, which Guernic has on the sonar, is our guardian angel. Hang onto it as though it was the first tit you ever tasted as an adult."

"Yes, sir," Oulahan said.

"And quit laughing," Stephens said. "That's an order, Mr. Oulahan."

"Aye, aye, sir," Oulahan said.

"Very well," Stephens said, and left the pulpit and went around to Guernic's chart table and spoke to the man with the beard. "Chief," he said, "do you have that spare chart of the Bosporus?"

"Right here, Captain. You need it?"

"I need it indeed. I am going somewhere with it—possibly the head—and read it again and have a good cry."

"I can't think of a better reason for bawling, Captain."

Stephens took the folded chart and stepped back up to the pulpit and spoke once more to Oulahan. "It may be a little silly, since I trust both Gottfried and Admiral March. All the same, rig for collision. I trust them implicitly, but I suspect that most of the other drivers out there got their licenses in Scarsdale, Westchester County, State of New York. And, as you know since it is your home town, precisely ninety-seven per cent of them are committable."

"Yes, sir, Captain. That is why I went to sea."

"Quit laughing, Mr. Oulahan."

"Aye."

With the chart under his arm, Stephens descended *Skate's* slightly grand stairway and entered the wardroom, where he found the British Captain Brown and the Italian Nicolai, whom he could never quite believe held any rank at all. They were drinking coffee.

"You stick with *Skate* long enough and we will make American sailors out of you yet," he said by way of greeting.

"I doubt if you will ever make one out of yourself," Nicolai said.

"That's my trouble; I'm a maverick," Stephens acknowledged, as Collingwood, a creature of habit, put down at his elbow a pot of hot water and a cup. Stephens unfolded the chart on the wardroom table and stared at it balefully.

"You know, gentlemen, this is one of the world's most important waterways. Without it the world might not function at all. From the times of the Phoenicians and Greeks and even"—he now glared at Nicolai—"your greedy damned Venetians, people have been fighting wars over it. Considering its importance, you would have thought God would make a better job of it in the first place. But, excusing His blunders, which I suppose is a theological necessity, why was it then necessary for man to screw it up even worse?"

"Mr. Oulahan told us a short time ago that we are going into the Black Sea," Captain Brown said. "Exciting, what?" He looked nearly as excited as Grant's Tomb and twice as dignified.

"I suppose he also told you what we're after," Stephens said.

"He did. You know, curious thing, I was introduced to the

man once. Naval affair in London. Can't say I was much attracted to him."

"Apparently his home folks no longer are either."

Nicolai looked somewhat distressed.

"Captain Stephens," he said, "I admit I have come to the point where I can tolerate—indeed almost enjoy—American coffee. But, now, don't you think it was somewhat impolite— not to say piratical—to shanghai us on this slightly insane, not to say dangerous, excursion to rescue a shopworn Russian politician? I cannot think of anything I want less."

"Capitano," Stephens said, "I want you to believe that politeness is a quality the American Navy believes in sincerely. The difference is that we don't practice it. What we do practice is orders. What I may believe personally is totally irrelevant. My orders say you are to be here. Therefore you are."

"Autocratic," Nicolai said with some heat.

"So was Caesar. And so, for that matter, was Mussolini."

"And so was Roosevelt," Nicolai retorted. "F.D.R., I mean."

"I'm not quarreling with you," Stephens said. "We can all hate the politicians of our choice. The only thing I hate at the moment is this abortion of a ditch."

"What causes your distress?" Captain Brown asked.

"For one thing, it's crooked. A cottonmouth moccasin would have to be agile to get through. A moccasin, sir, is an extremely agile—and bad-tempered—American snake which, under ordinary circumstances, prefers water over dry land."

"I do not suppose that making this passage submerged makes the problem any easier," Brown offered.

"You could not be closer to right if you had used a slide rule," Stephens acknowledged. "That is why, since I am at heart gutless and made even more so by being thirty-nine years old, I have turned the con over to my executive officer. It may be of some interest to you, sir, that in the American Navy running nuclear submarines is a young man's occupation. For the most part, in your entire career, you get only one command—which, by and large, is two years. After that you're on the shelf, so far as doing anything really useful is concerned."

"Good Lord, in the British Navy, they get more use out of us than that. Why, take me, for example; I was fifty-three my last birthday and now they are giving me the *Royal Oak*, Her Majesty's newest nuke." American slang always sounded a little strange on Captain Brown's tongue.

"Mazel tov!" Stephens said.

"What is that?" Brown cocked a shaggy, grizzled eyebrow at him.

"Yiddish, I think," Stephens said. "What it roughly means is 'enjoy it in good health.' "

"Oh, by all means," Captain Brown said. "In Arabic approximately the same thing is 'mawbruk.' It applies equally to new submarines, new automobiles, and new mistresses."

"Wonderful words, both of them," Nicolai said. "When I return to Istanbul I shall apply both of them to Marida."

"You'd better leave out the 'good health' part," Stephens said. "That dame is going to be the death of you."

"Like my paisan, who was named Horatius, how could man die better?" Nicolai said, and lifted his shoulders and eyebrows in total eloquence. "*Fearful odds* was his motto. I am proud to partake of his example."

"Mawbruk," Stephens and Captain Brown said together.

"You interest me by your comment that the American Navy either wears out or discards men in what I think of as youth," Captain Brown said. "Where do you go after you are forty and still have approximately the same number of years to survive?"

"If you get a good fitness report, they make you a captain, sew another stripe on your sleeve, raise your pay slightly—only slightly—and put you down behind a desk where you can grow a rump which requires a girdle—corset, perhaps in British—manufactured by a firm called Maidenform, without which the American gross national product would be a hell of a lot less than it is."

191

"And that is the end of the road?" Nicolai asked.

"Oh no. Not necessarily. If you are a good politician or so smart they can't ignore you, they may make you an admiral. This means bigger gold stripes and another slight raise in pay —quite slight, I assure you. However, admirals have a certain advantage; they are permitted to go around kicking the desk-fattened butts of captains and all lower ranks. On the other hand, they are forced to take some totally indigestible crap from politicians—particularly the one, who at any given moment, may inhabit the White House."

"Is that why we are here?" Nicolai asked.

"Your question is unfair—and possibly subversive," Stephens said. "I am a loyal citizen and am not, at the moment, pissed off at anything except this lousy ditch."

"I know you observed it was crooked," Captain Brown said. "And I can see by the chart that it is indeed. Also it has some clearly dangerous shallows in it, not to mention other navigational hazards such as cable crossings, prohibited anchorages and a nasty bit of fluff prohibiting ships carrying explosives from anchoring north of Haydarpasa Breakwater. Are we, by any chance, carrying explosives?"

"You can bet your bottom sixpence we are carrying explosives," Stephens said.

"Apart from these matters, which you appear able to manage successfully, what, Captain Stephens, especially annoys you about this waterway?"

"If I tell you the truth, Captain Brown, you are going to be insulted."

"I am an even-tempered man. Even my wife has difficulty arousing my anger."

"All right, then. You asked for it. Practically everywhere else in the world, traffic keeps to the right. Most of them do— more or less—even in Scarsdale, Westchester County, State of New York. I said 'most,' and I also said 'more or less' which saves me from committing a libel in reverse. But this damned gut called the Bosporus—the upper section of some-thing which has been called the Turkish Straits for generations and has been the fascinating object of numerous treaties and even more wars—operates on the British system. Traffic travels on the left. I recall from my somewhat distant youth—whatever you may regard it as in your green and beautiful island—that you once had a king—a custom which I find almost as objectionable as our own—who had sufficient human qualities to fall in love with a woman from Baltimore and renounced his crown in order to marry her. I am forced to qualify this too, not knowing the circumstances exactly, which the heavier burden may be—a crown or a woman from Baltimore. I guess it would be approximately six-to-five, and take your choice.

"However, although I am slightly tempted to admire him for turning the throne over to his brother, who in turn bequeathed it to a girl with a back end big enough to fill it, I am also forced to remember that once he attempted to set fashions. Specifically, for a time there, he had the creases in his pants pressed on the sides. This was peculiarly and exactly British, ignoring the plain fact that Providence arranged human knees to bend fore and aft and not port and starboard.

"That was a digression," Stephens said, only slightly apologetically, since he was sore at the world and did not really feel sorry for anything. "What I began to say, Captain Brown, is that I know Winston Churchill never made it this far in 1915. But some time or other, God knows how many generations ago—possibly when you were still colored blue and called Picts, and William the Conqueror had not yet showed up on the beach—you blasted limeys must have got in here and screwed up the traffic pattern forevermore."

"Hear, hear!" said Nicolai.

"Hell of a speech," Captain Brown agreed.

The squawk box beside the wardroom depth-and-course repeaters came stridently alive.

"Captain to the bridge!" it howled.

Stephens got up in a hurry, leaving his guests without

apology, hustled up the stairs, entered the control room, and stepped up beside Oulahan.

"What's up, Dick?" he said.

Oulahan looked at him, wearing a grin somewhat wider than a ready-made snap-on bow tie.

"We just passed Rumeli Burnu. In proper Turkish—in case you have not studied the charts—*burnu* means cape. We did it most correctly and legally on the port—or British—side of the channel. We are now in the Black Sea."

"Richard, if I have anything to do with it—and I suppose I do since I am still captain of this vessel—you are going to get a fitness report made of platinum. Carry on, bub, you have just become an old man of thirty-six."

XIV

THE express ran fast through the featureless marshes whose salt stench was heavy in their nostrils. Third class, for the disadvantaged of a classless state, was rank with the flesh of its burden. They sat together on a wooden bench, with Kirov by the window. Beside them, on the aisle, a fat woman had crowded in; between her knees was a cloth sack, and on her lap she supported a frightened baby whose yowls of rage and fear set Uzzumekis' teeth on edge. Somebody ought to choke the little monster, he thought, and did not think of the man he had choked.

Nobody paid much attention to Kirov beyond first curious glances. There were too many, too much engaged with their own problems, too much worn by the weight of toil, too much accustomed to the taste of their own lifelong misfortune to be more than passing curious about the misfortune of another. The baby was not alone in his uproar. On the bench behind them a man kept a brace of ducks which gabbled incessantly against the discomfort of having their legs tied and wings locked. Along the aisle on the other side a woman clucked futilely at a pig whose tether may have imbued him, rightly, with some apprehension for his future, which he voiced.

Uzzumekis hunched himself down, knowing that his size was remarkable and trying to minimize it. He had given the tickets to the girl, who sat next to the fat woman and baby, one in from the aisle.

Uzzumekis tensed when the train official came along the aisle, inspecting tickets. We could have trouble now, he thought, and there is not a damn thing in the world I can do about it if it comes.

But it was almost less than nothing.

"He has been hurt? You should take him to a doctor," the official said, peering at Kirov.

"Yes. In a truck accident," the woman said. "We are taking him home."

"To Bakhchisaray?" the official said, looking at the tickets.

"Yes. I do not think it was serious. He is cut and bruised."

Why doesn't she shut up? Uzzumekis wondered irritably. The next thing he'll want to do is put us off to see a doctor . . . or call one from somewhere else in the train.

"All the same he should see a doctor."

"He will. When we get home," the woman promised. She wanted to ask when the train would reach Bakhchisaray, but did not dare; the official might think she ought to know that —if she lived there. The official moved along the aisle, and, after a while, they breathed more easily.

It was dusk when the train stopped at Bakhchisaray and they, among a few others, got up. Trying to ease himself past the fat woman's spread knees, Uzzumekis woke the baby, who began to howl, and the fat woman looked up at him resentfully and called him clumsy and muttered a swear word.

"My pardon, madam," Uzzumekis said, longing to clout her.

They went into the station and the woman surrendered their tickets to the guard at the stile, who again stared curiously at Kirov's bloody bandages but made no comment.

Outside, Uzzumekis pulled his watch from his pocket and said, "We have six hours left. How do we go?"

"This way," the woman said. "To the wood."

"I am growing confident," Kirov said.

"I am not," Uzzumekis said. "Although now it is necessary to go only four kilometers an hour. The odds are a little better, that is all. A little better, but not good."

"You are a pessimist."

"No, a realist."

The town itself was not large, and the railroad station was on the eastern edge, with a few scattered houses lying between them and open farmland and beyond that low hills covered with scrubby woodland. Away to the south and west they could locate the city by a glow of light against the clouds. Sevastopol. A hell of a place to be anywhere near in my present company, Uzzumekis thought. A naval base, crawling with exactly the kind of people I don't want to talk to.

They were soon among the trees, which proved undergrown with brush that made progress difficult, as well as noisy.

"This is too slow. We've got to move faster," Uzzumekis said, after perhaps ten minutes of it. "Is there a road?"

"A little one. Mostly for the farms," the woman said.

"Let's get back on it then. It's dark and we can move faster."

"Do you think it is safe?" Kirov asked.

"Nothing is. Neither this nor that. We have to move faster."

"Can I get out of these odious rags? That man's blood begins to smell, as well as the reminder of love-making."

"Not yet. They've been pretty good camouflage so far. I don't know why smells should offend you—at the moment. You're no treat yourself."

"Precisely what do we do when we are in Balaklava?" Uzzumekis asked the girl.

"We go to the home of the man who was once my husband's foreman. He has promised me that the boat will be ready from eleven o'clock."

"What else does he know?"

"Nothing. Only that I need the boat."

"Does he know who will be with you?"

"No."

"Why was he fool enough to promise this?"

"He is not a fool. I believe he wants to sleep with me."

"That's not so odd. Has he?"

Her voice was frigid. "If he had, it would not be your affair."

"You're right. I apologize."

"As it happens, he has not."

197

"I still apologize."

"Once we are in the town, there should be no difficulty. It is a small place, except when the vacationers come."

"Good."

They had three hours left when luck smiled upon them. They became aware of a yellow glow of headlights coming behind them.

"We're going to have to flag this one and make him carry us to the town," Uzzumekis said.

"He won't stop," Kirov said.

"He will," Uzzumekis said. "I want you to get down in the road as though you had fallen. Melina will be bending over you. But be sure that you lie so he can see the bandage. He will have to stop."

"What will you do?"

"I will be beside the road, out of the light. With this." Uzzumekis took the pistol out of his inner pocket. "This is only in case he does not want to carry us."

"You would not harm another of my countrymen?"

"I will do what is necessary. No more."

The machine stopped. It could scarcely do otherwise without running over Kirov and the woman. The voice from the cab—it was a truck—was at first startled, then querulous.

"What is it? Who is there?"

"My father," Melina called. "He is hurt. Please help me."

"Why is he in the road?"

"Can't you see? He has fallen. Please help."

Grumbling, the driver got down. Uzzumekis now saw he was dressed in laborer's clothing as, in the light, he bent over to look curiously at Kirov.

"What is this?" the driver demanded.

"This," said Uzzumekis, stepping out of the shadow with the gun. "We need your help." The driver gasped and made as though to bolt, but Uzzumekis grabbed him by the collar with his left hand and struck him expertly with the gun butt. The man grunted, but did not go down.

"You are thieves !" he gasped.

"Not if you behave," Uzzumekis said. "We need to ride with you and so you have a choice. You can stay here, tied up beside the road and we will take your truck. Or you can drive us where the woman will tell you."

"I'll drive," the man said sullenly.

"Be sure you will," Uzzumekis said and then turned to Kirov who was now standing. "Get in the back. There is not room for all in the cab. I need the woman to tell him where to go. I need to be there to be certain he does not make any mistake."

The truck was ancient and grumbled about the necessity of moving. It would be just like the damn thing, Uzzumekis thought, to fall apart on us like Andrei's old bucket. It did not fall apart, although it labored in metallurgical agony, getting over the saddle that stood between Sevastopol and Balaklava.

"We are nearly there," the girl whispered. "Only a few minutes more."

"Stop," Uzzumekis said to the driver.

"Wha—" the girl began to ask.

"We can't take him into the town, nor where we are going. He would blab. Your man would be in unnecessary trouble. We leave him here."

"He would go to the police."

"Not the way I intend to leave him." He called to Kirov to get down and search the truck for rope. There was none. Uzzumekis shrugged out of his smock, awkwardly keeping the gun on the driver. "Here," he said to Kirov. "Take your knife and cut the sleeves off this thing. Then rip the body into strips—strong ones."

The driver stood sullen and silent beside the road.

"Do you know anything about a gun?" Uzzumekis asked the girl.

"Almost nothing. I couldn't . . ."

"You won't need to," Uzzumekis said. "Just point it at him for a moment." He handed her the weapon, took one long stride toward the driver, grabbed his clothing at the chest with his left hand and, with his right, sent a short straight punch to the man's jaw. The driver groaned and fell.

"Now," Uzzumekis told Kirov, "give me the rags."

They left him in the back of his truck, gagged, with his hands bound behind him and tied in turn to his bound ankles. Uzzumekis moved the truck to the side of the road and, before turning off the lights, looked at his watch. A quarter of eleven; it's going to be a tight thing.

"Now," he said to the girl. "We move. You lead."

"You are a rough man," Kirov observed.

"It's a rough world."

They moved to the edge of the town. There were few lights and apparently nobody about.

"How far?" Uzzumekis asked Melina.

"Five minutes, no more." Her voice betrayed the strain. She hurried on, and soon, by the smell and the faint lapping of waves, Uzzumekis knew they were on the water front.

"He lives here, just back of the docks," the girl whispered. "I take you first to where he moors the boat. It will be best if I go alone to his house, I think."

"You're right. Lead on."

Soon she turned from the narrow street and led them onto a wooden pier which rumbled hollowly under their feet.

"Here," she hissed. "Wait here." She vanished. In the dim light from shore, Uzzumekis saw the boat and heard it sloshing faintly at its moorings. It had a mast, he saw. I hope to God it's got an engine, too, he thought. The craft seemed to be some twenty feet long, and it smelled powerfully of fish. Hurry up, girl, he told himself. Now that it was nearly over, it was difficult to control the tension.

He heard steps coming over the planking and cushioned the pistol in his hand, but then he heard Melina's voice.

"We have come. We can go now."

The figure of the man with her was scarcely distinguishable. He did not speak but got down into the boat. After a moment, the engine coughed, spat, and then caught and was throttled back to idle. The man climbed back to the planking and began loosening lines. Well, it's been a hell of a trip, Uzzumekis sighed to himself, but here we are. He sighed again, this time aloud.

He did not see the second man until he was almost upon them. The voice was harsh, commanding.

"Stand as you are! Don't move!"

Light lanced out at them.

"Do not move!" the voice warned again. "Move and you die."

"Now, what is this?" Uzzumekis demanded.

"You don't need to ask that. You know. Comrade Kirov, it has been slow work. Now you will come back with me. Take those ridiculous rags off your head. They hide nothing."

The man with the light was standing near the edge of the pier. Uzzumekis saw the pistol in his hand just as he, firing through his pocket, shot him in the chest. The light went backward in a gleaming arc and fell into the water. The sound of its splash came just before the heavier splash of the man's body.

"Now, let's get out of here!" Uzzumekis hissed. "Where is the boatman?"

"He ran," Kirov said. "He's gone."

Uzzumekis cursed.

"Help me get these ropes off the boat and, you," he turned to Melina. "Get into the boat!"

They cast off, awkwardly but effectively.

"Now if I can get this damned thing in gear." He was talking to himself, aloud.

"Here," the girl said, taking his hand in the dark. "The lever is here, here beside the wheel. I know this much. Move the lever ahead, the boat goes back. Pull it toward you, the boat moves forward."

Here we go, the old ore-boat sailor from Back of the Yards, Uzzumekis thought. I wonder where the hell the compass is; there must be one. But the first thing is to get away from this God damned dock.

XV

FORTY miles off the Crimean coast, according to plan, *Skate* slowed to a two-knot hover, a speed which kept Chief Cate busy at his console to hold their depth of 200 feet. At any reasonable speed, *Skate* could keep her depth within a couple of inches, but slowed down, her diving planes were less effective and she tended to surge for which the chief of the watch was forced to compensate by minor adjustments of water into and out of the trim tanks. The slowdown was necessary to give the *Queen Zenobia* time to put the DSRV and Hale with a two-man crew over the side and take the miniature sub in tow. It was an awkward arrangement but necessary, for the *Queen* suffered certain disabilities which the DSRV was in condition to remedy, having both highly sophisticated sonar and underwater telephone.

"It'll also put her in a better condition to start to come to get us if any such thing should ever be necessary," Stephens said to Oulahan who regarded this as superfluous information since he knew it too. But then, he remembered, the old man has a tendency to talk slightly more than necessary when he is under pressure. However, it's all right with me, an innocent safety valve. Other guys might be running to the head every five minutes. Now that the pressure was beginning to be felt, Oulahan himself was standing watch on the underwater phone while Stephens was splitting his time more or less equally among Lieutenant (jg) Peter Zink, who had the con in the pulpit, Chief Guernic at his chart table, and Chief Cate at the console.

The time passed. It seemed like something over two weeks but it was in fact a little more than an hour and twenty minutes before Oulahan came from the phone and announced, "I have him on the horn."

Stephens went to the telephone and said, "Yes, John. You set?"

Hale's voice came hollowly back to him through the water. "We're set. Now what?"

"Got another line to the ship?"

"Yes, the boss is on it. The big boss."

"All right. I'm going ahead. Course zero-one-zero degrees. You follow until you're outside the limit. Around thirteen miles. After this you can hang onto me with sonar. I'll be coming out as briefed. From now on we'd better not use this thingamajig any more than necessary. Speed ten knots to the cutoff point; after that I'll be running dead slow."

"Okay. Good luck."

Stephens left the telephone and turned to Oulahan.

"We've got the watchdog," he said. "So let's get this over with. It's twenty hundred now. That'll give us an hour to spare on the other end, maybe a little less. I don't want to cut it too fine and, on the other hand, we don't want to hang around there any longer than necessary."

"We sure as hell don't," Oulahan said.

Under normal circumstances an atomic submarine, running submerged, is an extraordinarily peaceful, quiet and stable environment. To all outward appearance—except once when Nicolai came up from the wardroom and climbed up to the pulpit and was told to "get the hell off my bridge" by Zink—*Skate* remained so as she ran up to the Russian coast. Nicolai looked both shocked and hurt at this breach of *Skate's* usual courtesy, but he left. Orders were still given and received in subdued tones. Nevertheless, the tension was palpable. And it grew.

It grew also aboard the *Queen Zenobia*, where Admiral March, pacing from wing to wing of the small bridge, was having a grimly controlled case of the fidgets. He was also silently cursing Washington and all its works with particular attention to anything coming from the Pentagon, the Department of State, and, especially, the White House. *I ought to have something to be thankful for*, he thought, *and if I have* any blessings to count it's that we've got a calm sea running and it's dark. If it was rough, Hale would be having a miserable time back there at the end of that hawser.

Hale was, in fact, having a fairly wretched time but not particularly by the crankiness of his little craft. The DSRV, he found, had an ugly habit of yawing under tow, but that was supportable, though uncomfortable. What bothered him more was trying to estimate the true capacities of the DSRV if—he prayed not—he should have to use it under pressure. First there was the problem of how he could go about finding his target. And once he found it, what then? He knew, as Stephens had said, that if the DSRV was looking for him, others probably would too. And the DSRV, itself, was not immune to detection although, with its small size and slow speed, it would be a lot harder to pick up than the far bigger *Skate*. Then there was the question of sheer ability—and time —and batteries. He wondered if, under emergency conditions, he could appreciably strain the DSRV's passenger capacity of two dozen. Probably not much. That would depend partly, of course, on what condition *Skate* might be in; in plain language, which he didn't like but had to consider, that meant how many survivors he would have to take off. Submarines that had trouble also, as an essential ingredient of trouble, had casualties. Eight or nine miles to go—each way. That meant at least four hours out and the same back and a holdover for recharging. Jesus, what was he here for? A miracle?

On the *Queen's* bridge, Gottfried stood beside the helmsman studying the blackness ahead through binoculars. His eyes hurt and sometimes teared, so that it was frequently necessary to take a tissue to the lenses and to his eyes as well. He turned to the admiral.

"Sir, I think I'm picking up the white beacon. There's a flash off there. I may be wrong; its visibility range is charted at eight miles. No sign of the green one."

"Where?"

"Almost dead ahead. A little to port."

March took the glasses, staring at the nearly invisible horizon. He handed them back after five minutes.

"That's probably it. What time is it?"

"Twenty-three-fifteen, sir. According to that we should be about where we're supposed to be, maybe a little too close."

"Probably. We don't have *Skate's* navigation gear on this tub. I'll call Hale and tell him we're going to pull him off a little."

Gottfried was studying the blackness ahead again, where the shore should be.

"I'm sure it's the beacon, sir. I'm picking up more lights now."

The radarman sent a talker to the bridge to say he had the coast, a little more than 11 miles distant and no traffic that he could pick up from this distance at least. There was a stronger blip, bearing 332 degrees. Could that be the beacon on the windmill?

"It could be," Gottfried said, and called the engineroom. "We're coming about, but we've got that thing in tow. Give it ahead one third." Then to the helmsman. "Right rudder, easy. Come around to one-six-zero."

"Aye, aye, sir," the helmsman said, and the *Queen Zenobia* began a slow swing to starboard and out toward the relative —only relative—immunity from interference with Russia's unilaterally imposed twelve-mile limit. And a hell of a lot of good that will do us if they get really put out about this, Admiral March was thinking.

Aboard *Skate*, Chief Guernic came from the sonar room to report to Stephens that the *Queen* and her tow were dropping astern and turning.

"About time, Chief," Stephens said. "They were getting in too far. For a while there I thought they'd run up on the beach."

"Yes, sir," Guernic said. "But they're moving out now."

Stephens stepped up to the pulpit, dimly red lit to preserve night vision, and spoke quietly to Zink.

"Give the con to Mr. Oulahan," he said. "I want him to take the boat the rest of the way. I'll be going topsides."

"Aye, aye, sir," Zink said, both disappointed and relieved as Oulahan came up to the pulpit.

"Dick, rig for depth charge. Slow to three knots and cut down everything, including the air conditioning. From here in, we're sneaky."

If I had known it was going to come to this, Uzzumekis thought, I'd have either stayed in that Kraut prison or gone to the Pacific and let the Japs shoot my ass off. Here I'm practically doing it myself.

"Look, grandpa," he said to Kirov, "get that wornout flashlight from the girl and see if either of you can find anything that looks like a compass."

"A what?"

"A compass, damn it. The thing Columbus found his way around with."

They were clear of the harbor which, after all, had not amounted to much. Uzzumekis had been operating on ultimate simplicity, merely keeping the boat moving away from the few lights behind him. It was, of course, possible that any minute he would run into something, anything, a rock, a reef, another boat. It probably wouldn't matter what; if they did whack something, they were out of business and he was a long way from certain that they were in business in any case.

He was beginning to have a small, desperate fondness for the boat. The engine seemed to be a one or two lunger, but it ran with a steadfast chug. His eyes, now well acclimated to the dark, could make out the outlines: stubby, broad in the beam, a short mast. There was an awful stink of fish. He had found the throttle, a primitive affair, and by experimenting had found that he could coax a little more energy and thus, presumably, speed, out of it. But speed going where? Unless he had at least a rudimentary compass and the light to see it by, he could miss the rendezvous by a mile or ten for that matter. Uzzumekis was not normally a man to feel helpless, but now he did.

"Have you found anything?" he asked, impatient with his passengers, thinking in anger how impossible this situation was, how impossible even to conceive.

"The time," Kirov said. Uzzumekis was conscious of the dull, moving gleam of the flashlight behind him in the boat. "It is a quarter after midnight. The rendezvous is between one o'clock and twenty minutes later. Is it possible?"

"How do I know whether it is possible," Uzzumekis retorted. "I might have some glimmer of an idea if I knew where we are. All I know is it is wet."

Kirov chuckled, and it reminded Uzzumekis, in anger, how misplaced the old bastard's rare flashes of humor had a way of being.

"You will do well to find it then," Kirov said. "I would dislike going into court and being forced to testify that you have murdered two of my countrymen."

"I may make it three if you don't shut up—and find something to steer by."

Kirov chuckled again.

Suddenly the girl spoke. "I see the beacon. Behind us and a little to the right. I am sure of it. I have seen it many times."

That, at least, is some help, Uzzumekis thought. He slowed the boat and turned to look. It was there, all right. Every ten seconds a bright snarl of white light, flashing out of the murky dark. Could he estimate direction from it? Possibly— if he took into account the dim lights of the town behind them. Then, unexpectedly, he was a little heartened when he thought he glimpsed dimmer, quicker flashes of green more to the right. That could be the other beacon; if it was, that could help. It would be a guess and a meager one at that. But distance? What did he know about distance at sea? Brother, I wish I had spent a few more seasons on that ore boat.

And what did he think of these two people behind him? A job. An errand he had been given to do and had—thanks to some weird chances, a drunken truck driver, a crippled old

man who now, for all he knew, might be dead—got away
with so far. The girl . . . he didn't know . . . it was true he had
lain with her—you couldn't properly say slept with her since
it had been on the floor of a boxcar on a cold night in the
presence of a recently and personally killed corpse and a dirty-
minded old politician. A quick, mostly accidental lay in the
course of other more serious business? Well, no, he guessed
not. He had to admit she had been brave—and resourceful.
And, he remembered with a kind of speeded-up nostalgia for
what had taken place only two—or was it three—nights ago,
she had been unbelievably sweet and moving in her accept-
ance of them together. Oh hell, here she was. If anybody was
going to get her to where she had a reasonable chance of
safety, it had to be himself. The politician? The old bastard
irritated him more often than not. But, here again, the same
buzzing question : Kirov had pulled his weight; he hadn't
freeloaded except when Uzzumekis had forced him to stay
under whatever cover was available. He had guts enough
almost to fill his monumental belly. I guess I hope I get them
there. But how? Has that theoretical submarine got one
theoretical chance in hell of finding us? He turned again to
look at the beacon, hoping that by some miracle it would tell
him something impossible to tell.

"I fix us here," Guernic said, putting a pencil point on the
chart as he and Stephens bent over it. "We're two and a half
miles off the beach and inside what the Russians call a prohibited area. We wouldn't be popular here, sir."

"We never expected to be," Stephens said. "And we don't
expect to stay long. We're about to surface. What'll I see
when I get up there?"

"There should be that Karan light on the hill, the one
you're shooting for. White, ten-second flash. Should be almost
dead ahead."

"Dead astern is more like it, Chief. We'll turn her around
to one-eight-zero while we're coming up. What else?"

"The green three-second light at the harbor. It'll be on

your port quarter. At this distance there'll be about a twenty-four-degree spread between the two lights. That's as close as I can make it, Captain; I couldn't pin it any closer with a microscope. You may see some town lights, too—if the Russians stay up this late."

Stephens put a hand on the chief's shoulder. "Next time in port I'll get you a microscope—not that I think you need it."

He went and stuck his head into the sonar room where Lieutenant Grady Johnson was hovering over the instrument.

"You get anything?" he asked.

Johnson pulled off his headset as he turned, and the sonar's pinging came loud from the earphones.

"Had a ship on here half an hour ago. It faded out, moving west."

"What'd it sound like?"

"Destroyer, maybe. I couldn't be sure."

"Okay. Cut her down to passive now; we're through advertising."

"Aye, aye, Captain."

"A destroyer figures," Stephens added. "That navy base is just around the bend." Whew, Stephens thought, wouldn't it be dandy to surface under the keel of a Russian destroyer? If he's faded, good, and I hope to hell he stays faded. My mother shouldn't have bothered to raise her son to be a sailor.

He turned toward the pulpit, noting as he did so, the two helmsmen lounging in their comfortable swivel chairs, seemingly resting their butts with their hands scarcely on the airplane-style control wheels. But he knew they weren't goofing off and that their eyes would be roving over the depth gauges, inclinometers, cavitation lights and course repeaters banked above them. It didn't take much real work to handle *Skate*. But it did take a great deal of attention.

He stepped up beside Oulahan.

"Get her turned around and surface," he said. "This Chinese fire drill is about to come to a conclusion. What's your depth?"

"A hundred ten."

"When you make sixty take a look with the scope."

"Natch. Where'll you be?"

"On the ladder with the quartermaster. I want to hit the bridge fast. Come up on the planes as much as you can, and tell Cate not to blow any more air than he has to."

He turned to the talker beside Oulahan. "Pass the word for Chief Cummings," he said. "Get him up here on the double —and tell him to bring two good deck hands. The best he's got."

"Aye, aye, sir," the talker said, and spoke softly into his microphone.

Shortly Chief Machinist's Mate William Cummings came through from the engineering spaces where he kept his battle station as boss of *Skate*'s damage control organization. Chief Cummings was a short, broad man, with thinning blond hair, popping blue eyes, and an increasing tendency to gut since he had, on Guernic's advice, quit smoking. The job of damage control normally should have belonged to a commissioned officer, but Cummings was a man of such an enormous and apparently inexhaustible talent for making things work when they didn't want to that he had got damage control, among several other assignments, by natural inheritance. He also possessed other skills. Nobody had ever got around to counting them all, but among the lot—although it did seem a little incongruous—he was a superb seaman.

"Yes, sir?" Cummings said as he came into the con where Stephens stood beside Guernic at the radar screen.

"Just a second, Chief," Stephens said. Then to Guernic, "I want this screen guarded like it was your mother. We're looking for a small boat. That's our target; we're going to take the people off it. When you spot anything, get word to me on the bridge on the double. And tell Chief Cummings here. He'll be right beside you."

He turned to Cummings. "You got your men, Chief?" Cummings nodded. "All right, put them on the ladder to the main deck hatch. Have them take a heaving line and a boat hook. There should be a boat up there somewhere—two

210

people. When I pass the word down, get up there and get them aboard, then get back down and button her up. Once I see you've got them aboard, we're going under again. And fast. Got all that?"

"Aye, aye, Captain," Cummings said. He was grinning.

"And wipe that silly smile off your face, Chief," Stephens said, grinning back. It occurred to Stephens that his own grin felt a little stiff.

Normally the chore he had just assigned to Cummings would have been a job for chief of the boat. But it was so arranged aboard *Skate* that Chief Joseph Cate, now chief of the watch, could not be spared just now for anything else. He was at the console, sucking in water or blowing it out, playing *Skate*'s depth-keeping capacities with the virtuosity of Pablo Casals on a cello.

Stephens turned quickly away and went back to Oulahan on the pulpit.

"All set, Dick?"

"As I'll ever be."

"Okay. Cummings will crack the main deck hatch and grab our cargo. Pass the word not to crack anything else. The only holes in this boat are going to be that one and the bridge hatch."

"Aye, aye. Take a breath of fresh air for me. It's getting stuffy in here."

"Sixty-five, coming to sixty-four," the diving officer's talker repeated.

"Sixty-three, coming to sixty-two."

"I'll go now. If there's anything on that scope, sing out."

Stephens got down off the pulpit, circled around it and got his hands on the rails of the ladder leading to the sail. Above him a quartermaster's mate was already crouched under the first of the two hatches that would take them up through the sail, into the night, into open air. Into what else?

"Fifty-eight, coming to fifty-seven," a talker said behind them.

"Nothing on the tube that I can see," Oulahan called from

behind them. "It's blacker than the inside of a witch's brassiere out there."

"Fifty coming to forty-nine," the talker called.

"Anything on the radar?" Stephens called to Guernic.

"Yeah. The beach line. Nothing else yet."

"Forty coming to thirty-nine."

Hell, Stephens thought, was this all just for fun? His hands were tense on the ladder rails and slippery. Sweating like a damn pig, he knew with disgust.

"Thirty-two coming to thirty-one," the talker said.

"Permission to crack the hatch?" the quartermaster's mate above Stephens called down.

"Permission granted," the diving officer's talker called.

"Crack the thing. Let's go!" Stephens said and watched as the man spun the wheel which withdrew the locking bolts. The lower hatch sprang open with a gush of air and Stephens saw the man's hat leap off his head and sail upward into darkness. Stephens was on his heels as the man reached the second hatch and began undogging it. Then they were out of the pressure hull, swiftly, in darkness, by the feel of long knowledge, going up the ladders through two more levels from which sea water was still burbling out. As Stephens swung himself through the bend and onto the tiny bridge deck the quartermaster was already swinging open the doors which, when submerged, streamlined *Skate's* topknot.

"You've got the suitcase?" Stephens asked, as he straightened up in cool damp darkness.

"Yes, sir," the sailor said, opening the box which carried *Skate's* earphones, microphones, and course repeater to the bridge whenever she surfaced. "It's plugged in, sir. Do you want to take it yourself?"

"This time, yes," Stephens said, reaching for the headset. "Bridge here. I'll take the con now." From below he could hear the gush of air and burble of water being pumped overside as Chief Cate began blowing tanks just enough to keep *Skate* awash. Too damn much noise, Stephens thought, but it can't be helped.

Stephens, night glasses to his eyes, circled the horizon. He saw the white beacon sending its repetitive wink from the hill and, after a moment, much lower down and to his right as he looked at it, the feebler green blinking of the harbor beacon. Right on the money; thank the Lord for Guernic. But where the hell is that boat?

Where the everlasting hell are we? Uzzumekis was asking himself in baffled anger. He thought he was keeping the beacon dead behind him, but the darkness was confusing, and he wasn't sure, in any case, which direction he was taking from the beacon except that he was going away from it and thus presumably away from shore. But that didn't mean that he was necessarily going toward the submarine—if indeed the submarine had ever arrived.

I knew this whole lashup was impossible from the first, he told himself. It had to be thought up by a bunch of lunatics in the first place. And, he thought ruefully, I had to be a candidate for the loony bin myself to let them suck me into it.

"What time is it now?" he snarled at his passengers.

"Ten minutes after one," the girl replied, as the flashlight gleamed for a pale moment.

"What do you propose to do?" Kirov asked.

"Pray," Uzzumekis answered. "I suggest you try some of the same. Either that or jump overboard."

Kirov chuckled. "The praying, perhaps. The jumping I decline. This may end in disaster. That has been possible from the beginning, but I see no profit in anticipating it."

"What time do you make it?" Stephens called down to the con.

"Zero-one-ten, sir," his earphones replied.

Looks like it was all wasted, Stephens thought. What a bloody shame. We're in a lousy place to be. They've got to have radar in there, and if they ain't asleep they should have had a fix on us by now. Maybe they don't know what we are yet, but they sure ought to know we're here. I don't know how far I'm justified in exposing my boat and my people. Another ten minutes? Not any more than that. Then we hightail.

Suddenly his earphones began to clatter. It was Guernic's voice, and it was tense.

"Captain, we've got a blip! Fourteen hundred yards off the port quarter."

"What's it look like?" Stephens demanded, feeling the tension mount into his throat.

"It's small. It could be what we're after."

"Is it under way?"

"Yes. But slow. Five knots."

"Closing?"

"No." Stephens could hear the disappointment in Guernic's voice. "Crossing. Going to port."

Jesus! What a spot, Stephens thought. Nearly another mile closer to the beach. And we don't even know it's them. But we've got to find out. And that means turning around and heading in instead of out.

"Give me a course and bearing. We're going to have to run them down."

"Three-four-zero should intercept, sir," Guernic said.

I knew he'd have it plotted, Stephens thought. He called down to the con talker and told him to put Oulahan on.

"Dick," he said. "Spin her around on her tail and go after them. Starboard. Ten knots. I don't like this, and I don't want to waste any time on it. Tell Cummings to stand by. I don't want him to crack the hatch until we're alongside and I know who it is or what it is. Tell Guernic to keep giving me the bearing and distance. I'll tell you when I see it."

Even as he finished talking, he could feel *Skate* heeling into her turn, and soon, as she gathered speed, he could see the rising white wash of her bow wave. If they don't pick us up now, they never will. God damn it, why couldn't the blasted boat have been where it was supposed to be? Five minutes ought to do this.

He was straining his eyes ahead, covering a sector just to starboard where Guernic said the blip should be. Stephens' eyes were good at night but now he raged at them for failing to serve him better. Then he saw it, a small blob of blacker blackness in the black.

"Three hundred yards, sir," came Guernic's voice. "Closing fast."

"Dick," Stephens called to Oulahan. "I've got it in sight. It's a small boat. It could be them. Take the speed off her and come alongside."

Uzzumekis felt a moment of terror when he first made out the loom of *Skate*'s sail rushing down. His instinct was to turn away and run, and, before his brain took charge again, he was already jerking at the wheel. Then realization hit him like a fist and he reached for the switch and cut the little boat's engine as the monster slowed and came alongside.

"Uzzumekis? Is that Uzzumekis?" a voice called out of the blackness somewhere above him.

He stood up, grabbing the mast for support as the boat bobbed in the swell of the submarine's arrival.

"You're God damned right it's Uzzumekis," he bellowed. He turned to his passengers and spoke in Russian. "Get ready to do whatever they want you to do. You are still a lucky man, Kirov."

Leaning over the bridge, feeling a desperate sense of urgency, Stephens heard the clang of the deck hatch as it opened and then the sure-footed scramble of Cummings' sea detail. Now he could see that there were three figures in the boat. Wasn't it supposed to be two? Who was the other? A boatman? Well, one thing was sure, he wasn't going to leave any witnesses to *Skate*'s strange voyage.

"Chief," he yelled down to where Cumming's men already had a line aboard the small boat.

"Yes, sir?" Cummings yelled back.

"Get 'em all! And get 'em quick!" He turned to the

quartermaster's mate beside him. "Pack up and get below. We're getting out of here." He started down almost on the sailor's shoulders, and, as he hit bottom, the upper hatch was already dogged and the lower one was in the process of getting the same treatment. He was barely conscious of figures scrambling awkwardly down the other ladder from the main deck hatch. Good Christ, he thought, one is a woman. Cummings appeared at his elbow.

"All secured, sir."

"Well done, Chief," he said, as he was already turning to Oulahan. "Get her under. Emergency," he said. "As soon as you're under, turn starboard to one-eight-zero. That'll put us back about where we're supposed to be. As soon as you've got water enough get down to four hundred feet. And I want to see thirty-five knots out of this tub!"

"Yessir, Captain," Oulahan said, grinning.

"Passing one-seven-five coming to one-eight-zero," the call came from the helm.

They had 100 feet between the keel and the black surface off Balaklava, Stephens saw with satisfaction. They were back on their preordained course. There were 260 fathoms within 15 miles of the coast, and then they could get down where *Skate* felt her best. He could feel the smooth surge of power as the speed built up. We brought it off, he thought, inwardly hugging the boat, his crew and himself. I wonder if it's too early to call Hale to call Gottfried and tell him it's time to skedaddle.

"How far are we off the coast?" he asked Guernic.

"Four miles, sir," Guernic said. I suspect he's grinning, Stephens thought. Very unprofessional if he is, but it's hard to tell under all that bush. I'll wait a few more minutes on the good ship *Queen Zenobia*, I think. We could still be hit.

And just then, they were hit. The blow came out of the sea like a titanic fist. The shock drove Stephens' head forward against the periscope tube and stunned him. He was down on his knees, instinct driving him to fight his way onto his

216

feet. The lights were gone, he knew. He could hear the rattle and tumble of dislodged gear and the grunts of men.

"Get light in here," he thought he yelled, although what actually came out of his throat was more of a croak. "Get the battle lanterns on!"

He was on his feet and groping for the torch he knew was secured alongside the periscope housing. A dim blue battle lantern came alive alongside Chief Cate's console and Stephens stumbled down and crouched beside the chief. Stephens saw Cate was bleeding, blood dripping down his arm and hand, smearing the toggles of his realm.

"What's she doing?" he gasped.

Cate turned a dazed face toward him.

"Dropping."

"Blow everything. Get her up."

"I'm blowing." Stephens could hear the powerful rush of air, compressed at 2000 pounds an inch.

"She's not coming," Cate said. "She's down by the stern and I'm not holding her."

Skate hit bottom in 328 feet of water. She lay more or less level fore and aft, but as Stephens saw on the inclinometer, she was listing about nine degrees to starboard.

He set out to make inventory, to assay what had happened to his boat and what therapy it would need to mend her.

XVI

GUARDING his sonar, Lieutenant Hale was accurately aware of *Skate*'s progress, which he in turn kept reporting to Admiral March aboard the *Queen Zenobia*. He knew when *Skate* made her first turn and broke the surface at 0103 hours. While she lay there for ten minutes he found himself sweating from the sheer desperate need to know what was happening. He was baffled when she made her turn back toward the Russian coast. Christ, he's getting in close! he thought. But then she dived and turned back toward him and was getting deeper and picking up speed.

"*Skate* is under and coming out," he told the admiral.

"Thank God," the admiral said, and turned to Gottfried and clapped him on the shoulder, which was a very unadmiral sort of thing to do.

"He's done it!" he said. "Let's get this little old rust bucket of ours turned around and ready to haul ass. I am already sick of being a Panamanian sailor."

"Glory, glory!" Gottfried breathed. "Do you want to take the DSRV aboard now, sir?"

"No, I think not. We'll wait a little bit. Stephens will be coming out of there like a bat out of hell, and it won't take him long. But I want Hale's sonar to sit on him a little bit—just to make sure."

He went back to the phone to Hale.

"What's he doing now?" he asked.

"Down to one hundred feet and doing twenty knots, sir."

"How's he bear?"

"Three fifty-five true, sir."

"Good! Stay with him."

"Aye, aye, sir. He's still picking up speed."

The telephone was silent for roughly fifty seconds. Then

Hale's voice came on again. But this time, instead of jubilant, it was tight with sudden strain.

"Admiral! Something's happening."

"For God's sake, what?"

"I think something has hit him. There was a sudden—something like a jar, an impact. Just now."

"Is he still coming?"

"Yes. But slower. And going deeper."

"What's his distance now?"

"Just about seven and a half miles. But the speed is dropping fast."

Admiral March began to curse, then broke off and went back to Hale. His voice, usually either crisp or fierce, had gone hoarse.

"Keep a fix on him. A tight one!"

Gottfried was staring at the admiral, his face all at once drawn and gray.

"What's happening?"

"It looks like the bloody bastards tagged him. Hale got the impact and now *Skate's* slowing down." He turned back to the telephone.

"Distance and bearing now," he demanded.

"Seven miles and still three-five-five. He's down close to three hundred feet now."

"Still moving?"

"Dead slow, sir."

Time had lost any sense of reality, but it was actually just over five minutes from Hale's sudden awareness of the change in *Skate's* condition when he called to report.

"I've lost the signal."

"Lost it? What the hell do you mean, lost it?" the admiral snarled.

"I think he's hit bottom, sir. He may have come down in a depression that blanks him off."

"Give me the tightest fix you had on him last."

"Just under seven miles. Still the same bearing, sir."

The admiral cursed again and turned to Gottfried. "He's

down, I guess. As soon as Hale gives us the best fix he can make, I want it plotted tighter than a gnat's rear end."

"Yes, sir."

"Then get Hale aboard and make sure that damn little kettle is ready to go."

"Aye, sir. You're going to send Hale after him?"

"What the hell else did you think I would do? That's what we're here for. We've got to find him."

"God," Gottfried breathed, appalled, as the knowledge of what was expected of his shabby little vessel and the DSRV, in partnership, really sank in. He had considered it of course; in this business you had to consider ultimate possibilities. But really believe in it? No. But it had come. And now, right under the Russian noses, practically under the Russian guns, this untried, jury-rigged, pitifully inadequate little expeditionary force faced the duty of getting *Skate*'s people out. If, indeed, any of *Skate*'s people were still alive. Moreover, he knew, it was not a duty that could be declined—or in any way shirked—merely because it was impossible.

Ships are built and their men are steeled to heal themselves when hurt. If this were not so the oceans never would have yielded even a partial victory to seafaring men. By the time *Skate* hit bottom and took a list to starboard six minutes after she was wounded, the effort for survival was already under way. Lights were on again, now drawing direct current from the emergency battery banks. Stunned men were picking themselves up and getting back to their stations. Stephens knew that the next watertight compartment aft was still intact because he had called through and got a response when he ordered all engineering noise shut down. Whatever had hit him once could almost surely hit him again if it knew where to find him. *Skate* would issue no invitation.

"Try blowing her again, Chief," he said to Cate who, despite blood still dripping generously from a long and deep gash in his right arm, was still at his console.

Stephens heard the ferocious rush of 2000-pound air as

Cate tripped the toggles. Then he felt *Skate* begin to stir sluggishly. But she wasn't stirring the right way. Instead she was slowly coming up by the bow while the stern refused to budge.

"I'm not getting anything aft," Cate said. Aside from the fact that his normally gaunt face was now fiercely concentrated, the only deviation from Cate's normal composure was that this time he neglected to employ the usual honorific when addressing the captain of the ship.

"All right. Let her down. I'll have to go look." He turned to Oulahan. "You hold things together in here. Have the pharmacists find out how many and what kind of casualties we have forward. Send Johnson to make sure the passengers keep quiet. Tie 'em up and gag 'em if you have to."

There had not yet been time to pay much attention to the men in the control room, but as he turned to look for Cummings who had remained there after taking the fugitives aboard he was oddly struck by a figure braced against the sonar room door. It was quivering, he saw, pale as milk, eyes wide in terror; he could smell the fear coming out of it. In a bind like this he didn't expect the men to be happy; and neither was he. But this animal panic. Who was it anyhow? Then he remembered: the replacement communications man, a kid fresh from school, what had Guernic called him? Quill? That might be one to keep an eye on. The ship wasn't safe by a long shot, but it was necessary to guard what safety it had.

He saw Cummings standing near Guernic's chart table and called him. "Chief, let's go find out what they did to us." But the chances were, he considered, that there wouldn't be much they could ever do by themselves to get this boat afloat and alive and under way again. At least not while he himself was still alive. There was no time yet to tot up what all that implied. The thing now was to survey the damage and calculate the chances.

There's the DSRV, he thought. They must know about where we are. They were keeping watch on us. But it's chancy at best with only a makeshift back-up vessel and the necessity of even that staying outside the twelve-mile limit.

"Aye, aye, Captain," Cummings said and moved to undog the first of three watertight doors which would lead them toward the stern.

They stepped over the high coaming and into the compartment which was a tight-packed jungle of navigation gear— SINS, NAVDAC, their computers—the air-conditioning and scrubbing machinery—now silent—with even the ship's office cramped into a tiny left-over corner. Cummings turned to dog the door behind them. *Skate* was still rigged to withstand depth charging.

In the dim light, Stephens saw the taut faces of some of the fifteen men whom *Skate*'s battle bill required to be there in times of stress. He recognized a first-class named Janicek, a burly man with heavy features and a skin as dark as a Cherokee's, who, he remembered, was chief of the watch in this compartment.

"Any damage in here?" he asked.

"Some, sir. To gear. The SINS carried away, and I'm afraid it's a goner. Some other small gear. We got a hell of a punch in the tail."

"How are the men?"

"Five bunged up, sir. One is still out, cold as an ice cube. Could we get a pharmacist in here, sir? I don't like the looks of that one. Name's Gross."

"I know who he is. Call the con and tell them I said to send you somebody."

"Sir, can I ask what shape the ship's in?"

"That's what the chief and I want to find out. We're going aft. Dog the hatch after us, will you?"

"Aye, aye, sir."

Cummings was already undogging the door which would lead to the reactor compartment. The men around them stared in frozen tension as Cummings worked. Until that door was open they had no way of knowing what waited on the other

222

side. If it was sea water, they would all be dead in less than minutes.

It was not. The tunnel over the reactor, extraordinarily small because the compartment was taken up almost entirely by the atomic furnace itself and its massive shielding, was dry. And empty. Nobody lived with the reactor. It wasn't necessary, since the monster's output was controlled from the other side of the bulkhead. I've always been curious what, if anything, would happen if you put a torpedo into one of these things, Stephens wondered as they crossed over the shield toward the door leading to the engineroom. I know what the wizards say : nothing would happen, the core would simply disintegrate and drown itself in sea water. But then the wizards have never actually blown one up to find out for sure. And I wouldn't want to be too close if they did.

The door came undogged, and Cummings went through with Stephens on his heels. They stepped down into something that wasn't quite a shambles but was surely less than shipshape. Stephens turned and dogged the door shut behind him. The light was a dim glow, and at first all he could make out was the bulk of the engines which, in happier circumstances, fed the reactor's enormous power to *Skate*'s twin screws.

He heard noises unfamiliar here : a heavy thumping of metal, a slow hiss of escaping steam, a cascade of rushing water under pressure, the groans of a man. Out of the gloom appeared Lieutenant Gus Bartoli, *Skate*'s chief engineer.

"What've you got in here?" Stephens asked.

"A mess, Captain. One man dead; anyhow I think he's dead. The concussion apparently drove his head against something."

"Let me see him.

"He's here, between the engines. Here, here's a flashlight. You can see better."

Stephens knelt beside the sprawled body, a thin figure in blue denim pants and shirt. It lay with that peculiar receding flatness of the dead. The man's face was smashed so that

Stephens who thought he knew every man in the crew could not recognize him. He pressed the skull above the eyes and felt pulpy bone giving under the skin. He stood up.

"Not much doubt about that. What else?"

"Man with a broken leg, another with a bad back; I don't know whether it's broken. Assorted bruises and cuts."

"I'll get the pharmacists in here right away. What about the machinery?"

"The engines will run, but they seem to have come loose from the screws. Sheared the shafts, I guess."

"What about the stern compartment?"

"It's gone I think. We're getting some water in here through the after bulkhead."

"How's it holding?"

"All right so far. It could stand some work. And there's something thumping around back there. I don't like that."

Cummings, who had asked for the flashlight, was at the rear of the engineroom, stabbing the light from point to point against the bulkhead. Stephens and Bartoli went to join him.

"You're right," Cummings said to Bartoli. "It can stand some work. How many men can I have, Captain?"

"What you need. How many able-bodied men have you got in here?" he asked Bartoli.

"Six, I think. The rest need some patching up."

"All right," Stephens said to Cummings. "You take who-ever's here that can still work. I'll send you more."

For the first time he noticed that Bartoli's right arm hung limp in his sleeve.

"You look as though you could stand some patching up yourself. What happened?"

"Busted, I think. I got slammed into something. I don't know what."

"You'd better come forward with me. I'll send a party to bring the other wounded out. We'll leave the rest to the chief for now; patching things is his specialty. Okay, Chief?"

"Yes, sir," Cummings said. "I'll get with it, although I don't think it's going to come apart right away."

"How many men were in the stern compartment?" Stephens asked Bartoli.

"Seventeen. I haven't heard anything from them. I think you can count them out, Captain."

Back in the con, feeling infinitely weary, knowing that every man in the compartment had pleading eyes on him, feeling both helpless and guilty, Stephens stepped up beside Oulahan, who turned on him a look of somber inquiry.

"How bad?" Oulahan asked in a low voice.

"Bad. Eighteen dead, four badly hurt. Stern compartment entirely gone. Screws gone. Rudder and stern planes gone. We're out of business."

"What're we going to do?"

"You know. Pipe down and wait for the DSRV. We can do a little praying, too."

XVII

In a mood somewhere between triumph and total depression —more of the second than the first, he admitted to himself— Sobelov made an appointment and reported to the First Secretary. At least, this time, it was daylight which would save him from having to endure the bleakness of a man who had neither shaved, showered, nor had breakfast. It was going to be unpleasant enough any way one looked at it.

"Well?" the First Secretary said. The tone confirmed Sobelov's private expectations.

"Kirov got away. But not clear away."

"Comrade, that statement needs explaining. And before you begin to explain I will tell you something you know already: in the Soviet Union failure is not a virtue to be rewarded."

I know it better than he does, Sobelov thought; I have disposed of enough failures myself. Now I am one and I know what to expect. Nevertheless, until it comes, there remains a duty to be performed. He steeled himself to get on with it and knew that his face was as blandly impassive as always.

"They were successfully intercepted at Balaklava. My man, Gagarin, rightly predicted that they would attempt to escape through that port. He had found the fisherman who had been influenced to take them to a rendezvous with an American submarine."

The First Secretary's brow furrowed and grew blacker.

"Then why were they not stopped?"

"Because Gagarin was murdered on the dock. We have found his body. Probably foolishly in search of glory, he tried to make the arrest alone."

"You permit this kind of independent action in your bureau?" The First Secretary's voice, Sobelov considered, was colder than a Siberian winter.

"Normally not, of course. But the circumstances were . . . unprecedented. There were many holes to watch. And Gagarin was among the best of my men."

"A dead bumbler is of even less use than a living one. And after the murder?"

"They stole the fisherman's boat. He had run away, as had been arranged with Gagarin. Thus he could not stop them. Nor, probably, would he have tried once Gagarin was dead."

"You said Kirov did not get clear away. Explain that."

"We believe he got to the American submarine. In any case we have, this morning, found the abandoned boat in the sea some two miles out of Balaklava Harbor. Because we anticipated the arrival of the submarine our patrols were alerted. A torpedo boat, commanded by a Lieutenant Vasiliev, fired one acoustic torpedo—and struck the submarine."

"Do you mean to tell me you have sunk an American submarine?"

"I believe so, sir. It was in Russian territorial water."

"Nevertheless, as I suppose even you could guess, this sinking could start a war. I do not believe I ever told you that even Kirov was worth that."

"No, sir, you did not. But you did tell me not to let Kirov get away."

"And, evidently, he did not. Where is the submarine now?"

"We know within a mile or two. We are searching for it."

"Are there survivors?"

"We do not know of a certainty. We suppose probably there are since the torpedo was a small one guided by sound. Most probably it struck the submarine in the stern, where the propellers are, and disabled them."

"Why haven't you found it?"

"The navy is searching—with a device which I believe they call sonar."

"I know about sonar," the First Secretary said impatiently. "It seems to me strange that if the navy knew where the submarine was precisely enough to sink it, it should not also know where to find it now."

"I should think so, although of course that is not my field."

"I am beginning to wonder, Sobelov, precisely what your field is. Kirov has been allowed to escape. We do not know whether he is dead or alive at this moment. An American warship has been able to come through the Turkish Straits and invade our coast. It has engaged in piracy. Legally, I suppose, our navy was justified in sinking it. The Americans are fools, fools—but that, Sobelov, does not exempt you from the same category."

"Yes, sir."

"Find that submarine. If there are people alive, get them out alive. If possible get the ship as well. I want Kirov's body —alive or dead. I imagine the navy has salvage equipment at Sevastopol."

"I believe so, sir."

"Get them working. With everything necessary."

"Yes, sir."

"There are decisions to be reached, which also are not in your field. I must now consult."

The three of them, the First Secretary, the President, and the Chairman of the Council of Ministers, were assembled in the First Secretary's office.

"I know that we do not always agree. It is a disadvantage which neither Stalin nor Kirov—in their times—suffered, since each of them was everything," the First Secretary said. "However, this matter is so grave that this time we must get some concert of agreement out of this *troika*."

"It seems to me simple," said the President, who was a much fiercer man than his stooped figure and professorial features would indicate. "We have been invaded. That alone is enough to justify any measure. Kirov has been snatched from under our noses. Consider what capital the Americans would make of him if they could by some miracle rescue him.

I say find the submarine and then bomb it until we are absolutely certain that nothing remains alive. Precisely that!"

"And start a war?" The Chairman, a big man who had come up to his present eminence through the armed services and had, for the last ten years, directed the development of Russia's intercontinental ballistic missile program, knew precisely what Russia's rockets could do. By the same token, he knew pretty accurately what America's rockets could do in return. He was, of course, glad that, if America had rockets, Russia had them, too. But, out of a sure knowledge, he hoped to God that nobody, anywhere, ever got around to firing one in anger.

"How do you know that we won't be in a war anyhow—once the Americans discover what has happened to their pirate submarine?" the President persisted. "We may already have destroyed the submarine. I merely propose that we make sure."

"We could take the case before the Security Council," the Chairman mused. "Properly put, the case could be a devastating exposure of American methods. Piracy, invasion, kidnaping, hostile trespass on a peace-loving nation. It would be a shocking indictment to lay before the world."

"It would also make us the world's funniest joke," the First Secretary said curtly. "We cannot afford even to have this known at home. Think of it. Kirov slides through our fingers like an eel. A thieving submarine brazenly challenges all our costly defenses—and nearly succeeds. For all we know, has succeeded."

"Are we sure that we know the submarine is American?" the Chairman asked.

"Without actually seeing it, I couldn't be more sure of it," the First Secretary replied. "Less than a week ago an American nuclear submarine was in Istanbul. It left there ostensibly sailing westward. It had to be there through Turkish connivance."

"Perhaps we should protest to the Turks," the President suggested. "If they allow the Straits restrictions to be abused, we can feel free to do the same. But I still say find the submarine and obliterate it."

"I don't mind making free with the Straits," the First Secretary said. "The Turks have opened the door, and so I do not see why, in future, we should accede to the Montreux limitations on our naval vessels passing to and from the Mediterranean—even submarines. However, a formal protest would do us the same disservice as publicizing the affair in the United Nations. We can afford many things, but becoming a laughingstock is not one of them.

"I will tell you what instructions I gave at once when this was reported to me only an hour ago. I have given orders that the submarine must be located as expeditiously as possible. That is preliminary to all else. If there are survivors—and I am told that is a likely possibility—I have instructed that they be brought out alive, if, again, that is possible. Above all, Kirov is to be taken alive."

"What are we to do with the others—if we get them?" the Chairman asked.

"There lies the possibility of an embarrassment, I confess. Trial? Prison? Execution? Send them home? Make an example of them and, so doing, make an example of the United States? It is greatly debatable—but the debate can wait until we get them—if we do.

"I have also ordered that, if the submarine itself is salvageable, it is to be raised."

"Ah," said the Chairman. "I can think of few things more interesting than to have an American nuclear submarine to examine at leisure."

"But we must always remember," the First Secretary said warningly, "that if we should salvage the vessel, the Americans would surely learn of it. I have no doubt that they would consider this a provocation of the gravest order."

"Who, I must ask again, instituted this provocation?" the President asked angrily. "Did we invite the submarine here to be sunk? Did we sink it as anything but self-defense? I still say bomb it."

The troika were powerful men, the most powerful then in Russia. All power, all decision rested with them. But they recognized that their power was measurably diminished by the fundamental disagreement of their temperaments. If matters ever came to a clear-cut showdown among them, beyond any sort of compromise, the First Secretary thought he might win since he held the reins of the Party. But he was not entirely sure, and because he was less than positive he continued to tolerate their cumbersome makeshift.

"I say we do not bomb it," he said now. "That would be a direct confrontation, and the Americans could not easily avoid going to war over it. However, some sort of confrontation between the two governments has now become necessary. After all, we both know what has taken place and know, as well, that it cannot be ignored. But it must be kept private. Otherwise we court disaster."

"What do you want to do?" the President demanded.

"Telephone the President of the United States. He will not want this publicized any more than we do." He turned to the Chairman. "From our side, the conversation should be carried on by you. After all, technically, you are his opposite number."

XVIII

"I'm going with you," Admiral March said to Hale as, with Gottfried, they conferred on the bridge of the *Queen Zenobia*. The DSRV lay alongside, a low, humpbacked whale rolling slightly in a sea which they all gave thanks was running quiet. The throb of engines forward gave testimony that the generators were pouring overside a steady river of energy into the little rescue submarine's battery banks.

"No, sir," Hale said respectfully. "I think you had better not. With all respect, sir, my men are expert technicians. I need both of them."

"Damn it, I was in submarines when you were in diapers."

"I agree, sir. But the DSRV is a different kettle of fish."

The hell of it is, March thought, I know he's right and I haven't any business trying to horn in. All the same, I brought these people here. The trouble with command, he had often thought, was that you had to send other people to do the dirty work. He had probably exceeded his proper role by coming this far with the Kirov expedition. He had come, like a mule, he admitted to himself, because he felt from the beginning that the venture was harebrained, imposed on the submarine service by abysmal ignorance in quarters too powerful to be refused.

"How long can you last on a full charge?" he asked, giving in.

"About nine, possibly ten hours—that is, if I keep the speed down. The way I intend to go it'll use about three hours to the general vicinity of *Skate* and three back. That gives me about two hours of looking time there. Each time back here, the batteries will have to be topped off. I'll admit it cuts it fine."

"Too fine," the admiral muttered.

One of Hale's back-up crew came onto the bridge and addressed him. "They're full, sir. She's ready to go."

"Very well," Hale said. "I'll be aboard in a minute."

"What if you do run out of juice?" Gottfried asked.

"I don't intend to," Hale said. "But if I did I'd be back pretty close to you by then. I'd surface, and you could pick me up on radar and come and get me."

"The Russians might not like that," Gottfried said.

"They haven't shown any evidence of liking any of this so far," the admiral said.

"It's oh-three hundred," Hale said. "Permission to cast off, sir?"

"Granted," March said.

Hale left the bridge and went down the ladders to the well deck and over the side on a rope ladder secured to the DSRV's low, streamlined conning tower. He was less than two feet off the surface when he slid through the hatch and dogged it behind him. He was in an almost empty spherical chamber fewer than eight feet in diameter. Aft of him was another pressure hatch which, he knew, led into a similar and even more barren chamber. That was for his passengers—if I get any, he thought grimly. Another hatch, at his feet, led into the transfer skirt, a hemisphere of seven-eighths-inch steel whose lower rim he would have to maneuver to mate with and seal onto *Skate's* escape hatch—if he found her. Then the water would be blown out of the skirt and the three pressure hatches, this one in the DSRV and two into and out of *Skate's* escape chamber would be opened and then, God willing, they would be in business.

In the forward wall of this sphere was still another hatch which now stood open, and, crouching almost to his knees, he slid through. Unlike the two spheres behind him, this was jammed to the gunnels with equipment and means to read and control other equipment installed all over the boat, outside the pressure spheres and recessed into or extending from the streamlined, nonpressurized outer propulsion hull of the DSRV. This forward sphere was Hale's office, the very

233

center of his work world, and he never entered it without feeling again a great, satisfying swell of proprietary pride. Along with the pride was a constant nagging apprehension that he might not prove as smart as his vehicle, once the chips were down.

He knew he had everything the most advanced electronic sciences could pack into this space and put under command of his hands and brain. In essence, the concept of the DSRV taking living men off a helpless submarine was simple—the center sphere, its skirt and hatch amounted to an adaptation of the old McCann Rescue Bell—but in materialized reality it was an Orwellian fantasy. There were roughly ten kinds of sonar, counting the variations. He had sonar to track, sonar to reveal depth, sonar to feel to both sides and upward, sonar to home on an object, sonar to search out obstacles above and below and to both sides, sonar to tell him by Doppler effect whether an object was getting closer or moving away and high resolution sonar for the transcendently delicate job of mating the DSRV to the escape hatch of his target.

He had lights, ordinary illumination and high intensity search lights to spot his target and hold it in a shimmering glare at any depth in which the DSRV could operate. He had still cameras and closed circuit television cameras and could pan them, from his pilot's seat inside the forward sphere, to focus on anything he wanted or needed to look at. Under the DSRV's belly he had an articulated metal arm which he could control from his cubicle to—if necessary—clear away wreckage from the disabled submarine or to perform most other chores that a man could perform and some that no man could.

There were myriad sensors all over the boat, for velocity, direction, sound velocity, pressure and differentials in pressure. He had radio and he had underwater telephone by which he could talk to his mother ship or to the object of his search. He had, in a number of strategic places, thick conical plastic viewports by which he and his men could see with their own eyes what the electronic gear said was going on

234

outside. These viewports offered no danger of letting the sea invade the DSRV since their shape, with the small end inward and serving as eyepiece, seated itself tighter the deeper the DSRV ventured.

He knew he could make five knots maximum with his stern-mounted battery driven propeller, but he also knew that such a speed was hell on the DSRV's batteries. In any case, for this mission—which was furtive by its nature—he wanted to proceed slowly to preserve both battery and stealth. When it came to the delicate final maneuvering, he had thirteen different kinds of ballast tanks from fore to aft which could be variously flooded or blown to put the DSRV at any angle —forward or aft, port or starboard—which was necessary. And then there were the ducted thrusters—outlets and inlets through which integral small propellers drew sea water at one point and shoved it over the side at another chosen angle —to move him, inch by inch, port or starboard, forward or aft, to a precise mating with the hatch from which the rescued would have to emerge. And finally, like the old McCann Bell, he also had a winch inside the skirt under the center sphere which could reach down, guided by automatons, to seize the "bail," the approximation of a bucket handle, and pull the DSRV into a perfect seal on the rescue hatch.

And so he had everything. This thing, Hale knew, was built to operate down to 3000 feet and below and he had been that deep in her. This time he had no such depth to worry about, perhaps only a tenth of that. But he did suffer certain disadvantages, the first being that his only surface support was the makeshift _Queen Zenobia_ lying there off the twelve-mile limit pretending to be a disabled tramp—which nobody is going to believe for very long, he thought. Then there was the fact that he was between six and seven miles, presumably, from his target and that was about the limit of his effective range. Also, he knew, his target was not going to help him since helping him required sound and the Russians could hear sound as well as he could. And, of course, there were the Russians.

235

Akers and Pauer, both chiefs and both supremely competent, awaited him in the tight little ball.

"We'll shove off now," he told them. "*Skate*'s been on the bottom two hours and it's time to go get her."

"Are we sure she's on the bottom?" Pauer asked.

"She was the last time we heard her. Unless he's playing possum for some reason we don't know, he's still there."

"Course and distance, sir?" Akers asked.

"Three fifty-five ought to fetch her. Around thirteen thousand yards. We may as well get down to three hundred feet immediately. That's about where she should be. Four miles off the coast the depth runs from forty-seven to fifty-three fathoms. Out here it's seventy to eighty."

"Ought to be a cinch," said Pauer, who was a cheerful optimist.

"You'd better hope so," Hale said. "Two knots. Two reasons: I want to save battery and I don't want to attract too much attention." Few submariners put overpowering weight on formality and Hale less than most. First, he was a mustang and thus had come up through the ranks; second, his crews were tight little units in which every man knew exactly what every other man was supposed to do and respected his ability to do it.

The miniature submarine began to move and to go down. At three hundred feet, the fathometer told her she was still 112 feet off the bottom which was gradually shoaling, uneven in places, occasionally deeper gulches. *Skate* could have slid into any one of those, Hale suspected. If she had, it will make her harder to find. It will also make *Skate* harder for the Russians to find. Fifty-fifty.

In the second hour when they were four miles from their takeoff point on the *Queen*'s flank, he began to be aware that somebody else was also probing these waters. Sonar was repeatedly picking up the passage of surface ships, crossing and recrossing the area.

"Lots of activity up there," Pauer observed.

"Yeah. And not friendly," Hale said. He wondered how

susceptible his small, slow-moving, relatively quiet vessel was to being spotted by the searchers above. Some, of course. He wondered what they would do if they got a fix on him. That could be interesting.

Three hours out, six and a half miles from the *Queen*, they had an average of fifty feet under the bottom.

"Come to dead slow," he said. "Turn on the TV and the lights and let's get down to about ten feet off the bottom. We'll begin the search pattern. He's got to be in here somewhere."

At 0500 hours, just about three and one half hours after *Skate* went down, Admiral March, who had been on his feet nearly twice around the clock, went below to see if he could get a little rest. He did not expect to sleep, but he was exhausted, and since no word could be expected from the DSRV for some six more hours, there was little he could hope to accomplish by remaining on the bridge.

"Call me if anything turns up," he told Gottfried.

Nevertheless he was sound asleep, fully dressed, when a messenger came to wake him at 0830. He got up reluctantly and went to the bridge. Gottfried, who was just as tired but younger and more resilient, handed him the binoculars and pointed toward the hazy beach. It was full daylight now, a gray day with low clouds which seemed to offer the prospect of rain.

"They've been busy out there, Admiral," he said. "Had a few blips on radar before sunup. Now you can see them. And now it looks as though we may be getting a little company too." He pointed.

March saw a ship approaching from perhaps five miles off. It was bow-on, and he found himself squinting, trying to recognize the type.

"What's radar got on him?" he asked.

"Twenty knots. He's closing pretty fast, sir."

"Well, we could've expected it. How far are we off the beach?"

"Thirteen miles, sir."

"So we're legal—even by their peculiar standards. The problem's going to be how much they respect their own standards."

March raised the glasses again. The ship was appreciably closer, and visibly now coming on at a good clip. A destroyer? No, hardly big enough. Patrol boat of some kind. March felt a peculiar, not really unpleasant, prickle of anticipation. Pretty soon now they were going to find out something. He was glad they weren't going to get caught with the DSRV alongside; that would take some explaining.

"Got your signalman briefed on the spiel?" he asked.

"Yes, sir. If they'll fall for it," Gottfried said.

"They can go to hell if they don't," the admiral said. "We're broken down, but we're in international waters. They can't claim anything like a salvage right."

When the vessel was within a mile, March could see that it was a fast patrol boat, mounting some armament forward. Possibly three inch, he speculated.

But when the ship passed them to port about 500 yards distant, he knew better, because he recognized it.

"You know what that is?" he asked Gottfried.

"Yes, sir," Gottfried answered. "It's what they call the S.O.1. class. Around two hundred tons, rocket launchers and four twenty-five-mm. twin mounts."

"What you possibly don't know, in your youth," Admiral March said, "is that they copied it from us. We gave them some of the same things in World War II. Sold was the word for it, but they never paid up. That's a carbon copy, the bastards. Chased by our own boat, by the Lord!"

The patrol boat went on by, abruptly took off speed, and turned around their stern. It came up on the starboard side and lay hove to. A signal light was blinking from its wheel house even before it stopped.

"He's asking who we are," the signalman said.

"Tell him," Gottfried said. "Be sloppy about it—as if you didn't know the lamp very well and the code even less. I don't want any navy smartness now. Be stupid—and slow."

"Aye, aye, sir," the signalman said. With an Aldis lamp, haltingly, in international code, he spelled out, "Syrian . . . from Latakia."

"What registry?" the Russian lamp demanded.

After hesitation, the *Queen*'s signalman asked for a repeat.

"What registry?" the Russian asked again, this time in spaced longs and shorts.

"Panama," the *Queen*'s lamp said at last.

"Where bound?"

Again the *Queen*'s incompetent lamp needed a repeat and after two such requests finally got the question through its head.

"Sevastopol."

"Are you in distress?"

That took even longer, but finally the Russian got his answer.

"Not—in—distress."

"Why are you here?"

Even as he waited for an answer the Russian got slowly under way and began to swerve in toward them. He's going to want to talk by hand, March knew. That can be sticky. I wish I'd thought to bring along somebody who could speak Russian. Oh well, maybe it's just as well to play dumb. He can't do anything about it. Or can he?

"Engine repair," the *Queen*'s lamp at last spelled out with agonizing lack of skill.

A hundred yards away, the Russian lay to again, and a figure on the bridge began shouting through a loud hailer. Gottfried stepped out on the *Queen*'s open bridge and raised his shoulders and threw up his hands in a gesture of despair and utter ignorance. For half an hour the Russian lay there, wallowing slightly in the easy swell while the *Queen* companionably lay where she was and wallowed with him.

Then, abruptly, the Russian put on speed and ran off toward the beach without further exchange of unsatisfactory information.

"Whew!" Gottfried said. "The language barrier got him."

The signalman turned away from his lamp, grinning with delight.

"He'll be back. Or somebody will," the admiral said.

At 1100 hours the Queen's lookout on the port quarter—there were a dozen stationed all over the little ship—saw something heaving to the surface and yelled that the DSRV was back. It was. Slowly it maneuvered up to the Queen's starboard side where a half dozen agile line handlers secured her against rope fenders which the Russian had not seen since they had been prudently stowed aboard while he was alongside.

What's he got? What's he got? March and Gottfried and everybody topsides kept asking themselves in an agony of anticipation until the hatch opened. Hale came up the rope ladder, then Pauer. Hale swung over the rail and spoke to his crew.

"Get the chargers on her. On the double. And get a couple of men down there to relieve Akers."

He came wearily up to the bridge. Gottfried and Admiral March waited for him. They didn't have to ask the question. It was engraved on them. And Hale answered.

"We were running low on juice. Just made it back as it was. Those lights raise hell with the batteries."

"Anything at all?" the admiral asked, feeling the sickness of expected failure.

"I'm not sure, sir," Hale said somberly. "We got a little echo a couple of times. That could be him. Now I know about where, I can check it out for sure next time without all that fiddling around. What makes it tough is the gullies; that bottom is cut up in a lot of places. That's probably why the Russians are having trouble finding him; they're sure looking. We had echoes overhead all day."

"I know. They're busy," the admiral said. "We had a visitor out here, too."

"I'm not surprised."

"Did they pick you up?"

"They could have. I don't make a lot of noise but I do make some. I had one boat sticking with me for quite a while until I shut everything down. I may have fooled him. Maybe not, though."

"Could it be he thought you were *Skate*?"

"I don't know. I was under way, and *Skate* sure isn't. She's down, sir, and I'm pretty sure I know about where."

This changes things, the admiral was thinking. Nobody's fooling anybody any longer. It's a hundred to one they know *Skate*'s there and sooner or later they'll find her. It's at least fifty-to-one they know the DSRV is looking for her—or that something that isn't theirs is looking for her. They know we're here, and it's one-to-one they don't believe that crap we gave them. We're coming eyeball to eyeball on this. It's time the politicians and diplomats who got us into this take a hand, damn their black hearts to hell.

"Mr. Gottfried," he said, "we're going to break radio silence."

XIX

"THE troika wants them brought up alive. Therefore they must be," Sobelov said.

"To begin, I do not know that they are alive," replied Commander Nikolai Federenko. Commander Federenko was a salvage expert who had learned his trade during World War II in the Baltic, raising or otherwise disposing of ships sunk by the Germans or, occasionally, sent to the bottom by natural causes. The finest thing on his record was the reclamation of a 17,000-ton freighter torpedoed by U89, commanded by Kapitan Wilhelm Mueller, in the Kronstadt roads in late September 1944. It was fitting that a Russian escort vessel had caught U89 gloating on the surface after the torpedo attack and had sunk her for good, leaving only Kapitan Mueller alive to enjoy the amenities of a Russian prison camp for the rest of the war and some months thereafter. It had taken Commander Federenko only two months to put down a coffer dam around the freighter's port side, clear out the debris and the dead, get rid of the spilled oil, and weld in a durable patch to mend a forty-foot gash in the freighter's hull. The freighter thereafter made two voyages between Murmansk and New York to fetch P39 fighters which appreciably helped in the terminal devastation of Fortress Europe.

Now Commander Federenko was aboard a destroyer escort in the company of the moderately disgraced head of Soviet state security, five miles offshore from Balaklava. They were after *Skate* and Kirov's corpus—one way or another—and only incidentally intent upon reclaiming Sobelov's good name if that was possible.

The destroyer escort was slowly cruising a rectangular search pattern, while her sonar sent down pings and the operators listened for a significant echo. To both port and starboard other vessels were engaged in the same work. The day was gray and lowering, which agreed exactly with Sobelov's state of mind. I protected him for years, he thought, what kind of gratitude is this?

"We could saturate this area with depth charges," Federenko said. "That would take care of the problem."

"That has been suggested. And rejected," Sobelov said. "They want the people—particularly him—and the vessel."

"Like all politicians, they know little of the practical considerations. First, we need to find the thing—"

"And it had better be done quickly."

Federenko was exasperated. From three o'clock in the morning of the day before yesterday, he and the ships and men under his command had been doing nothing else. He had this destroyer escort, another like it, two patrol vessels equipped with sonar and, back around the cape in Sevastopol Harbor, a salvage ship fully equipped and waiting only his summons. He knew the depth of the water to the foot and had divers waiting to go down into it. He had everything except the location and now this man from Moscow was telling him to hurry up and get that.

"And then there is the matter of that ship out there," Sobelov said, pointing toward the gray rim of the horizon and the faint rising and falling blob which was the *Queen Zenobia*. "I am not certain that their explanation bears much relation to truth."

Federenko shrugged and turned his hands upward. "Neither am I. But it is in international waters beyond doubt."

"Syrian . . ." Sobelov mused. "An arms shipment would be plausible."

"That has been checked," Federenko said. "There are arms for Syria on the docks in Sevastopol. But there is no Estimated Time of Arrival registered for this particular vessel. What do you want me to do? Take it in tow? Sink it?"

"Not yet. Can't you discover more about it?"

"Get me somebody who speaks Arabic—or American English."

"So you think?"

"I suspect the same as you. However, until I get orders, there is not much I can do about it."

Sobelov was pondering, as it now seemed to him he had been for months—although in fact it was only weeks. I am tired, he reflected, and I have trouble coming to me.

"What do you do when you find it?" he asked.

"That—at the beginning—is relatively simple. We send divers to explore the condition of the ship. They should be able to make a sound assessment of whether it is salvageable."

"I remind you, Kirov comes first."

"You don't need to remind me. It has been said often enough. But I should remind you that opening a submarine is not so simple as opening a jar of caviar. In the first place— given the reasonable assumption that living persons are within this particular submarine—they are not co-operating with us. If they do not want to be found—as I assume they do not—then our problem is multiplied. Do you want me to give it to you in detail?"

"How else?" Sobelov said.

"All right. American submarines, like ours, have escape chambers forward and aft. I am going to assume that the forward escape hatch is the one we are interested in—since, as I am informed, we fired an acoustic torpedo which would naturally attack the screws.

"Normally a submarine disabled in such shallow water as this would release from its forward escape hatch a buoy which would come to the surface and locate the vessel for rescuers. The buoy would also contain a telephone. No such buoy has been released. You agree?"

"I agree. Yes," Sobelov said, thinking this idiotic and impossible assignment became worse by the hour.

"To go on. If the buoy had been released, our problem would be immensely simpler. We would then know precisely where the submarine was and that it needed and desired succor. We could then undertake practical steps toward rescue, but I must advise you, Comrade, this too would impose very serious difficulties upon us."

"Why so? Do we not have submarine rescue equipment in our navy?"

"We do, naturally. We have three vessels specifically built and equipped for submarine rescue. However, none of them is here. Two are in the Baltic and one is in Murmansk."

"Why not here?" Sobelov demanded impatiently. "It is here we need one—and at once."

Federenko shrugged.

"I do not dispose of our shipping, Comrade," he said.

"And so what do we do?"

"We make an improvisation. We do have in Sevastopol one of our nine Atrek class, submarine support ships. These are converted freighters primarily intended to supply submarines at sea. However, they mount heavy hoisting equipment and other useful devices. Our ship, the *Bakhmut*, is at our disposal. I can have it here on two hours' notice."

"Why isn't it here, then?"

"To explain that, I need to explain another difficulty. There is a device, developed in the United States in the 1930s, which they call the McCann rescue chamber. It is in effect a diving bell, although more complex. In use, the rescue vessel puts down five anchors to hold it firmly and directly above the disabled submarine. The rescue chamber would then be winched down to the escape hatch of the submarine."

"This is technical," Sobelov protested impatiently.

"What else did you think? Do you want me to go on?"

"Of course. Forgive me. I am concerned."

"Who is not? Well then, the rescue vessel would lower the escape chamber to the surface. Divers would go down and attach the cable from the escape chamber's winch to the submarine escape hatch. And then the escape chamber, having its own motor, would wind itself down to the hatch. Simple. No?"

"Perhaps. Go on."

"Not so simple, in fact. It would depend on many things.

But, given that the submarine was upright—and its occupants alive and willing—the escape chamber would seal itself to the hatch. Water would be pressed out of the lower section, thus leaving a dry area. The people inside the submarine would open their own pressure hatches and emerge into the rescue chamber. Under extreme circumstances, it might be possible to take off eight men for each descent and ascent. You follow me?"

"I do. There is more?"

"There is—and what remains may mean disaster," Federenko's tone was grimly professional. "While we do have rescue chambers patterned upon the McCann principle, they are specifically designed to seal on Soviet submarines, not American submarines. I do not know that our rescue chamber could be made to fit. It might be necessary to make emergency alterations in its configuration—and even these may not work."

"Why, then, don't we get on with it?" Sobelov demanded.

"For one reason, we do not yet have the rescue chamber here. I have ordered it flown from the Baltic and it will arrive within hours and will be put aboard the *Bakhmut*. The *Bakhmut* carries all the necessary welding and other equipment to change our escape chamber suitably—if indeed that is possible. But first we need to find the submarine and determine precisely what alterations are needed. This is a difficult business, Comrade."

Federenko knew he was talking his own esoteric art to a person who could not possibly understand it; in part, perhaps, because Sobelov's own esoteric art was dealing with the peculiar things which went on inside men's minds and souls. This fellow, he thought, is a professional killer and by no means a saver. He thought it with distaste.

"This is not totally hopeless," he added. "If we knew where the submarine is, it could work. But it could work only if the persons inside—assuming they are alive—would help us. We could not, under any circumstances, compel Kirov to come

246

up into the chamber. Moreover, he is old and fat, and the matter requires some exertion."

"You could not go in and get him?"

"Impossible. The rescue chamber accommodates a crew of one. He must stay with it."

Sobelov weighed one impossible against another and found that, whichever one it turned out to be, his career was near to being a finished chapter.

"It is possible to accept Kirov dead," he said cautiously. "You can, of course, get the ship?"

"If I find it, I can get it. It is partly a matter of weather. In calm, such as this, the work would go more easily. But it would take weeks, months more probably. We would get lines under the submarine. Then we would sink flooded pontoons—tanks, in a manner of speaking—down and attach them to the cradle of cables under the vessel. Then we would pump the water out of the pontoons and they would float and—hopefully—carry the ship to the surface. We would then tow it into dry-dock."

"What then?"

"Carry out the corpses," Federenko said.

"Make sure you get them," Sobelov said.

XX

PROBABLY no psychological test the Navy or Submarine Service could devise would have adequately plumbed the fact that the core of Howie Quill's being was an utter determination to live and—as its corollary—to do so unfettered. Since utter life and utter freedom are manifest impossibilities, Howie customarily went as far as he could to fill his soul's tall order by compromising as little as possible with the inescapable impositions on him by the world he lived in.

Most people, of course, nourish somewhere inside a yearning for personal life and freedom from confinement. But here most people differed from Howie by much more than a mere matter of degrees. Most people compromised more or less gracefully with things like responsibility, creditors, wives, children, mortgages, honesty or honor. The difference between them and Howie was that *his* life and *his* freedom were more than the core of his being; they comprised practically all of it.

To some, if they had fully recognized it, Howie's special dedication might have seemed selfishness or cowardice or both. It never had seemed so to him; in fact he didn't think about it but merely obeyed what to him was natural law— the only law he did pay attention to—his personal well being.

Thus, in his eighteenth year, as a senior in high school, Howie found out about girls and was delighted with his discovery. Although his first seventeen years had been active, he considered that he had never encountered any tactile sensation quite as stimulating as the touch of Virginia's silky young breasts against his chest, her smooth young thighs and her eager young body struggling against his.

However, he was unready one night to find Virginia crying on the Quills' front porch. He was annoyed, because he thought she must be jealous at his having taken another girl to the senior prom, for which Virginia, as a sophomore, was not eligible. Her message was different. She had missed two periods, and he knew what that meant, didn't he? She wanted to talk about running away and getting married.

"Married!" Howie was appalled. "Jesus Christ, Virginia, I'm only eighteen years old!"

"And I'm only sixteen! Anyhow, you were old enough for—for that!"

"Why the hell did you do this to me anyhow!"

"Did to you!" she gasped. "How about me!"

In the end Howie's father, who was the only physician in their small Nebraska town, aborted Virginia, who later, in pain and shame and tears, told her mother.

Howie's father, who had done the deed to preserve the honor—or at least the safety—of his son, went to prison for five years. He went, in part, because Howie, traded his own immunity by the county sheriff, testified against his father.

The Navy never knew it—not until it was too late—but Howie's getting into the Submarine Service was in fact merely a perfectly normal expression of his compulsion toward self-preservation.

When the dean kicked him out of the University of Colorado—for being caught trying to compound LSD in the chemistry lab—Howie confronted an ogre in the form of his draft card. He considered burning it as a public spectacular but abandoned that temptation when his car radio told him of a case in the East in which a young man was sentenced to prison for a similar act of arson : Howie had no desire whatever to share his father's unhappy condition as a convict.

On the other hand, he had even less admiration for the idea of going to Vietnam. Vietnam was out—absolutely out. He got a sickening weight of lead in his stomach at the mere thought of it.

And so he enlisted in the Navy on the theory that, even if he did get sent to Vietnam, the Navy was likely to be well offshore hurling long distance shells or carrier aircraft at the foe and, except for the pilots, not much subject to retribution.

After boot training, he put in for Sub School on the grounds that, in peacetime, the submarines were even less likely to come to grips with anything lethal. Moreover, submarines sounded glamorous, and Howie was fond of glamour, although somewhat down the scale from his fondness for himself.

Howie did extraordinarily well in Sub School, being bright among his other qualities. Moreover, he earnestly desired not to flunk out, since he also knew the Navy did operate patrol boats in the rivers and canals of Vietnam, which he considered altogether too close. He demonstrated particular aptitude for the several media of communications and eventually emerged from school rated ST 3/c (Sonar Technician Third Class).

Howie was assigned to *Skate* for his qualifying cruise. He reported aboard in Naples in March. He had perhaps six months of on-the-job training ahead of him before he would likely have earned his dolphins and with them a raise in rate to second class. Chief Cate and Chief Guernic took his schooling in hand. They gave him a battle-station watch on sonar. He was just past his twenty-first birthday and exactly six weeks in *Skate* when a Russian torpedo tore off her stern and she sank. He had been standing in the sonar room door, breathing quickly with the excitement of getting away from the Russian coast, when the missile struck. The concussion knocked him off his feet and into a tangle of bodies. He had just struggled upright in the darkness and was cowering at the entrance to the sonar room when the emergency lights came up and Captain Stephens happened to notice him, ashen and trembling without control.

At first Howie could not know what had come to pass, nor what it meant. All he knew was a cold, unthinking terror. But, being at the center of things in the control room, he gradually became aware. They were sunk. *Skate* was not going to move again. They were under 300 feet of water—trapped there. They no longer had conditioned air to breathe—and even if they had, he knew, his lungs would still be constricted by fear. He felt a wild impulse to throw himself against the main deck hatch and, with sheer terrified muscle, batter his way to light and freedom.

A species of hysterical resentment swelled up inside him to match the icy, paralyzing foreboding. Were they going to stay down here to die like trapped rats? He wanted to run at Stephens and smash that maddening calm out of him, force him to do something. He got me down here, he felt in the wrench of his anger; it's up to him to get me out, damn him. Why doesn't he do something? Ordering men to their bunks, for the love of God! What's he want of me? Just to lie down and fold my hands and die? I'm damned if I will, he thought. And still he knew, at the center of his quivering soul, that was probably precisely what he was going to do.

It was in that condition that Cavanides got to him. Cavanides had come into the control room, barefooted like everybody else, and seeing Howie Quill near the sonar, stood for long minutes eying him speculatively. Through the caul of his terror, Howie gradually became aware of that questioning stare. At length Cavanides came and stood near him and, after another measuring time, spoke to him.

"Do you know where we are?"

Howie found that he could not speak. His throat and tongue simply would not work. He nodded, a spasmodic bobbing; that was all.

There was a rumbling sound overhead, growing louder and louder until it went beyond with a menacing throb.

"Those are Russian ships up there. Hunting for us. Did you know that?"

This time Howie could not even nod; the Greek's voice seemed to come thinly from a vast, unreal distance.

"We are going to die here—in this tomb. Did you know that?" Cavanides said. "Do you want to die? Now?"

Howie Quill shuddered and felt the cold creep higher. This, he recognized, was not something your father could do for you as proxy.

"The captain intends to let us die—rather than call for help," Cavanides' far-off voice prodded at him again. "Did you know that?"

"Shut up!" Howie managed to croak.

"But help is possible," Cavanides persisted, with calm lack of mercy. "Those people up there are not murderers. Your captain prefers to believe they are killers. They are not. But they cannot do anything for us unless they can find us."

"Get away!" Howie said.

"You may as well know the truth," Cavanides said. "You are young, but death does not honor youth. You have to accept that as fact—or do something about it."

"There's nothing to do," Howie succeeded in wrenching from his despair.

"Perhaps not. Perhaps something. One does not die by choice—not when other choices are possible. Listen to me." Cavanides' voice became a whisper.

Chief Guernic, coming from his bunk to relieve Chief Cate at the useless console, was intent upon what he was doing. But, by long habit, he saw and heard and smelled things around him by a sort of instinctive peripheral awareness. He was passing the cubicle which housed the sonar, and the door was minutely ajar. He sense a glow of growing light and, unmistakably, the breathing of the cooling fans. And there was human movement inside. He pulled up abruptly. Who the hell is that? he wondered. And what the hell is he doing?

He stopped, looked, listened, considered. He turned, barefooted, silent, and eased the door wide. A figure was bent over the instrument and it was coming alive. The fans were working and the lights afire but it had not yet begun to ping.

"Belay that!" Guernic snapped. "Turn that damn thing off! At once!"

He heard a strangled gasp and the figure began to straighten up.

"Shut it down!" Guernic demanded.

The lights went out and the fans whispered dead and, cringing, the person turned.

"Quill?" Guernic said. "Come out of there, craphead! What the hell do you think you're doing?"

Guernic had considered Quill a good-looking kid when he came aboard. He had begun to like him, as much as he could like any boot, for the kid had been smart, attentive, and bright about learning the job. What he saw now was a metamorphosis, and he crossed the con spaces and found Cate.

"We got something here, Joe," he said. "I think it's something for the captain."

"What?" Cate asked, turning his gaunt, deep-lined face.

Guernic jerked a thumb toward the starboard side.

"That boot was warming up the sonar. He's scared shitless. Maybe he didn't know what he was doing. Maybe he did. You take him over."

They, Stephens and Chief Cate, got it out of him, but it wasn't easy. At first it was flat denial. It veered, not too slowly, toward the snarl of a frantic, cornered but dangerous beast. It ended in whimpers.

"Take him away, Chief," Stephens said at last, feeling sick. "I'll do something about Cavanides, whatever is necessary."

XXI

THE hour was unprecedented, but so was the purpose of this gathering in the privacy of the family dining room in the White House. It was three o'clock in the morning of May 2, and the President of the United States, needing a shave, sat at the head of the table in pajamas, turned half away from the table, with his knees crossed, pulling thoughtfully at his chin with his left hand while frowning at a sheet of dispatch paper in his right.

In addition to the President, also needing shaves but otherwise clothed for the day, sat the Secretaries of Defense and State and Admiral Michael Engel, the Chief of Naval Operations. They, too, were frowning.

"This came in clear language?" the President asked Engel.

"No, sir, Mr. President. Top priority, top-secret code. It was relayed through Rhodes. It was delayed there. I got it an hour ago."

"Why Rhodes?"

"We have a communications ship there, sir." Wouldn't you think he'd know it was coded, the admiral thought irritably. Maybe he's just vamping until ready.

The message was Admiral March's advisory saying that *Skate* had been sunk at one-thirty A.M. the same day about four miles off the Russian coast of Balaklava, that the DSRV had been unable to find her in the first attempt, that the *Queen Zenobia* already had been once accosted by a Russian patrol vessel, that, indeed there was a danger of being driven out of the area entirely.

"How long now since the sub was sunk?" the President asked.

"There is an eight-hour time differential, sir." Engel said. "That would have put her on the bottom a little more than twelve hours."

"How long can she last?"

"That depends on her condition. And upon what the captain decides to do about it. If he can save his ship, he will."

"And if he can't?"

"He has orders not to let his ship be taken."

"What does that mean? How could he escape capture?"

"Sir, destruct charges were planted aboard *Skate* while she was in Istanbul. If capture appears imminent, he will destroy the ship."

Defense sat forward and spoke his protest: "That ship cost me sixty-nine million dollars. Why can't *we* salvage her?" The President scowled. "Get your mind off money. The *Skate* was cheap figured that way. The new ones cost twice that."

Admiral Engel was patient with ignorance, especially when it emanated from Defense, his civilian boss.

"Getting a submarine up is a job of weeks, or months, depending on conditions: how much damage, how deep, what kind of bottom she lies on, the weather topsides. Moreover, there remains the political question. You know more about that than I do. But that is Russian water . . ."

State felt he had to voice his worries, which were many.

"If we sent a salvage fleet there, the Russians would know why it was there as well as we would. What is worse, they would be forced to make their knowledge public. And so would we. The situation could no longer be concealed nor tolerated. It is already too near to becoming public knowledge—the British embassy has twice inquired in the Department. They want to know the whereabouts of Captain Brown; it seems the Admiralty wants him there for the launching of the *Royal Oak*. It is difficult to evade a direct question. And embarrassing."

"That brings up another thing," the President said, measuring State with cold disapproval. His voice was calm, but the fangs in it were almost visible. "Why the hell, Alec, were you stupid enough to keep those people on the submarine when it left Istanbul?"

State flushed. He hoped he wasn't visibly cringing. He had

taken this kind of abuse before, but it got no easier with practice. He wondered why he didn't throw up his hands and go back to Milwaukee, where, considering his eminence as chairman of the board of a giant corporation, nobody was likely to treat him with disrespect.

"There were what seemed to be sound reasons, Mr. President," he began, knowing beforehand that it wouldn't do him a nickel's worth of good to remind the head of state that he had been advised of the proposition ahead of time and had approved it. "First, they were already guests aboard the ship. We hoped, if they stayed aboard and the mission was successful much of the free world could feel that it had shared in Kirov's rescue. No small profit—propagandawise. Second, to put them off summarily would attract curiosity—as well as being discourteous."

"I'll bet your ass they now wish you had been downright rude," the President said. "I know every man enjoys the privilege of being an idiot, but, Alec, you are abusing the privilege."

After a moment he turned to Admiral Engel, wearing that calculating look which often forecast that somebody else was going to get clawed.

"If you had that bunch of foreign kibitzers aboard the *Skate*, why didn't you send some other submarine?"

Admiral Engel didn't feel like being bullied. On the other hand, you couldn't just walk over and belt the Commander-in-Chief in the chops. Besides, he could probably lick me, the admiral thought ruefully. But he wasn't going to be stampeded.

"*Skate* was the only available vessel to do the job," he said, and omitted the "sir" deliberately.

"You mean to say Defense here has spent God knows how many billions on those hot-bellied tubs and you had nothing else around to do a little work? What kind of organization is that?"

"Yes, sir. The only other nuclear submarine in the eastern

Mediterranean at that time was *Triton*. She and *Skate* were engaged in fleet exercises in the same area."

"Did *Triton* also have aboard a herd of so-called allies?"

"No."

"Then why didn't you send her instead?"

"*Triton's* too big for the job. She's almost twice as long as *Skate* and displaces more than twice as much. Getting *Skate* into the Black Sea was tricky enough. Putting *Triton* through that needle's eye could have been impossible."

"All right," the President grunted. "That makes sense." He turned toward State again. "I don't know whether to fire you or not." He paused, pulling at his chin again—and asked at large, "Did they get Kirov?"

"No way of knowing—until we get into that submarine," Engel answered.

"You know," the President mused, "the way people mess things up around here I often wish I could go back to Oklahoma. While I try to save the country, you boobs seem to be trying to wreck it. Who got the idea in the first place that Kirov was worth it?"

"You did, Mr. President," said Defense, committing lese majesty and not caring if he did. He was fed up.

The President quirked a shaggy eyebrow at him and for a moment stared with intense malevolence. Then he relaxed and a slow grin tugged at the corners of his mouth.

"I guess you're right. Thanks for reminding me."

Admiral Engel returned to action on the front which preeminently engaged his attention.

"Mr. President, we've got a hundred and twenty men down there, plus the four guests, plus Kirov and his escort. That's a hundred and twenty-six, counting those who may be dead. For all I know, they may all be dead, but if there are living people we want to get them out . . ."

"Even if we have to go to war to do it?"

"I can't answer that. You are in a better position than I am to doubledome the Kremlin. Is there a possibility you could make a deal with them?"

257

"With what for trading cards?"

"Let us move in close and take the men off and, if he's alive, toss Kirov back to them."

"Do what with the submarine?"

"Salvage it—if you can make that good a deal. If not, blow it up as we leave to make sure nobody else does."

"I'd look pretty silly crawling to the Kremlin—if, for example, your little kettle of a rescue sub has already found *Skate* and is taking the men off. The Russians would chew me out, naturally. How much time can we spare—that is before we take any action here?"

"I don't know."

"Can we give it another day's grace?"

"Possibly," Engel said, then added in bitter afterthought, "If they're already dead we can give it grace forever."

"It's a gruesome thing to think about," State said hesitantly. "But if they are dead it would solve the diplomatic dilemma. If there was nobody alive that we had to rescue, we would never have to admit one of our submarines had ever been there."

"You're God damned right it's a gruesome thought!" Admiral Engel growled in unaccustomed fury. "What do you want me to do. Leave them down there to rot?"

After lunch in the White House the President was notified that the Chairman of the Soviet Council of Ministers most urgently desired to talk with him, and, if agreeable, the call from Moscow would be put through on the hot line from the Kremlin at two o'clock that afternoon, Washington time.

"So," the President mused, "we're going to lock horns on this, are we? That telephone is getting busier than a party line in the Panhandle." Actually this was only the second time the hot line had been used in this administration. The only other call on that telephone had come only the week before from the Secretary of State in Istanbul.

The hot line to the Kremlin had, until recently, consisted of a teletype affair, which previous Presidents had found adequate for direct exchange of views. This President, however, found the reading and sending of messages a cold comfort, although undoubtedly efficient. But his temperament demanded human contact as close and direct as possible and so he had insisted that the system be changed to voice telephone, with scramblers to prevent busybodies from eavesdropping on any conversation or debate between the heads of state in Moscow and Washington.

"One of the troubles here," the President told State and Defense, "is that we don't know just how much he knows. I'd better shadow box some until I get some idea. Naturally, he has to suspect that we know a lot more than he does.

"Well, get the interpreter and get him down to the Situation Room. He can warm up the line by getting acquainted with his opposite number. I'll be down at two sharp."

The interpreter, whom the President didn't know because he had never needed his services before, was seated on the far side of the booth with pads and pencils before him and his hand on one of two duplicate red telephones. He scrambled to his feet as the President entered and stood stammering.

"I hope you settle down when he gets on the horn," the President said. The interpreter was a wispy little man with thick glasses. He was going bald, the President noted, although he was still quite young.

A man with a headset stood outside the glass doors, evidently speaking into his microphone.

"What's his job?" the President asked.

"He signals when the line is open," the interpreter replied.

The President sat, frowning, tapping the small table between them with his fingertips, brooding in thought. I'll just have to play it by ear, admit nothing unless it appears they've really got the goods on us. Then he became aware that the man beyond the glass door had his right hand up with thumb and forefinger forming a circle. Then suddenly, the man dropped his arm. The President reached for his telephone.

Immediately he heard a baritone rumble entirely unintelligible to him. That must be him. Sounds like him anyhow; the way he sounded at the UN. He noted with satisfaction that his interpreter was taking notes as the Russian talked.

The rumbling voice paused, and immediately the Kremlin interpreter began translating. That voice was high and light and prissily exact.

I don't know why they don't get some he-men and teach them to translate, the President thought irritably. Instead, they get these damn faggots. You lose all sense of the guy you're really trying to communicate with. If I wasn't so ancient I'd learn Russian myself. This straining everything through somebody else's tonsils just about defeats the whole idea.

The formal greetings back and forth were got over quickly and the Chairman got down to business without further delay. The President listened again to the baritone rumble from 6000 miles away.

"Mr. President," the interpreter's prim voice came over. "A situation has arisen here whose potential consequences are so grave that we, the First Secretary, the President and myself, believe it is absolutely essential that we communicate with yourself. The situation is too delicate for an exchange of notes."

"Tell him I can't see how I can help him until I know what the situation is," the President told his interpreter. If he thinks I'm going to spring it first, he's got a long wait coming, he told himself.

Again the rumbling voice followed by his translator.

"Early this morning a pirate submarine invaded our territorial waters in the Black Sea. Naturally, since our coastal defenses were anticipating some such violation and were alert, they detected the vessel's approach. They sank it."

"Tell him I can understand that he regards this so-called invasion seriously. But I can't tell, not yet anyhow, where we fit into it."

The heavy, somehow melodious voice again, with the interpreter bringing up the rear.

"My people are mortally certain that it is an American submarine and that it was sent here on a mission of kidnaping one of our very important leaders."

"What makes him think it is an American submarine?"

Back and forth, the voices traded the line.

"An American nuclear submarine was in Istanbul last week. It left there under circumstances our people consider suspicious. We know the submarine approached our coast off Balaklava. Three weeks prior to that arrival, my predecessor vanished from Moscow. He was kidnaped by an American expatriate who had lived in Russia since World War II. The two of them made their way south to Balaklava. A little more than one hour before we sank the submarine, one of our security agents was murdered on the dock. A fisherman's boat was stolen. We are convinced, indeed almost categorically certain, that my predecessor was aboard that submarine when it was struck and sunk."

Kirov, all right, the President thought. Who does he think he's kidding describing Kirov as a "very important leader?" After all, they'd dumped him, hadn't they? Kidnaping? Kidnaping, my foot!

The Chairman's voice was changing in timbre, growing harsher, more demanding, angry.

"Mr. President, this act cannot be tolerated!"

"Ask him what he wants me to do about it? And what he intends to do?"

The growling voice was going again.

"That is why I have telephoned you personally," the Soviet interpreter vouchsafed. "This is a very grave matter. If it becomes public knowledge the consequences are virtually impossible to predict. It is my belief that we should find the submarine and, if there are survivors, take them off. We want my predecessor back. I myself favor rescue. But I assure you, Mr. President, not all of my colleagues are so mercifully inclined. Some powerful voices believe we should find the submarine and destroy it utterly. Others desire to lay the matter before the Security Council."

"That last alternative, I should think, is precisely what you don't want, Mr. Chairman," the President said. "You seem to fear a public confrontation. I would agree with that, I think.

"On the other hand, any overt effort to destroy this submarine would, of course, be unlikely to be tolerated by the owners, whoever they may be. I should think the mere fact of having torpedoed a submarine going about its peaceful business would already have brought your apprehension about consequences almost to the breaking point. Mr. Chairman, if you are interested in my advice, it is to tread very softly indeed. And you seem not to know exactly where the submarine is."

"We do not—yet," the Chairman acknowledged. "But we will—surely."

"You know approximately where it is?"

"Of course. Knowing where it was struck by the torpedo we can calculate its position—subject to some variables. It lies approximately four miles off the coast. We will find it. I am completely certain of that."

"You say this submarine is four miles out. That's beyond the three-mile limit and your jurisdiction over the submarine —if you ever did in fact have any—should have terminated at three miles."

"Mr. President, you know that our territorial limit is not three but twelve miles."

"I know that is what you assert. But no international law that I am aware of supports it. You imposed the limit unilaterally where, for most of the world, the recognized limit is three."

"Mr. President, that is pettifogging . . ." The deep voice now sounded clearly furious.

"Mr. Chairman, if what I said amounts to pettifogging, it is no more so than that one-sided pretension that you can legally claim and enforce a twelve-mile territorial limit. This talk then becomes absurd."

"Mr. President, let us avoid a quarrel—at least for now.

262

That could too easily come later if this contretemps is not settled in a manner which my country can accept.

"Now, if this vessel's approach was innocent—as you seem to suggest—although frankly I am unable to believe that. But if it was innocent—or even if it was not—it now appears to be disabled and helpless. Why doesn't the captain reveal himself, so that we can rescue his people?"

"Perhaps whoever is down there off your coast is not quite as convinced as you say that your intent is merciful. On the other hand, he may be dead, since you confess you hit him with a torpedo. But I should think any submarine commander in the condition you describe would have orders not to betray himself if he could help it."

"Mr. President, I urgently suggest you dispatch new orders to him."

"Mr. Chairman, I assure you earnestly that I enjoy no communication whatever with any such submarine as you describe. None whatever. I will investigate to whatever degree is possible. Meanwhile I suggest that this conversation is not getting us ahead in the least.

"But I warn you once again. The situation you have brought to my attention with your contention—which I must say stands unproven—that an American submarine which you admit firing upon lies disabled somewhere off your Black Sea coast—this situation is dangerous. I suggest you make an earnest effort to restrain your more impetuous associates."

That, at least, was the truth, the President thought as, head down and trying to sort out the variables in the strangest gamble he had ever ventured into, he went to the elevator and his office.

Something I really do not have—but wish to hell I did have—is any kind of communication with the *Skate*.

XXII

COMMANDER Stephens looked at the ship's clock mounted on his stateroom bulkhead. More than twenty hours now since *Skate* had hit bottom. He had a throbbing headache and he knew the air was going foul. Possibly worse—or at least as bad—was temperature. When the reactor was shut down, it went subcritical but that did not mean it had gone entirely dead. The hot stuff inside was still emanating decay-heat which, in turn, flowed into the heat exchangers and was passed along to the turbines to radiate a dragon's breath to the rest of *Skate*. The bulkheads were going slimy with condensed humidity, and comfort was not here.

He longed to order the scrubbers into action, but dared not—not with the noise of screws—sometimes the fast, fierce rush of destroyers, sometimes a lower, slower rumble—passing back and forth overhead.

Three hundred and twenty-eight feet, the depth gauges said. They're looking for us, all right, he knew, but then, why wouldn't they? They had to know they hit us. So then they've got to wonder how bad they hurt us, whether they killed us entirely, whether we can still get under way, whether anybody's alive down here. They can't know all the answers and they can't, not yet anyhow, know exactly where we are. To know that they have to know all the X-values of a really complicated equation : course, speed, rate of descent, exactly in what way the explosion had affected each of these factors or all of them taken together.

And he suspected, although he did not know that any more than the Russians did, that *Skate* might have come down in some sort of trough which gave the submarine a measure of defilade from the fingering sonars.

Meanwhile, until the people up there gave up—which he doubted they would do considering who and what game they sought—or the air situation got really terminal, he was damn well going to maintain a silent ship. He didn't even need passive sonar since they were in water shallow enough to hear the searchers' screws with little strain on the ears.

What was the maximum endurable level of carbon dioxide build-up in their general situation? You could only generalize, of course. He remembered or half remembered some sort of self-study some boat had made of its circumstances in World War II when they'd had to take over thirty hours of Japanese depth bombing before they could get up and get a gulp of new air. Something about growing lassitude, a rise of irritability until people were popping off about nothing, ready to kill. Anger to the level of idiocy, anger at everything. Then, progressively, a loss of will to keep on taking it, resignation to death, even the half-hearted eagerness to get it over with. That had been in hot seas, somewhere near the equator, and they had thought the heat was a major contribution to the deterioration of men's brains and wills. But they had their own heat problem here—out of *Skate's* quiet but sizzling guts. Not scientific, of course, but who knew what exactly was scientific for a certain boat in certain waters under a certain level of strain? Something a little more clinical had been done later, he remembered, the fairly precise clocking of what carbon dioxide did to a man. There was a kind of elation, a euphoria for the first day, then the downhill glide, steepening all the way, into defiant anger, disorientation, confusion, coma and the hereafter. The real problem, apparently, was carbon dioxide poisoning; that would get you before you starved for oxygen. In any case he knew there was plenty of oxygen aboard. Any skipper with any sense at all would come into this kind of a situation only with things to his best feasible advantage, and so, naturally, *Skate* had come here with her oxygen bottles stuffed and ready to bleed. It was the carbon dioxide; you couldn't get rid of that without the scrubbers and you couldn't run those without nailing yourself like a pinned butterfly for those waiting sonsofbitches upstairs.

Inactivity by *Skate*'s people was a paramount he had striven to maintain as soon as he learned, too quickly, that *Skate* was as good as done for as a functioning mechanism. She had gone on down to bottom because she was already bound for the bottom when hit, and sheer inertia, more than intrinsic flooding, carried her the rest of the way. Once down, she was down for good until or unless somebody came to get her. The quick instinct to blow tanks and get to the surface had demonstrated that; she had risen by the bow—enough to make it obvious that she could never get herself to the surface on anything like even keel. She would merely stand upright on her shattered and flooded tail like some enormous, grotesque guppy gulping at the surface of a giant's aquarium.

He had dead men back there, he knew. Eighteen to be precise, seventeen shorn off in the stern compartment, one in the engine room just forward, two wounded who might yet die. The dead had died the second the torpedo struck—he was almost certain it must have been a small acoustic torpedo homing on the noise of *Skate*'s screws. There was nothing left to do for the dead; it was impossible, here on the bottom, to go through a proper burial at sea, with readings from Scripture, prayer, rifle salute, and taps—and then the plank tipped up so that the body, sewed up in tarpaulin with a shell at the feet to give it weight against the fish, could slide over the side to its rest—if, indeed, it was to be repose.

But something, he had thought, back there at the last bulkhead beyond which lay the sea, might be useful—at least for those who still were alive and so he had repeated a part of that brief and loving ritual:

"Unto Almighty God, we commit the souls of our brothers departed and we commit their bodies to the deep. In sure and certain hope of their resurrection and eternal life . . ." He had quit at that point, because he suddenly remembered that, although he knew his crew man by man, he now realized he did not know who was Jew and who was Christian.

The only reason the rest of them were alive was that when he surfaced to pick up her cargo, *Skate* had been rigged for depth charge with all her watertight openings buttoned up—except for the hurried opening of the hatches to the bridge and, once their guests were alongside, the brief cracking of the main deck hatch to hustle them below, but she had been all buttoned up again and on her way down when the torpedo tore off her stern.

So now he was keeping everybody whose activity was not essential, in his bunk; the best way to delay the inevitable poisoning of the stuff going into your lungs was to do as little as possible physically. He couldn't imagine a more difficult brand of idleness to endure, not when your every instinct was a rebellious will to do something about it. He had always admired his crew, but now his admiration had been swelled by a surge of gratitude that was something close to love. They were picked men, superbly trained, but now their quality was being superbly tested. He knew that tension was growing throughout the boat; it had to be. Every time the rumble of a screw went overhead, the iron had to sink deeper into a man's gut. And, in this modified hell, they lay in their bunks and took it.

All but that one scared kid, terrified into treason. It made him sick to realize that when and if they ever got out of this he'd have to do something about that.

Meanwhile he himself had things to do. It was time to tour the boat again—and after that remained a chore he dreaded but knew must be done.

He climbed the stairway in the dim emergency light being drained from the ship's batteries and stepped into the con where Lieutenant Commander Richard Oulahan was keeping watch with Chief Joe Cate. They had nothing much to do except keep in periodic consultation with the technicians who were, as usual, keeping constant stewardship over the condition of the air in the boat—now a melancholy duty since there was nothing they dared do to improve it.

"How's it stand now?" Stephens asked Oulahan. "Much worse?"

"CO-two's climbing, natch," Oulahan said. "Around three

per cent now. We can stand that for a while, but if it goes much higher, we're in trouble."

"We're in trouble already. We can't run the scrubbers with those bastards prowling around upstairs."

"Captain, you ready to make an estimate on the chances of the DSRV finding us—in time to do any good?"

"They've got as good a chance as the Russians, maybe better. They can get down where we are to look. And their guess at our position should be as good as the Russians—or maybe a little better. They've got one other advantage over the Russians: they'd know we wouldn't dare call—which might give them a slightly more optimistic presumption that somebody's still alive down here."

"How're the passengers taking it?" Oulahan couldn't keep a slight tinge of the professional's contempt for the amateur out of his tone.

"I'm seeing the lot in a few minutes. And I've got to figure out what to do about that Greek. He's a guest. So do I put him under arrest—or what?"

"Your problem, Captain. And I don't envy you. Personally, I'd shoot him."

"And make all that noise?"

Stephens moved over to Chief Cate who, as his personally delegated Chief of the Boat, was his right arm and factotum in many matters dealing with health, morale, discipline and all concerns, social and mechanical, involved in the smooth and efficient interlocking of officers and enlisted men and the boat as a team.

"What have you done with the kid, Chief?"

"He got sort of wild, Captain. Hysterical. I had the pharmacists look at him. They gave him a shot in the arm and I locked him up in my room. Took away his belt and anything in the room he could bang around and make a noise with. Anyhow, he'll be sleeping it off for hours now. Anything else you want me to do about him?"

"Technically he's under arrest and in the brig—although,

I suppose, we're all in the brig. Too bad. He hadn't qualified yet, had he?"

"No. Newest man aboard—but he'd been doing fine—until this. Sort 'em and re-sort 'em. And you still don't know."

"I hate to see it. Chief, let's take a gander aft."

"Aye, aye, sir."

The chief, a lean, almost gaunt man, his short black hair going a little gray, wearing a look of calm and immense competence behind his thick glasses, led the way back through the narrow passageways and up into the tunnel and over the heavy shielding of the reactor.

"Good thing they didn't hit us here, Captain," Cate said.

"That's probably pretty much on their minds. Nobody quite knows for sure what a busted-open reactor would do to the water it was busted open in. This is their water. They'd probably hate to think they'd poisoned it with their own torpedo."

"I'm not going to worry about their worries."

The watertight door to the engineroom, next to the last compartment in the boat, was closed and dogged on the other side. Both Stephens and Cate knew that the compartment aft of the engineroom was no longer a compartment at all but merely a tangle of rubble and corpses. The chief tapped softly on the door, and, after a moment, they saw the locking wheel turn on their side and heard the dogs, resembling the locking pinions on a vault door, being withdrawn. They stepped over the coaming. Beyond them at the after end of the engineroom stood *Skate*'s last watertight barrier between the boat and seventeen dead men and the eager sea. And, as Stephens knew, that barrier was no longer any too watertight.

Chief Cummings came up out of the gloom of the emergency lighting. He looked both greasy and tired, and his normally bulging eyeballs appeared to be out an extra quarter inch.

"What's it look like, Chief?" Stephens asked.

"Bulged some and a little leakage around pipe fittings."

Cummings, usually cheerful and profane, looked haggard. It was hot, for, although the reactor was shut down, some steam still leaked into the compartment from the strained turbines, the heat still generated by a reactor ordered to loaf—"decay-heat" they called it. Sweat cut little creeks through the grease on Cummings' face, and he mopped it out of his eyes.

"It's holding so far. But if we were any deeper we'd have hell's own job holding it. And probably couldn't."

"How bad are the leaks?"

"I'll show you, Captain. Over this way."

Stephens followed and now became conscious of a new sound, sustained, ugly, threatening, rushing noise.

"Here, this is the worst one," Cummings said. "That's a fresh water line. The blast must've ripped it out just behind the bulkhead and strained the fitting. It's bringing in enough sea water to be irritating, but it's not getting any worse. We got a sleeve clamped around it and welded it, and I think that'll hold it. Best we can do, so far."

A thin stream of water was sizzling around the jury-rigged repair and shooting half across the compartment with a malignant hiss.

"How about the door?"

"Buckled some, but it's not leaking. It'll hold, I think—it had better. But we're shoring it just to make a little more sure."

"She groans some, doesn't she?" Stephens observed, conscious of an almost inaudible straining of the metal as it shouldered back against the sea which demanded entrance just three points under nine times the pressure it would have exerted at sea level.

"Yeah, she's a grunter, and I can't blame her. But my only real worry is the condition of the junk back there. If the wreckage is mangled enough or loose enough and a depth charge went off anywhere near the stern it would be good night Mabel. Even a current setting the wrong way would ram us with our own wreckage. You got any dope on the currents here, Captain?"

"The chart doesn't show anything. But I doubt if there's much. We're not near any river mouth that amounts to anything."

"Keep a grip on your left one; I got one guy in this detail doing that and nothing else. I wish we had a hunchback we could massage."

"Anything you need, Chief?"

"Yeah, about eight ounces of straight bourbon."

"You'll get it. I doubt if Josephus Daniels' ghost carries much weight down here."

"Aye, aye, Captain. Thanks." Cummings' smile was there, but it was weary.

As he left with Cate, Cummings' men were dogging the engineroom door behind them again. He knew what they were doing, all right, Stephens thought, sealing themselves in their own tomb in case that bulkhead gives. Not out of any special thought of heroism, merely instinctively fulfilling an obligation to the boat, the whole boat. If the bulkhead did collapse, he'd have lost twenty-nine men, nearly a fourth of *Skate's* crew. The butcher's bill was too high already.

Back in the con, he paused to speak to Oulahan. "I'm going up to the wardroom and talk to the passengers," he said.

"Shoot the Greek, Captain," the exec said.

"I'd like to."

In the wardroom, Stephens slumped into a chair and, seeing Billings in the pantry, asked, "You got any hot water?"

Billings began to look apologetic but, seeing Stephens' tired smile, managed something like it on his own. "Captain, you got to be kidding, sir."

"I wish I wasn't, Billings," Stephens said, then remembered something he had overlooked in the press of more urgent matters. "What's the food situation?"

"Well, Captain, so far it's been mostly sandwiches and canned fruit. There's still plenty of fresh water, but nobody's using it for baths; the exec, Mr. Oulahan, he saw to that early."

"I mean more for the long pull; we may be here a while.

How long can you feed without getting into the freezers? The last thing I want is to be sitting here in a boatful of rotting food."

"We locked up the freezers right away. Mr. Oulahan, he's got the keys. That stuff'll keep a week if they're not opened."

"Good. Well, feed as much as you can the way you've been doing. First, you better use up all the fresh stuff in the refrigerators before it spoils. We can't dump garbage now." Christ, he thought suddenly, we can't flush the heads either; the boat's going to stink like a sewer pretty soon—and, God, with a woman aboard on top of everything else.

His headache had grown thicker, a tightening band around his skull, and he was immensely tired. And the heat; it's even too hot to sweat.

"Billings, where's Collingwood?"

"Battle station, Captain. Aft, I think, with the damage control party."

"I should have known and that reminds me. Billings, do something for me, will you?"

"Sure, Captain."

"Go to the chief pharmacist and tell him I told you he should give you a quart of bourbon. Take it back to Mr. Cummings in the engineroom with my compliments. That working party is pretty tired. Then, when you get back, Billings, will you round up the guests, all of them—the lady, too. And tell them I'd like to see them in the wardroom?"

"Aye, aye, Captain. On the double." Billings left, feeling a curious sympathy for the captain. I'm scared enough for my own self, he thought, but he's got to be scared for the whole boatful. The old man looks tired as hell.

Left to himself, Stephens tried to organize his tired brain. How did he handle this? He couldn't ignore them. They didn't owe the ship anything—well—the Greek, damn his soul. They hadn't asked to be in this fix—except Kirov, who in a sense was the cause of it all . . . But then Kirov hadn't sent *Skate* on this mission—and the woman. Oh, Christ!

Mueller was the first to arrive, erect, austere, fully in uni-

272

form, looking so absurd in his bony bare feet that Stephens felt a silly impulse to giggle.

"How does it go, Captain Stephens?" he asked.

"The ship is safe—for the moment. I can't answer beyond that."

"I know. This is a hard business for a shipmaster." A little professional warmth seemed to soften those rigid features for a moment—and then vanished back into their customary tight reserve.

Nicolai came in. It couldn't be said he looked gay. Not somber either but a kind of effervescent pugnacity; it was clear that Nicolai was going to want some answers.

Brown arrived, collapsed his lanky frame into a chair and looked with quick curiosity at Stephens. "Blasted inconvenient, Captain, wouldn't you say?"

"Blasted, Captain," Stephens aroused himself enough to say.

Cavanides came, sat down carefully, saying nothing. Stephens caught himself staring. The sonofabitch looks sullen, he thought. Maybe Dick's idea is the best way to handle him —but that might be doing him a favor. We may all be here for the duration; shooting him would be letting him off too easy. Besides—there would be the noise.

Uzzumekis arrived, his towering bulk at first hiding the slight figure of the woman behind him. Stephens rose though it was an effort, and stayed on his feet until she was seated between Brown and Uzzumekis, who was at Cavanides' right.

Kirov was the last, escorted personally by Billings with some visible awe. The awe would have to spring from something other than the Russian's present appearance, maybe from recognition of what a mogul this one once had been, more likely from the painful present knowledge of the fix they were all in because of him. For the moment, Kirov was merely a fat old man, impassive, cold blue eyes without expression, a pig's face still seamed with coal dust, shapeless in a peasant's stained and shapeless work garments.

Stephens eyed his new guests with freshly aroused curiosity. He had not seen them before except in those moments when they were hauled sloshing aboard from what had looked, in the dark, like a battered fishing boat. They had vanished below—and ever since he had been totally involved in dealing with disaster. How, he wondered, could this one man be worth it?

Of all the matters he had to deal with—without, for the most part, the means to do it—one that chivvied him unmercifully was the incongruous presence of the woman. Submarines were men's ships, and he had a bothersome instinct—perhaps old-fashioned—that getting into a jam was a man's prerogative and that women should be kept clear of tight spots. He looked at her, wondering what they could possibly do to help her if she got hysterical. She looked calm enough, for now anyhow, though drawn and somber, sitting quietly with her hands folded in her lap. He couldn't guess her age, thirty-five maybe. And her appearance wasn't special one way or another, scarf over her hair, eyes gray and direct, a shapeless heavy black skirt and jacket, flat rubber-soled shoes. What was a woman doing mixed up in a thing like this anyhow?

Uzzumekis? Mostly Kirov's escort gave an impression of bigness and brawn and a kind of cold and wary self-possession. This one was tough, Stephens guessed, as he would probably have to be, considering the job they had given him. He noticed, with a little surprise when the man's lips parted slightly, that one of his front teeth was stainless steel. Somehow, though Uzzumekis seemed to be unaware of the woman beside him, Stephens felt, with relief, that the man was taking protective responsibility for her.

Well, get on with it, he thought. He did not get up, but leaned forward with his elbows on the table and said, "I won't waste your time or mine on politeness, except to say that I regret the circumstances you are forced to share with the ship. I have called you together to outline those circumstances, as best I know them, for your information. You will

274

be uncomfortable, very likely increasingly so, but I can tell you the ship itself is safe for now. However, it cannot either surface or get under way. We were struck by some missile, probably a torpedo, probably small, which smashed our screws and rudder and flooded the aftermost watertight compartment—"

Captain Brown quirked a shaggy eyebrow and interrupted with quick curiosity. "A small missile? Why do you say small, Captain?"

"If it had been big, we wouldn't be here now."

"I have a question, which I consider legitimate," Nicolai spoke up. "If we are both dead in the water and dead on the bottom, what, my Captain, are you doing or propose to do to get us out of here? The conditions you describe sound desolate."

"They're bad enough," Stephens acknowledged. "But possibly not hopeless, although for the moment we appear to have no alternative but waiting. You have all heard the screws of ships passing above. I assure you, they are not likely to be friendly. So far as I know they have not yet located us..."

He turned to Kirov. "You, sir, are probably better equipped than anyone else here to make an educated guess at the intentions of your—of those people up there—" He gestured overhead with a thumb as Uzzumekis translated. Kirov nodded, considered a while, and then spoke as Uzzumekis listened intently.

"He says first you may be wrong in assuming they haven't located us. He says you shouldn't underestimate them, because they are highly trained and very good. The fact that they hit you with one torpedo should have been enough to prove that to you . . . The old bastard seems sort of proud of it," Uzzumekis added. Kirov, watching Stephens' face closely, nodded, permitted himself a quick, warmthless smile, then spoke again.

"He says," Uzzumekis translated again, "even if you are right and they have not yet exactly located you, you can assume that they sure enough will. He said again that you should remember the excellence of Soviet technology. But he says it would be wrong to suppose that they will necessarily bomb us when they do find us . . . The way he puts it is that they would probably want to salvage the ship. They would probably want to examine the equipment to see if you have anything they don't—which he says he doubts. Nevertheless, he says, the ship would be quite a prize . . ."

You would, you old scoundrel, Stephens thought. Quite a prize is right. Sonar, SINS, NAVDAC, long-range underwater phones, those other new gadgets. Don't be so damn sure Soviet technology has them all already. And I could assure you that one thing your slobs will never do—though it's pointless to scare the rest by rubbing your nose in it—is get this ship in one piece.

Kirov was speaking again. Though totally self-possessed, Uzzumekis was slightly grimmer as he translated.

"He says that, of course, in the case of a ship salvage operation, none of us can expect to come up alive, since lifting a vessel of this tonnage is a laborious process. He says he hopes you will all believe he is sincere that he regrets that we are in this bind because the submarine was sent here illegally to pick him up. On the other hand, he begs you to remember that he knows it could not have been out of pure mercy that your—our—government decided to rescue him. He says we both know it isn't because we love his big blue eyes. He says that the U.S. knows, as well as he does, that—even out of a job—he is a commodity of great political value and that, considering the pickle we are all in, it would be silly to kid one another . . ."

Through his fatigue, Stephens felt the stir of anger. "You can tell him for me that it is equally silly to act snotty—whatever the Russian word for that is—about the relative merits of the U.S. and the country from which he is taking it on the lam. Nobody has any illusions about his big blue eyes. I was sent here to get him; that's all, no more. I'll still get him out —if it's humanly possible."

Kirov permitted himself another cold smile as Uzzumekis himself wearing a grimly amused satisfaction, translated. Kirov thought it over briefly and replied.

"He says you are optimistic if you think you are going to get him out alive—now that they know approximately where he is. The Soviet Union will never permit it. They may not want him running the country any more, but they won't want him running around loose either."

All this, while informative, was exhausting, a waste of time and an irritation. "Ask the old goat one more question then," said Stephens. "Satisfy my slight curiosity if he will. Why the hell did he go over the hill in the first place? We could have got along without him."

Kirov, no longer mocking, seemed to give the question grave consideration and, for once, seemed to be bidding for respect in turn.

"He says it is a fair question, particularly considering the difficulty in which it has placed you. He says he gave it much thought and decided only after long debate and, at times, much doubt. He asks you to believe that he loves his country and decided to become a fugitive with the greatest hesitation and regret. He says it would be useless to spell it out in detail, here and now, but he says he disapproves of many of the policies of the government which has succeeded him. He says that while he stayed in Russia he was powerless to change anything and that, after much pondering, he decided that working from outside—perhaps, say, with men of the nature of Marshall Tito, he might be able to do something. Then, finally—maybe you saw him smile a little—he says that he was to most intents a political prisoner in his own land, and, you must forgive him if it sounds like vanity, but the power of command is a habit hard to break . . . and humiliation is difficult to endure. He says you may not consider these noble motives, but it is hard for an ex-boss to be always noble. He would rather be boss again."

"Noble or not, it'll do for now," Stephens said. "Thank Mr. Kirov for his information—and his patience."

"You will excuse my impatience then, although I do not believe I can be accused of it after listening in silence to all that only moderately informative talk," said Nicolai, a glint of anger in his dark eyes. "I asked a question and I would like an answer. How do you propose to escape?"

"I don't know that you will escape. I can't promise it," Stephens said coldly. "And Mr. Kirov's talk, whatever your impatience may lead you to believe, was more than moderately useful."

"It should not, I think, be necessary to remind you that I am not in this jeopardy by my own intent," Nicolai said. "Until the last minute we were not informed of our destination and even then not of its insane character. You—or your government—got me into this without my agreement, or even my knowledge. Your obligation, your government's obligation, is plain. To spare nothing. Why did you drag us here in ignorance?"

"Your question may be justified," Stephens said coldly, at the same time feeling the weight of guilt and grief he could not admit. "Those were my orders."

"Your orders! Do you consider those orders less than criminal, less than murder?" The Italian was angry.

"Capitano, you are supposed to be a military person. You know what orders are. I do not propose to explain them . . ."

Nicolai sputtered into resentful silence.

"Now," Stephens said, "I will try to outline our circumstances—which, incidentally, may have been slightly modified by Mr. Kirov's information.

"Just now, as you know, we are disabled. We are also being hunted. However, except for being immobilized, our main machinery is intact. We could provide fresh air, light, air conditioning, remove this heat, and furnish food for an almost indefinite period. We are not doing it simply because we are being hunted, and a silent ship is hard to find. I intend to keep it silent until there is some radical change in our situation." He smiled grimly. "Those also are my orders. We

278

are not to be taken. That's why you are presently uncomfortable. I am sorry."

Kirov was watching him curiously, and Stephens paused to let Uzzumekis interpret. The old man grunted and said a few words.

"He says not to be concerned about his discomfort although he admits a bath would improve his disposition ... Says he finds he no longer likes coal dust as he did when a boy ..."

"Okay, he'll have to stay dirty. Now, there are certain options. They are extremely limited, but I think you may have the right to know what they are.

"We lie in three hundred and twenty-eight feet of water. That leaves about three hundred feet from the escape trunk to the surface. We carry a device called a Steinke hood, a simple device which permits a man to breathe and rebreathe his own air on the way to the surface. Men have escaped at nearly the same depth—from the American submarine *Squalus* in 1939. It is possible that, using the hood, even an untrained person could make it to the surface alive ..."

"Then why ... ?" Nicolai again.

"Listen!" Stephens stopped him. They could feel the throb first in their bones, then hear it increase, swell in malevolent urgency until it went overhead with a roar.

"A destroyer—that's why."

"Why is that not good? Ships nearby on the surface to pick us up?"

"You may forget. My orders are not to be taken. Now, to go on. You perhaps do not know it—I'm sure you don't—it was another thing you were not told, but we did not come to this rendezvous alone. We were accompanied by an escort vessel, a merchant ship. It is not a U.S. naval vessel, but it is commanded by U.S. naval personnel. The ship has been converted for this mission into what we call an ASR—Auxiliary Submarine Rescue. It carries a highly qualified submarine rescue team—"

"I say, that's cheerful news! They should be alongside soon, right?" Brown broke in.

"I'm afraid not right, Captain. It's more complicated than that, as you know. We lie roughly four miles offshore in almost exactly fifty-four fathoms in Russian territorial waters in what the Russians have designated as a Prohibited Zone. We are being hunted. Do you really believe the Russians would tolerate a standard rescue mission here?"

"No, of course not, Captain," Brown subsided as again the angry churn of screws passed above them.

"Then what may be expected of this rescue vessel—a rescue vessel that cannot even approach?" Nicolai again.

"Quite possibly your life, Capitano," Stephens said in cold anger. "The ship carries a DSRV. Those initials, with which you may not be familiar, designate Deep Submergence Rescue Vehicle. The DSRV is a small submarine, equipped to seal itself to the escape hatch of a disabled submarine and take off the personnel. The vehicle is new. It has been proved in practice, but never under these conditions. The DSRV is there, if possible, to attempt the rescue of this ship's people—if it should get into trouble. As it has."

"Then why in the name of God hasn't it come?" Cavanides' voice, breaking in for the first time, was tense, close to going out of control.

"Because they don't know precisely where we are," Stephens said in deadly calm, as his eyes turned toward the Greek in contemptuous appraisal. "And I do not intend to call them, although I could. As, Mr. Cavanides, you know I could, as, indeed, you terrorized one of my men into trying to call the Russians less than twenty-four hours ago. Mr. Cavanides, if you were a member of my crew, instead of a guest, you would now be in irons. As it is, you are under arrest.

"I am not empowered to take summary action against you. But I will tell you that boy you subverted will, if he lives, have to stand a general court-martial. And, since, as captain of this vessel, it is my responsibility to dictate the order in which people may be rescued, I make you this personal promise. If and when the personnel of this boat are rescued, you will be the last man, except myself, to leave."

Stephens stopped talking and sat staring at Cavanides, thinking in icy anger that he would like to take Oulahan's advice and kill him. This fragment of a man. In that moment, he could have done so.

The Greek stared back, face white, lips twitching, eyes burning with rage. Slowly he stood up, bracing his hands on the table. Look at the shit, Stephens thought, as the Greek half turned as though to leave, then suddenly swung around to face him down the length of the table. The man swayed, Stephens noted, and his hands were shaking.

Then, as screws again raced overhead and Stephens half cocked his head upward, listening, he turned back to see a pistol in Cavanides' right hand, and, he noted almost idly, though the hand still trembled violently, the weapon stayed trained more or less down his middle line. The lunatic blaze in those eyes, the whitening tension of a knuckle as the trigger finger tightened. He's really going to do it, the madman. Stephens felt the conviction stabbing into him and his muscles tightened to receive the blow.

He hardly saw it as Uzzumekis' big body swung, his right arm looped across his chest and through Cavanides' elbow, then with the swift precision of a striking snake, twisted down and under as his left arm went up and around Cavanides' neck and clamped on his throat. Cavanides croaked, the gun went off—a deafening blast in the small room—and a gasp of pain came out of his clenched throat as Uzzumekis' powerful right arm doubled the gun hand up behind the Greek's back. They heard the bone crack. Cavanides screamed as the gun clattered to the deck and Uzzumekis' left arm tightened visibly. Cavanides' tongue came out of his gaping mouth.

"You want me to kill him now?" Uzzumekis spoke, almost conversationally calm.

It had been too quick. Stephens had hardly had time to

ready himself for it, and then it was over. He looked at the body writhing in the crook of Uzzumekis' elbow and thought, with chill amazement, that he had just had his life saved. Then another thought hit him, that shot. The noise. Maybe Cavanides had got him after all, him and all the rest.

"No, better drop him, Mr. Uzzumekis. I don't think he'll be more trouble." He turned and spoke to Billings, frozen in the pantry doorway. "Billings, get Chief Cate for me, will you? Better get the chief pharmacist, too."

Uzzumekis, almost negligently, dropped Cavanides back into his chair. The man's head fell forward onto the table, his body collapsed and he lay sobbing.

"He's got a busted arm," Uzzumekis remarked. He bent down to pick up the fallen pistol, looked at it with curiosity, and slid it down the table toward Stephens. "I guess, Captain, you'd rather have charge of firearms around here."

"I guess I would. Thanks," Stephens said.

Chief Cate and two pharmacists had come and gone, taking Cavanides, trembling and wordless, to sick bay to set his arm.

"What do you want me to do with him, Captain?" Cate had asked.

"Patch him up, Chief. Then same as the boy. Only put a guard on him."

"I say, that was something, wasn't it?" Captain Brown observed thoughtfully. "What do you suppose could have got into the fellow?"

"Cracked. Couldn't take it," Stephens said shortly.

"Pity. Service should never take in a fellow like that. Unreliable."

"I speak for myself," Nicolai spoke up, after an admiring and somewhat awed inspection of Uzzumekis. "Hereafter I propose to take it."

"To get on with it," Stephens said, through the abominable throbbing of his headache, wishing to hell this would be over with so that he could get back to the concerns of his wounded boat. "The DSRV has a reasonable chance of finding us.

282

Unlike the Russians, they knew precisely the course I intended to take after picking you up." He nodded at Kirov. "Moreover, he operates submerged and thus has a better prospect of locating us. I have to warn you, however, that the DSRV will be operating under tough conditions. It is a short-range vehicle, slow speed, and, since the mother ship cannot feasibly stand in closer than twelve miles, the rescue sub will be operating at the limit of its range. Also, of course, it is vulnerable to Russian detection and attack."

"Can you estimate the prospects?" Brown asked.

"Not with any accuracy. Also, you have to know, even if they find us in good time, not everyone goes at once. The DSRV should need at least four round trips to empty this ship. The prospects decline for each succeeding trip." He looked around the room in cold appraisal. "I say once more, as captain, it is my responsibility to determine the priority of rescue." He nodded at the woman, then at Kirov. "Naturally, they go first."

Kirov looked inquiringly at Uzzumekis, who translated. Kirov spoke shortly and Uzzumekis spoke for him.

"He says of course the woman goes first. As for him, it is a question which should be pondered. He is aware that he is the cargo you were sent to pick up and, therefore, your masters must be anxious to receive the cargo intact. On the other hand, he says, he is old and wearing out—I can tell you for myself, the old goat is pretty rugged—and he himself should consider again whether his hope to do something for his country was, maybe just an old man's dream."

"Tell him he'll have to leave that to me," Stephens said.

"How long do we survive without running the machinery?" Mueller, who had been long silent, observing in austere detachment, asked. It was a professional's question.

"I can't say exactly. Depends a lot on the individual, of course, as you must know. My technicians calculate somewhere in the area of fifty hours." He looked at his watch. "As of now we have been down twenty-two.

"But that brings up another matter. Mr. Kirov gave us his

283

opinion that they will not bomb because they will want to salvage the boat. In extreme circumstances I could consider taking that chance—particularly if those search boats seem to be laying off for any considerable time. I can tell you, however, in the simplest way I know that they will *never* take this boat." Kirov looked inquiringly at Uzzumekis, then, getting his answer, asked a question.

"He wants to know if you would destroy it—and yourself —first?"

"Tell him he can take that any way he likes."

"And that would mean, naturally, we would all go with the boat," Captain Brown observed in shaggy composure. "A pity. All these fine young men—but then I suppose, of course, that is an intrinsic of their service—and they are aware of it."

"They all know there can be circumstances in which a man may have to stay down and die," Stephens said. "But that does not necessarily apply to you people. If this comes to the last ditch—as you must know it may—I propose to offer a chance to those who want to take it. Say the DSRV does not find us and that no hope remains they will. In that case, there are the Steinke hoods. We are deep, probably almost at the limit for a trained man. You people are not trained, but it is conceivable some of you could survive the ascent. In that case, I intend to let you try—if you wish."

He looked around the room, gazing intently through a pain grown close to the limit of tolerability: Kirov, Brown, the woman, Uzzumekis, Mueller, Nicolai. It wasn't much he was offering, he knew. The chances that it would really work for any of them were odds he would never bet in a poker game or on a horse.

"And, of course, each of you would have to figure out for himself what he preferred—this or what you would come up to. You must know that anything waiting for you up there would be Russian. It is not a choice I would care to have to make for myself." He looked around again, and the guilt and shame were with him, compounding the very real pain in his

284

skull. I've never been so goddam tired, he thought. He lifted his head. "I think that's everything I have to say."

Kirov, whose usual composure could not be compared with either that of Captain Brown, who probably felt that seeming unflappable was merely the thing one did, or of Mueller, who may have felt that seeming to be fashioned of cast iron was the only conceivable mien to show all lesser creatures—including wives, children, and subordinates—now asked Uzzumekis to straighten out what had been going on. He didn't ask often, and Stephens had an uneasy feeling that most of the time he didn't need to. Kirov's composure was a special kind, no pose. Stephens suspected he was quiet to keep from interfering with the receptive capacity of his pores. Kirov sighed and spoke and Uzzumekis did his duty.

"He says that while his countrymen may have expected many things of him during his lifetime and surely suspected him of many more, probably the last thing they would ever expect would be to see him coming up out of the Black Sea like a pregnant sturgeon surfacing for the sun. Much as he thinks the spectacle might arouse amazement and cause a good deal of comment, he feels he must decline—with thanks. He has for a long lifetime been willing to sacrifice anything for his people—but if they want the circus they will have to go to Moscow."

"Hear, hear!" Captain Brown said, with open enthusiasm. "Very little point, really, in surfacing in those waters. Humiliating. Worse for him, of course."

"Nobody is asked to decide now," Stephens said. "I wanted you to know the possibilities. I guess I owe it to you." He found himself gazing at the girl. Shame was sour in his throat, though he knew it wasn't his fault she was here. Why in the name of God had she got here? She was looking down at her hands, silent, sad, with a great quietness in her. Stephens caught Uzzumekis' eye and nodded toward her. Uzzumekis touched her arm gently; Stephens had not before seen him give her more than a glance. Now he spoke to her quietly, and she looked up at him and spoke and then turned her gray glance on Stephens. What was in it, sadness surely, sorrow probably, resignation maybe, trust, not exactly. If she visibly gave anybody here trust it was to Uzzumekis, and even that was tinged with something beyond identifying.

"She says there is nothing there for her, not any longer. She is sorry she gives you trouble."

"I'm getting accustomed to it," Stephens said shortly. "Only the kind we've stuck her with sets badly. You?"

"Hell, Captain, I've got two murder raps waiting for me on the beach," Uzzumekis said. He stared at Kirov, not with animosity. "And I've got him. They might pass up the killings with twenty years. But personal travel agent for Mr. Big? No thanks, I'll take mine here."

Nicolai, who had been, for a man of his volatility, extraordinarily pensive, decided it was time to have at least a tentative opinion.

"I am a man of faith," he announced. "I have decided to place that valuable commodity in your little submarine. However, I am also a man of prudence, and, even with a thing as priceless as faith, I prefer to hedge a little. The little submarine first and I promise you I will be on my knees praying for its successful journey . . ." He paused for a moment of gentle confusion. "I mean, of course, journeys. After all, I might not be in the first relay.

"But should the little submarine regrettably fall on evil times—I think it would be necessary for me to shift my little remaining faith to your—what did you call it, Captain, hood? Yes, that is it. Hood. After all, the Russians should bear me little ill will—particularly, my Captain, if you would be so generous as to furnish me with testimony to the innocence of my presence here . . ."

"Glad to do it," Stephens said shortly.

Kapitan Mueller spoke up, his voice harsh, his eyes on Nicolai.

"Have you ever been in a Russian prison?"

"No, Herr Kapitan, but there are worse things than prison, surely."

"You will not believe that after you have experienced it. The Russians sank my boat in the Baltic in the autumn of 1944. I was on the bridge and was thrown into the sea; the rest of the crew went down with my boat. A violation of my principles but unavoidable. I was in prison until the beginning of 1946. I have, quite naturally, little desire to sit here and suffocate, particularly when it is necessary to go about like this." He looked with distaste at the knobby nudity of his feet. "But if this is the alternative to rotting in a Russian jail—I take this." He folded his arms.

Nicolai regarded the German officer with warm sympathy and spoke as though to a child.

"That, Herr Kapitan, perfectly illustrates the pigheaded, not quite to say suicidal obstinacy of the German race. Our man Mussolini was not a bad fellow in many ways, but I have long believed that the cachet of his essential stupidity was to throw in our national lot with your man who was clearly a psychotic lunatic and bent upon hauling everybody about him along to perdition.

"As for me, although not entirely without physical courage—I believe I proved that admirably when I went back to Marida in Istanbul—early and clearly discerned the difference between being courageous and merely being stubborn. One should not ignore the true portents of the course of coming history. I saw them like a vision at Kasserine Pass in 1942. I was captured. The less discerning might say I deserted, since I threw away my rifle and ran down a hill waving my handkerchief, but that would be unjust. It was already clear that my little rifle was not likely to accomplish much for my fatherland.

"I spent the rest of the war in Montana. Technically I was a prisoner of war, but I assure you, gentlemen, I have fond memories of Montana. Travel teaches a man many fascinating and even enjoyable lessons, such as the taste and tenderness of Montana beef. It even teaches the essence of true humanity, to love your fellow man. Wars would become unnecessary if men traveled more, observed more and learned

287

that there is warmth and nobility in all nations. Now, there was a girl in Missoula . . ."

"Bah!" Mueller said. "To desert in the face of the enemy . . ." His voice could not carry the weight of his contempt.

Nicolai waved a softly reproving forefinger.

"But recall, Herr Kapitan. While I was learning many instructive and broadening—and some delicious things about Montana, you in your cold submarine were pursuing your stubborn and futile course toward inevitable self-destruction. Who was right?" He lifted his shoulders, hands palm upward. It was the eternal gesture of questing man's futile search for the genuine 24-carat truth of his condition.

Stephens found himself grinning in spite of the headache. "Gentlemen . . . young lady. This has taken too much time. I must get back to the ship. I ask you—no, I tell you—return to your quarters and remain quiet. I want no noise. I want no physical exertion. I demand your patience and such courage as you can muster. If escape is possible—good. But please remember that I will direct the circumstances of that escape. All of them. It may be that you regard my country as the champion of democracy, which it claims to be, and which it often is, in fact. It is a virtue which we sincerely admire. It is also one which the Navy leaves at the dock. Please do not get the notion that you have any vote aboard this ship. The only word that counts here is mine." Stephens got up.

As the others began to rise, Stephens saw the imperturbable Uzzumekis seem to wince. The man settled back in his chair and spoke.

"Captain, would I be out of order to borrow the services of those corpsmen or pharmacist's mates or whatever you call them in the Navy for a few minutes?"

"Of course," Stephens said. Damn, he thought, now I've got a sick man on my hands—and it has to be this mammoth. "What seems to be the trouble, Mr. Uzzumekis?"

"Nothing much. But that little bastard with his popgun seems to have nicked me slightly when it went off. It may need a Band-Aid or something."

He started to rise again, got all the way up, then, like a storm-struck oak, he swayed—and crashed to the deck.

"Billings!" Stephens yelled as he started around the table. "Get the chief pharmacist!"

It may have taken Stephens four seconds to negotiate his way around the chairs and people to where Uzzumekis lay. By the time he made it, the girl was down on her knees beside the toppled giant.

Christ, Stephens thought as he hit the deck beside the moaning girl. Blood was gushing like a geyser high up on the inside of Uzzumekis' right thigh and already had formed a pool on the deck.

XXIII

Lieutenant J. N. Hale owned three compelling reasons, although he was not aware of them as such, why it was impossible for the idea of surrendering the search for *Skate* to enter his head : one, he was proud; two, he was stubborn; three, he was constitutionally incapable of leaving other submariners to drown like kittens tied up in a sack.

Moreove, he did not believe the DSRV could miss in the long run. The little sub's antennae were too sensitive for that. Some of the stuff was for long shots; others, so to speak, for the making of portraits. The little DSRV, he felt deeply, was simply too well educated to miss.

Nevertheless, he was dead exhausted when he brought the baby submarine for the second time alongside the *Queen Zenobia*. He got his hands on the ladder, heaved himself over the rail, ordered the chargers into action and sent men down to relieve Akers and Pauer. Somebody else, certainly fresher, could monitor the charge pouring down to the DSRV's batteries in a steady river of energy. Then he turned to the bridge ladder and mounted tired hand over tired foot.

"Nothing?" Admiral March's voice grated with fatigue as he met Hale at the head of the ladder. Hale had been more or less on his feet for twenty-four hours, groping for *Skate* with his bag of tools—more than ample to astound King Arthur's Merlin—bolstered by a submariner's instinct which defied definition. For about twenty-seven hours before that he had either been getting the DSRV ready or lying nine-tenths awake, stewing over whether everything would work. (After all, Merlin must sometimes have wondered, too.) He did not doubt the DSRV; he doubted himself, since he was sure the little vessel's electronic innards must be smarter than he was. Admiral March's strains had not been nearly as physical as Hale's, but his anxieties were as abrading, and, moreover, he was much older.

"Nothing," Hale said. "But we've combed the area pretty thoroughly. There's not much space left where he could be, and we should fetch him next time out." He hoped that didn't sound as fatuous to the admiral as he was afraid it did to himself. It couldn't be the DSRV's fault; it had to be his own. He had now missed her twice, and the knowledge hurt, as he had expected it would.

"There's a lot of action up there, sir. Our Russian buddies are looking, too. They've got one advantage; they're on their home grounds."

To Hale it was utterly unthinkable that the Russians might pick up *Skate* before he did.

"Don't you think you ought to let somebody else spell you the next time she goes out?" Lieutenant Commander Gottfried asked. "After all, you've got other men qualified in the DSRV. They know it, too. And you look like hell."

"They don't know the boat as well as I do," Hale said. "Besides they haven't been down there to run the search patterns Akers and Pauer and I have. Better leave it to us.

"Incidentally, you had any more interruption out here, sir?" he asked Admiral March.

"They sent that patrol boat out again to look us over; hung around an hour just before dusk and then shoved off without a peep. After all, we're still outside their twelve-mile limit."

"Maybe they haven't quite figured us out yet. Or what to do about us," Gottfried said.

"I wouldn't bet a plugged nickel on it," the admiral said. "Maybe they're a little spooked yet. A little hesitant about actually precipitating a hassle with Washington. Although they've got a solid excuse if they want to take it. After all, legally we're under false colors—a pirate ship—on what they'd have to define as a hostile mission."

"Who the hell knows what goes on in the Kremlin's mind?" Hale asked out of his weariness, forgetting that he was addressing an admiral.

"This is getting tight enough out here, so that I hope somebody in Washington is at least getting a glimmer of what's on their minds. If things go according to pattern, they're probably now shaking rockets at one another."

It was getting close on their second midnight, and *Skate* had been down more than twenty-two hours.

"With everything shut down—which he damn well will have done—if he's alive—things will be getting kind of foul and stinking in that boat, not to mention hot. But it should be survivable for maybe another twenty-four—maybe more than that—depending on how bad he's hit," the admiral said. "When do you want to shove off again?"

"Soon as the charge is in. Should be a couple of hours yet."

"You're really pushing it, lad," said Lieutenant Commander Gottfried, who was at least ten years younger than Hale. Damn it, Hale thought, I wish these guys who outrank me in everything but age wouldn't insist on calling me a snotty-nosed kid. First, that red-assed Air-Force major, now Gottfried.

"It's a good thing you surfaced in the dark," the admiral said. "I can't even imagine what the Russians would do—or maybe I can—if they sent their snoopers out here and found you alongside in broad daylight."

"I'm not so sure they won't one of these trips, sir. When my batteries are down, I have to come up, no matter what time of day it is."

He felt himself sag with weariness, barely on his feet.

"I sent Pauer and Akers below for a little rest. They're the best I've got, and besides, they know the ground now. And I think I'll hit the sack, too." He turned to Gottfried. "Dave, send somebody for me when she's ready, will you?"

"Sure, lad. Would you like a shot before you turn in?"

"Would I? Yes, sir!" Then instinctively Hale turned a slightly apprehensive eye on the admiral. After all, he knew he served the only dry Navy in the world. Or did he? He seemed to remember from somewhere that their current inhospitable hosts, the Russians, were also teetotalers when afloat.

"Send him a double, Mr. Gottfried," Admiral March said. "*Queen Zenobia*'s not regular Navy, not yet."

Two hours and the double scotch, Hale recognized, had done something for him—but a long way from enough—when he straddled the *Queen*'s rail and scrambled down her low freeboard to the sloshing almost nonexistent freeboard of the DSRV at 0230 hours. The little sub was ready to go again but he was a long way from sure that Akers or Pauer or he were.

Let's see now. In two trips, running almost to the absolute limits of both batteries and brain, they had searched two patterns, one dead ahead on 355, where he had last heard the echo of *Skate*'s stricken descent. That had taken them out nine miles toward the coast, which he reckoned to be at least a mile and a half closer in to land than he supposed *Skate* lay. But he had been trying desperately to cover every possibility, for example, damage to the stern turning her inadvertently as she went down. On the second trip he had followed a general course line ten degrees to the right, or 005. Nothing. What was left? Cut it down the middle. It might be the last hope.

"We'll take her in pretty much as usual," he told Akers and Pauer. "Out there where we've been at the end of the pattern there's a spread of maybe two miles where conceivably we haven't covered everything. As a matter of fact, I know we haven't, or we'd have had her by now. And those goddam gullies ain't helping us any. We'll get down to three hundred right away and run a close zigzag pattern. As soon as we're six miles from the ship, I want everything put on, sonar, TV, searchlights. This time we want her—and want her for real. Base course three-five-nine. Got that?"

"Aye, aye," Pauer said. "Sir, I think the Russians have picked us up a couple of times. But they've never held on." Pauer's face was haggard with fatigue and perhaps something

293

more, but whatever it was, Hale didn't think much of it was fear—although, of course, perhaps some.

Commander Federenko was on the bridge of his patrolling Destroyer Escort, where he and the increasingly distraught Chief of State Security had thus far kept a futile twenty-one-hour watch.

"We make no progress, Comrade," Sobelov complained. "This should have come to some conclusion—or at least some definite information long ago. If I ran my duties the way the navy does, my head would have vanished long ago. In fact, years."

"I explained the technical difficulties to you when this first began," Federenko said coldly. "You will forgive me that your bureau had more than a fortnight to find Kirov before you did find him and then allowed one of your agents to be murdered and the man to slip through your fingers?"

"That is no longer relevant," Sobelov reminded him. "I am aware of my error and am prepared to pay the cost of it. I urge you not to incur a similar debt."

"I am trying not to."

"Naturally," Sobelov snapped.

"Now, there is something else about what you suppose to be the navy's lack of efficiency," Federenko said with something that might have been a gleam of tired satisfaction. "We have not found the nuclear submarine—that is regrettably true. But I do not think we are entirely empty-handed."

"And what may that mean?" Sobelov demanded.

"We have been getting sonar contacts."

"With what?"

"We are not sure. It is small and slow, and it has, thus far, proved to be impossible to hold. But it is moving in these waters."

"Why then, in the name of heaven—which normally I abjure—have you not been able to hold contact?"

"I explained that," Federenko said impatiently. "It is small, slow, mostly silent, and extraordinarily elusive."

"All right then, Comrade, if you have only this will-o-the-wisp, what can it conceivably mean to us?"

"Ah," Federenko was as pleased as a man in his depressed state of mind could be. "It may be some kind of rescue vessel."

"Rescue vessel! You mean a submarine?"

"We hear rumors of such things."

"It can't be permitted. Does it have a chance to beat us?"

Federenko lifted his shoulders in the manner of one who has been asked a question both impossible and absurd.

Lieutenant Hale, and Akers and Pauer were two and a half hours and five miles out from *Queen Zenobia* at 310 feet with everything working, zigzagging slightly from their base course moving at two knots, prowling by vision and feel and all their electronic gear into one empty declivity after another in the sea floor. For the first time, far surmounting his own fatigue of body and mind, Hale felt the clutching hand of despair and death—not his own death but the deaths of those he had sought with determination and stubborn courage.

And Akers suddenly shouted.

"I've got something! Something!"

Hale, as though roused from the dead, was instantly alert.

"Where! What have you got?" he croaked.

Akers was stammering and yelling at the same time.

"An echo. An echo. Bears ten degrees right. Three hundred yards."

"How big is it?" Hale demanded, professionalism suddenly rising above his quick intense hope.

"Not much. Just a pip."

"Probably another God damned rock!" Pauer said out of the depths of uncounted disappointments.

Hale was already turning the DSRV onto Akers' range and bearing.

"Get the lights on it!" he ordered. "And get onto the viewports." He cursed the water, its dark and blinding murk, and moved ahead dead slow, holding down his longing to charge ahead and then Pauer yelled.

"It's *Skate!* The sail's in sight. Five-seven-eight!"

The fatigue, but not the fear, went out of Hale in a huge, surging catharsis. And at once, through this uncontainable joy tempered with uncertain apprehension, the instincts of his profession asserted themselves.

"How's she lie?" he demanded.

"Down in one of those damned gullies," Pauer said in disgust. "As near as I can tell, listed to starboard. Probably the reason we missed her so long. Nothing but the sail is visible from here."

"Can we get down beside her? Find out what shape she's in?"

It struck them all with dread that this might be a dead ship and all within it and they may have sought and found it in vain. The thought wouldn't bear support.

"I don't know how much clearance around her there is in the gully."

"Well, we're gonna try it," Hale said. "Keep a lookout. I want to go directly over the bow first—in front of the sail. Keep the lights down on her. I want to see if she's smashed forward—and what it's like around the escape hatch. Then, look sharp. I want to see the stern. If she's in fair shape forward, we've got a chance to get somebody out of her. Sing out when you see anything."

"Aye, aye."

"Akers, keep the television on her. Especially on the hatch —and then on the stern. Goddamit, we found her!"

Hovering, moving glacially slow, the DSRV drifted over *Skate's* bow and settled in front of the sail with the escape skirt almost over the submarine's hatch.

"It looks secure," Pauer's voice called up from the port bottom viewport. His voice was tense.

"How much list? Can you make it out?" Hale called.

"Enough," Pauer called. "Maybe as much as nine or ten degrees. Can we handle that, sir?"

"We'd damn well better!" Hale said. "Now, keep a lookout. I want to see the stern."

The DSRV drifted clear of *Skate*, found a squeeze-through depression in the gully along the port side in the gully and eased toward the stern of the submarine. As they reached near it, Akers on the television gasped.

"Sir, the whole ass end of her is gone !"

Hale felt his heart sink. She could still be a dead ship.

"How much of the ass end, for the love of God?" he yelled.

"Both screws, both rudders. The after compartment is a heap of junk, waving in the breeze."

Well, Hale thought, if she ruptured as many as two compartments, there could still be people alive ahead of that, but it was a lead-pipe cinch that *Skate* had to have some dead ones, too. How many there could be no way of knowing, except to get her open and find out.

"All right, look alive," he called. "We're going to try to make a seal on that forward hatch. I'll nurse her around. When we get up there, Pauer, take a spanner and hammer out the signal, so they'll know it's us. Don't beat on it too much. This close they should hear us easy—if there's anybody down there to hear. And we don't want those other people upstairs listening."

With infinite care, Hale eased the DSRV up and out of the depression on *Skate*'s port quarter, rose behind the sail, turned out to starboard, and moved away 100 feet to give a turning radius which the baby submarine could well manage with her extraordinary maneuvering ability. He nursed the little vessel in ahead of *Skate*'s sail toward the flat flange around the submarine's escape hatch set into the upper surface of her pressure hull. Below that, he knew, was another upright pressure chamber, set like an egg inside the pressure hull, big enough to accommodate four or five men at a time. This escape trunk, as it was called, would also be sealed at its lower end by another heavy hatch.

Hale's job was to maneuver the DSRV so that the gasket surface of the lower skirt would settle down precisely on the flange around the hatch. Then its haul-down winch would have to be secured, without any direct assistance from human hands, to the submarine's escape hatch bail. Once the winch had pulled the DSRV down to a tight seal on the submarine —and only then—could he blow the sea water out of the DSRV's inundated lower skirt and blast it into the DSRV's own ballast tanks. Thereafter the pressure of the sea would hold the two vessels mated in unbreakable orgasm—until Hale chose to break it.

With the skirt dry, Pauer and Akers could open the lower hatch in the DSRV's central sphere, descend into the de-watered skirt, retrieve the telephone in *Skate's* hatch, and call to whoever was inside. With his pumps, Hale would equalize the pressure between the two vessels. Thereafter, *Skate* could undog her own two hatches and living beings—if such there were—could begin emerging to live again.

Hale knew the maneuver sounded simple enough. He also knew it was in fact enormously difficult, particularly with *Skate* listing at a fairly stiff angle. It was a job for a seagoing maestro who had never done it before except in practice. The DSRV crept. It had for guides its own high resolution sonar, exquisitely tuned for these distances, plus the human eyes of Chief Pauer, on his hands and knees, staring down through the mistily lighted water of the DSRV's bottom skirt, staring at *Skate's* deck as though watching a peep show.

"How is it?" Hale called softly, controlling his desperate urgency.

"Just about," Pauer answered. "Easy. Easy. Slow. A little port. Inches. Half inches. There!"

"Drop her astern," Hale spoke to Akers. "Ease her down. Easy."

There came a rush of water as Akers nursed ballast into the DSRV's after trim tanks. Then a muffled thunk, and she was down. The thunk made almost less noise than Hale's explosive sigh.

"Secure the winch," he called to Pauer.

"Aye," Pauer answered. Then, after moments that could have served for hours, he called up, "Winch secure and tight, sir."

"Dewater the skirt," Hale told Akers. "We're on her. Thank God!" It was as close to a prayer as ever he had uttered.

As the water sank in the skirt, driven by highly compressed air into the DSRV's main ballast with Akers at the controls, Pauer crouched face down over the tiny viewport in the bottom hatch of the little sub's middle pressure sphere and watched it recede. At length, in an agony of waiting, he could see the submarine's upper hatch.

"Skirt's dry," he called up to Hale at the DSRV's control console in the forward sphere. "Permission to crack the hatch?"

"Permission granted," Hale said in what he hoped was a normal voice of command—but whose strain confessed that it was not quite that. He prayed the seal was tight and that when Pauer opened the DSRV admittance hatch he would not find his own baby vessel full of sea water. That would finish things—for everybody.

Pauer undogged the hatch with some care, having in mind thoughts somewhat similar to Hale's. It stayed dry below. He swung his feet over and got them onto the few rungs of ladder and, straddling *Skate's* upper hatch, fumbled for and got his hands on *Skate's* telephone and spoke into it, "Ahoy, *Skate*—Baby's here."

For perhaps half an hour Commander Stephens had known something was on and around his vessel. At first he could not know which of his hunters it might be; after all, he knew there were two. At this close range, within scant feet, the sounds were audible, and at least once *Skate* had been touched with a noticeable thump. A heavy-shod diver on deck conceivably could have made that noise. But even through his blinding headache and the fatigue, he didn't think it was. In any case, instinctive hope would not permit him to credit that. It had to be Hale and the DSRV. For him, as for Hale, there had to be the consuming concern whether Hale could successfully seal on and dewater the skirt. If he couldn't nothing had been accomplished. If the DSRV wouldn't mate and seal they were as dead as ever, as though sealed between themselves and rescue as by the time-locked, sixteen-inch-thick vault doors of the Chase Manhattan Bank in Rockefeller Center. All the same, professional reality or not, hope was no more suppressible than life.

The certainty came with Chief of the Boat Cate, who came aft from the forward torpedo room, gaunt and impassive as ever, still wearing his bloody sleeve, and reported with a matter-of-factness that might have meant that he expected it all the time.

"The DSRV is latched on, sir. What's the priority?"

"How many people aboard know it?"

"I don't know, sir."

"Keep as many as you can quiet. The last thing we need is a rush."

"The DSRV wants to know how many survivors we have."

"All right, Chief, I'll come forward and talk to Hale. You got him on the horn or one of the chiefs?"

"Pauer. But he's got Hale."

Stephens knew he was stumbling as he passed down the wardroom stairway, passed through enlisted men's quarters, waited while Cate undogged the door to the forward torpedo room, knew that eyes followed him every step, knew that now he had to begin making choices. That first choice, he knew, was arbitrary: first he got rid of the unfit. The agonizing choices would come later when he would have to play God among the fit. That is, if the DSRV ever got back.

"Joe," he rallied himself to say in a low voice as they came into the torpedo room and before he took the telephone that led up into *Skate's* bottle-shaped escape chamber. "You're going to have to take this first load."

"Hell, no, I'm not, Captain. I'm chief of this boat."

"That's exactly why you're going to have to take them. They're going to be the toughest bunch to handle. I need you to take them." And privately he was thinking that Joe had two kids in college. "All right, I'll get on the horn."

"Stephens here," he said. "Pass this word to Hale. I've got twenty dead. Seventeen in the stern compartment and out of reach. Three in the boat, and I guess we'll have to leave them. There's eighteen wounded, three I think serious. Two prisoners, one wounded, one a crew member. Another passenger wounded. I have five other passengers. That makes one hundred and seven alive to take off all together. The wounded prisoners and passengers add up to twenty-four. I've got to send an escort, and I'm sending Chief Cate. That makes twenty-five."

"That makes a full load," Hale's message was relayed back to him.

"I know it," Stephens' voice was tinged with impatience.

"A full design load. But this is not a design situation. It would take another three full trips to get everybody off this bucket and I suspect you know damned well, Lieutenant, you're not going to take three more loads out of here. You'll be lucky if you make one more."

"Captain, I don't think she'll do it."

"Listen, by God, she is going to do it! I'm unloading my crips, my prisoners, and my freeloaders this time because I have to. I've got able-bodied men down here. I'll never in God's name get 'em all out. Somebody's going to die down here. You are going to take every breathing body you can into that thing and then get back for more—if you can. That's an order, Mr. Hale."

Hale's voice was desperate. "But I can't, Captain Stephens!"

"You can! And you will! It doesn't matter if they don't breathe good going up; what matters is that they breathe at all after this. Blow some ballast and that'll take care of the weight. That's an order, Hale."

"Aye, aye, sir," Hale said. Privately, in despair and rage, he was damning rank and the privilege of command to some everlasting white hot hell. Which, knowing the circumstances of *Skate*'s present situation, he did not much doubt that Stephens would before long be frying in.

Stephens, trembling with anger and fatigue, turned to Chief Cate. "Chief, get a working party up here and round up the first load. The guests, the prisoners including that jerk Cavanides with his busted arm, Quill—I want you to prefer my charges against both of them as soon as they're up—the wounded including that big bastard Uzzumekis, the girl, Kirov, the rest of the guests—and I'll pick the ten other able-bodied passengers. I'm keeping Cummings, of course, because somebody's got to keep this boat from caving in as long as possible. Move 'em quietly but move 'em fast. And keep this door dogged."

Thank God, I've got a crew that doesn't panic worth a damn, Stephens thought as Cate left on his errand. Still, I don't want a crowd in here. It's not easy watching somebody else get away, knowing that maybe you yourself never will.

Now it was time to do some deciding. The cripples, the prisoners, the guests had to go. But he had bullied Hale into taking ten more than he was supposed to. But who? It was up to him. Was this a moral question? Or merely eenie-meenie-minie-mo? With Cummings and Guernic he would play selfish and keep them, one for the sake of the boat, the other for the sake of his own sanity.

The door was undogged. It was Billings, bringing the woman, and Cavanides, his broken arm in a sling, pale and speechless. Stephens looked at him with loathing.

"Help the girl up the ladders first," he told Billings.

As they mounted, Stephens turned to Cavanides.

"I promised you'd be the last man but me off this boat. Instead you're the first. You're going partly because I can no longer stand the smell of skunk. You are also going because you are a prisoner of the United States and I have preferred charges against you which will be carried by your escort. These include assault, attempted murder, and sabotage. If you make any further trouble, he has my orders to shoot you."

Billings reappeared back down the ladder from Hale's DSRV, his dark face expressionless. I guess I just made a choice, Stephens thought to himself. He turned to Cavanides. "Get up that ladder," he snapped. "There are better men waiting."

"I need help," Cavanides said.

"You'll get none. Get *up* that ladder!"

Cavanides made it, painfully, as awkwardly as a crab, using his two good feet, his good left hand and the doubled elbow of his slung right arm, the fear in his heart and the hatred in his head.

"What you want me to do next, Captain?" Billings asked.

"Fetch two more, the Englishman and the wounded officer, Bartoli."

As Billings left, Cate returned with Nicolai and with Gross, who stumbled and wore a vacant, wondering look. It's probably a concussion, Stephens thought, from the thing that cold-cocked him back there in the navigation department.

"That kid is out on his feet," Stephens told Nicolai. "I can't spare my men. You help him up that ladder and be quick about it. And I hope that Marida screws you into the same condition when you get to Istanbul."

" I hope she does also," Nicolai said as he guided Gross's fumbling hands on the ladder, going up with his feet only a rung below the sailor's supporting the sagging body with his own. He turned his head, "Captain, I am deeply grateful."

"Don't thank me. Keep moving!"

Billings returned with Lieutenant Bartoli, his broken arm slung like Cavanides' and with Captain Brown.

"Billings, go fetch another couple," Stephens said. "Captain Brown can help Mr. Bartoli, can't you, sir?"

Brown was plainly embarrassed.

"Captain, I really shouldn't accept this. It strikes me as unsporting. Moreover I am the senior officer aboard this boat."

"I sympathize, Captain," Stephens said kindly. "But it isn't your boat. Kindly help that officer up as quickly as possible."

"You are a brave man, Captain."

"Good luck with the *Royal Oak*."

The door was undogged again, bringing Mueller and a man whose face had one eyeball missing, the rest smashed beyond recognition. But Stephens knew he was the big handsome young talker who yelled depths under the keel in really shallow waters. Name's Gilmore. Guernic brought this pair, the cigarette imperiling his beard.

"Thanks, Ray," Stephens said, then turned to the German. "Herr Kapitan, I'll appreciate your guiding this man. He can't see much."

The tall German, austere but absurd in his bare feet, was at his most formal.

"Captain, as you know, I lost my own boat in nineteen forty-four. All lost but me. I feel it is improper for me to . . ."

Stephens was on the verge of losing his temper.

"Two at a time, is it? That was your boat, and if you feel it was a disgrace, kindly carry your disgrace out of here. *This* is my boat. Kindly give it your help by getting your ass up that ladder and give that man what help he needs. *Achtung!* On the double !"

"Sir . . ." the German said.

"Get ! Or I'll have you carried."

Quill arrived under tow by Cate with another man who gasped with the grating pain of four broken ribs.

"You think you can make it, son?" Stephens asked the wounded man. "It'll probably hurt less than being man-handled, but I'll get you help if you have to have it."

"I'll try it, sir," the man, a signalman named Lusk said. He got his hands on the rails and a foot on the first rung and pulled—and screamed. Then he choked the scream and Stephens could see him biting his lips as he pulled up, one piece of agony at a time. Stephens turned to Quill.

"You know you're going to a general court, don't you?" he said, not unkindly.

"Yes, sir," Howie Quill said. He was pale and involuntarily quivering. He blurted, "Captain, let me stay—I—I can help—"

"Sorry. I can't let you off that easy. Up the ladder, boy—

maybe you couldn't help it. Some can't, if that's any comfort to you. Up the ladder!"

They came by pairs, except for the man from the nav compartment who had seemed at first might have a broken back. Now it was almost certain. He appeared to be paralyzed from the hips down and had not been able to walk at all. Billings and Guernic carried him. Stephens remembered his name was Rundle.

"We're going to have to hoist him," Stephens said. "Billings, you're both young and strong as a bulldozer. Take a line and get up there and lower it. The chief and I will get a bight under his arms and the chief will guide him up and take what weight he can but most of it is up to you. Can do?"

"Can sure as hell try, sir," Billings said, and vanished into the blackness above. And it worked, although Stephens saw that the palms of Billings' hands were bleeding when he came back down again. That's one choice that was pretty easy, he thought to himself. But another able-bodied one I've got to send is a pharmacist with plenty of morphine. That's going to be a load of the sickest chickens you ever saw. Maybe the girl can help; she seems calm and pretty capable.

It seemed endless but eventually it did end—nearly. They were all up: broken arms, broken skulls, torn flesh turning black, broken legs—one man with both out of commission—the limping, the blind, the broken.

All but one. Where the everlasting hell was Uzzumekis with his crazy name, his mighty body, and the Greek's bullet down his leg through the femoral artery and the tourniquet that was all that stood between him and the hereafter? I hope the bastard doesn't lose that leg, Stephens thought; who could manufacture a phony that would support that giant? And what a giant.

And where is Kirov?

He went looking for them himself. He found them in the wardroom. Kirov, the fallen god, sat in Stephens' own armchair, looking down on Uzzumekis, filling almost the full length of the wardroom transom. Kirov had a Navy towel and a stainless steel Navy bowl filled with water with which he was bathing Uzzumekis' gray but composed face.

"What the hell is this?" Stephens demanded. "You're holding up the parade, for Christ's sake."

"He won't go," Uzzumekis said.

"The hell he won't go! What does he think we came after? Tell him to get forward and I'll get about six man mountains to come and carry you."

"Nyet," Kirov said calmly, and spoke to Uzzumekis, who translated.

"He says he is deeply sorry—and I think the old shithead means that at least. He says this is a tragedy between our two countries. He says he now realizes he was a fool. He says he does not intend to compound the foolishness. He says there must be leaders in America, as insane as he was, ever to consent to this."

"Tell him I'll have him carried, fat as he is."

Uzzumekis translated and Kirov spoke at length and Uzzumekis, though obviously in considerable pain answered for him.

"He says it would be useless to try to force him because he has a pistol—to tell the God's honest truth I didn't know he had it or I'd have taken it away from him long ago—and the second your carriers appear he will kill himself."

"What does he think he intends to do then?"

Uzzumekis translated again and then again for Kirov.

"He says this man is badly hurt—I guess he means me—and needs help and you should take me at once . . . As for him, he wants time to think—and intends to take it. He considers if you took him now it would make clowns of the leaders of his country, which he admits they are, but more serious, it would also make a clown of his country. He will consider; he knows your little submarine will come again. If he can see his way clear, he will go on the next trip."

Stephens was close to rage, in fact he was all the way there.

"Doesn't the pigheaded old goat know I command this ship?"

Kirov nodded gravely. Once again Stephens had the uneasy feeling that Kirov understood language through his pores or some other extrasensory organ.

Uzzumekis was speaking for him again.

"Yes, he knows that, and he is deeply sorry for the things you must do. But in this he has the upper hand. You cannot take him against his will. You command the ship, but not his soul."

"All right, tell the bastard he has cost us twenty dead men, created traitors, wrecked a ship, and smashed up eighteen other men better than himself, including you. That's a fairly high price for whimsy."

Kirov nodded and spoke.

"He says he knows. There have been worse follies in history, but he admits this one is beyond forgiveness. He will think and if he can convince himself, he will go with the little submarine's next trip."

"There may never be a next trip," Stephens said grimly. "But, now about you; I'm going to get you out of here."

"You can't," Uzzumekis said with hard finality. "This man —Kirov—is my responsibility. I have to stay with the old sonofabitch because I'm the only way you can talk to him. He's mine; I fetched him. Besides I'm not as bad off as you may think. Us Lithuanians are tough."

"Jesus glittering Christ!" Stephens exploded. "All the way to this sinkhole of hell to find a couple of pigheaded mutineers. All right, maybe you can survive until the DSRV's next trip. And then, by God, pistol or no pistol, clown country or no clown country, leg or no leg, you're getting off my boat! Now I'm going to find some better men than either of you to send off."

He left, fuming. But away down under the rage, he knew that here were two good ones, two that couldn't be duplicated.

He found Cate waiting in the forward torpedo room.

"Chief, I'm going to lighten ship. I want these men in here on the double: Guernic, he's too good a navigator for the

Navy to discard; Pete Zink, he's not only a damned good officer but he's got a new baby; Billings, because he's a hell of a man and asks nothing in return; Jackson, he's among the best of the pharmacists and that load of cripples is likely to need attention on the way out; Jensen, the sonar boss, because they're rare; West, Turner, Kauffman; the two reactor men, Phillips and Majewski because they're rarities and we don't need them any more, and yourself. And be quick about it. Zink's an officer and, I suppose, technically in command. But you're running that show and I'll tell him so."

"Listen, Captain . . ."

"Listen, my ass. Get 'em in here and get them up in that DSRV on the double. Before you close the top hatch, ask Hale and pass the word down how soon he can be back."

"How about the Russian?"

"He's having a streak of Russian—just take my word for it."

Guernic protested, as did others. Stephens simply said, "Ray, I want you off this boat. I've known all along you'd burn it up some day with those damned cigarettes, but this ain't the time. Now, get!"

The hatches were closed; he could hear the blast of air and the muted grate of metals as the DSRV disengaged. He went back to the wardroom and began making a list. Seventy-two left, counting those two stubborn sonsofbitches, one lying on the transom, the other bathing the shot man's face. Two more trips—if the DSRV could make that many.

He had made out the priorities. Damn it, being God was no job for a man, especially not for one boob enough to get shot down by an armful of smashed crockery. Tiredly he got up and made his way aft to see how successfully Cummings and his working party were holding back the sea.

XXIV

In the nine hours Lieutenant Hale needed to find his way out to the *Queen Zenobia*, unload his overloaded and already gasping passengers from the DSRV, get a charge back into his batteries, and grab a couple of hours' rest, other actions having to do with *Skate* were going on in the world. But Commander Stephens, lying helpless on the bottom in his dark, increasingly foul, increasingly toxic, increasingly torrid, little world had no way of knowing what they were. Although, knowing some of the rules of the game, he could have made some educated guesses. For example, he knew the Russian hunt would still be on.

When the DSRV returned, mated to *Skate*, sealed and dewatered her lower skirt, Hale had been in more or less continuous action for some sixty hours—barring about four out for some dubious rest on his returns for a recharge; he couldn't guess how many more he could endure, but he was still determined to last until the job was done.

Thus his tired voice was nearly as croaking as Stephens' when it was strained down through the equally worn-out lungs and larynx of Chief Pauer.

"How'd you make out with that overload?" Stephens called up into the darkness of the gut leading into the bowels of the DSRV.

"We made it," Hale sent the word back down. "That's about all you can say for it."

"Nobody could ask you to say more. I've still got seventy-two, including the old man, Kirov and his escort—that guy with the weird name; he's wounded; that crazy Greek you hauled the last time shot him in the leg—and bad."

"I'll get you all with this and one more trip—provided I can get away with one more—there are some things you ought to know about, Commander."

Commander Federenko, the salvage expert, and Sobelov,

the Chief of Soviet State Security, entertained a mounting suspicion about the *Queen Zenobia*'s activities lying there offshore—or rather about her apparent lack of any activity whatever. But with a rash of orders, counterorders, suggestions, and impatient demands for explicit information coming from Moscow, they didn't quite see what they could do about it.

They were still out in the destroyer escort in the gray light of midmorning May 3, futilely pinging for a contact and getting nothing but an occasional elusive echo of something slowly fiddling about down there. This, too, roused their distrust but none of the four patrol vessels had been able to hold the contact, and, in any case, it was too small and too slow to be the game they sought—*Skate* with Kirov aboard. It could have been a big fish, but all the same they had an uneasy feeling there was something about it fishier than a fish.

"That fellow has been holding there something over thirty-four hours now," Sobelov said, leaning on the bridge rail and staring out at the *Queen*. "He claims he is Syrian and disabled on his way to Sevastopol."

"But he is off course for Sevastopol—at least ten kilometers," Federenko said, musing.

"What can you really expect of a Syrian? That is—if he is Syrian. Somehow I suspect if he is a Syrian, I am a Laplander."

"I suggest we go out again now and observe him for a time."

"A good suggestion," Sobelov agreed. "But he will probably still pretend he does not know the code well enough to answer questions. Why can't we board him?"

"We could, naturally—but he is still clearly in international waters. What is more, we have not received an order to board."

"I wish we would receive such an order," Sobelov agreed gloomily. "It may sound disloyal, but I sometimes suspect Moscow does not know it's own mind."

"Nearly everybody suspects that. Well then, let us go." He turned to the DE's officer of the deck. "Take us out to the strange trawler. Come in on her port side, turn around the stern and come up slowly on the starboard."

"Yes, sir." The OOD spoke to the helmsman and rang the engineroom. The DE began to put on speed. The hour was 0910.

At 0930, they slid along the Queen's port side—seeing nothing of particular interest even though both were staring through binoculars. They turned aft and came up slowly to starboard—the side away from the land.

Federenko suddenly grabbed at Sobelov's arm.

"Look!"

"Where? What?" the man from Moscow demanded, startled.

"There! Amidships!"

Then Sobelov saw. A low, black, humpbacked shape was heaving up alongside the Queen, scarcely visible against the Queen's untidy hull.

"Bring the ship in nearer. Fifty meters. Then stop!" Federenko yelled at the OOD. And soon, the DE lay wallowing, looking down the Queen's throat, so to speak.

"What is it?" Sobelov demanded.

"I think I know. Watch! We shall see."

And they did see.

A hatch opened in the top of the ungainly shape. Head and shoulders appeared, then the rest of a body. It was a man and it reached for a ladder hanging over the Queen's tail and climbed, with evident infinite weariness to the rail where hands reached down to help it over.

Admiral March, with squinting eyes and a fiercely set jaw, was staring out at the rolling Russian DE.

He recognized the type, Petya class, 1050 tons, mounting 85 mm. guns, which was pretty heavy stuff for a DE, he reflected. Janes Fighting Ships said the class also carried rocket launchers, and he could see plainly enough that she mounted torpedo tubes, which looked a little undersized to him. I wonder if he's the sonofabitch that got *Skate*. (As a matter of fact, she was.)

Gottfried spoke beside him, his voice tight with sudden new strain, a strain he realized now, he had been expecting for a day and a half—and probably even before they approached this coast.

"They found us," he said and added with vast and deep feeling. "The sonsofbitches!"

"I knew they would—sooner or later," Admiral March replied. "Get the crew and passengers aboard and start the charge going. I don't know how many Hale got—but this is going to take at least two more loads. Maybe three."

"What do you think they'll do, Admiral?" Gottfried asked.

"I don't know what they'll do. But you can sure bet they want to do something! Carry on. I'm getting on the horn to Washington." He turned toward the radio room.

"We're still outside the limit, sir," Gottfried said.

"Maybe they don't give a shit," Admiral March said over his shoulder. "Or maybe they do."

Sobelov and Federenko watched as figure after figure appeared in the hatch and was helped aboard the *Queen*. One, they saw in amazement, was a woman. Others, plainly hurt, had to be carried or lifted in slings.

"What is that thing?" Sobelov demanded.

"Obviously a submarine. We know the Americans and French have been experimenting for years with small submarines. Mostly for deep oceanographic research. This is something else. Clearly a submarine designed particularly for rescue. We knew they were working on it. We are working on our own, as a matter of fact. But I did not know they had it operating. Clearly they are trying to pull them out from under our noses. What are we going to do?"

"I am not sure yet. Get the radio man in here. At once!"

When the radio operator appeared, Sobelov snapped him

to attention. But first he asked Federenko, "Would you recognize Kirov?"

"Who would not?"

"Watch those people like an eagle. If Kirov appears on that ladder, shout to me!" He turned again to the communications man. "Get this to Moscow at once! Fullest urgent! Fullest secret. ADDRESSED CHAIRMAN COUNCIL OF MINISTERS. MESSAGE AMERICANS EVACUATING SUBMARINE SUNK IN OUR WATERS WITH RESCUE SUBMARINE. AM CLOSE ALONGSIDE. IF KIROV APPEARS PROPOSE TO BOARD AND SEIZE HIM. AWAIT FULL ORDERS URGENTLY. SOBELOV."

The radio operator was quivering.

"But, sir, our radio is not powerful enough to reach Moscow."

"Relay through fleet headquarters at Sevastopol, dumbhead! Move!" Sobelov snarled.

He turned back beside Federenko and stared at the *Queen* and her low-slung companion.

"Anything yet?" he snapped.

"No," Federenko said in a low, awed voice. "I would know him. How can they dare?"

"How many have come up?"

"Thirty. Nobody who resembles Kirov."

"If he comes we are going to board and arrest him. Get your guns trained on that ship," Sobelov said, all the mildness vanished from the round face and the eyes behind the pince-nez. Now he looked as dangerous as, in fact, he was.

"There appear to be many hurt. Perhaps he is wounded—or dead," Federenko offered.

"That would be suitable," Sobelov said coldly. "How many does such a submarine as the one we sank carry? Its usual complement?"

"I do not know precisely. Something over one hundred."

No more figures were emerging from the DSRV's hatch. In all, thirty-eight had been taken aboard the *Queen Zenobia*. Then three men went down, and cables were strung over the *Queen*'s side and down through the hatch.

"That means they will have to make other trips," Sobelov said with sudden satisfaction.

"How do you mean, Comrade?" Federenko asked.

"It means we wait for them to leave and track them from here, idiot. Thus, we at last find the big submarine which your stupidheads had been unable to find in nearly two days."

"It was your stupidheads who let him get away, if I may remind you." Federenko's tone was chilly.

Thus, when the DSRV pulled away and down to take off her second cargo of Skate's marooned men, she had company all the way. Lieutenant Hale knew it, Pauer and Akers knew it and so, by that time, did the Pentagon, the White House, and the Kremlin.

Once the Russians knew what they were after and had a bellwether to lead them, it would be impossible to shake off their sonar. From now on it was a matter of bulling ahead and praying for luck. Nobody involved thought there would be much profit in praying for pity.

Thus when Hale's voice told Stephens there were some things he ought to know about, Skate's captain was not very much surprised, but he was interested indeed.

"They caught me on the surface, preparing to unload our passengers," Hale told him. "Broad daylight, but it couldn't be helped; I was out of battery and damn near out of air."

"They take any action?" Stephens asked.

"Not that I know of—not just then. Just sat there and kept the glasses on us from about fifty yards away, like a lecher in the front row at the Lido. I know their radio was busy, but we couldn't read it."

"Anything later?"

"Sure. They chased us out here like a pack of hounds after a raccoon. You're treed, sir, and you can expect guests of some sort before long."

"You shouldn't have come back."

"You were still here," Hale said, without drama. "Anyhow, March intends to empty *Skate*, come hell or high water. Meanwhile, he's been talking to Washington, yelling at it, I suspect."

"All right, Mr. Hale—and thanks; we'll start sending men up at once."

Stephens remembered the agonies of his last few hours, trying to make choices. It wasn't going to be easy for the DSRV to make a third and final trip. And there was a good chance it couldn't at all, although it was unlikely the Russians would do anything immediately about *Skate*. He simply had to hope that old Kirov had been correct in his estimate that they wouldn't bomb because they would be desperately eager to salvage *Skate* to see what went on inside her. They couldn't do that or even seriously begin in a mere matter of hours. Still, now that they knew her track they might very well do something about the DSRV. That would be just as terminal for the third and last load.

How did you separate the sheep with a reasonable hope of salvation from the goats who were to be left with an extraordinarily minor hope—if any? What were the criteria? Personal friendship? No, certainly not; and most of them were his friends anyhow, enlisted and officers alike. Family responsibilities? That was certainly a factor. He knew it had influenced him in sending both Chief Cate and Lieutenant Zink away in the first load. Something else had entered his decision to send Billings in the first load. It was hard to define that. Billings was a good man, he knew that. But it was something more than that. He remembered how Billings had calmly come back down after getting the woman into the DSRV; he could simply have bolted and stayed up there in the rescue chamber and refused to come down. Instead he had returned and voluntarily gone about the work of gathering up the wounded. He didn't know whether it would make textbook sense to reward a man for unselfish courage, but at least he could justify himself on grounds that Billings was big and brawny and could help with what was unquestionably going to be a difficult job of unloading the wounded.

There was another consideration and it was touchy. That was the problem of balancing—one against another—the ultimate relative worth of men to the profession they all served. Some men, like Chief Cummings, he had to hold back because *Skate* desperately needed them here and now to preserve what was left of her watertight integrity for the sake of the rest. He had made his choices, meeting real resistance from only one, which he could have expected in any case.

"Dick, you're taking this load," he had said, finding the executive officer prowling the boat with Andrews, the chief pharmacist, making sure the dead were really dead.

"The hell I am, Captain, sir," Oulahan had said.

"The hell you're not. I'm captain of this boat," Stephens said.

"No." Oulahan managed a weary grin. "You might still come down with the grippe."

"Don't argue with me. You know how things stand. I've got to have somebody in charge of this load."

"Anybody can do that, Dave," Oulahan said. "Besides, the DSRV scares me. Gives me claustrophobia."

"The time for kidding is over. They're going to want a report on this excursion. You're going to make it."

"You can make it yourself, Captain. It's the captain's job anyhow. I hate paper work."

"Cut it out, Dick. I'm too damn tired. And I mean it. You take this load."

Oulahan regarded him somberly. Stephens couldn't read him, probably for the first time in what seemed like many years. Exhaustion? Possibly. Reluctance to see a job less than finished? Probably. Anger? That's possible too.

Oulahan abruptly turned away. "All right, Captain," he said, moving forward.

And so his choices had been made and now that the DSRV was sealed down again, the men were already swarming up the ladder. He couldn't know whether his choices were the best. Only God could know that and possibly He didn't know either. The unsolvable equation was that there wasn't a bad choice in the boat.

He had sent Oulahan for the reasons he had stated, which were sound enough—but not quite honest. He feared that if he held him back to the last load—and its ultimate necessity—he would have a real officers' country mutiny on his hands and he didn't know whether he could take that. He sent only one other officer on the DSRV's second trip, Lieutenant (jg) Jerome Kastner, the weapons officer. That decision wasn't capricious; he had no weapons he could still use; a boat in *Skate*'s condition wasn't likely to be using torpedoes, particularly dummy torpedoes.

Holding back the other officers until the last certainly did not mean to Stephens that they were more valuable to the boat than enlisted men. It did perhaps imply that the gold braid on their sleeves somehow seemed to indicate that they owed a shade more responsibility—but only a shade. No, he had to admit to himself, officers by and large got more comfort, more dignities, more privileges out of the Navy than enlisted men did. So that decision possibly could be branded sentimental; officers had got more and therefore they ought to give back more when the pinch was on. Didn't make a hell of a lot of sense, he told himself.

Now, there remained that one other problem, Kirov and Uzzumekis. Christ, what a name! Kirov, that muleheaded old coal miner—and the cause of it all. No, that wasn't exactly fair. Kirov had merely indicated a wish to leave his country. And Washington, delighted to be of service—to itself—had thought up this disastrous grandstand maneuver, not to please Kirov, but to please itself.

He went to the wardroom and, as he expected, found Kirov and Uzzumekis still there for the entirely sound reason that the wardroom transom was the only approximation of a bed on the whole boat long enough to hold Uzzumekis' extended frame, and with his leg in the shape it was, it would be a needless cruelty to bend him.

"How's the leg?" he asked Uzzumekis.

"It'll do," Uzzumekis grunted. Stephens didn't think it would, but, for the moment, he didn't say so. But what he thought privately was that he wanted this giant of a man off his boat—and quickly—and he damned well intended to have him off, Kirov or no Kirov.

"Has the old man done his thinking? Is he ready to go now?"

Uzzumekis contrived the pale shadow of a grin.

"As you know, he's stubborn. Keeps saying he's seventy-seven and that's too old to go around making a joke of his country."

"All right, I'll pitch him out a hatch and see what sort of a joke he thinks that is. They're taking off the second load now, and I want you on it. You need a doctor, maybe several."

Uzzumekis spoke with more force.

"Captain Stephens, I don't think you really get it. At home, I'm a deserter in the face of the enemy. Probably, in some ways, I was also a spy against my own country. I can't go home without this old bastard. He's not only my responsibility, but he's my ticket to a clean bill of health at home. Besides, I'm beginning to like the old fart. But as long as he's waving that popgun around, I don't see there's very much either you or I can do about it. But I'll get him persuaded and we'll go in the next load," he promised.

"Nyet," Kirov said and smiled his cold, blue-eyed smile.

"Anyhow," said Stephens, "I'll be back in a moment. That leg must hurt like hell. We've been too busy around here to take proper care of our guests. Just hang on a minute."

He climbed from the wardroom and went aft to sick bay, where he found Chief Pharmacist's Mate Jeff Andrews, whom he was holding for the last load for the same reason he was holding Chief Cummings. The boat, in its straits, badly needed them now.

"Chief," he said, "in the wardroom, on the transom, there's a guy about the size of a grizzly bear. He's got a hell of a

318

bullet hole in his leg and I want him off on the DSRV this trip. The hole's turning black and so is his leg. We'll all be off this thing in about nine hours, but I want him off now. I told him I'd get somebody to give him a little something to cut the pain. But what I want you to do is slip him something that'll really knock him out in less than five minutes. Figure about enough for a full-grown Percheron stallion. Then we'll get about six guys and tote him up to the escape hatch, get a harness on him and hoist him into the DSRV. Can do?"

"Can do, Captain," Chief Andrews said, and turned to his medicine cabinet. "Count on it; I'll have him colder than a witch's tit in a jiffy."

When Stephens went back to the wardroom, Uzzumekis was snoring, while Chief Andrews, hypodermic in hand was gazing down on his handiwork with a look of thoughtful satisfaction. Stephens had a half dozen men waiting outside the wardroom door, gazing in curiously.

"Is he out?" Stephens asked.

"You couldn't wake him up with a baseball bat."

"Okay, men, heave him and let's go. He's heavy as a buffalo, but try not to bend him. He's got a sore leg."

As the working party left with its burden, Kirov looked up at Stephens and grinned. "Da! Very good," he said.

"I didn't know you could speak English, you old fake."

"Da. A little."

XXV

IT was four o'clock in the morning, May 3, in Washington when his apprehensive valet-masseur tiptoed into the bedroom of the President of the United States and fearfully but firmly tapped him on the shoulder. The valet knew that the President often worked until one A.M. or later, but that when he quit and went to sleep he wanted to stay that way until he had finished his rest, which would be something like seven A.M. The President grunted and rolled over, and the valet tapped him again. The President came up roaring like a bull walrus.

"There are gentlemen here to see you, sir," the valet said or tried to say.

"What time is it, for sweet Christ's sake?"

"Four oh five, sir," the valet said.

"Then who said they were gentlemen? Who are they?"

"The Secretary of State, the Secretary of Defense, and Admiral Engel, sir. They said it was urgent."

The President rolled over, got his extensive legs over the edge of the high bed, and let his feet fumble for his slippers. "I guess it must be, then. Fetch me my robe. Where are they?"

"The family sitting room, sir."

"All right. Tell 'em I'll be right in."

The President went to the bathroom, splashed cold water on his face and hair and shoved that thinning crop back into some sort of order with his hands. He took a quick glance at the mirror and made a command decision that he looked like hell.

However, by the time he reached the bedroom door, he was back in form. He knew what they were here for, and he was ready for business. He began to move with more speed and purpose. He noted automatically as he entered the formal and rather ornate room that his waiting guests didn't look any better than he did except that, at least, they had on pants and shirts.

"What's up?" the President demanded.

"They want you on the phone again, Mr. President," State said.

"Come on, Alec, who wants me on the phone?" he said without patience, although he knew perfectly well who wanted him.

"The Chairman, sir. They have the call set up for four-thirty."

"Damned if I know why those people can't call at a decent hour," the President grumbled. "The guy before them promised to bury us. This bunch has a new method, electronic mortuary science. What's new that I have to know before I talk to him?"

"You know most of it, Mr President," Defense said. "The only thing is it's moving faster." He turned to Admiral Engel. "You'd better run over it, Mike."

"The DSRV got its second load off, sir," Admiral Engel said. "They should be alongside the support ship pretty soon, or maybe they are already."

"They get Kirov this time?"

"No. After the Russians found *Skate* and Captain Stephens knew they had found him, he broke radio silence briefly. He said that Kirov was still refusing to go but that he would, if necessary, load him forcibly on the next relay."

"How could he break radio silence? He's on the bottom, isn't he?"

"Underwater telephone, sir."

The President pulled at his chin and frowned.

"I'll never understand this. Kirov says he wants to get out. We're willing to help him and go to considerable lengths to help him get out—the Bureau of Budget will eventually have to figure out what lengths we did go to. So now he balks like a mule. Why?"

"I don't know, sir," Admiral Engel said. He had been sim-

321

mering ever since this began, and now, since it was the time it was and what else he knew, he let some of it boil over. "It won't only be the Bureau of Budget, sir. I lost some good men down there—and I may lose more."

"I know that," the President said, and let, for a moment, a baleful glance rove from State to Defense. "Anything else?"

"Yes, and I don't like it," Engel said. "Within the last three hours—so Admiral March reports—the Russians have anchored a ship over where *Skate* lies. March says it looks like a salvage ship."

"What's that mean?"

"Who knows? Certainly they'll want to send divers down to look her over. It's a reasonable guess, depending on what shape she's in, that sooner or later they'll want to raise her."

"How long would that take?"

"Depends on a lot of things, sir. Weather, luck, how she lies—but weeks at the minimum. However, you can write that one off," he added, and now his tired unshaven face—beyond its day-to-day blandness—wore a look both grim and sad.

"Why?"

"Captain Stephens' order are not to let the ship be captured."

"What can he do about it? He's helpless, isn't he?"

"No," Engel said, and, if they were sufficiently acute, President, State and Defense might have read the grief behind the shortness of his answer.

"One more thing. Have the Russians done anything to molest or interfere with the support ship? Anything serious?"

"Nothing physical, not yet anyhow. But they keep a picket ship close alongside all the time now."

"All right." The President got up, tied his robe, rubbed the stubble on his chin. "It's four twenty-five. I'll go down and talk to the damn poltergeist. It's a good thing they don't have Phonevision."

A Marine guard was waiting in the hall to escort him to

322

the elevator, and they dropped to the Situation Room. The scene was getting to be familiar. The glass-walled, sound-proof booth, the technician with his headset stationed outside the door, the little, worried-looking interpreter waiting at the table inside, the two red telephones. The President entered the booth while the Marine guard took up post outside the door, with his back to the booth so that he could see the rest of the room. This place was as secure as any in Washington, but those charged with the safety of the President of the United States had long since, for a very sound reason, given up taking any chances whatever.

The President entered the booth, sat down and fixed a glum eye on the telephone. How was it going to be this time, he wondered. Now that we both know, more or less, how things stand. This time, I should think, they know almost as much as I do and maybe a little more, about their part of it any-how.

Outside the man with the earphones suddenly gave the signal. The interpreter hitched his receiver on one shoulder, picked up one of his half dozen sharpened pencils and pulled a yellow note pad toward him. Good thing he can write, the President thought; last time his notes were pretty good. He picked up his own telephone. Once more he heard that rumbling voice and half liked the sound of it. Might be a pretty fair skate, he thought—if he wasn't on the other side.

Then the Soviet interpreter began translating, and the President winced. How in the name of anything am I sup-posed to believe anything that comes out of that mouth?

This time the Chairman's greeting was brief and formal; the President's reply equally brief, formal, and even more guarded. After all, he called me; I didn't call him, he thought. And, he knew from that baritone inflection that this time the Chairman was really sore. Moreover, hadn't there been a note of triumph, satisfaction at least, in the baritone? Thinks he's got a full house, does he?

"Mr. President," the interpreter's voice said, "the last time

323

we spoke you lied to me. Lying to me is one matter; lying to the Soviet Union is another."

The President scowled and glanced up at his own interpreter.

"Tell him that neither the United States nor I like to listen to that kind of gu—No, tell him that neither the U.S. nor its President is prepared to be insulted. Tell him that, if he thinks I lied, I want to know in what precise way he thinks I lied."

The baritone voice again and then its echo, "Mr. President, you assured me that you had no communication with an American submarine sunk in Soviet waters."

This time the President grinned slightly. "Tell him that was the precise truth. I did not then have any communication with the submarine—direct or indirect. I still have no direct communication with the submarine."

Again baritone and its obbligato. "You also, Mr. President, lied by implication when you refused to admit that an American warship had illegally invaded Russian waters."

Hell, the President thought in disgust, it's like being bitten to death by a parakeet. But he had his temper under control, which was in some ways remarkable considering the size and temperature of that famous, not to say notorious instrument of leadership.

"Remind him that I reminded him that I can find no sound reason for accepting his twelve-mile limit in the first place. It's his, not mine. As for not telling him that it was an American submarine, tell him now that, of course, it is an American submarine. Ask him if he ever heard of a game called poker? If he hasn't, there must be some Russian game in which it is both accepted and sensible not to bla—no, not to admit everything a man knows at once."

The baritone rolled again and was interpreted. The Chairman, it appeared, was unready to discuss games of chance, although both participants knew that they gambled every day—for immense stakes.

"Now, Mr. President, we come to a more serious matter:

your submarine kidnaped and attempted to make away with a Soviet citizen of the first rank . . ."

The President interrupted, somewhat impatiently.

"Mr. Chairman, if you are going to repeat that nonsense, I propose to terminate this conversation. Kidnaped? The man asked for political asylum, an international convention of which you may have heard. The United States was prepared to grant it and prepared to assist him. Don't try to make something out of this which it clearly is not."

The other end of the line got busy again.

"Mr. President, I ask you directly: Has Mr. Kirov been taken alive off that submarine? If he has, we propose to take him back."

"Mr. Chairman, to my knowledge—and please do not out of this build up another of your visions about lying—to my knowledge Mr. Kirov is still on the submarine. Also, to the best of my knowledge, he is still alive. That is the best I can do for you in the way of information."

"Why has he not been taken off?"

"That, Mr. Chairman, is Mr. Kirov's business. I will not presume to answer for Mr. Kirov. So don't waste our mutually valuable time asking questions that both you and I know are manifestly unanswerable and foolish."

The President's temper was by now slipping a little, perhaps because he was still tired and it was after four in the morning and the air conditioning in the booth was too chilly for a man in thin pyjamas and robe.

"Don't try to take him off, Mr. President," the voice warned. "It will not be permitted."

"And how do you propose to stop us, Mr. Chairman?"

This time the baritone rumble went on for a long time and carried a tone which the President recognized as both cold and menacing. He knew he would have to rely on the interpreter for its content, a prospect which he did not relish for, although he knew the Chairman probably meant what he said at this stage, he also knew he would have trouble believing it after it had been strained.

325

"Mr. President, we are in our own waters. Within those waters lies an American submarine which, however you choose to interpret its mission, came on what was—it cannot be denied—an act of war. Also plying those waters, again illegally, is a small American submarine which for the last forty or more hours, has been making repeated trips to the sunken submarine. It delivers its cargo to a small ship lying almost at the edge of those waters. The small ship is obviously either a United States vessel or a ship under United States command. We choose to believe that it is a United States ship and that it is flying false colors which, in international law, renders it a pirate ship on the high seas. The courses open to the Soviet Union are obvious."

"Mr. Chairman, do I need to remind you that weapons under your command sank an American submarine in waters which nobody but you can claim with any legality are Soviet territorial waters? The United States is as free as the Soviet Union to proclaim what is or is not an act of war."

"Mr. President, argument is without point. What does have point is that the vessels involved are here—not there. If you wish me to set forth the alternatives open to the Soviet Union, I will now do so. First, if you should by some miracle succeed in transferring Mr. Kirov to the pirate support ship, we will board that ship and take him off. On the other hand, since we too possess submarine rescue equipment, we can go down and take him directly off the sunken submarine by our own means. Or we can so harass the support ship that it will be forced to withdraw, which would leave your rescue submarine marooned with no place to go unless its captain chose to come into the port of Balaklava and surrender himself and his passengers. And there are other alternatives which, as you will clearly recognize, would be more drastic."

Scowling, the President replied. "Mr. Chairman, your suggestion that Soviet rescue equipment could go down and rescue—as you describe it, since there is no evidence whatever that Mr. Kirov wants to be rescued by you—the threat is arrant nonsense. They wouldn't let you in and you couldn't get in. If, by 'more drastic' measures, you contemplate some further act of violence, I urge you—most vehemently and seriously—to refrain. You have already and are continuing to interfere intolerably with the legal missions of United States vessels, including the sinking of one. I warn you, sir, keep your hands off those vessels. You have gone too far already. Venture no further!"

This time the replying baritone carried a note of inquiry, almost of unease, although its echo carried no more feel of human sensibility than in any other of the preceding exchanges.

"Mr. President, you threaten the Soviet Union."

The President's tone was menacing, which he hoped— without much real hope—would come through in translation.

"For openers—no, he wouldn't understand that," he told his own interpreter. "Mr. Chairman, you sank one American submarine. I must advise you, which you doubtless already know, the United States possesses forty-two of another type of submarine which is called Polaris. Except for those in training or in port for refit, most of them are on patrol. Each one carries sixteen Polaris missiles, any single one of which is capable of erasing a large part of any Russian city. You can't find those submarines; they are not easy game such as the one which came near your coast and you trapped and sank. Each of them, however, is capable of reaching you with the utmost ease. Is your man Kirov worth the price?"

"You threaten me with rockets, Mr. President?"

"I do."

"Don't forget, Mr. President, the Soviet Union is not unequipped with rockets. Let us not destroy one another over an issue which is comparatively trivial."

"I don't consider it trivial, Mr. Chairman. But if you do, I urgently advise you to keep it trivial. I think there is, at this juncture, not much more to say. Good night, Mr. Chairman."

At five A.M. in the White House family sitting room,

State, Defense and Admiral Engel were uniformly drawn, bearded, rumpled, gray-faced, and appalled.

"Was that a bluff, Mr. President?" State asked at length. He was tense and haggard and his eyes reflected a vision of something too awful either to contemplate or comprehend.

"Mexican standoff, I think," the President replied. "I just want to get that crew off the submarine alive. Hell, if he had asked politely, I'd have given him Kirov."

"It's still going to cost me another man," Admiral Engel said evenly.

XXVI

ONCE Hale was away with the second load, Stephens confiscated a little time to take stock of what remained to be done. As a profoundly personal matter, he was grateful that he didn't have to make any more choices between who was going to be saved and who might not. Wrong or right, executioner or savior, sinner or saint, he had chosen and he could quit thinking about it—more or less.

Hale had said the Russians had him treed, and he believed that judgment because his own judgment said it had been inevitable. He had got Uzzumekis off, by stealth and against the giant's will, it was true, but he had believed that if he allowed him to stay he would die. He might very well die anyhow; Stephens was no doctor and neither was Chief Andrews, but Andrews was about as close as you could come without membership in the Arizona State Medical Association, the state from which he had come. And Andrews, inspecting the wound had agreed with him that it was bad and dangerous and rapidly becoming more so. Thinking of Uzzumekis—brother, with a name like that!—reminded him of the big man's last speech about what he thought awaited him at home if he didn't fetch Kirov. He hardly shared Uzzumekis' own opinion that he would be shot or imprisoned as a deserter and traitor. Moreover, Uzzumekis had more than fulfilled his contract to deliver Kirov to *Skate*. Still, you never could be sure what knucklehead officialdom might do at home to make an example, to cover up or distract attention from its own boobery, to excuse the loss of *Skate*. There were those in both the first and second loads who could and would stand up in court and testify to Uzzumekis' behavior aboard *Skate*. Particularly, Oulahan's defense could not be ignored. But he thought he had better add his own weight in whatever way he still could; if the third load got off he could send his own fitness report on the expatriate American; if it did not, the time was approaching when he would break out the underwater telephone and call Admiral March on the *Queen Zenobia*. March trusted him and Stephens trusted March, and if March marched into the Pentagon and demanded that instead of a court-martial Uzzumekis should get a medal, he was going to be listened to. Perhaps.

Of course the best thing he could do for Uzzumekis—or for the President of the United States, for that matter—would be to deliver Kirov alive and kicking. But if he did bring off that unlikely feat, it was a dead certainty that the fallen Russian deity would be kicking.

As for the other thirty-two men still there with Kirov and himself, there was still some slim chance for them. They would be nourishing that hope, he knew. As who wouldn't? Still, the crew all knew, had always known, that there could come a time when a man *knew* he had to stay down and die. None of them had cracked yet; he doubted if any would.

God, the air was foul in this boat! He thought he might be getting used to the heat, but that undoubtedly contributed to the accumulating poisons. He longed to light up the reactor and get things functioning. He went back to the one technician he had kept back to monitor the state of air in the boat. A fairly useless errand, he told himself.

"How's it coming, Chapman?" he asked through his own growing lethargy.

"It stinks, Captain, as you know," Chapman said. "No problem about oxygen. That'll last as long as we do. But the Co_2 stands at four point five per cent. I've been checking men. A lot are pretty well along. Depressed, not too rational."

"Anybody close to coma, as far as you can tell?"

"I don't think so. But it's different with different people. Chief Andrews went with me. He thinks they may hold out awhile yet. To tell the truth, Captain, I don't feel too good myself."

"How many hours are the worst ones good for?"

"Who knows, Captain? Four, six, ten at the outside. I wish we could start her up."

"So do I, and maybe we will before long. Keep a grip on your left one."

"Aye, aye. But my grip's loosening."

"So is mine. I'm going aft."

He went back forward through the control room and got pock-marked Lieutenant Grady Johnson, the most senior officer next to himself still aboard, out of his bunk, where he was obeying orders by lying flat and poisoning the already toxic air as little more as possible.

"Grady, take the control room for a while, will you? There's not a lot to do there, but I get uneasy when it's not manned."

"Okay, skipper. You know I got the God damnedest headache I can remember since I got plastered on New Years two years ago in New York. Lasted for three days. Greatest liberty I ever made."

"You'll make another—and I hope your hangover lasts a week."

"Let's not kid ourselves any more than necessary, Captain," Johnson said.

"It's too early. Hale's been gone only three hours, but in about two more I want all the men rounded up and into the forward torpedo room. That's rushing it, but some are getting punchy—to put it mildly—and I want to make sure they can all navigate—or that somebody's still got enough muscle and savvy to make them navigate."

As Johnson rolled out of his bunk, Stephens turned and started aft again. Irritably, he knew he was shuffling, almost staggering and he cursed with brief hot anger when he lurched and bumped an elbow against the chart table as he passed it. It felt like a day's work to undog that door and the next one into the reactor compartment, to crawl over the shielding above the great seven-eighths-dead furnace. He thought he hammered at the door to the engineroom, but his fist managed only a feeble, slow-paced tattoo. Nevertheless it was heard and, in dazed fascination, he watched the wheel turn and the locking dogs slowly withdraw. The door swung open, and Cummings' face, so grimed by grease and sweat that its sick weariness scarcely showed through, peered owlishly out at him.

"How're your men?" Stephens said.

"They're alive," Cummings croaked. "Not much more."

"How's the bulkhead?"

"Holding. We've done all we can for it, Captain."

"All right, Chief. I want you to get them all forward. Can they make it?"

Cummings shrugged.

Stephens forced himself to look around at Cummings' working party. Some hunched against the bulkhead, arms loosely around knees, heads lolling. Collingwood, the big cook, lay prone on the deck between the turbines, and Stephens wondered where they had put the dead man who had once occupied that space.

"I guess they can, Captain. They'll damn well have to."

Stephens looked at his watch. Hale had been gone nearly three hours and if he was having any luck ought to be somewhere closing on the *Queen Zenobia*. Stephens was trying to force his head to function. Say three hours and a half, if the Russians hadn't done anything to the DSRV en route, say his batteries held up, say Hale himself held up, they ought to be unloading before long. They'd probably get the chargers going even before they got the passengers off, but charging was going to take a minimum of two hours before the DSRV could start back—if it could start back—if any one of several dozen other things did not come to pass. But whatever way you looked at it, unloading the passengers was going to slow things up. Christ, I wish I could think. The only reasonable guess—if it was possible to guess at all—was that it would take another seven hours before the DSRV got back. Well, they all knew there came a time for a man to stay down and die—but not without protest, not for the lack of trying, even when there wasn't much to try with.

"You're damn well certain they're going to damn well have to," Stephens said. "Let's get 'em moving. When everybody's out, dog down this door. Leave everything else open. Whatever air's left in this boat is going to be all the same mixture. Here, lemme help."

"I can move 'em," Cummings said. "Where do you want 'em?"

"Forward torpedo room. Under the hatch. All except you. I want you to stick with me."

Together, Stephens and Cummings kicked, pulled, pleaded and persuaded, cursed and dragged the men to the door. Those who could still best move painfully boosted and shoved others over the high coaming of the open door. Collingwood was the hardest to rouse, but at last he, too, was in motion.

A procession of grease-grimed apparitions, they crawled blindly forward on hands and knees. Cummings and Stephens were the last two out.

"You sure we got them all?" Stephens asked as they turned to dog the door.

"All but the dead one," Cummings muttered. "But I guess I'd better look." He stumbled back over the coaming and it was five minutes before he reappeared and hitched himself out of the damaged compartment. That sick after bulkhead was *Skate's* only wound which might yet yield to the sea. It took both men to dog down the door.

On the bridge of the Russian salvage ship *Bakhmut*, the pinging sonar was picking up a steady echo. Federenko nursed the ship to a spot directly over it and hove to. Without anchors, it was ticklish work holding the 4000-tonner in an exact position, for, though the sea still held its miraculous calm and the breeze was still light, the ship wanted to drift; her high sides amounted to a sail responsive to the faintest zephyr.

It is obvious I can't hold the ship here, Federenko told himself. It is necessary to put down an anchor until the other four anchors can be put down to hold the ship precisely. He spoke to the officer of the deck.

"Steer directly into the breeze, south southeast. All ahead slow. I want to be exactly three hundred meters upwind from the target. Order out the anchor sea detail. I will tell you when I want the anchor put down."

By voice radio, he called the four escort vessels. "One ship on each bow, one on each quarter," he ordered. "Keep station on me. Station your anchor details. Meanwhile, each of you put a line aboard me. I have the target."

These orders were scarcely necessary, for the captains of the several small ships knew exactly what Federenko wanted. They had done this work before.

Very slowly the *Bakhmut* forged ahead into the breeze. Federenko's orders to the sonar room were exacting and sharp.

"The instant we are three hundred upwind, advise me. The very instant!"

The word came.

"Drop the anchor!" Federenko said. Chain roared out of the forward hawse pipe, and far below, in slightly more than three hundred feet, the *Bakhmut's* hook bit into the mud.

"Let her drift back on the chain until we are again directly above the target," he told the OOD. He called the escorts. "Now. Now take out cable from me and shackle to the anchors you carry. When I signal, drop the anchors, starboard, and port bows, starboard and port quarters. Each three hundred meters. Be sharp about it!"

The work went swiftly, as swift is measured in terms of precise maneuvering at sea. Within ninety minutes, the *Bakhmut* was firmly anchored at five points, exactly over *Skate:* The salvage ship's own anchor forward, another on each bow and quarter. Nothing short of a hurricane could move her from that position.

Federenko turned to the landsman, Sobelov, who had been watching this work in utter fascination as well as eagerness.

With the satisfied expression of a man who knew his job and had just performed it superbly, Federenko pointed a stubby forefinger straight down.

"He is there," he said. "The submarine is there. Mr. Kirov is there."

"My congratulations," Sobelov said. His brow furrowed slightly. "Does there remain any possibility of error?"

"None whatever," Federenko snapped.

"What is the next procedure then?"

"Get a diver down to inspect the ship."

"What possibility that the diver can enter the submarine?"

"Very slight. They will not admit him. After we inspect the ship I suggest you make contact with your masters in Moscow and ask what they wish us to do."

"Hmmm," Sobelov said. "They want Kirov. Also, if that is possible, they want the ship." Then sharply, "Need I remind you, Comrade, they are your masters also?"

"Both assignments will take some time. If we can get the ship, they can have Kirov, but in that case, I fear, they will have to take him dead."

Stephens had halted in the control room with Cummings when he heard the *Bakhmut* drop her anchor. The roar of chain was even more audible to him than it must have been aboard the Russian salvage vessel.

"That cuts it," he told Lieutenant Johnson. "Get me a radioman in here. On the double—if you can find one that still makes sense."

Soon a communications man appeared, stumbling, dazed, poisoned with carbon dioxide.

"Get the phone working," he ordered. "You know the call for *Queen Zenobia?*"

"Yes, sir," the sailor mumbled.

"Get her," Stephens said. "I want to talk to Admiral March."

Stephens watched the boy—and, damn it, he is only a boy,

he thought with pity—fumbling with the instrument. But, sooner than he thought the kid could possibly manage it in his condition, he heard the admiral's sharp, anxious voice, sounding hollow through seven miles of sea.

"Admiral, this is Stephens. Somebody just dropped a hook off my port bow, a little abaft. I can now hear a ship backing down on me. There are other ships in the vicinity. Not being up there, I can't swear to it, but I suppose it's the goblins."

"It is." The admiral's voice was tense. "We can see them from here."

"Has Hale arrived yet?"

"Just surfaced and cracked the hatch. We'll have him out of here again in two hours. Can you hold out?"

"The men are in bad shape, but I don't know whether Hale should come back. In fact, I think he shouldn't." Even as he said it, Stephens' tired brain was fighting with itself. Hale and the DSRV represented three lives; he had ten times that many more.

"He's coming to you anyhow," March said. "He is, or somebody else qualified is coming. But the way he's taken this over, I'm afraid he'll insist. He knows the road."

"Admiral, I've got some pretty sick cases here. I'm going to fire up the reactor and get the scrubbers going. If we don't clean up the air in this boat there won't be anybody strong enough to get up the ladder."

"Go ahead, son. I know who is out there. Any noise you make now is not going to make any difference. Did you send Kirov this trip?"

"No, the mule-headed sonofabitch has a gun and threatens to commit suicide when I try to force him. I'll get him to you if I can. Excuse me, sir, I'm going to get things working. When they are I'll call again."

"All right, son. Good luck."

And we are damn well going to need it, Stephens thought as he turned to the reeling Chief Cummings.

"Come on, Bill," he said, feeling a vast pity for this man

336

and all the others but knowing that the time for pity had run out twice over. "Can you make it?"

"Sure," Cummings mumbled. "Whaddya want, Captain?" The voice was slurring.

Jesus, Stephens thought, I wish he was drunk, not poisoned. He grabbed the chief by the arm, knowing his own grip was failing, and both stumbled back through the open door, through the crowded and half-wrecked navigation and communications and sickbay compartment, back across the reactor, through the door—which it took all of both men's strength to open—into the engineroom with its perilously buckled bulkhead at the after end. They had to go there, for that was where the reactor controls were.

"Concentrate on this, Chief, for Christ's sake!" he gasped. "Let's get this thing fired up."

It was a fumbling work of agony, and it seemed to take hours, but at last they had energy in the boat again and staggered back forward, forgetting this time to dog down the door which was their only reasonable assurance of watertight integrity in what was left of *Skate*.

Stephens found the air-conditioning technician slumped over his desk, head down. Sleep or coma? he wondered. If it's coma, Cummings and I are on our own and there isn't much of our own left. He shook the man and shook him again, and then again. At last Chapman stirred and looked at him with blank, uncomprehending eyes.

Stephens left Cummings with Chapman and crawled forward. Walking, by God, is for babies and the blessed, he thought foolishly. He found Chief Pharmacist's Mate Andrews in sickbay, far gone but conscious.

"Chief, you got anything that'll get a man going—at least for a little?"

"Dunno, Captain. I c'n try. Who? Who?"

"You, Cummings, Chapman and me. Hurry up. We're gonna get this air cleaned up if we can move."

"Th'nk God," Andrews said and with half-seeing eyes began fumbling with his medicine chest.

"Hurry up, for Christ's sake," Stephens gasped.

"This might," Andrews muttered. "Stimulant. Call it amin . . . aminoph . . . oh shit . . . aminophline. Helps resp . . . respir . . . oh shit . . . respiration." He pulled out a vial and began fumbling for hypodermic syringes and needles. With unsteady hands and a wavering eye, he sucked a dose into the tube and squeezed out the air and turned toward Stephens.

"You first, Cap'n."

"No. You first! *You* got three more to fix up."

It hadn't been any wonder cure, Stephens thought dimly, as he and Andrews fumbled back toward Cummings and Chapman who, this time, they found on the edge of passing out. Andrews got a shot into each, while, in impatience, Stephens waited for the drug to take hold. And, after seven minutes, woodenly timed by Stephens, it visibly did so.

"Now," Stephens said. "Let's get this air washed. If we don't we're gonna have dead men aboard this boat." He didn't know it yet, but he had one dead already. Collingwood, the cook, had got his big frame forward as far as the last door to the forward torpedo room and there on the coaming had collapsed and died.

Neither Cummings nor Chapman, Stephens realized, was anywhere near his normal level of efficiency as he knew he himself was not. But, with stubborn fumbling, they made the thing work. Suddenly the boat was full of the powerful rush of air as the blowers came on, then the scrubbers that absorbed carbon dioxide, then the unit that did the same for carbon monoxide—a lesser peril where there had been no combustion since *Skate* hit bottom, then the one that did away with freon gas. Then, at length, the coolers which would leak more freon, which, however, would be no problem now since the system which produced it also destroyed it, as the whole system would also destroy the stifling heat.

Skate, in whatever peril she might be from above, was a living entity again.

"How long will it take to clean this boat?" Stephens asked Chapman.

"Can't say, Captain," the air expert mumbled. "I never had to bring one back from this close to the edge. But she's livable now and will get more so."

"Okay, carry on," Stephens said. "I'm going forward and count heads."

It was in the course of this survey that he discovered Collingwood had not made it.

He called the *Queen Zenobia* again. Stephens could not say that *Skate* was alert again, but the first thin beginnings of awareness and strength and a renewed will to live were fermenting in the minds and arteries of her men. Stephens could feel it growing in himself and he knew it had to if he was to complete the remainder of his work.

"What is your condition?" March asked.

"We're functioning," Stephens said. "It was close. I've got another dead man. It was that close."

He did not quite hear the admiral's next words, for there came an intrusion, unmistakable to his ears. It was the almost simultaneous dropping of four more anchors.

"Sorry, sir. I didn't hear you. They just put down more hooks. That takes away any doubt—if there was any. They're here to get us."

"I know. We saw the other four taking station on the big one," March said. "What I said before is that Hale just shoved off. He ought to reach you in three hours, not much more."

"You know that bothers me, sir. Hale has been magnificent but he must be close to the zombie stage. And those bastards can give him trouble."

The admiral's answer was somber. "I recognize magnificence when I see it. But I doubt if they can give him much trouble, unless they're willing to attack. That could be, but it's a calculated guess that they won't. The White House fella, has, I understand, talked to the other people twice. The last time he got tough. Maybe he was bluffing. I don't know. But they don't either."

"Well, let's hope they study their hand for awhile. Give Hale three to get out here, two here and three back and they can have what's left."

"What about Kirov?"

"You can tell the Pentagon to tell the President, who can tell Moscow, if he thinks it's worthwhile, that their man has had a relapse into patriotism. So far, he won't budge. I'll lasso him if I can which will be tough. But I've found out one thing about him. He can speak a sort of pidgin English and understands a lot more. I'll have one more chat with him."

The admiral lapsed into silence, and Stephens remembered an obligation.

"Admiral March, this Uzzumekis I sent you in the last load. How's he doing?"

"The doctor says he'll survive—maybe without the leg. He's getting the most care of any wounded aboard this ship. That girl, you can't pry her loose from him. Why?"

"Uzzumekis was a deserter in World War II; he also thinks perhaps he spied for the Russians. He thinks he's got his lumps coming unless he delivers Kirov. I want to say, as a minor matter, that he got shot in the process of saving my life. He also delivered Kirov to *Skate*, which was all the responsibility he really had—it wasn't his fault we got a torpedo in the butt. What he went through delivering Kirov, I don't know; you can probably get the details from the woman. Oulahan, Chief Cate, the pharmacists can tell you how he acted aboard this ship. I say that Uzzumekis—silly damned name—has paid his bill about six times over. If those jerks in Washington try to make a spectacle of him, Admiral, for God's sake, stand up for him. Will you?"

"I promise you that, Dave . . . and something else . . ."

At the telephone, aboard the *Queen Zenobia*, the admiral found himself unable to speak and silently cursed himself. What could a man say to a man he had ordered to go where Stephens was and do what Stephens was doing and would do? And he did not, for one second, doubt he would do it. He got control of himself.

"You, Dave. Are you going to be all right?"

"I guess so, sir. I know the drill."

Aboard the *Bakhmut*, Commander Federenko came from the sonar room and spoke to Sobelov, who stood on the bridge wing, glowering down at the water under which *Skate* was invisible to his straining eyes. So far, for so many weeks, he had pursued this man, and now he was within a hundred meters of him—and virtually helpless.

"They have all their machinery running," Federenko told the Chief of Soviet State Security.

"What does that mean?" Sobelov demanded.

"They're not getting under way. I imagine it means only that they know we are here and no longer care how much noise they create."

"What are you going to do?"

"I am rigging to send divers down to inspect the hull. What else do you expect of me? What has Moscow said?"

"To raise the ship when we can. They are willing—not willing, but they appear to feel forced—to take that as second prize."

"What about Kirov?"

"If the little submarine takes Kirov off alive and tries to put him aboard the support ship, I intend to write my own orders and take him off. You are keeping the pickets out there?"

"Yes. Naturally. But will it not be risky to board that ship?"

"The risk is Moscow's concern. As for me, I am finished in any case. Also as for me, it is a matter of pride, professional pride. I was sent to get him; I intend to have him."

"You grow reckless, Comrade."

Stephens went to his stateroom, opened his little folding desk, closed the door. He needed privacy, a commodity which

341

was seldom his. His mind was in New London with Peg and the kids. He could see them in the yard, which he had so painstakingly plugged with zoysia and had with such pride seen mature into luxuriant turf. He could see Peg's face, big-eyed, wide brown eyes, not exactly beautiful maybe, by somebody else's standards, but infinitely beautiful and infinitely precious by his own. He knew her patience and her courage and the wonderful resourcefulness of her spirit. He knew the comfort and the excitement of their love-making. He knew the marvels she worked with the $13,000 a year they paid the skipper of a $69 million submarine. He knew that she took pride in him, in his work, in the profession he served. He knew the kids worshiped him, as he did them. They had been married fifteen years and every single year had been a wonder to him—a highly undeserved treasure.

And now what was he to do with it all? Tell her about insurance, the mortgage, the few U.S. bonds and where they were? Advise her about the future? Tell her to marry again? Tell her he loved her and always had? Hell, she knew that.

He got as far as pulling a piece of Navy stationery before him, wrote "My darling," and choked on it and crumpled it and threw it in a corner. He tried again and failed again.

Tell her what he was doing and why he was doing it? Her heart was going to be smashed anyhow, as his already was—except for the will to do the work he still had to do. Leave her with the memory that he was a sort of modern kamikaze to no purpose. But there was a purpose; he knew that. And she might accept the purpose with her mind, but, knowing her, he knew her heart never could. The bitterness would be planted and it would grow . . . and grow . . . and fester. She was a Navy wife, and a Navy wife knew her husband went in harm's way. She would be crushed when she knew he had died doing his job, but eventually she and the kids would recover from that. But a death for which a man apologized in advance would be something else again, incomprehensible and in the end unforgivable, a slow, paralyzing poison. Nothing more admirable than a willful suicide. He crushed the last sheet of paper and threw it aside and got up and went back to the boat.

He had made his last choice, the hardest one.

Hale, half an hour from *Skate*, spoke to Pauer and Akers.

"We know where she is. We know what's upstairs. We don't know whether they're going to mess with us, but we'll sure find out. We'll make as little fuss as possible. Keep the lights and television shut down until we really need them. We'll home in on sonar until we're within a couple of hundred feet."

"They can track us on their sonar anyhow," Pauer said. These three, now, had been riding this circuit too long to bother with the likes of "sir." Titles were for when things weren't hurting.

"I know that, but what can they really do except try to sink us? And we're pretty hard to hit."

"But not impossible," Akers said.

"I never said impossible," Hale retorted. "All I said was hard. Also, even if I didn't tell you before, the admiral told me they've been talking between the White House and the Kremlin and That Man has been doing his godawful best to keep them off our necks."

"I hope his godawful best is godawful good," Pauer said.

"We can stop the little submarine," Commander Federenko told Sobelov. "Sink it—a simple matter. We know course, speed, depth."

"I don't doubt we can," Sobelov said sourly. "But my orders say we don't."

"What do your orders say about boarding the support ship which you are so determined to do if Kirov gets aboard?"

"If I see that man alive, I'm going to get him," Sobelov said. "I promise you!"

Stephens, touring *Skate* from stem to stern, feeling more aware and strong as the air-cleaning machinery steadily cleared her of poison, went into the forward torpedo room and counted heads.

"How're they doing?" he asked Lieutenant Grady Johnson.

"Perking up some, Captain," Johnson said. Stephens deliberately ignored Johnson's uneasy air of awe as he answered, almost as though he was talking to somebody desperately ill, embarrassed in the presence of something he himself had yet to face, perhaps not for years—but also, of course, perhaps today. But not, in any case, by an act of his own will.

"What's the head count?"

"Thirty-one . . . since Collingwood died." He looked at the corpse laid out on a stretcher under the torpedo racks.

"I wish he could have made it," Stephens permitted himself to say. "I'm going to take a look around . . . I think we've got everybody. Just want to make sure."

"Aye, aye, Captain." Johnson had never said it with such quiet respect.

Returning from the engineroom, where he noted with interest that the bulged after bulkhead was still holding, Stephens thoughtfully dogged the forgotten door. Damned sloppy, he thought, but then remembered Cummings and he had been on the verge of unconsciousness the last time they went through that door.

It was then he was stopped and stood listening intently. There were noises outside the hull, aft of the sail. Was the DSRV back so soon? He looked at his watch. No, impossible, not for another twenty minutes at the earliest. Anyhow, Hale knew the routine too well by now. He wouldn't be fooling around here a hundred feet aft of his target on the forward hatch.

So it had to be something else. And who else could it be? It had to be from that overshadowing watchman upstairs. Divers, he guessed. Clumping with their lead-soled shoes, prowling about his boat—*his* boat—like jackals tearing at a lion's kill. A moment of pure rage shook him. But then he calmed. Why wouldn't they? And, with a kind of satisfaction, he thought a hell of a lot of good it's going to do them! They may dirty my deck, but they'll never carry it home.

The DSRV, still blind but for sonar, was almost on her target when Hale ordered Pauer and Akers to turn on the lights and television. The screen before Hale came alive. Pauer and Akers were at port and starboard viewports. The first thing Hale saw were the white numerals "578" springing up in the hazy glare of the light beams. Home again, he thought, rather smugly, home again for the last time. This isn't going to take long, not too long, anyhow.

Then he saw something else, a snaky wavering line of black almost dead ahead to starboard.

"Diver!" Akers yelled. Hale felt some small tenuous, momentary resistance on the starboard side and Akers yelled again.

"Jesus Christ! We cut his lines! He's over the side!"

"Color him dead," Hale said with quiet exultation. Being a mustang and thus relatively old in the service as well as relatively old compared to the kids he commanded, Hale's set of useful clichés was relatively out of date.

He was maneuvering the DSRV, with now familiar shifts of weight and movement, delicate, gentle, precise, minute, down to grapple and seat and seal on the escape hatch, when he saw the second one. Good Lord, he thought, I'm almost face to face with the bastard. The figure was grotesque in the DSRV's lights, the monstrous, bulbous metal helmet, the single staring eye of the face plate, the slow-moving arms, like the tentacles of an under-endowed octopus now frantically tugging at its lines.

I guess the lad must want out of here, Hale thought with grim amusement. Can't say I blame him.

The DSRV was settling into her seal, athwartship of *Skate*.

"What'll we do about the other one?" Akers yelled.

"Forget him," Hale said. "He's the one that got away."

There did not remain many chores which Stephens knew

345

he had to do. About the second one, he was quietly—and now calmly—certain. The first was a stinker and had been ever since he had heaved alongside the fishing boat and Chief Cummings had hauled its occupants aboard. Kirov. Damn him. He knew where he would find him. He went to the wardroom and, now that *Skate* was functioning again, paused in the pantry, to fetch a cup and heat a little stainless steel pot of water on the hot plate. He carried these delicacies into the wardroom and put them down on the table and, with a steady hand, poured the steaming virgin brew into the cup. He sat in his own armchair, commander of a ship about to be abandoned.

Kirov sat impassive where he had been ten hours ago when, with a kind of clumsy tenderness, he still had been trying to nurse Uzzumekis.

Stephens measured the man thoughtfully. Looks as fat as butter and as hard as H-11 steel, he thought. Look what the bastard cost me—us—I ought to hate his guts. But, strangely, he only sorrowed; he did not hate.

Kirov had his gun laid on the table before him. Stephens studied it curiously. Snub-nosed, looks about like a ·38. Useful, he thought. I wonder how it was Uzzumekis never discovered in all that time that the man had it.

I've got plenty of guns, too, he reflected. Nastier even than that little hunk of steel, deadly as it may be. But what use would it be to point a ·45 to threaten a man whose only intention with his ·38 was to use it on himself, he thought helplessly? Jump him? How? He was ten feet away with his back to the bulkhead.

"You told me you speak a little English?" he asked coldly.

"Da. A little."

"I think you understand more than you speak. Is that correct?"

"Da." A short, acquiescing nod of the head.

"I will do most of the talking then. When I say something you do not understand, will you let me know?"

"Da. Correct."

"All right. The small rescue submarine is now attaching itself to this ship. Soon men will be going aboard—I mean climbing into it. They will go to safety. You understand?"

The blue eyes, which seldom revealed much, now seemed to be digesting Stephens' words, not considering a prospect, but shaping an unfamiliar pattern together. Finally he had it.

"Da. I under—understand."

"This is the last voyage it will make. The last without question. I want that to be most clear in your mind. Do you understand?"

"Da. Correct." No hesitation.

"I want you to go with that little submarine."

"Nyet. I"—Kirov was working on it but at last he got it out—"impossible. My country . . ." He seemed to be working on more but bogged down on it.

"I have heard that argument before—through Uzzumekis." Stephens was losing patience and knew he was being anything but clear.

The blue eyes became a little less stony, imperceptibly so.

"Ah—Uzzumekis . . . He is good?"

"As good as he ever will be. Yes. Good. Alive. You understand?"

"Da. Good. Very good."

What a hell of a conversation this is, Stephens thought, in frustration. I wish I could trade him for anyone I lost.

"Do you understand the cost . . . the price . . . the penalty . . . oh hell . . . do you understand that if you do not go with the little submarine you are going to die?"

It was another time for Kirov to puzzle over the words and Stephens filled the space with a flat statement.

"Your people"—he pointed a finger upward—"cannot save . . . rescue . . bring you up alive. Do you understand that?"

"Da. I understand."

"Do you want to die?"

"Nyet. But I am old man. My country . . ."

"Your country, my ass!" Stephens suddenly yelled in exasperation. "You left your country!" and was instantly sorry he had lost his temper.

"Is it your thought that your people up there"—finger pointed upward again—"can take this ship? Study it? Use it? Learn its secrets?"

Kirov shrugged massively.

"You were informed by me—through Uzzumekis—they could not have the ship."

"Da. I understand . . . but . . ."

"No *but*. The ship will not still be here. You understand that?"

"Da. But it is impossible you can take it away."

"You are mistaken. I intend to take it away. Do you understand?"

"Da. I understand . . . you would die . . . you would smash it."

"Da!" Hell, he's got me doing it, Stephens thought in disgust. "I will smash it. If you do not go now you will go with me when I smash it. Do you understand that?"

"Da. I am sorry."

"Do you understand . . . oh hell, this is pointless . . . do you understand that you have already cost more than twenty dead men?" Stephens used ten fingers twice.

"Da. I am sorry. Of my own also some. Two. Me too, it does not matter . . . you . . . I I am sorry."

And the old bastard probably really is sorry in his peculiar fashion, Stephens thought. He refused, now, to think of Peg and the children.

Kirov spoke. "You will smash it when?"

Stephens looked at his watch.

"Three hours . . . four hours. Do you understand?"

Kirov nodded, otherwise unreadable.

Christ, what a companion for this sort of work, Stephens thought. It's hopeless. What are we going to talk about for the next few hours? Music? Baseball? Movie stars? The essential elements of pigheadedness? The difference between a late-come glory of patriotism and a plain job that had to be done? He felt lonely.

"Excuse me, I must see my men," he said, and got up and left.

In the torpedo room he found Lieutenant Johnson and Chief Cummings. Otherwise, except for Collingwood's body, the place was empty.

"Everybody aboard?" he asked.

Johnson nodded wordlessly.

"Okay, shove off," Stephens said.

Without warning, Cummings grabbed his arms.

"For the love of God, Captain! I wired those things myself! Set 'em and leave 'em. They'll go off. I guarantee it! Listen to me! I guarantee it!"

Stephens pried himself loose. "I believe you, Chief. But it's necessary to make sure. And you know it. Now, shove off. That's an order!"

That enormous shibboleth of command; anybody with one rank over another could use it. Could conjure with it. It was a dirty trick on human dignity and the human heart—but it worked. Should you pity the one who submitted to it or the one who used it? And how would he know? All Stephens knew was that he had a little work yet to do.

The DSRV was gone. Stephens went to the telephone and called the *Queen Zenobia*. Admiral March's voice, now cracked and grating, came to him.

"They're on the way," Stephens said calmly. "You should have them aboard not later than oh-six hundred."

"And then . . . All right, God damn it! . . . And then when?"

"As soon as you're clear. You don't get Kirov; I do. Admiral, I suggest you advise the Russians at once. No use blowing them up, too, just because they're greedy. If they won't believe you, get the White House to tell them."

For the first time, a hot-line call originated in the White House Situation Room directed to the Kremlin on a no-delay top-urgency status. It was seven o'clock in the evening, May 3, Eastern Daylight Saving Time and two o'clock in the morning, May 4, Moscow Time. The President, who was waiting in the booth with his interpreter for the call to go through—unusual, in fact, unprecedented for him—spoke to the interpreter out of a grim unease and a depression deeper than he felt qualified to plumb.

"For once, we're getting *those* bastards out of bed in the middle of the night."

The communicator outside the booth signaled, and the President spoke to his interpreter savagely. "Now, for God's sake, don't sound like that sissy voice that speaks for the Chairman."

The President heard the deep baritone of the Chairman's voice and guessed it was the beginning of the usual exchange of courtesies.

"Tell him to cut out the crap," the President said curtly. "I want to tell him something for his own good, and he doesn't have much time to listen. Paraphrase that but not very much."

The baritone began again, sounding taken aback, not too sure whether it should be angry.

"Give him this exactly," the President told the interpreter. "Mr. Chairman, you have ships, five to be precise, anchored over the United States submarine. I have no desire whatever to save your ships. But also I have no desire to kill your men. If you want to save your ships and your men (the President looked at his watch) you have exactly two hours and thirty-five minutes to get them clear of the area."

The baritone rumble came again and was interpreted. "Mr. President, are you threatening me again?"

"Mr. Chairman, you are at liberty to disbelieve me. They are your ships and your men. But in precisely two hours and thirty-three minutes, now, the United States submarine *Skate* is going to blow up. It will take with it anything on the surface within a radius of one half mile."

350

"Am I to believe this, Mr. President?"

"God damn it to hell, you obtuse sonofabitch, Mr. Chairman, get those ships out of there!"

"And Kirov?"

"Kirov goes with *Skate*. So does the captain. Now do you believe me?"

The baritone was soft and brief this time. The President looked at his own interpreter. "I don't want to listen to that interpreter's voice again," he said savagely. "*You* tell me what he said."

"He said, 'Two brave men.' That's all he said, Mr. President."

Aboard *Skate*, Stephens stood in the control room, listening to the small destruct charges go off, counting them as they blew.

One, sonar. Two, second sonar. Three, NAVDAC. Four, underwater telephone. Five, radar. Six, SINS. Seven, Eight, Nine, Ten: all the little, delicate, secret things which did not take much to be destroyed—but which must be destroyed absolutely.

Kirov stood beside him, watching with curiosity.

That was the lot, Stephens believed, counting back over them in his mind. He reached for the big button but Kirov grasped his arm and spoke.

"Nyet. Wait."

Stephens turned and saw that Kirov had his hand outstretched. He hesitated, shrugged, thought, well, why not? and took it.

"Da. Okay," Kirov said. He was smiling.

Stephens reached for the big button again.

They all saw it go, a mountainous upswelling of the sea and moments later the shock reached the *Queen Zenobia*.

"I'm going below," Admiral March told Lieutenant Commander Gottfried. Gottfried, just in time, reached out to steady the admiral as he stumbled.

Gottfried spoke to the OOD. "Set two-two-eight. Straight into the Bosporus." His tone was savage.

To his embarrassment, the interpreter was forced to listen for the first time in his career while the President of the United States voiced an opinion seemingly addressed to himself. "He's a stupid sonofabitch," he said. "But so am I."

THE MAN WHO PLAYED THIEF

Don Smith

He could swallow his pride—but if he didn't find the diamonds it would be all he would have left to swallow.

It was a £2,000,000 diamond heist. The criminals were in jail and Scotland Yard was satisfied. But the insurance companies weren't. They had paid up and now they wanted the diamonds tracked down.

So they hired Tim Parnell, adventurer-private eye, to spring one of the thieves and follow him to the stones. And follow he does, in a spectacularly daring and unique adventure.

Swift, tough-paced, filled with explosive action, the novel moves relentlessly against a rich backdrop of the Côte d'Azur and the international elite of criminals.

CORONET BOOKS

OPERATION STRANGLEHOLD

Dan J. Marlowe

He wasn't a good man; he wasn't a bad man; but his name was Earl Drake—and that was the difference.

Drake simply hadn't expected any visitors—which is why he was so wary when Hazel told him about the two men at the door. They didn't look like hoods and they didn't look like cops; and Drake didn't like anything about them when they started to get rough with his woman. He shot one in the arm—and that quietened them down; enough, anyway, for him to gather that they were from the central government and that his friend Karl Erikson was rotting in a Spanish Jail.

He liked Erikson. But he had other things to think about right then. Such as—whether some fool had blown his cover; and whether he wouldn't have to run hard and fast to make sure that his own past hadn't caught up with him again.

CORONET BOOKS

THE INTIMIDATORS

Donald Hamilton

NAME: MATTHEW HELM
CODE NAME: ERIC
MISSION: No. 15—THE INTIMIDATORS
REMARKS: It was a double mission this time. Firstly,
to terminate a top-notch enemy agent. Secondly, to
locate the missing fiancée of a Texas oil millionaire
who had disappeared in the infamous Bermuda
Triangle.

Somehow these two were connected. Matt Helm
didn't know how. And it was only after a few members
of the international set disappeared into the Triangle
in their turn that things began to clear. Most people
assumed them to be dead. But dead they were not;
and, very much alive, they proved to be part of a
deadly little game.

CORONET BOOKS

ALSO AVAILABLE IN CORONET BOOKS

DON SMITH

☐ 18625 9	The Payoff	35p
☐ 15474 8	The Padrone	30p
☐ 15685 6	The Man Who Played Thief	30p
☐ 18830 8	Corsican Takeover	40p

DAN J. MARLOWE

☐ 18286 5	Operation Stranglehold	30p
☐ 19476 6	Operation Endless Hour	35p
☐ 18601 1	Operation Whiplash	30p
☐ 16474 3	Operation Fireball	30p

DONALD HAMILTON

☐ 18779 4	The Intimidators	35p
☐ 02009 1	The Silencers	35p
☐ 10767 7	The Menacers	35p
☐ 15472 1	The Poisoners	35p

All these books are available at your bookshop or newsagent, or can be ordered direct from the publisher. Just tick the titles you want and fill in the form below.

....

CORONET BOOKS, P.O. Box 11, Falmouth, Cornwall.

Please send cheque or postal order. No currency, and allow the following for postage and packing:

1 book—10p, 2 books—15p, 3 books—20p, 4–5 books—25p, 6–9 books—4p per copy, 10–15 books—2½p per copy, over 30 books free within the U.K.

Overseas—please allow 10p for the first book and 5p per copy for each additional book.

Name...

Address..

....